Southern Cross

"For most American readers the first big novel about Australia they encountered was 'The Thorn Birds'. Now there is another one, so richly romantic, so dramatic a blend of true history and what might have been, that it could almost be called an Australian 'Gone With the Wind'."

Publishers Weekly

"A PASSIONATE HUMAN DRAMA ON THE ONE HAND, *SOUTHERN CROSS* IS ALSO A COMPELLING HISTORICAL NOVEL THAT BRILLIANTLY RE-CREATES THE EARLY TURBULENT DECADES WHEN AUSTRALIA AND ITS PEOPLE STRUGGLED FOR SURVIVAL. IT IS A STORY THE READER WILL NOT SOON FORGET."

Book-of-the-Month Club News

"ENTHRALLING, ACCOMPLISHED . . . THIS IMPECCABLY WRITTEN TALE, HAUNTING AS *THE FRENCH LIEUTENANT'S WOMAN*, OFFERS A COMPASSIONATE PERSPECTIVE OF THE PALACES AND DUNGEONS OF THE HUMAN HEART."

Cosmopolitan

Southern Cross

by

Terry Coleman

BALLANTINE BOOKS • NEW YORK

All rights reserved. Published in the United States by Ballantine Books, a division of Random House, Inc., New York.

Library of Congress Catalog Card Number: 78-26876

ISBN 0-345-28365-1

This edition published by arrangement with The Viking Press

Manufactured in the United States of America

First Ballantine Books Edition: October 1980

Contents

PART ONE

PART TWO

Part One

cove, the woman returned to the spot before the house where she had first waited.

Still she stood there. The trees became silhouettes, no longer green. The light was between what a lands-man calls twilight, when a person may see to walk easily over uneven ground, and that darker state which a sailor calls nautical twilight, when shapes are only dimly visible at a hundred yards. Then the cor-vette moved to her mooring and the captain strode up the grassed slope towards Government House.

When she began to wait the woman had stood in golden sunlight, and the house, with its verandas and shading trees, in cool shadow. But when the man at last approached she stood in a dusk that was almost night, with the house no longer obscure but lit inside with the soft light of mirrored candelabra and sending that light faintly on to the lawns behind her. Against the night sky, her long hair was darkness made visible by the faint haze of the harbour lights before her, and by the stars above. Through her slight muslin gown the house lights shone, penetrating, tracing, and trans-luminating the petals, ferns, and quatrefoils of the embroidery, so that she seemed herself the source of light. The man took the woman's outstretched hands in his, drew her to him and clasped her, raising her a little so that she came up on her toes. They held each other. Then she withdrew enough to be able to take his head in her hands and regard his features. Post-captain Nicolas Baudin was commander of the French corvette, and Susannah's lover. He was not returning from a long absence—the separation had been for only ten days while he prospected the neigh-bouring inlets for the specimens of mahogany and blackbutt tree that would be required of him on his return to Europe—but he had sailed with his mem-ories of her, and her name, every hour in his mind. He loved her; and she saw this. The moment of that perception is one that reveals a woman's soul. He knew that she would cherish him. The winking points of the Southern Cross looked down on the broad bay, on the cove with its ships riding easily, on the town, on the domain, on the lawn, on the two figures on that lawn, on the translucencies of the woman's dress, and on the man's transfigured face, which he lowered and buried in her hair.

"My love?" she said.

He raised his head a little.

"How clear a night it is," she said. "Your stars are clear."

He was so intent on her that he hardly glanced up. But he was a navigator and had explained the southern heavens to her, showing her stars seen in no northern sky. The Southern Cross, which he had especially shown her, lies on the edge of a gap in the Milky Way, on the edge of a black void that sets off the brilliance of its five points. The southern skies are less crowded than the northern, just as the southern oceans run for many thousands of miles unbroken by land. But those south seas enclose one entire island continent, then called New Holland, and on one fragment of that continent Susannah and Baudin stood embraced.

This was in the year 1802. Susannah was the daughter of Philip Gidley King, captain-general and governor-in-chief of His Majesty's colony of New South Wales. Baudin commanded two French men-of-war of thirty guns, which both now lay in the cove. Britain and France had been at war and would be again—those long wars that began with the French Revolution and ended with Waterloo. It did happen, on that evening, that the two powers had been for a few months briefly at peace, in the interval, as it were, between two acts of a drama. But that news had not reached the ends of the earth, and it was on the ends of the earth that Susannah and Baudin found themselves. There was nothing farther. There is nothing farther. How they came there must be told. All around them was the spirit of this last, loneliest place, its apartness and its grandeur. But neither the genius of the place nor any sense of her own insignificance under so vast a heaven, awed Susannah.

She took Baudin by the hand and led him towards the house and towards the light. She was eighteen and he was her first love: he was twice her age, and she was to be his last. It was a night she never forgot, and it determined the whole course of her long life.

2

───────⟊⟐⟑───────

Transported Beyond the Seas

SUSANNAH AND BAUDIN WERE OBSERVED as they entered the house by John Easty, the governor's head gardener, who lived in a cottage within the domain. Easty was a man whose memory went back as far as there was any colony to be remembered. In 1787, as a private soldier, he sailed with the First Fleet of convict ships from England to Botany Bay. The convicts were the first settlers. Before them, only Captain Cook and his crew had seen that bay, when they discovered it in 1770. Easty remembered some of the officers of the First Fleet. One of them was Lieutenant King, who became the colony's third governor. Easty remembered, the day they sailed, how the lieutenant's little daughter was held up at the dockside to wave good-bye. That was Susannah, who was three at the time. She came out much later. He could remember some of the felons. He well remembered George Bryant, who in 1802 was still in the colony. He had become quite friends with Bryant, as far as a soldier and a felon could be friends. He remembered Bryant and other convicts telling him about their trials.

Trials in 1786 were apt to be brief. One summer

day at the Old Bailey, in the City of London, Mr. Justice Hotham got through six. All the offences were capital. First, Mary Abell, alias Tilley, of Islington, was put up.

"Why alias Tilley?" asked the judge, looking up from his nosegay of sweet flowers, whose fragrance was supposed to refresh the judicial mind and repel the miasma which floated up from the prisoners in the dock. The prisoners did stink. Mary Abell stank. She would, after four months in Newgate jail, waiting for her trial.

"Because, my lord," said Mr. Rhodes, counsel for the Crown, "she has committed other crimes under that name, which—"

"Mr. Rhodes," said the judge, "you really must not tell me that. She is charged upon indictment with one count, although that, God knows, is enough." It was. Mary Abell was a whore, which did not matter and was no concern of the law. She was a procuress, which could hardly help appearing in the evidence, but that did not much matter. What mattered was that, failing to procure enough girls for her uses, though the wretchedly poor were easily enough procured, she cruelly kidnapped Ann Shore, aged twelve years and four months, and deprived the said Ann Shore of her freedom, and brought about the death of Ann Shore. The indictment did not say all that, because the girl, having already escaped from the house of Mary Abell, had drowned herself. Such a death could not be charged to Mary Abell. It was no murder. But it was an evil kidnapping. The prisoner wept, and not a man in court believed her tears. The jury did not retire. The foreman said "Guilty," and the judge, turning to the woman, said to her, "Do you think there will be mercy for your soul?" She was hustled away.

Put up Henry Abrams. He did not know his age, but thought twenty-seven, and was indicted for the very thorough highway robbery of Fleetwood Bury, Esquire, whom he had deprived of one pair men's leather breeches, value ten shillings; one linen ruffled shirt, five shillings; one man's peruke, two shillings; one pair leather boot-garters, twelve pence; one gold repeater watch, ten guineas; and One Proper Coin of the Realm called half a guinea, value half a guinea.

"In that order?" said the judge. "Breeches first?"

There was a little, permitted, laughter in the court before the verdict of guilty was pronounced.

And so on. Robert Spencer, for forging cheques in the name of the Earl of Harington: Guilty. Jane Bowing, for stealing a tub with a hundred oysters in it at Billingsgate; it being strongly urged against her that she had been defended from arrest by a gang of girls, one of whom had a knife: Guilty. William Pearce, for that, having been employed at His Majesty's Mint in the cleaning of sovereigns, he did feloniously steal forty-seven of the objects of his work: Guilty.

Then came George Bryant, aged sixteen, for having taken and carried away with intent at the time of such taking to deprive the owner permanently thereof, one blue broadcloth cloak, with fur collar, lined with blue silk, and buckled with a silver buckle, the property of James, Lord Bishop of Peterborough, from his London residence: Guilty. Bryant was exceptional. Not only had he stolen a bishop's cloak, no less, but he was the only prisoner in court that day to have chattels with him. The other prisoners were penniless. Bryant's chattel was the cloak, which had been too good to sell, as no receiver of stolen goods would touch so distinctive a thing, and some even had religious scruples, or said they had. It was of course the bishop's, but the bishop would not reclaim it for fear that it might have attracted to it the taint of prison fever, which might communicate itself in turn to the bishop. Now prisoners could indeed have chattels, and, if they did, this was written down in the court record. A prisoner might have forty guineas, evidently stolen, but if they were not the subject of the indictment brought against him they were his to take with him to prison, or to exile: that is, if the jailers had not already, in the broader interests of justice, in their turn robbed the prisoner. Bryant's chattel had survived his jailers because it had to be produced in court. Since it was unclaimed it was his. Since it was his it had to be written down: "George Bryant. Chattel: One bishop's cloak," and while the clerk was doing this, the judge looked at the prisoner for the first time.

"Where do you come from?"

"Dorchester, sir."

The judge remembered Dorchester, a county town one hundred and fifty miles from London, a western provincial capital in its own way, a town laid out by the Romans, with broad, straight roads. He had been on assize there. He knew Weymouth too, a watering place on the coast, six miles away. It was a place much loved by the king, and the judge had been there as the king's guest at a place called Gloucester House. He remembered the name. But what he most remembered was that, one morning five years before, he had bought at a Weymouth linen draper's five pairs of women's gloves, for a woman who lay deep in his affection. The recollection of this touched the mind of the judge, and he looked again at the boy and at the cloak. The court had completed its business. Counsel were waiting, the clerks sat still, the ushers' hands were on the doors. All were waiting His Lordship's pleasure, but all wanted to get away.

"Put it on," said the judge.

The boy looked up helplessly around, until a clerk motioned to him what to do, and Bryant took the cloak and draped it over his shoulders, and looked up. He did not know whether he was being mocked. He was not. The assembled counsel, clerks, and ushers had already seen that the judge was not playing with the prisoner, and they kept silence.

"Very well," said Mr. Justice Hotham. "George Bryant, I wish you better for the future. And"—this to the clerk—"let it be recorded that I wish that he *shall* have the cloak, and that whoever robs him of it may count on my displeasure. You know who should be told. See they know."

The judge's chance recollection of a chance happiness saved that cloak for George Bryant. It was a small affair, of course; or so everyone thought.

The judge said, again to the boy, "I wish you well," and then the court rose.

In those days each prisoner was not sentenced at the end of his own trial, but at the end of the session all were brought back to be sentenced together. That was the end of the assize. There were no more prisoners to try, and so next morning they were all brought back. All were cast for death. Mary Abell, alias Tilley, wept throughout. Pearce, the thief of the sovereigns, and Henry Abrams, the thorough highwayman, both joked with their friends in court. They joked to keep up their courage, because they were in real fear of their lives. Most sentences of death were known to be only formal. That was why the judge could wish the boy Bryant well the evening before, and in the morning tell him he was to be taken to a place of execution and there hanged by the neck until he was dead. In that year, no fewer than two hundred and twenty-two crimes were capital. You could hardly hang one-eighth of the population of London, which would have been the result of a literal interpretation of the law. And so almost all sentences were commuted to transportation, but a flagrant highwayman or a thief in the Mint itself could not count on that mercy. Mary Abell, had she been a man, would have died, but the law was kinder to women. In the end only Pearce, the thief of the sovereigns, was told to resign himself to death. Early one morning he was suspended outside Newgate in the sight of God and in the face of a large press of men and women assembled for the entertainment. The other five, with Abrams the thorough highwayman marvelling at his luck, were condemned to be transported beyond the seas, and were shipped in chains down the Thames and into the English Channel, where at Portsmouth they met the other five hundred and eighty-two men and one hundred and ninety women who were to be the convicts of the First Fleet bound for Botany Bay, in New Holland.

As they waited to sail, an impresario with an eye for the idea of the moment presented at the Royal Circus Theatre in London an opera entitled *Botany Bay,* in which the hero has this aria, this snatch of song:

> *I'll kill them tyrants one by one*
> *And shoot the flogger down;*
> *I'll give the law a little shock,*
> *Remember what I say.*
> *They'll yet regret they sent Jim Jones*
> *In chains to Botany Bay.*

The governor of that First Fleet, Arthur Phillip, the man to whose office Philip Gidley King was eventually to succeed, was a mild Christian gentleman. He was born the son of a German immigrant and teacher of foreign languages, and had raised himself to be a captain in the Royal Navy. But for the twelve years before 1787 he had been retired on half-pay, farming down in the New Forest in Hampshire, hardly expecting to sail again, certainly expecting no high com-

mand. Not that Botany Bay was so high a command.
Nobody wanted it until this gentleman farmer was
made the most casual offer of it by the secretary to
the navy, who was by chance a neighbour. Whereupon George III, by the Grace of God, caused a commission to be drawn up in which he called the
gentleman farmer his trusty and well-beloved servant,
recited that he had especial confidence in his prudence,
courage, and loyalty, and gave him despotic powers
over a continent.

"I would not," said the governor to the secretary of
the navy, over a glass of punch three days before they
sailed, "I would not wish convicts to lay the foundation of an empire."

"Convicts is what you have got."

"I think convicts should ever remain separated
from the garrison soldiers, and other settlers that may
come in from Europe."

"None will come." And the secretary was right. In
the first two decades, fewer than one hundred did.

"Then we shall be a fragile colony. I should wish to
show clemency." So he did wish. He wished indeed to
retain only two offences as capital—murder, and unnatural crime, by which he meant sodomy.

"You must hold out a little more terror than that,"
said the secretary. But then, the governor did have in
mind the holding out of some terror. Though he would
desire only two crimes to be capital, yet those guilty
of such crimes he proposed not to hang but to deliver
up to the native blacks, to be eaten.

"Cannibals?" said the secretary.

The governor assented.

"Cannibals. Who might, then, acquire a taste for
white meat greater than your tribute to them of the
occasional assassin would satisfy?"

But by then the Home Office in London had already

received just such a modest proposal from the governor-designate and had, for reasons unstated, declined it. Excessive clemency was to be avoided, but no one was to be eaten.

So, on a fine Sunday morning, they sailed. One day out, in light breezes, John Easty, a soldier on the convict transport *Scarborough,* gazed astern at the Lizard, the last of England. One month out the rum measures were suspected, complained of by the sailors, and found to be one-third short. Two months out, a large shoal of flying fish flew on board. Three months out, they lay in sight of Rio de Janeiro. From Rio they sailed eastwards across the South Atlantic to the Cape of Good Hope, which was then Dutch. Easty and Bryant had become friends. Bryant had kept the bishop's cloak. The judge's writ ran as far as Portsmouth. No one had dared to take it before then. But at Portsmouth, when the prisoners were taken on board the convict ships, they were stripped, sluiced down with buckets of salt water, compelled to dress in slop-clothes of yellow and brown, and their own clothes, even if still good, were thrown overboard. Easty had saved Bryant's cloak, mostly out of the kindness of his heart, and would return it to him at the end of the voyage, minus the silver buckle. It was understood Easty would keep that.

From Cape Town they made eastwards again, in the roaring forties, through the heaviest seas they had ever seen, under the sharpest lightning, and towards the reddest skies, until, eight months and one week out from England, they came to New Holland. Captain Cook had said the climate was that of the south of France, and the gentlemen of the Admiralty, and the prime minister, relied upon his judgement. The men of the First Fleet found a very complete harbour, in which a thousand ships of the line, all the navies of the world, could safely shelter, and then they discovered the cove which, on January 26, 1788, they named Sydney after the British home secretary of the day. But they had not found the south of France, only a magnificent desert.

3

The Hundred Hungry Days

THE MARINE SENTRIES shuffled backwards and forwards on the dirt path in front of what would one day, if they ever completed it, be Government House, but was still, a year after the colony was established, only a wooden shanty, a bit larger than the others of the town. There were four sentries, Luke Hines, Richard Aske, James Baker, and Joseph Hunt, and only the last had boots. The others wore the ruined remains of boots, cracked uppers from which the leather soles had long ago fallen away and been replaced by wooden slats. The leather uppers and wooden soles were bound together with canvas strips wound round and round. Only Joseph Hunt had boots, and the others knew why and said nothing. The uniforms of all four were no longer recognizable as uniforms. The red cloth was faded and torn and no longer even patchable. Only Joseph Hunt had eaten meat in the last week, and that had been salt pork—meat from pigs brought from England, animals from which they should have bred, but almost all the colony's livestock had been slaughtered for food. The flour in the government stores was low. The crops planted had shriv-

elled in the ground. Only a few orange trees, planted
in the domain, were flourishing. Of the four sentries,
only Joseph Hunt was not hungry.

Richard Aske gazed at the barren lawns of struggling grass, and over the barren government farm,
where no crops grew, and then at the distant, barren
hills.

"We'll starve," he said, "unless we're lucky."

"We'll be lucky then," said Luke Hines. "A black
cat crossed our path the other day, James Baker and
me, when we were down by the stores."

"Black cat's lucky," said Richard Aske.

"Lucky for us," said Luke Hines. "Poor beast went
almost mewing down our throats."

"Like rabbit pie," said Baker. "As good as. Only,
that was two weeks ago, and that, I b'lieve, was the
extermination of the breed in the colony."

"There was a woman," said Hines, "ate grass on
Greenhill, and died; and when the surgeon opened
her, there was only grass."

Aske said, "It will be a hundred hungry days for
us."

Only Joseph Hunt was sanguine. The stock was
slaughtered and the crops shrivelled, but he was sure
the supply ships would come. Since the colony was
established, no single ship had come. The First Fleet
had been the only fleet so far. But Hunt was sanguine.
The other three said nothing, and then they separated
and drew themselves to some sort of attention as the
first of the governor's guests began to arrive, walking
up the slope from the settlement. They were the officers of the colony and its magistrates. The more
provident or dishonest still had good shoes.

The governor still had clothes because he had
come out with three uniforms. There were servants.
The governor's table had silver and fine china, but
little food. The governor had put his own supplies into

the common store. He tried to govern his colony with mercy, and often pardoned the larcenies of half-starved men. His own table had silver and china, but for food only a broth, a thick soup with very little meat in it made to go a long way. The governor said Grace himself, and then each guest produced from his pocket a hunk of bread, which he placed on the polished walnut table beside the solid silver spoon. In Sydney, even at Government House, the unwritten rule was "Bring your own bread."

"The Irishmen, sir," said Lieutenant Johnston of the New South Wales Corps, among general laughter, "have set off for China." The lieutenant's colleagues had known what he was going to say and were delighted to observe the governor as he received the news. The lieutenant had a reputation as a wit. The Corps was getting to be a law unto itself in the colony, even this early. The governor was a captain in the Royal Navy, and he had practically the powers of a viceroy over every man in the colony—except for the officers of the Corps. They were certainly, in the end, under his command, and had come out to guard the convicts. But they were not from his own service. They were soldiers, who wore red coats, and in the day-to-day running of their own affairs they pleased themselves. If the governor cared to give a direct order to their commanding officer, that would be that. It would be obeyed. But in practice he was unlikely to do so, because, at the other end of the earth, he was dependent on the Corps to keep order.

Governor Phillip waited for the laughter to die down. "Poor men," he said. "I tried to save them." The governor and Lieutenant King, Susannah's father, had gone to the Irish when they heard of this belief of theirs that a colony of white people flourished three to four hundred miles south-west of

Sydney, white people in a country that the Irish nevertheless believed was China.

"Only a tolerable walk, sir," said Johnston. "So the Paddies are reported to have gone to China, fourteen of them, with bits of boiled beef over their shoulders gone rotten from being saved so long from their rations, and bags of biscuits at their belts, and each man with a screw of paper full of sugar stored in the crown of his hat. The sugar to put in the infusion of tea they propose to brew with the leaves they pull off the bushes as they cross the Chinese border."

"It was a wild and cruel fancy of theirs," said King, "and they would not be reasoned out of it." The soldiers were indignant that the governor should talk to Irish convicts at all, because to do so was to lower not only his own dignity but also his subordinates'. They would have flogged the Irishmen out of their fancy, and one Corps officer said as much. The governor looked bleakly round his table. Only King and another naval lieutenant, his own men, appeared in sympathy with him. The navy was an unfashionable service, because in it a man might rise by his own exertions and luck, whereas in the army a commission was bought. In his earlier years, the governor had met lieutenant-colonels fourteen years old, who had attained that rank by purchase. But he was continually amazed at the resource and humanity of his own officers when he compared them with their counterparts in the military. He had once requested the Corps officers in the colony, when they saw the convicts diligent, to say a few words of encouragement to them, and when they met them idle, or straggling in the woods, to threaten them with punishment. To this their commanding officer replied that this was not in his written orders, and that he considered it no business of his officers to associate in any way, however slightly, with criminals. Except, the governor sup-

posed, to order them flogged. He was sick of the in-
cessant dignity of the military officers. He was
dismayed by their insensibility.

He thought the Irish had cruelly deluded themselves, but even though he put this down largely to
their Papism, he would not flog a man for his delu-
sions. For what else kept a man alive in New South
Wales? The Irish pined most for home, and their
Celtic imagination was the most easily stirred. Many
Irishmen had no idea how far they had come, no idea
of the shape of the world, and no idea where New
South Wales lay in relation to Ireland. Sailors told
them that if you sailed south from Sydney it got
colder. The Irishmen knew Ireland was colder than
New South Wales. Therefore they reasoned that if
you sailed south you would come again to Ireland.
Some put out in open boats, bound for Antarctica,
and were never seen again. Now these Irishmen,
fourteen of them, had conceived the idea of China. It
was a delusion—spread by a half-mad old woman—
which had been nourished by hope until it was a conviction. And New South Wales itself nourished delusion. It was a continent like no other, with plants
like no other, and animals nowhere else found. Away
from the coast, there were few trees, and most of those
were eucalypts. Eucalypt could be scrub, or it could
grow to trees two hundred feet high. When the hot
wind blew, bark hanging from the trunks in strips
rustled and chafed and almost moaned. The outback
moaned. It was a fragment of another planet, and
on it men took on other minds. Few could stand
the loneliness. Perhaps the sailors did better because
they were used to years of solitude at sea. But all of
them, for more than a year, had heard nothing and
seen nothing that they had not brought with them, or
that was not already on the land. Delusion was their
only hope, and the governor, surveying his dwindling

stores, sometimes thought hope itself was a delusion.

"What of the gold?" he asked.

"The mine is being searched for," said King.

A week before, a convict had come into the commissariat and tried to buy food with ore of some sort, which he said was gold. He was refused the food, but the governor did send a detachment of soldiers to seek out the mine. The man was leading them to it. The soldiers were searching without much hope, since large freshwater rivers, quarries of limestone and even marble, and mines of various rare ores were proclaimed by the convicts every day. No claim had once proved true. But the chance of gold was worth a search. The officers were also asking among the convicts for a goldsmith who could assay the stuff brought in, which was certainly yellow and heavy. But gold in New South Wales? The man said it was, and insisted that he had found another Peru. It might be so, or it might be as insubstantial as the Irishmen's China. The governor and his officers ate their broth.

Outside, Joseph Hunt took his three colleagues into his confidence and promised to make them rich in a way which could gain them boots like his and fill their stomachs. They hesitated.

Next morning in the convict barracks, John Orton, a common felon, earnestly told his mates and his guards that John Orton was no more than an alias, and that he was by rights Count Grigori Orlov, favourite for many years of the Tsarina Catherine II, who had of course been his mistress. This was a tale thought unnecessarily flamboyant. Count Orlov already had a greater fame. He had been a prince of pickpockets. He had once dipped a jewelled snuffbox valued at £4000 from a royal duke, and he had enjoyed a remarkably long run. In the London of the 1780s a felon was judged like a play—the longer the run the more estimable the criminal, and Orlov had run for ever. For fourteen years, in fact, before he made the mistake of passing himself off as a member of Parliament, entering the Commons chamber, and rising to speak. The Speaker, not quite recalling his constituency, said, "The member for? . . ." to which Orlov replied, "For Saint Petersburgh."

That morning too, in front of the barracks, a funeral cortège was drawn up—a dray to carry the coffin of Captain DuCann, late of the New South Wales Corps, whose principal achievement in life was to devise an iron man-collar with long spikes each side of the neck, so that gangs of convicts wearing it looked, as they approached, like herds of horned cattle. As his representative at the funeral the governor sent Lieutenant King, whose order of precedence in the dusty procession to the burying ground was being disputed by Lieutenant Johnston of the Corps. There was no doubt that King's naval rank was senior to the military, and no doubt that as governor's representative he had to take precedence. King did not care to brawl by a coffin, in public, watched by private soldiers and convicts, but the midshipman with him was zealous for the honour of the service, and was quietly reasoning with the military officer, who was shouting about his honour. It was hot. King approached to end the matter, saying he would be perfectly happy to bring up the rear, at which Johnston was determined he should not have that privilege either, and howled at him, "Damn your soul and uniform, King, go first. Go first. I shall be delighted to see any navy man go before me to the grave."

Two weeks later a broken key was found by the night patrol in the lock of the government storehouse. The shaft of the key was discovered after a search at daybreak next morning under the bed of Joseph Hunt, and in his quarters were found two pairs of new boots and twelve ounces of government tobacco. In the house of the bootmaker, quantities of flour, meat, spirits, and tobacco were found, which he admitted he had received from Hunt. Hunt, being in danger of his life, informed on six of his fellow soldiers and turned king's evidence at their trial. The six included his three colleagues of the guard at Government House—Luke Hines, Richard Aske, James Baker, and three others, Brown, Dykes, and Jones. Hunt betrayed men he had himself seduced into the robberies. At half past two they were pronounced guilty by a court of their own officers and sentenced to death. The six stood to attention under the high sun beside the storehouse while the warrant for their execution was taken for the governor's signature. He was a long hour before he brought himself to sign it, and then the paper was brought to the execution place and read aloud to the men. They had already been degraded of all the badges and numbers of their regiment, and now the brass buttons of their tunics were cut away. All wore new boots, from which the laces had been removed. The convicts assembled for the spectacle kept silence. A woman offered the six men rum, which all took, except James Baker, who asked for water. The hangman trussed their arms and placed the rope around their throats. Dykes wept, and Aske said a word to comfort him. Luke Hines squared his shoulders in the bright-red coat made by the tailor—for a leg of bacon—only three days before. The governor did not attend. He refused the invitation of the Corps captain in charge, saying that with the signing of the warrant he already felt executioner enough. There was no drop. The hanging was strangulation by slow struggle. Though the governor did not go, he could not avoid seeing, from his window, the new and vivid-red coat of Luke Hines as at first it jerked, and then as it twisted in a half circle slowly left and then right.

The hanging was by the store the men had robbed.

Easty said, "The gallows was erected before the sentence was cast upon them, before they had any trial."

Lieutenant King glanced at him, and said, "They were the flower of the regiment."

"Sir," said Easty, "Joseph Hunt was the occasion of all their deaths as he was the first that began the robbery, but he received a free pardon."

The convicts maintained their silence. The soldiers looked down at the red dust. The six dying in front of them were six men known to them all, and in so small a colony, six out of so very few. There was hardly a soldier present but shed tears, officers and men.

"What did poor Aske say to Dykes," asked King, "before they were turned off? Did you catch it?"

Easty answered him. "I think he said, sir, 'Such is life.' "

And such was life in the colony in March of 1789, a month before George Washington was inaugurated as first president of the United States, and less than four months before the Paris mob stormed the Bastille. Next year the Second and Third fleets limped into Sydney Cove, trebling the population and bringing food and supplies. The hungry days were over. The *Lady Vane* transport put into the cove carrying London newspapers and the Twelve Apostles, young women sent out by a religious society in London and so named by the sailors. Most were found pregnant by the reverend inspector who visited the vessel in order to certify the young women's high state of moral improvement. The newspapers, arriving eight months late from England, carried an item which amused the governor for days. Washington, D.C., had at last been laid out, three years later, as he never tired of remarking, than his own city of Sydney. But Washington, D.C., was still on paper, and it was also, as he was uncharitable enough to perceive from the news-

paper account, situated on a swamp. The projected
great avenues, he said, if they were ever built, would
for fifty years lead only to other swamps; for more
than fifty years he was right. Not that New South
Wales was a flourishing settlement. There were no
swamps because there was so little water. Avenues
from Sydney would have led to arid deserts. The
searchers for the gold mine had long ago returned,
having found nothing, and in their absence the fraudulent ore had been assayed and found to contain a
mixture of sand, redstone, and powdered red brass.
The discoverer confessed the brass came from two
doorknobs. "Gold!" said the governor. "Doorknobs is
all the gold there ever will be in New Holland." Everyone agreed.

Two of the fourteen Irishmen returned half-
demented from China, the other twelve having fallen
victim to starvation or aborigines. The two survivors
were apprehended at the outskirts of the town and had
the misfortune to be brought before Lieutenant
Johnston. "Arrah there, Colonel," said the first Irishman, "and long life to ye." This counted as insolence,
and the lieutenant set about having them flogged, selecting as scourgers two convicts of bodily height and
power, who inflicted alternate strokes with the cat-o'-
nine-tails. Each Irishman received fifty strokes, after
which one man died.

Fifty was a commonplace punishment, as Lieutenant
Johnston said when he was summoned by the governor
to give an account of himself. The governor had wished
to rule by clemency, and now saw the colony reduced
to a state of near savagery, a savagery he felt as much
in himself as in the felons. The execution of the six
marines, which he had countenanced with such great
reluctance, signing the warrants after agonizing over
those men and the power he had over their lives, but
also having to consider the example he must make of

those who looted the stores of a near-starving settlement, had been on his mind ever since. And now a
man had been flogged to death for believing an old
woman who told him China was within walking distance, and for a few words of greeting to Johnston.
The governor could not arrest Johnston. It was within
the power of any officer summarily to order a flogging
of fifty lashes. More required a magistrate. But the
governor was angry, and brought Johnston before him
as nearly under appearance of arrest as he could,
having him conducted into the room by an escort of
two naval lieutenants.

"You may order a punishment of fifty lashes, Mr.
Johnston, but did it not occur to your mind that these
were men exhausted by months of privation, and probably starved?"

"We gave water to the one who asked, sir." Mr.
Johnston at this point said, as further evidence of his
concern for the state of the two men, that he had ordered a surgeon to be present.

"Bring him," said the governor, and the surgeon
was brought, and read from his notes.

"The first man," he said, "uttered a piercing scream
at the first lash, and continued to bellow at every suc-
ceeding lash. The skin was lacerated at the fifth lash,
the blood came at the sixth, and ran at the eighth. He
asked for water at the tenth lash, which was given. I
am of opinion that he was sufficiently punished at the
twenty-fifth lash. He fainted at the thirtieth. More
blood appeared than I had previously discerned on any
other criminal."

"He fainted, but was still flogged?"

"Yes, sir."

"And the second man?"

"The skin lacerated at the ninth, and there was a
slight effusion of blood. The prisoner subdued his sense
of pain by biting his lips. The skin of this man was

thick to an exceptional degree. Both his mind and his body must have been hardened by former punishments. He did not cry out, but at the eighteenth he began to writhe. Still he did not cry out. He was a criminal known to be 'flash' or 'game.' After the punishment was completed he stood and shook himself like a bear, and said 'Domino.' "

"The first man fainted and was continued to be flogged?"

"Yes."

"Did it occur to you that after the thirtieth stroke Lieutenant Johnston might have been flogging a dead man?"

"It was not the first who died, sir, but the second."

"The harder man died?"

"An hour afterwards. He did not speak after the punishment, but sat and looked to sea."

"And this word 'Domino' that he said, when he was cut down, what was that?"

Lieutenant Johnston explained that it was a word spoken by the winner at the game of dominoes.

"At the end of the game he says 'Domino'?" asked the governor.

The surgeon said, "It is an ejaculation of completion."

"Yes," said the governor. There was nothing he could do except take the extreme step of court-martialling Johnston but there was no charge that would warrant that.

"Go back to your duty," he said. "Get out."

Then, as the lieutenant and the surgeon left, he called back the surgeon.

"There is blood on your coat? Is that blood?" It was only a tiny spattering, but it did appear to be blood.

"I could not remove it, sir. As the scourgers flourished their cats, to clean them after each stroke, a little blood and flesh flew from the instrument."

"How far away were you standing?"

The surgeon reflected. "About thirty feet, sir."

For the next two days the governor rode round his city, taking stock of what he saw, and then wrote a dispatch to the secretary of state in London:

The crops are now fair, but there is not a barn, granary, or storehouse in which to preserve them, nor are these even thought of yet. There are too few mechanics in the colony to erect them. Our boats have gone to ruin and decay. Nor is there any place of public worship. There is a tendency to evil not so much among the felons as among those appointed to guard them, which the greatest diligence on my part has been unable wholly to check. Officers grow overweening in brutality. Men become beasts. Even the Sacred Character of the Redeemer, were He to appear in the colony in its present dark state, might well find gentlemen readier to prepare for His head a second crown of thorns than to welcome Him as their Saviour.

The under secretary in London, when he read this, did not pass it to the secretary of state but put it aside. There were other matters to think of. War with the French was imminent. The under secretary glanced again at the letter he had put aside. "Deluded," he said to himself.

4

---∽◦⊱∾◦∾---

Felons' Gala and the Night of the Wives

BENNELONG, AN ABORIGINE, sat at a side table in the governor's dining-room eating lamb chops daintily with his fingers and a knife. When he had finished he reached instinctively to wipe his hands on the fabric at the back of the brocaded chair on which he was sitting but Easty, who had been charged with his training from the moment of his capture, looked hard at him and Bennelong grinned, dipped his fingers in the finger bowl, and dabbed them on the napkin.

"Might think he'd dined in good company all his life," said the governor.

It had not always been so. The first time he was brought to the governor's table he bowed to the company, as he had been taught, ate his food cleanly, as he had been taught, and then sat back and threw his plate and knife out of the open window. The governor said they had expected too much too soon, and must persevere. They had persevered, until Bennelong was now perfect in all the usages of civilization, not excepting the finger bowl. The time of the Hundred Hungry Days was well behind the colony. There was now abundant food, though when Bennelong first appeared there had not been, and the servants murmured at the amount he was fed. He was sturdy for an aborigine, five feet eight inches tall, and in the famine-time a week's ration kept him content for barely a day. Since it was the governor's policy to keep him content, he was fed as much as he could eat.

Bennelong's introduction to good society had given the governor pleasure. His commission as governor enjoined him to conciliate the affections of the natives, to encourage the convicts to live in amity and kindness with them, and to punish those who wantonly hindered their pursuits or destroyed their persons. He had always assured his superiors in London that he did everything possible to prevent their being offered insults, that he would teach them the advantages of civilization and how to sow corn so that they might not die of starvation in the season when the fish were short, and that when he had time he would himself go among them. "And mix with them myself," he wrote to the secretary. The governor well remembered the day, a year after his arrival, when he and a party of twelve white men went to the north shore of Botany Bay, twenty miles from Sydney, and were surrounded by two hundred and twelve aborigines who, when he offered friendship, laid down their spears and stone hatchers, sat beside their weapons, and afterwards brought some of their women to receive gifts of beads, kettles, and little bells. He was inclined to forget that he and his party of twelve had first set out to find the murderers of two convicts who were speared while they were cutting rushes. But he knew that the aborigines were treacherous. They could invite a man to eat with them, and then, after a convivial meal, kill him. There were few escapes by convicts into the interior, because a man unarmed or alone was invariably murdered, as most of the Irishmen had been. He chose not to believe tales that an aborigine woman

who had given birth to a half-caste child, fathered
by a convict, had tried to darken its skin by holding it
over a fire. It died, but the aborigines would have
killed it in any case, as they always did any white
man's child, and the white men, with so few white
women, had many children by aboriginal women. The
white man had also, as the governor well knew, taken
the aborigines' land. The governor's honest mind,
when it contemplated aborigines, led him to act hu-
manely because he was a Christian who believed in
the equality of all men in the eyes of God, and because he had not been untouched by Rousseau's concept of the Noble Savage. He believed that in his
natural state, from which he departed only to decay,
Man was good and happy. So he was delighted when
Bennelong was captured, submitted to instruction,
wore European clothes, declined all spirituous liquor
and drank only water, and showed pleasure at a portrait of the Duchess of Cumberland. The duchess was
sister-in-law of George III. Easty did not tell the governor that Bennelong, when first shown the portrait,
said of it, as he had been instructed by the servants to
say of any female convict who took his fancy, "Now
there's a flash covess. I like to dab it up with her."
Covess was the feminine of *cove,* and meant a likely-
looking woman: and the rest speaks for itself. Bennelong's command of English was rapidly increasing,
which pleased the governor. He overlooked Bennelong's habit of absconding for the night to pursue
women of his own kind, only finding it strange that on
such occasions the man should leave his European
clothes, of which he was so proud, in a thrown-off
heap on the floor of this or that drawing-room. One
day Easty found Bennelong with his ear half-bitten
through by a man whose woman he was dragging off,
and had it secretly sewn up for him by a surgeon.
After a year Bennelong was no longer guarded but

was allowed to live in a brick hut on the eastern point of the cove, appearing at the governor's for dinner. The part of the cove where he lived was named Bennelong Point.

When Governor Phillip returned home to London he took Bennelong with him, to demonstrate that aborigines existed, to show that they could master both etiquette and English, and to be presented to the monarch. Black men were not then unknown in London. Negroes were fashionable as ladies' servants. The great Doctor Johnson, of the Dictionary, had such a servant, Francis Barber, to whom he left £1500 in his will, a fortune. Nor were blacks slaves. English shipping might flourish on the slave trade, as it did, but in England a black was a free man like any other subject. Not, of course, that Bennelong was a Negro. It was much noted that Bennelong was much closer in his features to an Indian than to any African Negro. He was fitted out like a gentleman in a red tailcoat and doeskin breeches, and was altogether one of the attractions of the season, behaving, except at a concert of music by Handel, in a most genteel fashion, chatting to all and learning to make an excellent bow, a most excellent bow, a most excellent leg.

Lieutenant King had returned to England on leave at the same time, and was employed in conducting Bennelong from town house to town house. To the Handel concert King brought his daughter, Susannah, then aged ten. She did not see him at his best. He made his leg when presented to her, which was elegant enough, but when the music began he was so affected by the clavichord and by the singing of an admittedly indifferent soprano that he covered his ears and gave a great howl.

He was instructed not to howl at his presentation a few days later to George III. His Majesty chose to receive Bennelong, along with Lieutenant King, in his library. The king was expecting a savage. When he saw Bennelong in the dress of an English gentleman, he could think only to address him as a gentleman, and asked with which books written on the topography of New Holland he was familiar. Bennelong was mute, merely making repeated legs until he was escorted from the room. His Majesty asked the lieutenant to remain.

"Now, sir," he said, "tell me. I have read dispatches from New Holland, which speak of hardship. But is not a fine colony to be made there?"

"It is, sir," the officer said, "so fine a harbour as I never before saw. But inland a mile, sir, and it is beyond all description a wretched country."

Few men spoke with candour to George III. He liked this young officer. "Wretched?" he said. "Wretched, you say?"

"Sir," said the lieutenant, "every man, almost, laments himself of being there."

"Ah," said His Majesty, "ah—but they said as much of Virginia, when that was first settled. We have lost Virginia. I will be very frank with you: I was the last to consent to the separation."

The lieutenant had the good fortune to have served in that lost American colony, and so monarch and naval officer talked for half an hour. Conversation pleased George III, and the young man—though he had said Sydney was a wretched place, and though the king had strangely American hopes of his new southern colony—also pleased him.

"And when," asked the king, "do you return?"

The lieutenant did not at that moment intend to return at all. He rather looked for promotion in the navy, and some command. Again he said what he thought, and told the king he believed he had already done his part in New South Wales.

"I should have thought so too," said George III, "if

you had not done it so well." Now this was either great courtesy on the part of a monarch, or an empty compliment (but he was not given to such things), or more likely an expression of hope, because he wished the young man *would* do well. Whatever it was, the fact is that he had no knowledge at all, at that moment, of whether the lieutenant had done well, or done badly, or done anything. But it was decisive. When in 1800 another new governor was required for this new Virginia, George III remembered Philip Gidley King. And that is how he returned to Sydney as governor, and how Susannah, his daughter, came there too.

Six months out from London, on a warm summer evening, the convoy of King's ship and four convict vessels entered the great harbour. It was already sunset, so the fleet anchored for the night in open waters. They would wait until daylight to enter the cove. On board, as his flagship rode at anchor, King entertained the ship's officers to dinner in the great stern cabin. Toasts were drunk to the monarch, to the colony in whose waters they lay, and then, as was the custom, the last toast was proposed by the youngest lieutenant of the ship's company.

"To His Excellency the governor, and to Miss King, the governor's lady."

Susannah had never been toasted in that way before. Nor had she ever been referred to in that way. She was at first surprised, but then she inclined her head in acknowledgement to the officers who drank her health, and to the young man who had proposed it.

When his officers left, and Susannah stood to leave with them, to go to her cabin, King called her back.

"Susannah. Wait."

The officers said their good nights. King resumed

his place at the head of the long table, and motioned his daughter to take her place again, at the side.

King was a widower. Susannah's mother had died when she was three years old. She was his only child. Little more than six months before she had still been at her finishing school at Bath.

King poured himself a glass of port, leaned back in his chair, and regarded his daughter. She was sitting with her back very straight, and her head high. She waited.

"That young man who proposed your health is seventeen," he said. "It will be years before he has any command."

"He is very young," she said.

"Dear Susannah, you are younger still."

She was sixteen.

"And from tomorrow," said King, "you will be the first lady of this colony. You will receive my guests. Government House is not a palace, but it will be yours to run. It will be your house."

She looked down at her lap, at the folds of her dress. He rose and walked round the table to her, and kissed her head. She still sat, and then suddenly reached up and encircled him with her arms.

"I shall do it," she said.

King nodded. He knew very well she would.

"Now go to bed," he said, and then, as she rose to go, he said, "Susannah. It is a very young colony. Younger than you."

But even in so young a colony there were already two traditions. The first was that a play should be given, of course by the convicts, in a theatre newly built by them, to celebrate any great event. The coming of a new governor was such an event. The second was that, the day after the arrival of a convict fleet bringing women convicts, the ticket-of-leave men, convicts who had completed four years of a seven-year sentence or eight years out of fourteen, should be permitted to visit the new women's quarters, in a strictly orderly and supervised manner, to select wives. The play was given on the night of the governor's arrival. The wiving was to be the next day.

The play had a fetching prologue, written by an author who had at home gained by his works great praise and little cash, and had in the end been driven so to desperation by the dilatory payment of a celebrated publisher that he accosted the man in Fleet Street, was once again refused, and in uncontrolled fury dragged the man to the banks of the Thames and threw him in. Alas, he had mischosen his man. The publisher had the ear of those in high places, the warrant for the poor hack's arrest was issued from Downing Street itself, and the penal colony of New South Wales acquired a writer of spirit. This was his prologue:

> *From distant climes, o'er wide-spread seas we*
>   *come,*
> *Though not with much éclat or beat of drum:*
> *True patriots all, for, be it understood,*
> *We left our country for our country's good.*

Much laughter in the boxes. Susannah was delighted.

> *But, you inquire, what could our breasts inflame*
> *With this new passion for theatric fame?*
> *Your patience, sirs; some observations made,*
> *You'll grant us equal to the scenic trade.*
> *Too oft, alas, we've wept th'unwilling tear,*
> *And petrified our hearts with real fear.*
> *Macbeth a harvest of applause will reap,*
> *For some of us, I fear, have murdered sleep.*

This was greeted with silence by all. Many had murdered sleep. Many never knew a lasting peace of
mind. The prologue continued:

His lady, too, with grace will sleep and talk,
Our females have been used at night to walk.

Back to laughter.

Sometimes, indeed, so various is our art,
An actor may improve and mend his part.
"Give me a horse," bawls Richard, like a drone;
We'll find a man will help himself to one.
Grant us your favour, put us to the test,
To gain your smiles we'll do our very best;
And, without fear of turnkey lockits,
Thus, in an honest way, still pick your pockets.

The officers were amused, the governor diverted,
and Susannah delighted. She applauded, clapping her
white-gloved hands. Next day the seamstresses and
dressmakers of Sydney received visit after visit from
ladies wanting gloves made up—cotton gloves, silk
gloves, but always white gloves. Within a week, white
gloves became a fashion in Sydney. It was this more
than anything else that told Susannah that she was indeed first lady.

After the play, the audience all went home in high
spirits, where the officers found that their quarters had
been looted in their absence of all eatables, drinkables,
shoes—of which there was still scarcely a pair to be
had in all Sydney, for want of both shoemakers and
leather—and of anything transportable and saleable.
All feather mattresses had disappeared. The play had
been called *The Revenge.*

A few men were apprehended the next day, and
each endured fifty lashes. Susannah, walking near the

hospital, caught a brief sight of a scourged man being carried there from the prison. He was writhing, and calling out. King wished she had not seen this so soon, but knew he could not keep it from her. It was a thing of everyday occurrence. He did, however, keep her from the wiving, which was less difficult to do since the women's prison, called the factory, was fifteen miles out, at Parramatta. The newly arrived women had been taken to the factory the previous day. There was generally a substantial difference in the criminality of a transported man and a transported woman. The male convicts were not saints. Those from the cities, and most were from London or Liverpool or such places, were a pack of lying, thieving rogues. Some were violent, but few were murderous, few evil. The women were worse. There were some who had simply been unlucky, but on the whole a woman, to be transported, had to be a more persistent, hard, pitiless criminal, a whore who would strip her drunken client of all he wore and leave him naked in the frozen streets, or a kidnapper of children. The women were not only worse but were also under less restraint than the men. On board convict ships carrying females —for once a woman became a convict she was no longer, By Authority, to be called a woman, but a female—there were no soldiers to mount guard. The females were not chained as men often were. It was much lamented that the means of disciplining females were few. Females could scarcely be flogged, though a few were. The master of the *Orion,* in the First Fleet, had tied Mary Abell to the rigging and ordered twenty-five lashes, which the boatswain laid on with a will because she had bitten half through the tongue of one of his shipmates. That was the Mary Abell convicted of abducting a twelve-year-old girl. But such a flogging was unusual. Furthermore, the seduction of the ship's crew, on a voyage of many months, was taken for granted. The females were certainly wanton. Very few, however innocently convicted, retained after the voyage an innocence of any sort.

When they arrived in the colony they were most welcome. In 1800 there were five men to each woman in New South Wales, so the two hundred who sailed with Susannah were eagerly awaited. The colony was conducted on Christian principles. The officers had a wholesome horror of unnatural offences, offences to which females, though depraved, were known to be a preventive. Therefore the lawful union of male and female was held to conduce to the best interests of the colony. So a ticket-of-leave man might also have a ticket of admission to the factory, under strict supervision, and on the explicit understanding that his visit was made with the purpose of selecting a wife. The union envisaged was that of holy matrimony, but it was not inquired too rigorously, and sometimes not at all, whether either partner was previously married in England.

So, the day after the arrival, tickets were given in batches to the males. Each was allowed an hour—to view, converse, invite, and strike the bargain. It was remarked as a sad fact by the magistrate conducting the factory, who was also a clergyman, that the females did most of the viewing and made most of the terms. The magistrate was assisted in keeping order by his subordinates, corporals in the New South Wales Regiment. Things could not proceed too far while the reverend magistrate was present, but on the day after the governor's arrival, while the viewing was proceeding, he departed at dusk for the governor's banquet, whereupon the corporals were cozened, coneyed, traduced by promises, and stupefied by liquor, and males and females became men and women again. Then followed a reckless lasciviousness which, though he could not for a moment have countenanced it, would not much have surprised the governor. The ground was strewn with copulating forms, the more delicate seeking the privacy of kitchens, lofts, or stables. Women rolled from one man to another, and bargained themselves for liquor, for food, for any possession a man might have upon him.

Two hundred women had newly arrived, all declaring themselves single. Three hundred men presented themselves with tickets. It should have been the night of the two hundred wives. That is the name the convicts gave it. The next day, fifty-eight couples did present themselves as candidates for Christian marriage, and were, after the proper time prescribed by the Church for the publishing of banns—banns thirteen thousand miles from any ears that might need to hear them—joined in the sacred bonds of matrimony.

But, before that, dark word of what happened that night came to the ears of the Reverend Peregrine Judd, and he, in black habit, came to the governor.

"The females comported themselves, Your Excellency, like . . . like wanton colts."

"Fillies, Mr. Judd, I take it; fillies. You do see? And fillies are pretty chaste, you know. Ever tried to take a stallion to a filly? Ever *seen* a stallion with a filly, come to that? I suppose you must have done; and been forcibly impressed with the—what would you say, Mr. Judd?"

"By the animality, sir."

"Men and women, if we bring them here, and if *you* give them tickets, are likely to be animals, and a great deal more ingenious and various than animals. Marry the fifty-eight fillies and save their souls."

But it was a strange thing that among these deplored animals there were both men and women who, finding in each other a personal attachment they had not known before—for which they had had no opportunity, coming as they did from teeming lodgings and filthy alleys—stood by each other faithfully. Two such were George Bryant, the boy of the cloak, now about thirty, and Jane Broad. They married, not with the fifty-eight couples, as not wishing to be precipitate, but two months later.

5

The Summons to the Tuileries

IT WAS SO LONG since he had worn full-dress uniform
that, when he received his astonishing summons to the
Tuileries, Nicolas Baudin had to borrow the sword,
his own having long ago been sold. His had been the
sort of service that rarely called for full dress, and,
for that matter, he had not for two years worn even
the seagoing uniform of a lieutenant of the French
Navy. These two years he spent in his Paris lodgings,
writing the memoirs of past voyages. He was poor.
He was the son of a small provincial merchant and
had entered the French marine when Louis XVI was
still alive and king of France. For fifteen years he had
held the rank of lieutenant, unpromoted. He had no
connections. He had made one bad error, which
haunted him. But it was forgotten by almost everyone
except himself, and it had not been an error of seamanship. He was, and he knew it, a much more than
good sailor. But by January of 1802 he had not for two
years been at sea.

"Who," Napoléon Bonaparte had demanded three
days before of an aged admiral whose loyalty and

43

judgement he trusted, "is the best navigator we have? I am thinking of the South Seas."

The old man said straightaway, "Baudin."

"Why?"

"He was under my command twelve years ago. I know him. Bougainville will know him." Bougainville was a great man, old and full of honours, the navigator who gave his name to the crimson bougainvillea, a man as renowned as Captain Cook.

"And *where* is this Baudin," said Napoléon, thinking he would probably be cruising off Martinique or somewhere equally remote, not likely to put into a French port for months or years and therefore useless to his present purpose. "What is his command?"

"To my knowledge, he has none."

"And that man, you say, and Bougainville would say, is the best navigator in France; and he has no command?"

The admiral explained.

Baudin was found rapidly, and in due time presented himself at the Tuileries, the royal palace of the guillotined king. Napoléon had moved his quarters there only a month before. He was not yet emperor; that would take another four years. But he was first consul. He was the man who was making an empire out of a revolution, which was thought by some to be treason to the revolution, and by others a miracle.

Baudin entered the great room knowing nothing. Napoléon did not greet him, but regarded him for ten seconds, which is a long time. He knew Baudin to be older than himself, and now he saw, as he had often seen in his officers of the marine, that a life spent largely at sea is a hard one. Baudin was also not of a sailor's build. He was not tall, well short of six feet, but neither was he broad. His hair was dark, his eyes hazel, or a shade darker than hazel. His life was in his eyes. He could keep the other features of his face impassive, but never his eyes, which revealed his mind. Bonaparte took this in, and then motioned him to a window, where there was a globe, a chased and gilded globe. His finger traced the ports of Canton and Macao, and the island of Timor.

"For two centuries Europeans have formed settlements here."

Baudin assented.

"And for two centuries this," said Bonaparte, indicating the sketchy contour of New Holland, "has been forgotten?"

Baudin let his silence assent again, though for two centuries that land had been not forgotten but unknown. It was only thirty years since the east coast had been mapped at all. In the lifetimes of both men in that room it had been thought possible that a vast, new, unknown continent lay somewhere in the Pacific, much farther north than New Holland. There was room for one. It was only in their time that Captain Cook had disproved that thesis, and mapped a fragment of the eastern coast of New South Wales.

"Well"—and Napoléon sat—"we shall come to know the coastline of that great south land." Baudin was thinking that he had himself come close to that coast twelve years before, and never touched it, having to retreat before a tempest. He was thinking of the mocking story put about by the English that other French navigators had also come as close, and had been deterred by the croaking of the monstrous New Holland frogs.

"Baudin," said the first consul, "I am told you are as good a navigator as I have. I have also been informed that you have spent most of the last few years cruising the Indian and Pacific oceans collecting botanical specimens for the emperor of Austria, or for his nephew of Hungary, and that you appear to have

stocked the more exotic gardens and glasshouses of
Vienna and Budapest."

"I am an officer of the French marine, sir, and I
carried out those expeditions with the leave of my superiors. It was a leave I did not want. I would have
served on any French ship, but none was offered."

"Two are offered now. You will take two corvettes,
and do for me along the coasts of New Holland what
you did for Vienna and Budapest. And, as well, you
will chart, survey, and bring back specimens of these."
Baudin found himself taking tinted engravings of emus
and kangaroos held out to him. He had never seen
such creatures. He had never heard of the first consul's sudden interest in zoology.

"Sir, to do that we shall have to put in at Sydney to
victual, and Sydney—"

"You are perhaps reminding me that we are at war
with England? Captain Cook sailed in time of war, a
British ship with passports from the former government of France and the present government of the
United States of America. You seem to have gone
about the business of the emperor of Austria, with, you
say, the approval of my admirals, and we are, you
will recall, at war with him too. Well, we already have
passports from the English, who have sent them along
with a learned quotation to the effect that even in
times of war men in search of the truth need fear no
enemy. Voltaire, they say."

"Sir, Cook was sailing what I understand to have
been a sort of collier brig. I am to have two corvettes?
Two men-of-war, each of thirty guns?"

"Baudin, you have been a lieutenant for some fifteen years, and I begin to see why. In part I see why.
You will take command of these ships with the rank
of post-captain, you will select your own officers, you
will rename your ships, let us say, *Géographe* and
Naturaliste, you will make France's name honoured

in all the countries you touch on, you will make us beloved of those uncivilized people to whom you will be taking nothing but benefits, and you will show, oh, the great and liberal designs of the Consulate for the pacification of Europe."

Baudin hardly heard these last words. He had never been an ambitious man, but now he had just received the greatest preferment of his life. He had been given *carte blanche* to explore the only utterly unknown continent of the world, and knew that should he remotely succeed he would leave at least a name to posterity. He said, with some passion, that with God's help he would do it.

"You must not," said Napoléon, "confuse even the first consul with God."

Then he said, "I shall not dwell further, Citizen Baudin, on what solely concerns your inner conduct, so to speak." Baudin bowed. That matter of the past again.

So there they were. Corvettes, passports, surveys, emus. And of course more than that. Baudin could never remember the first consul's exact words, nor were those words later embodied in any formal orders, but he was told indirectly, though plainly enough, that the great southern route to China and the East was the concern of France as well as of Britain, and that Sydney commanded that route. He understood. Ten years later Napoléon would order the taking of Sydney, though by then he would lack the ships to do it.

As Baudin left his presence, Bonaparte called after him, "Outward bound, take on wine at Tenerife."

6

---⌒⊙⌒---

The Sighting of the French Sail

BY 1802 SYDNEY had a town clock. The loss of eight
sheep and a hog killed by lightning was no longer a
public calamity. As early as 1790, shops opened in the
town. Houses were numbered by 1796. There was
progress. The colony was a flourishing gaol. It could
also be said by its presence to be guarding the southern trade routes. The other things hoped of it had
failed. South Sea pines proved too brittle or downright
rotten to provide masts for His Majesty's ships. The
southern flax of which so much was hoped, since it
had a longer fibre than the Baltic flax on which for
years Britain had perilously depended for the ropes
and rigging of its ships, would not make even a decent
cat-o'-nine-tails. The knotted cords tended to fray
soon after the fiftieth lash. By 1802, six convicts had
suffered as many as a thousand lashes each but, as
one despairing officer remarked, they were so little
reclaimed by the lash as if so many drops of water had
been poured upon their backs. He might also have remarked that four of them, if not reformed, were at
least so crippled that they could never again work,
only steal.

Bennelong had returned from England civilized, and continued to wear the clothes of an English gentleman. He went so far as to bring back lacy petticoats that he made his wives wear for decency's sake. They obeyed until they were ridiculed by their own people. Bennelong's noble savagery had been so thoroughly civilized out of him that he took to drink. He was no longer asked to eat at Government House. Easty tried to look after him, but found the man intractable. Captain Johnston of the Corps, a few days after his promotion from lieutenant, found that his elevation had given him a new sense of concern for the safety of the convicts and went round announcing he would shoot the Bennelong fellow the next time he saw him drunk. He was only prevented from doing this by a direct order from the governor. Bennelong was not given new Western clothes, and his old ones soon wore to rags. In the end he took to the bush, living alone in the outback, and was not seen for months at a time.

Governor King continued to be irritated by the atrociousness of the military officers. Two women, Bridget Rose and Margaret Murphy, on no more than suspicion of stealing a gown and selling it for liquor, were ordered to be chained together and to remain chained until the gown was restored. King released them when he heard of it. Then there was the affair of John Macarthur, formerly a London corset-maker, who had risen to be a lieutenant in the Corps. Macarthur, with farsightedness, had devoted himself to sheep-farming for profit, but overstepped himself when he picked a quarrel with the lieutenant-governor and wounded him in a duel. King took the opportunity to be rid of the man and sent him to England for court-martial, together with a report intended to put a final stop to his military career. He wrote that Macarthur's chief employment during his years in the colony had been that of making a large fortune for himself, helping his brother officers to make small ones, mostly at the public expense, and generally sowing discord and strife. He had also wounded the lieutenant-governor. That, thought King, sealing the dispatch, should be enough.

What with all this, the governor could not help reflecting that few of his magistrates and even fewer of his officers were gentlemen. He often consoled himself by conversing with those few of the newly arrived convicts who, back in England, had been, if not gentlemen, at least more like gentlemen than his colleagues in the administration of the colony. These conversations were known as his "At Homes."

"Well, Mr. Burgoyne," he would say to a man brought before him, "and what were you sent here for?"

Mr. Burgoyne would explain that he had suffered the misfortune to be acquainted with a person of bad character, and that—

"But, Mr. Burgoyne, come to the point. I don't want you to go round here and then back again and round the other way." Here the governor traced circles on the table with his finger as he spoke, and fixed the man with an amiable stare. "Really, sir, you are not at the bar of the Old Bailey now. Come to the point."

The point was that Mr. Burgoyne, having the misfortune to introduce himself to a royal levée at St. James's Palace attended by the lord chancellor and some of the greatest quality in the land, had cut off and made away with the insignia of the Order of the Bath, encrusted with brilliants of the first water, worn by the Duke of Buccleuch.

"So you are of the better class of pickpocket, Mr. Burgoyne?"

"Though Your Excellency may doubt my assertion, I solemnly assure you I was innocent of the charge."

"Oh, I dare say, Mr. Burgoyne, very innocent, no doubt. Quite innocent, I dare say."

"I am happy you should think so, sir."

"Yes. And what trade were you brought up to, Mr. Burgoyne?"

To this the man replied that he had no trade at all, since he was, though now regrettably declined, a gentleman by birth. The governor nodded and nodded and gave the man a scribbled note to be a clerk at the commissary stores, where, he said, there were no brilliants of any water. This kept the man off the road gangs and out of fetters.

It was one afternoon in late June when Sir Harry Browne Hayes, knight, made his appearance and he, though not only a transported felon but also an Irishman, was as near a gentleman as could be got.

He was shown in while the governor was putting the finishing touches to a watercolour of a black man, whom he had portrayed standing on a rock of flat sandstone at the east side of the cove. The pencilled outline was complete, and the governor was tinting in the colours.

"A moment, if you please," he said over his shoulder. Sir Harry did wait a moment but then, when he caught sight of the painting, he stepped over to regard it.

"A fine thing, sir," he said. "A very fine thing. To the life. It is a gift you have, sir, to get so near the life."

The governor put down his brush and turned round.

"Indeed?" he said.

Sir Harry apologized. "I beg your pardon, sir, to have come between you and your work. But at home, in Cork, the walls of my house were covered with fine paintings, though I could never myself as much as

draw a mouse, or not so that even a cat would recognize it. I beg your pardon, sir."

"Not at all, not at all," said the governor. "But now
I fear I must ask you what came between you and
your house in Cork, with its fine paintings. Pray, Sir
Harry, why were you sent here?"

"I am an Irishman, sir."

"I am sorry for that; but, Sir Harry? . . ."

"Sir, I was a freeman of Cork and high sheriff of
that city."

"But even for that, Sir Harry?" And the governor,
making his circles on the table, was saying don't go
round here and back again, when Sir Harry volunteered that he had been condemned for abducting an
heiress.

"Ah," said the governor, waving him to a chair.
"You were of course innocent? Quite innocent?"

"Oh, no, sir, quite guilty, very guilty. Though she
was a Quaker."

"Ah," repeated the governor, and, dismissing his
escort and calling for a decanter, he was soon settling
down to chat with Sir Harry as if with a member of
his own club in London. A gentleman was rare.

"Not at all for the money, Sir Harry, I take it,
though she was an heiress?"

"There was a matter of twenty thousand pounds
that she had, sir, and a man could not say, knowing
of such a sum, that his conduct might not be swayed,
but it was mostly for Mary Pike herself, for she was
as fine a woman as a man could wake to see as his first
sight of a new day. But she was never of one mind.
First she would, and then she would not, and seeing
the poor woman's hesitation . . ."

"There was nothing you could do but make up her
mind for her?"

"It was so. But there no violence offered to Miss
Pike, except the forcing of her from her father's house,

and she assented to that, sir, as you might say, afterwards. Three months we lived together, as man and woman, and going openly to assemblies and other public companies, where the natural gaiety of her was a great thing to see; and a great thing for me in company to have it said behind my back that such a fine girl was mine. There are some things a man likes to hear said behind his back, and him not intended to hear. There *was* the sin of pride in it."

"And the, ah, forcible marriage was taken exception to by the father?"

"A marriage there never was, though I offered it, and me having her already too. We lived as man and woman, and such a woman, who could hold out her wild arms to me at dinner with the lord mayor himself, and take me away, in the eyes of the company, between the soup and the roast, to her bed. She was a dear wanton. But she was halfhearted in the deeper things. We lived as man and woman, not man and wife. She would not be my wife. Sir, the indictment said, 'Carrying off with intent to marry,' and I would not demur at that indictment as all my friends cried out to me that I should. I would not deny the intent. It was always my dearest intent. I was a widower, sir, and I wanted a wife. If I had wanted *Mary,* not marriage, it would never have come to the assizes. So there's the outcome of an honourable intent."

Sir Harry laughed, and the governor leaned forward to refill his glass.

"But you were thinking," said Sir Harry, "that the money went with the marriage? No marriage, no fortune? I do not blame the natural course of your thoughts, sir. It is very likely, but it is not the truth. Banker's daughter though she was, she ran through two-thirds of her fortune unasked. I never asked a penny of it, but she gave it. But she was a Quaker, and thought it a sin to marry having been abducted,

as if the good God could read between the lines of a
marriage register but not see between the sheets of her
bed. And I could not carry away her mind, much
as I tried. I said the abduction was on my soul, not
hers. Still she asserted that we were living in sin, a
state from which we could not marry, even to cure
that sin. It was a Quaker logic that escaped me. The
Irish Church, being older, is more conversant with
man's frailties. So I told her. And as for living in sin,
sir, I denied that premise, given my intent to marry.
'Living in the sin of abduction, then, Sir Harry?' she
would say, 'living in abduction,' and she was not to be
moved."

"But what brought you here, Sir Harry? Who laid
the information?"

"Zealots, her brothers. Broadsheets all over Cork,
five hundred pounds reward for my discovery, and I
walking at liberty past the whole town every day and
all the world knowing me and smiling with me. Then
some poor man in need, God rest his soul, took the
five hundred, and I was taken. Do you know, sir,
when the day came in court, Mary Pike spoke as
clearly against me as if I were a man she had
observed, but did not know. But I swear she did it
without malice, for she would have thought that a sin.
I knew the jury, all of them, and they said, as I saw,
that she was unembarrassed on the occasion. When I
was brought in guilty, I asked the judge to hang me
that day, but he would not, and then, while I waited
three months in gaol expecting my death, I had the
'Dead March' in *Saul* played every day on a barrel-
organ as I dined. A man should prepare his soul."

"But you are prepared for Heaven, not New
South Wales, Sir Harry. And what became of Mary
Pike?"

"I never heard. Gay at other assemblies, and in
other company? She was a dear wanton."

The governor was asking what he could do to make his guest's stay in the colony less arduous, and Sir Harry was requesting the loan of books from his library, when a ship was signalled in the bay. King begged Sir Harry not to disturb himself, and by all means to finish the decanter, but to excuse him while he attended to his duties. He went to see the ship.

She was a French corvette, in tatters, only twelve of her crew fit out of one hundred and eighty, and unable to work herself into the cove. King sent sailors to bring her in. The men were received at the hospital with care, and the officers by the governor and his daughter, Susannah, with all sweet help and gentle visitation.

7

---◦◦◦◦---

The Sandalwood Bed, and the Conception
of Australia

BAUDIN WAS FIT IN TWO WEEKS, and he owed much
of his recovery to Susannah. She was a woman of
vivid spirit and, besides, having been brought up in
decent English society in the last decade of the eighteenth century, the century of the Enlightenment, she
spoke better French than he did English, and was almost as competent a botanist. So she was with him a
great deal. He insisted, as soon as he could insist on
anything, that they should speak English. It was all
very well, he said, for a man in a fever to be nursed
in his own language, but now he was well he should
speak hers. She laughed at his pride, and he
laughed at it himself. She undertook his further instruction in English, in his turn he instructed her in
astronomy, and they were altogether happy. He was
tender with her. She touched his heart, and, when she
saw this, there was no defence left to her, or to him. A
wound which had afflicted his heart for ten years—for
he was a man who remembered and remembered, and
tormented himself with remembrance—was at last
solaced. He truly loved Susannah, and within a month
they were grateful lovers. He could remember days as

intense, but never happier. He could even bear a ten days' absence from her to prospect the nearby coast for specimens of timber-wood, and to trap the required kangaroos. It was from this brief expedition that Susannah watched him return, at the beginning of our story. She waited for him in the dark, and then took him to the house. Her father was away for the night at Parramatta.

Susannah was a beautiful woman. She stood quite still, by the great bed in her room, while he looked from her windows into the cove. There were the lights of his own ship, the *Géographe,* and of his second vessel, the *Naturaliste,* which had reached Sydney some weeks after him, and the lights of an American trader, a beautiful ship, he thought, as trim a merchantman as he had ever seen. She was the *Caroline,* out of New York. Yankee captains were learning that sugar, tobacco, muslins, silks, and above all rum, commanded a price in Sydney. Susannah was dressed in Chinese silks and Irish linens that had come in the cargoes of American ships. The bed too was of American pine, pine that had been the gift of an American skipper who desired the governor to enlarge his licence to import West Indies sugar. The wood had been worked by a convict as a labour of love, because he had been a cabinet-maker before a thief, and longed to make fine things. It was a fine bed. At its head he had set an inlay of red sandalwood, from Djakarta. He said it was the kind of sandalwood which had lined King Solomon's temple. The bed was always known as the sandalwood bed, and had always been Susannah's.

Baudin closed the shutters and turned to her. The whole length of the room was between them. She was lit by the three candles in the gilt candelabrum she still carried.

"Put it down," he said.

She placed it on the rosewood chest, and then
stood as before, and smiled directly at him. Baudin
always told her that her hair was black, but it was
brown, though so dark a brown as to be black in any
light but open day. Her dark eyes and all her features were, he had often told her, those of Raphael's
portrait of Saint Cecilia, which he had often seen in
the cathedral at Bayeux before the Revolution. Susannah was no saint. Her time as a girl in London and
Bath, as a daughter of a lieutenant in the colonies,
had not been easy. In England she was not the governor's daughter. There she was poor, and lonely, and
it had made her wary. This wariness she hid under an
assumed assurance that was almost coquettish. She
had not acquired naturally, but had been taught at
her finishing school, the assurance of a lady. She had
been *taught* how to walk through a doorway, and how
to hold her head high. This she did with such style that
it might have been to the manner born, but she knew
it had been taught. And she could at times seem to
flirt with her father's aides, though she did not know
she did this, or with the man who held her horse,
or with a ferryman. She did smile directly at any man,
in the most trivial of transactions. She could be proud,
and hurt, and so preserved this wariness. She was always, as it were, remembering to walk through door-
ways with her head held high. Baudin loved her, but
that did not stop him from seeing this touch of the
coquette in her. He saw it all the more clearly. He was
older than she was, and wiser than he had been a few
years before. He loved her most when she was grave.
In repose she was grave, and her gravity moved him
to tenderness and sometimes near to tears of gratitude
for the great gift she was to him; a gift he had never
expected again. But he was now wise enough to see
her coquettishness for what it was, for an uncertainty,
a tentativeness. He had the sense to know she was

whole-hearted. He was a fortunate man to know this, because it was true. She stood by the bed with a smile that a jealous man, or a man less happy—a man made less happy by the smallest doubt—might have thought a mocking smile. He walked across to her and loosened her long hair. He unfastened her silk dress, and she moved her shoulders, held her arms straight at her sides, and let the slight garment slip down her arms and over her hips onto the floor. He loosened the waistband of her linen slip, and let that fall. He knelt and removed her shoes. He rose and kissed her eyes, and took her hands in his for a moment, and only then did she move onto the bed and lie waiting for him.

When he came to lie beside her, arched above her, she held out both arms to welcome him, and spoke his name. As he entered her, he spoke her name again and again, making of the words a litany of hope and faith. He was not a man of any formal religious belief. These were the only moments of his life in which he felt the gift of Grace, and she was as beyond herself as he was.

They slept for a while, perhaps for half an hour, until he awoke and woke her. She laid her hand on his head, a touch almost of ceremony, and then moved towards him and held him. They talked drowsily. She lay, with her eyes closed, her hair over her face, and her arms thrown wide on the pillows. He raised himself, lightly kissed the parting of her legs, and then her forehead, and then with the edge of his right hand traced a course from her throat, down across her belly, towards the slightly raised knees.

"Terre Napoléon?" she said.

He smiled. When they had first met, at any rate as soon as he was sufficiently recovered to walk with her in the gardens of the domain, he had told her, most indiscreetly—so indiscreetly that they both knew then that a great intimacy had already grown up between them—that he would on his charts mark New Holland as Terre Napoléon.

"Napoléon's land?" she had said. "So much for your passports then? So much for your botany? So much for your kangaroos? And of what will my father then be governor?"

Of the corner of a continent no one had ever mapped, he could have said, and that continent as large as North America and much less known. In that continent, which might be a waste or as rich as Europe, her father had a commission as captain-general and governor-in-chief of a tract of unknown land stretching westwards to the 135th meridian of longitude, more than a thousand miles west of Sydney. The frontier was a notional line over which, he would have guessed, no man would ever walk for another twenty years, and that would have been a good guess. But he did not say anything like that, partly because he did not wish to be discourteous to a British governor whose kindness to him had been so great, and partly because he already loved that governor's daughter. But "Terre Napoléon" he certainly intended to mark on the charts he would present, on his return, to the first consul. That had been the conversation in the garden.

In bed, Susannah now said, "Nicolas, you have circumnavigated the world?" She knew he had, and when he returned to France would have done it a second time. When he returned to France—they had rarely talked of that. Her mind ran from the thought. Her mind fled from it. But the return would have to be soon.

Susannah had the gift of abandon, of a carnality that was right with a true lover, and this is a gift beyond words. She took his hand, guided it gently to her maidenhair and between, below, and said, "You have circumnavigated me. You discovered me. So name me."

"Not for Napoléon," he said, and then went on. "The Frenchmen who came to New Holland before me—"

But she interrupted him, took his hand and kissed it, and said, completing his sentence, "—and who ran away because of the frogs?"

"Those who came before me," said Baudin, "called it Terre Australe, the southern land."

"I am your southern lands?" she said. "That will not do. A name of any consequence must be in Latin."

He was almost asleep. He touched her shoulder. She understood, and turned with her back towards him, and he covered them both with the bedclothes, and curled himself around her, with his face in the nape of her neck.

Then, into her hair, he murmured, "I will say, *Australia*. Is that Latin enough for you? I shall call you Australia." She moved her head in assent, took his arm and placed it round her, and they slept.

What will not be believed is that the next day, at dinner, when her father had returned, captain-general of Terre Napoléon, Susannah expressed the view, in front of Baudin and two of his officers who were there, and before Sir Harry Browne Hayes, who could not possibly be invited to the governor's table, but was— what will not be believed is that she said, addressing the table at large, that Australia would do very well for a name for the whole continent. Better than New Holland, seeing there had been no Dutchmen for years. Much better than New South Wales, because who could name a continent after Wales? Australia would do very well: did not Captain Baudin think so? Whereupon the gentlemen all agreed, and, what was more important, Sir Harry Browne Hayes said he would willingly abduct a continent of that name, and so told his convict friends, and they began to use the name in what was known as the "flash language." It became current. It was settled in a year.

At the dinner table Baudin returned her smile, and spread both his hands open towards her in a gesture which was entirely comprehended by the governor, and very well understood by Baudin's fellow officers, and by Sir Harry Browne Hayes. All this was fifteen years before a future governor of the colony, in a dispatch to Westminster, suggested that Australia, which did appear to be the given name, the name generally used, might be a good name to adopt, did they think, for the whole continent?

8

Them that Sells, and Them that Drinks

ON A BARREN PLOT a mile from Sydney, twenty feet from his shack which was in turn only twenty feet from the Parramatta road, Henry Abrams sat in the heat of the day drinking one glass of rum, and then refilling the glass and with a muttering of words tipping the contents slowly onto the ground beside him where a rough cross of wood was planted in the earth. All this was plainly visible from the road, and the governor, on his way home from Parramatta, ordered his carriage to stop. He watched as the man went through the same ritual for a second time, but could not hear the words he uttered.

He got down from the carriage.

"Take care, Y'r Excellency," said the sergeant of his guard. "The man is mad drunk."

"No, the man is despairing drunk."

He walked across the red dust to the man, who was pouring another libation over what the governor could now see was a fresh grave.

"I loved you in this life, Retty, though I showed it little enough. I had little to share, and I didn't share that much. But I'll share this now, if you'll take a drink from me."

He looked up and saw the governor and sergeant, and pointed to the earth. "She does take it down, you see." He watched, and the governor and the sergeant watched as the rum soaked into the sodden patch at the foot of the cross.

"She does, you see."

"What are you?" asked the governor.

"I'm Henry Abrams. And that's Retty. But no more of that. It's too late for reason now."

"I know him, Y'r Excellency," said the sergeant. "Abrams, a highwayman that was. Came out First Fleet and pardoned two year ago, but never prospered." Then to Abrams the sergeant said, "She was your wife that drowned?"

Abrams refilled the glass with care, and offered it first to the sergeant and then to the governor, who shook their heads. "We put out in a boat," he said. "But that was afterwards. First there was Ellen Breen, and we revelled the day in the town. I don't know that I liked Ellen, but we were all day in the town. And at four we came back to the water, where there was a boat. Ellen got in the boat, and that was when Retty came round."

"Came round?" said King.

"Came round. Came round the cove to find me, and saw Ellen in the boat. She did use language then, and all but pushed me in the cove, and Ellen hit Retty with an oar, but she missed. And all the time Retty cursed me, by the child that was in her, that I'd be damned for Ellen, and I dare say I am."

He drank. "First Fleet we both was, and then ticket-of-leave, and then the king's pardon, and then my own land." He gazed at the arid patch around him. "But it would never yet grow.

"Were you First Fleet, sir?" This he asked of the

sergeant who seemed to him, as wearing a uniform, of greater authority than the other man who was standing watching.

The sergeant said, "What happened with the boat?"

"Capsized. We all know that. Capsized near Breakfast Point. We made peace, and after Retty cursed me again she came into the boat too. I think Ellen was asleep. But you see, we lost an oar. Ellen hit Retty with an oar, which was the one that was lost, because it floated away."

He poured another glass for himself, and another for the grave. "I sculled out to Breakfast Point, with one oar, and then Retty saw the second, where it had drifted, and she reached for it and fell, and took the boat with her, and us all in the cove drowning. I never saw Retty again, and Ellen drowned asleep. I was the fullest of us all but I did swim. I was the fullest of the three of us, and I never knew rum did float."

He looked up at the sergeant's red coat. "Were you in the First Fleet? There was an officer there spoke wise words to me. Wise words. He was always saying the same, mind, but he did say—this was when we was in the chain gangs, and in the heat of day, like now—he did say, 'Abrams, you have a precious gift, denied to many. You have peace of mind. For,' he would say, 'the remembrance of your past vices is for the moment absorbed in the greatness of your present punishment.' Wise words. Damn fool that he was, saying always the same. Damn fool."

The man poured more rum straight from the bottle into the earth, watching until the last drop soaked in.

"Rum," said the governor. "Blasted rum."

"Oh, rum," repeated the man on the ground, looking at the governor as if aware for the first time who he might be, and then waving his hand out over the water to where a cutter loaded with kegs was moving away from a supply shop. "But this colony is made up

half of them who sells rum, as you sees," gesturing towards the cutter and the ship, "and half," taking the
bottle and with infinite care, tipping the last few drops
into the grave, "and half of them that drinks it."

The governor did not need to look twice to know
that the cutter was Johnston's, recently promoted major and now commander of the New South Wales
Corps. He knew Johnston of old. He knew well that
the major and his officers made far and away the
greater part of their income from a monopoly in rum,
a monopoly they enforced with the rifle butts of their
troops, who simply stove in any casks found to have
been acquired from other sources. King was disposed
not to see many things that he did see. He relied on
the good sense of Johnston not to allow his greed to
carry things too far. Johnston, in his turn, ought to
have known, and knew, that a letter from the governor to London could have him recalled—though that
would take perhaps a year. The governor, looking out
into the cove at the cutter and the supply ship, and
then at a brig lying off the mouth of the cove, waiting as he knew to enter the next day with another
cargo of rum, resolved to say a few quiet words. Johnston was asked that night to dinner.

"Major Johnston," said the governor, having taken
him aside beforehand, "what was the asking price, per
gallon, of the master of the *Solent?*" That was the ship
already in the cove, discharging rum. The governor
had never before asked such a question.

The major assured him that a dozen kegs would,
naturally, be delivered to Government House the next
day if the governor wished. He never had before, but
the major considered himself a reasonable man and the
governor's hint, as he took it to be, a reasonable one.

"No, Johnston, I was just wondering about the asking price."

"Twenty shillings," said the major.

The governor had made careful inquiries and found the figure to be eight shillings. He said nothing of that.

"Ah, and what will it fetch, would you say? A fair figure?"

"Thirty," said the major, "but some of it is poor stuff and will not make that."

The governor had heard eighty shillings was already being extorted from the publicans of Sydney, and guessed that the price would rise before it fell. He also had information that the quality was excellent.

"A plentiful supply?" he inquired.

The major attempted a light answer. "The colony does have a thirst."

"I have seen the results of that thirst. But shall we say we have enough for the moment? It would be better if the ship that works in tomorrow were to discharge no rum here, and I shall be obliged if you will see that she does not."

Johnston had already begun to negotiate with the master of the second ship. "I shall require that order in writing, sir," he said.

"No," said the governor, "I do not think that you will, on reflection, find that necessary at all. Now, let us go in."

At dinner the conversation was not about rum but wine. Baudin's third lieutenant, Pèlegrin, who was only a boy of twenty, was saying he had met two winegrowers from Bordeaux. The governor knew them: they had come out on a Dutch merchantman the year before and had by all been thought slightly mad in their enthusiasm at the colony's future as a producer of wine. Now they had met the French lieutenant and communicated their enthusiasm to him.

"They told me," said the officer, "that no other part of the world they knew, not one of the great wine regions of France, could grow a vine with such force as New South Wales."

"Nowhere else so fast?" said the governor.

"So they said."

"So they told me too. But the trouble is, the first north-westerly off that desert that none of us has yet explored, and the whole lot shrivels up. So, as I remember it, they moved away somewhere up-country." The governor recalled giving them his formal permission to go where they liked, only not to get made into stew by the aborigines, and off they went carrying their cherished cuttings with them, which they had brought out in the Dutch ship.

"Well," said the lieutenant, "they found the slopes of a valley where everything has flourished. North of the city. Fifteen miles north. I tasted their new wine and thought it more than fair. Not quite this"—the governor's guests were drinking a Burgundy from the same Dutchman that had brought the French wine-growers—"by no means this, but fair wine, much fairer than I have drunk in some French inns, and some French ships."

Major Johnston, whose thoughts were on a cargo of West Indies rum waiting in the cove, a cargo he could not now touch, drank a great deal of the governor's good Burgundy and kept a stubborn silence.

The governor wished the wine-growers success. England was, he supposed, the only maritime power in the world in whose empire no wine of any consequence was made. France, Spain, Portugal, Holland, all had their vineyards either at home or somewhere in their overseas possessions, and England, he thought— though his tone of voice hardly showed any great concern for it—must spend a fair part of her wealth on Madeiras and Burgundies and Sherries.

The French and English officers were now very easy with one another, easy enough for Pèlegrin to remark that if England had her own vineyards she wouldn't have needed to try, twice each, to take the

Canary Islands and the Cape; and for the governor to reply that, as for the Canaries, they were probably worth the taking, but, as far as the wine went, he would not risk a sloop for the Cape.

Johnston, summoning the footman to refill his glass, growled at this, and Susannah, whose misfortune it was to have the man next to her, turned to address Baudin across the table. Had he met these French wine-growers?

"No. Just a forger."

"Plenty of those," said the governor. "Good climate for those."

"From Paris," said Baudin.

"French? Didn't know we had any French convicts. Must try and do something for the fellow. Could he teach a smattering of French to the daughters of the garrison? What's his name?"

"Morand," said Baudin. "And he's persuasive enough. He did put it rather well, saying all he'd ever done was wish to associate himself with the Bank of England. . . ."

"Laudable enough wish," said the governor.

"But without, as he put it, having first gone through the formality of opening an account there."

The evening was well enough advanced for them to laugh at this, and to be highly entertained by what followed.

"Notes of hand for five pounds," said Baudin. Notes on the Bank of England, only he got slightly confused in his etching of the plates, and Britannia came out sitting the wrong way round."

A voice from next to Susannah interrupted the laughter.

"Subvert the whole economy," said Johnston.

"What?" asked the governor.

"Undermine the whole economy. Damned rogue intended to print a million of the things, useless paper, honoured for gold, and the whole economy of England crashing round our ears."

Susannah laughed helplessly. Baudin had to look away for fear he might do much the same. Pèlegrin buried his face in his napkin, and the governor gave a great roar of laughter. This was all a pity. For once, Major Johnston was on the fringes of the truth. Morand had intended to print a million notes, with the precise, mad purpose Johnston had expressed.

"I'll give him a ticket-of-leave tomorrow," said the governor. "He can teach the ladies how to sketch too." But Johnston was on his feet in half-drunken anger. First his rum lost to him, and now this mockery. It was too much humiliation, and he turned furiously to Baudin, who was the only man at the table who had managed to keep his face, and then to the governor. "Your Excellency will know," he said, trembling, "that the brig standing out in the cove, the brig whose rum is not to be introduced into the colony, has already contracted eight hundred gallons to Captain Baudin, who will be enabled to sell it at a vast profit?" And with that he threw his napkin in Baudin's face.

Out of the silence which followed, the governor said, "Major Johnston, it is with my knowledge and permission that Captain Baudin has revictualled his ships for their return passage, and with that knowledge and permission that he has contracted for rum from that brig. Now, sir. . . ."

Johnston realized the enormity of what he had said and done, bowed to the governor, and apologized to Baudin, saying, with the weird echo of some form of words he had got from a manual of etiquette as it pertained to insults, "I am in your hands." Phrases such as "the demanding of satisfaction," and the "putting himself at Baudin's disposal," slurred across his mind.

Baudin, anxious that Johnston should be humiliated no further, replied, "I beg you to think no more of it."

Johnston left. Baudin, by his gentle conduct, had made an enemy, because such generosity is rarely forgiven. By intending not to humiliate Johnston he had placed him greatly in his debt and therefore greatly humiliated him. The governor by his laughter had made a scourge for himself and his successor; and Susannah, by hers, had engendered an enmity that would last longer than she could have dreamed.

9

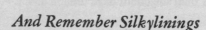

And Remember Silkylinings

GOVERNMENT HOUSE WAS BUILT in the Italian style, with colonnades, but to it there was attached, in the English style by an English builder, an orangery. The builder was a man who, some years before, while in the employment of the Crown Estates in London, had stolen many tons of ready-cut Portland stone from the Crown's yards. He did this openly, getting his wagoners to call at the government depot with their drays and teams of horses, and to present an order signed by himself. His signature was known and trusted. For many years he had been patching up Kensington Palace and other royal residences, and collecting many tons of cut stone to carry out the work. But he began to use more and more of the stone to build handsome houses on his own account, which he sold at a handsome profit, until one day he was found out, and transported. In New South Wales he was put to the making of Government House, and, since he had often worked at Kensington Palace and admired the orangery there, he built another at Sydney. It was elegant but it was not needed. In Sydney, orange trees need no shelter to grow. The orangery was not used, fell

into disuse, and was overgrown outside by vines. No
one went there. But there it remained, an arched summerhouse, aside from the residence, and the vines gave
shade. What was intended as a shelter for orange trees,
to warm and encourage them, became a summerhouse
for Nicolas and Susannah, to shade them. At one end of
the orangery the builder had placed a marble table,
six feet long. He wished, after all, to make something
not of Portland stone. The curiously olive marble, almost like onyx, came from the hold of a Spanish ship,
and the builder gave it to his masons to fashion after
a design he sketched in pencil on the white wall of the
orangery. The masons did well. The table top was
smooth. Its four legs were shaped like those of a lion,
with lion's paws.

It was the orangery and this table which Nicolas
and Susannah discovered. On an afternoon a few days
after the naming of Australia, she sat on the table, and
leaned back, supporting herself with her hands on the
table behind her. Her head was thrown back so that
her hair spread out, also behind her. Nicolas stood by
an archway. Outside it was full afternoon. Inside it was
cool. The table was cool through Susannah's dress.

"I must tell your father," said Nicolas.

"My love, he knows," she said, to the ceiling.

"He knows, but I must tell him."

She stayed as she was, then first turned her head to
look across at him, and then, without moving, closed
her eyes. There was already a language between them
that takes years to grow between others, or never
grows. With most it never grows. It could be direct,
and then it was mostly she who was direct, either
speaking to him in words that were most open or else
holding out her arms to him, again openly. Or it could
be indirect, as in a feigned withdrawal, a silence, or a
closing of the eyes. It was the most subtle of semiot-
ics, a language of silences and signs shared by them.

She closed her eyes, and he crossed to her, and waited,
and then let his hand fall on the line of her hair as it
fell from her brow, and from the back of her head,
and behind her shoulders. She never showed she felt
this, unless with the faintest of smiles.

This is a moment at which the manner of her dress
matters least, but whatever she wore became part of
Susannah, so this is how she was dressed. She could
have been Greek. It was a time when a woman wore
as little as women ever have worn. The farthingales
and frills and wigs of ten years before were all gone,
and so was almost everything gone. Ten years before it
would have been unthinkable not to be nipped in at
the waist by tight lacing: in 1802 it was as unthinkable
to be constricted in that way. Ten years before everything would have been elaborate: now everything was
simplicity. By those in England who did not fight, the
French Revolution and the wars that followed were
felt mostly in the changing cut of women's clothes.
The Revolution took away the old, and put the new
in its place. The new felt the need to be pure, and
purity was Classical Greek. Susannah's hair, at all
times of the day and on all occasions, was her own.
She had no wigs. On her face she wore no colouring.
The Directory was mostly known not as a French political institution but as the name of all that was new in
fashion. Her dress was in Directory style. It was muslin, so high-waisted that the fabric was shaped over
her breasts and then fell sheer. She wore no petticoats, only a linen slip. She wore no stockings, and her
silk shoes were without heels. She wore no decoration,
not even a bow of flowers between the breasts. That
year, a woman's dress of silk or muslin might be a
little embroidered, as Susannah's was. It was a fashion
often too cold for London, but it might have been designed for the climate of Sydney. It was a line cruel
to a woman of no figure, but fortunate for Susannah.

She was a woman in white muslin and a little linen, leaning back on a table of olive marble and throwing back her head so that her dark-brown hair fell straight.

When she smiled, Baudin caressed her lips with his fingers, parting them a little, so that he touched, no more than touched, her teeth and the tip of her tongue. He leaned to brush his cheek against her hair, and parted her lips with his lips, and then he raised his head a little and looked at her. Sometimes they were silent. At other times he talked to her, and now he talked.

"I shall come into you," he said.

She said nothing, not a word, but opened her eyes to look into his for a moment, and then let her head fall back again.

He caressed her hair, and she smiled.

"But if I stay here, your hair will keep me," he murmured to her. "Or"—not kissing her but letting his lips rest on hers for an instant—"this will keep me."

She made again the almost imperceptible movement of her head which meant yes, she agreed that he must not be kept there.

"Or here," he said, touching the line of her throat; and again she agreed, showing this by the smallest arching of the neck.

"Or I should be kept here." With his right hand he caressed not her breasts, but her side, and at that she moved, in agreement, yes, but by now involuntarily.

"And so," he said, and let his hand fall in one caress from her side, to her waist and then her hips, then down to her knees and to her ankles, and then he was kneeling on the floor of the orangery before her. It was a soft floor to kneel on, because it was carpeted with the petals and leaves of the flowers and plants a gardener had grown there many years before, which were now dried and powdered and half an inch thick on the floor. Baudin slipped off her shoes, which were so insubstantial they could scarcely be called shoes, rather slippers, and kissed her toes and the insteps of her feet, and then held both her ankles in his hands. Raising himself slowly, he caressed the line of her calves with his lips, and then his head was between her knees and she held it there with the lightest sideways pressing of her parted legs. The muslin dress of the Directory was light but long, and full in the skirt, so that Nicolas, when he rose from Susannah's ankles, buried his head under the dress, and the muslin was a canopy over his head. His hands were at her waist, and he held her there as his lips travelled up from her knees, and he stroked the inside of her legs with the hair of his head.

She said one word, his name, and he took his hands from her waist, embraced her hips with his arms, and kissed her gently between the legs, kissing her softly and then exploring with his lips and entering with his tongue. His senses were surrounded by the airiness of muslin, the scented musk of Susannah, and the silkiness of her.

"Nicolas, Nicolas, Nicolas," she said.

He rose, and she slid herself towards him on the marble table, and, no longer supporting herself on her arms, lay back on the table with her hands behind her head, and then, standing, he entered her. She no longer closed her eyes, but looked into his, and at his hands where they held her, and at his body as it moved and moved into hers, and then she held out a hand to take his.

He said, "Lie still a moment then," and, taking her hand, entwined his fingers in hers. In the summerhouse, what was happening? To say merely the conjunction of two bodies would have been the most bitter of misapprehensions. It was their minds and spirits

that were one. He was a Frenchman and an officer of
the Republic, but he was also, and could never wish to
be free from it, a Roman Catholic. He was a man
of the Age of Reason and yet, in spite of all that reason, his whole instinct told him that he had a soul.
With his dear love Susannah, how could he not at least
hope that he might have a soul, and that she might
have? No man enters a woman he truly loves without
that hope. And what was she? She, but that was the
last consideration in the world, was the governor's
daughter, and that was nothing to her. At that moment, it was nothing to her. It was not on the fringes
of her consciousness. She was a girl, she was a
woman, and as changed since she met Baudin as a human being can be changed, realizing worlds she had
not guessed at. She was also an Englishwoman and a
Protestant. She would have been hard put to say what
a Protestant was. But whereas Baudin would go to his
priest, and expect the priest to intercede between himself and his God, Susannah took it for granted that
she could, if she wished, pray to her God alone, without intercession of saints or priests. Priests of the Established Church in eighteenth-century England were
men of pleasant education who could be asked to
dinner. She would never have thought of a priest of
the English Church as a man in whom she could con-
fide her greatest longings, sins, and hopes. She would
not have thrust so great a burden on a man one could
ask to dinner. She never did pray, though later she
would, but she too believed in an immortal soul. Of
Baudin's soul, of the soul of the man she adored and
loved, she had no doubt. She would not have used the
word "soul," but that was the idea that was in her
mind and body, and her mind and body were at that
moment one. So they held hands, and lay still.

He began to move inside her again, she put up her
arms at first to hold his waist, and then his shoulders,

and then his head, bringing him closer to her, and then she averted her head, a gesture he knew so well, and moments (or how long?) afterwards, she tossed her head, exclaiming "Oh my dear love," and came with that exaltation on her lips and in his ears; and at this he too was moved beyond himself and splashed helplessly into her.

Perhaps five minutes later, Susannah and Nicolas —lovers disentwined—stood in the arched doorway of the summerhouse, and she turned in his arms to rise on her toes and kiss him on the brow. They had been half an hour in the orangery. Whatever an observer might have thought, though there was no observer, it was not done wantonly or recklessly, or, if there were colours of recklessness or wantonness, they were nothing to set against the knowledge of both that all was done, at heart, discreetly, soberly, fittingly. Nicolas said, for the first time, "We shall marry." And she said, *"Oh yes,"* and they walked in sunlight hand in hand over the lawns of the domain towards her father, not disguising where they came from, and he, for his part, showed no surprise, because he had none. When they reached him he embraced his daughter and then offered his hand to Baudin. Yet neither had spoken one word to him.

Baudin looked at King, drawing himself up as if to form words to speak, and then both men smiled.

"Sir," said Baudin, and then stopped, because he was in shirt and breeches, and Susannah, as he saw at a glance, a glance he had not thought to make before, was, as plainly as could be, a woman who has just made love, which showed not only in her dishevelled hair but in her eyes. Then he began again. Her father had noticed all that before Baudin, in his great happiness, had given any thought to appearance.

"Sir," he said. "I do fear this may be unexpected—"

"Nicolas," said King. "My dear Nicolas. I do assure you it is not."

Both Baudin and King could have laughed for joy, but they postponed that until necessary words could be spoken.

Baudin said, "I am asking for your daughter."

The governor glanced at Susannah, knowing he did not need to. He said, "There is nothing that could give me more happiness. Nothing." The two men laughed, and the governor—officer, gentleman, and Englishman that he was—put a hand on Baudin's shoulder, and then both hands on both shoulders, and nearly embraced him. He did again embrace his daughter.

"Nicolas," he said, "there are a few things. Before dinner, would you care to take a glass with me in my room?"

There were a few things, and more than they could have expected. It was now known that France and England were at peace. Both Baudin and King, as naval officers, knew that this might be an uneasy peace, but even if they supposed that war might break out again, what was a war between nations that could not be settled between gentlemen? If these two gentlemen ever met at sea they might be obliged to slaughter each other, but that really was to take matters to absurdity. This they agreed. Such an event was unlikely. Apart from that, even in war the civilities were observed. During the late hostilities, even trade of a sort had continued between Britain and France, though some of that trade had the tinge of smuggling about it. French brandy was still procurable in England. And safe-conducts would of course be granted. Susannah would have no difficulty in obtaining a passage to France, and once there she would marry Baudin. She could not sail with the *Géographe*. That would be too precipitate, and, besides, it would be stretching the proprieties for the daughter of an English governor to

sail aboard a French man-of-war. But the governor
expected to be recalled the next year, and Susannah
would return with him to Europe. Probably all would
still be peace. If there was war, that would scarcely
last long; and even if it did, Susannah could of course
join Baudin in Paris. If there was war he might be
called to sea again, but a woman who married a sailor
knew that. And of course there was this: that she was
an Anglican and he a Roman Catholic, but she knew
that too. Their children would be Catholic, but the
governor was tolerant in religion and expected his
daughter would be. And if there was a peace, Baudin
would either flourish in the French marine or, if he
chose, he might come to live with King in London or
in the country. There *were* things to be talked of, but
they would all resolve themselves—so these two gentlemen told themselves over their Madeira. They could
not know that the war had already broken out again.
They could not foresee that it would last another
thirteen years. They could not foresee that French
naval power would be broken at Trafalgar in only
three years' time. They could not foresee, that day at
the end of the earth, the early death of the governor
so soon after his return to England. They could not
foresee so many things, but all was agreed as if they
could.

Meanwhile, in the time left to them in Sydney, Susannah and Nicolas haunted the house and the domain,
illuminating it with their love and with the instinct of
their attraction to each other. This was so strong an
attraction, having so much a life of its own, that they
did not at all need to be close before it was felt by
them, and evident to all around. It was there if they
walked in the garden twenty yards apart, she stepping
onto the lawns from the east wing and he from the
west, and, knowing each other to be there but not ap-

proaching more closely, walking parallel paths. He
was as aware of her, and she of him, as if they held
each other. It happened the first time by chance that
they left the house this way, at the same time but
apart; and then it happened not by chance.

At breakfast she said, "Shall we be two paths?"

So they strolled their parallel walks, over the lawns,
by the cedars, downwards to the cove, until she
turned to face him, and then ran towards him with her
gown flying behind her, and did not so much fall into
his arms as give herself softly into them, even at a
run, and then say, with her head on his breast, when
she was breathing again quietly, "You are a magnet."

"We are magnets," he said. "We are fortunate.
We have been happy. But magnets have two poles,
north and south. And if you take two magnets, as you
are one and I am another, the northern pole of one
will seize and clasp the southern pole of the other.
That is us. But put north to north and the two poles
do not attract. They chase each other away. They
fight." She did not understand, so, on the chart table
in his cabin on the *Géographe,* in the cove, where he
had often before shown her charts of the seas and
plans of the stars, he demonstrated for her, taking two
tiny bar magnets, showing first how one moved to bring
the other to it and hold it firm, so that it took the
strength of her fingers to pull them apart. But then he
reversed the bars, and one fled from the other until,
by his manoeuvring, the first bar turned the other,
and held it again.

"So they can fight," she exclaimed.

It was in his cabin that Baudin and Susannah fought,
when he told her he must sail on a certain day, in two
weeks. Two weeks to that day. She asked for longer,
confidently expecting that he would delay, but he
could not. She did not comprehend.

"You won't?"

He shook his head. "I cannot."

"You refuse?" She took her hands from his.

"I do not refuse. I must. There is no choice. If I stay here another week after that day, I may lose three months on the passage home." He explained the prevailing winds, the monsoons, the precarious seasonal tempests of the southern seas, and the peril of the passage to the Cape of Good Hope which he must make, but she swept the charts from the table. She was a girl again, with all her unsureness, a girl with her father away God knew where, her mother dead, a little girl bewildered by their absences which seemed to her the withdrawal of love. In her mind, at the moment, she was losing Nicolas as she had so often lost her father as he said good-bye at the outset of so many voyages.

"Go," she said. "Go away. I shall never see you again. You will forget. I shall be forgotten."

He tried to be gentle. He was gentle. "That *is* nonsense," he said, taking her by the shoulders, doing all in his power to reassure a frightened girl he loved. Alas, her father, too many times saying good-bye, had often touched her shoulders in just such a way, and she whirled on Baudin and struck him, twice, full in the face. This was a side of Susannah he had never seen. He was astonished, and put up his arms to defend himself, and when she struck at him again he caught her wrists. As he did she pulled him down, taking him off-balance. He fell, and, as he did, Susannah, curling her body into a half circle to break her own fall, struck him in the chest with her knees. She meant it. He caught his breath with the shock, released her, and stumbled to his feet in amazement.

"Susannah?"

She lay on the floor as she had fallen. He stooped, but rose when he saw her eyes full of bitter anger. He turned and walked from the cabin onto the quarterdeck. It had not been a silent scuffle. There is little privacy even for the captain on board a corvette. As he stepped from his cabin the midshipman of the watch, divided between duty and sense, looked inquiringly at him from the flush deck, twenty feet away. Baudin shook his head and the boy walked away. Baudin closed the door to his quarters and leaned over the rail. For the first time he noticed the pain in his right side. When he re-entered the cabin ten minutes later, Susannah still lay where she had lain before, no longer in fury but asleep. He sat and watched her as she slept for half an hour. Then she stirred, realized where she was, saw her lover sitting with his face away from her, as if looking through one of the cabin lights, but seeing nothing. She came and knelt before him, laying her head in his lap, saying not a word. He caressed her hair, took the shape of her head in his hands, and his heart went out to her at that moment as never before. She never uttered the hint of an apology. She only said, "I did not know it would be that soon."

Two days later the ship's surgeon, told by Baudin some cock-and-bull story about a fall against a capstan on the quay, examined his captain and announced that he had come by three cracked ribs. "Nothing much, sir, for a capstan. I should say you will feel it for a week or so, and then it will go. You may catch your breath every now and again. Nothing to that, though. Shouldn't lie on my right side for a bit if I were you."

Baudin dined every evening now at the governor's table. King laughed at the story of the capstan, not disbelieving it but amused that a British capstan, if not the government of New South Wales, knew a Frenchman when it saw one coming, and couldn't read passports signed by some secretary of state in London enjoining all who owed allegiance to the British Crown to accord safe-conduct to French botanists,

even though they might come in corvettes. Baudin
would have said nothing whatever, except that as he
reached for the salt he had been unable to hide a
sharp twinge. Susannah had not realized either. There
had been no bruise. Afterwards she said to him, "I did
not know." The whole strange violence of that moment
in the cabin brought them closer than ever, and she
accepted that he did have to leave.

Two days before Baudin sailed the governor gave a
masked ball in his honour.

"No one," said the governor, as they discussed the
arrangements, "is going to assassinate me, I take it?"
It was only ten years before that the Swedish King
Gustavus III had been stabbed at a masked ball at
the Stockholm opera. Baudin knew Stockholm, and so
did the governor. Both had put into that brilliant port,
that harbour of the wooded islands, in high midsummer, sailing through Baltic seas, where at that time of
year the sun hardly sets, where light becomes twilight for the space of only three or four hours, and
sunset and dawn are hardly separated. Both Baudin
and the governor, in their previous service, had paid
courtesy visits to the Swedish king. He had entertained
both. He had taken both to Drottningholm, his summer palace a few miles from Stockholm, and there
shown them his own opera house, not the city opera
where he was to be assassinated but the elegant, narrow theatre built for the court.

"Turned into a granary or something, after his
death?" asked the governor. "Wasn't it?"

Baudin only knew that the present king of Sweden had no taste for music.

"Drottningholm," said the governor, "Queen's Island. Strange we should both have been there. So far
off." It was far: not from Europe, but from Sydney it
could hardly have been farther. But it was not strange.

Sweden was still the remains of a great power, and it was to be expected that both French and English men-of-war would pay courtesy visits. What was strange was what the governor said next, when the ladies had left the table and the port had been round twice.

"Those," he said, "were summer nights. The summer nights of my youth."

Baudin refilled his glass.

"I cannot think that I have ever told Susannah," said the governor, "or why I haven't. Her mother may have. I don't know, but I doubt it, because she was little when her mother died. It was my first command, and there I was with a new ship, frigate, a thirty-four, and a new wife. And so I took her to Stockholm. It was there Susannah was conceived. We were always sure of that."

Baudin smiled.

"Summer nights," said the governor.

Baudin proposed a toast to summer nights and to Susannah, and the masked ball was settled. It would be a farewell to him, and a commemoration of that summer night, whenever it was, long ago.

"No one," said the governor, "will assassinate me. They're all scared to death of my deputies who would succeed me. So am I."

Susannah's maid dressed her for the evening. The masked ball had been obliged to admit a small compromise. The gentlemen would be allowed to wear uniform, with the token disguise of a mask. There were still hardly enough men's clothes in the colony to permit more than that. The women were luckier, or more ingenious. Wigs could hardly be counterfeited, and were not, but the hair could be powdered, and picture hats, in the style much painted by Gainsborough, could be devised. Above all, the simple,

clinging dresses of the Directory were abandoned for
that night, and the old full skirts—of what was after all
only the fashion before that—were adopted. Most of
the women who had come in the first years of the
colony still possessed such gowns. The servants still
wore them. Few convict women had anything else. So
full skirts were to be had, and there are few extravagancies to which a full skirt will not lend its shape.

Susannah stepped naked into a creation of pleated
frills, into a skirt layered and bunched and puffed and
festooned with ribbon, and, which was her own touch,
lined at the hem with paper so that as her maid drew
the skirt around her waist, and as Susannah moved to
view herself in the long pier-glass of her dressing-
room, the skirt rustled against itself and against her.
The paper was from the five quires of tissue paper
carried by the *Géographe,* to make tracings of charts;
the ribbon from the twenty-five ells of silver fringe
and gold fringe carried, along with snuff-boxes, drums,
and tambourines, to trade with the natives. Then Susannah put on high-heeled shoes. For years she had
not worn either a skirt that fastened at her real waist,
or shoes that raised her heels. She swirled around and,
what with the unaccustomed weight and momentum of
the skirt and the unaccustomed height of the heels, all
but fell over. She recovered herself and laughed, and
regarded her long reflection in the looking-glass—the
skirt, and above the skirt her undressed body, bare
breasts, bare arms, and neck as yet unadorned. She
extended her arms as far as she could by her sides,
raised them above her head, and said aloud, "This is
how I am for Nicolas. This is how I look to Nicolas.
This is how I shall be for Nicolas. This is how I shall
be for Nicolas tonight." She spun round again, and
caught glimpses of her shoulders, admiring herself,
knowing Nicolas would admire her, and that Nicolas
loved her.

Her maid, being the daughter of a convict and therefore more proper, reproached her animal pride and exhilaration.

"Shame, ma'am."

Susannah stopped spinning so suddenly that her skirt continued to move and rustle round her of its own volition, and looked at the girl. She knew Mary had men of her own. "Mary," she said, "why not? Now, dress me. No, the hat first. No, first the powder."

Her maid was unwilling, and there she showed sense.

"To muck up such hair as yours, black and just brushed shining, and cake it with this tack, is nothing but wicked." It was true. The tack the girl spoke of was only bad flour, adulterated as usual in the colony with a little chalk.

"Leave it off," said Susannah. "The hat then."

The hat was pinned in place.

"Now my necklace."

A silver necklace was placed to encircle her throat, and fastened at the nape of the neck, and from it a pendant hung so that its single diamond fell between her breasts.

"Now the bracelets."

Three bracelets were slipped over her extended fingers. The bracelet nearest the wrist was the gift of Baudin.

"And now cover me."

It was warm. The maid placed a thin basque, with sleeves, over Susannah's arms and shoulders, and tied it at the back. That was all. Susannah viewed herself again, tossed her hair from her face, heard the music begin from below, and descended to welcome her father's guests. All evening, wherever she moved, the paper rustled in her skirts and the candles shone in reflection in her hair.

At the ball, all the softness was provided by the

women, most of whom showed their shoulders. All
the colour was provided by the men, who showed
their uniforms. The female shoulders of New South
Wales in 1802 were white. It was November 16, a
month to midsummer, and the Sydney sun was nearly
tropical in intensity, but no lady would display herself to the sun. No lady would, if she could prevent it,
allow the sun to see her face. At the ball nearly all the
women adopted as fancy dress the extraordinary
hoops, farthingales, and bunched petticoats of forty
years before. One or two braver women had gone
back another hundred years to Nell Gwynne and become for the night orange sellers (a trade they would
have despised, whatever its prospects) and kings'
mistresses (an honourable estate to which many would
have aspired, had there been monarchs in Sydney).
So their skirts were all of unfamiliar fullness, and their
shoulders were all alike bare because that was fancy
dress, and white because they were ladies. The gentlemen were more glorious. The British naval officers, the
aristocracy of the colony, wore the full dress of the
time, the blue cutaway coat, single-breasted, with
white breeches, white stockings, and black shoes with
gilt buckles. The blues were many in shade. Only
those officers recently arrived from England wore un-
faded coats. The governor's was probably the most
faded of all, but he was rather proud of that. All coats
had high, turned-back cuffs, but, just as there were
few blues that were dark blues, there were few whites
that were doeskin white. The breeches were as likely
to be of canvas as doeskin. The governor did have
doeskin, but it was, to say the best of it, a creamy
white, or, to tell the truth, off-white with age. What
predominated was the blue and the gold, the blue of
the naval uniforms, and the gilt in the trimmings of
the coats, on the braided pockets, at the sleeves, and
in the epaulettes. The officers of the New South Wales

din. She half withdrew when she saw he was with one
of his officers, but he called to her to come in.

"Susannah, is Mary Bickaith the Mary who is your
maid?"

A nod.

"She's on my ship saying she is no convict, that she
wants to sail with us, and that your father wouldn't
refuse to listen to her, or words to that effect. Now,
I can get her off quickly, and that will be that. Or I
can, I suppose, talk to your father. If she's your
maid, what do you want me to do?"

Susannah said, "It's true she isn't a convict."

"How then?"

"She came here with her mother, who was. Her
mother stole some cloth. That was four years ago, or
so Mary says. Mary came here with her mother. It
was either that or go into a convent, and Mary is no
nun."

"And her mother?"

"Dead last year."

"And you didn't know of this? That she would
come to me?"

"I did not." Susannah's temper nearly took fire, until she saw that Baudin had only meant to ask
whether she would approve of the girl's going, and not
whether she had connived at it. She made that motion
of looking down and quickly up again which, he well
knew, signified, "I didn't mean that," words she was
never able to bring herself to say plainly. She said,
"Mary does want to go home, and I know how badly
she wants it. She is always talking about Suffolk. If
you want to go and ask my father, I wish her well."

"All right." Baudin turned to his lieutenant, who
had been conspicuously hearing nothing, and said,
"Take off that sword you are carrying, go and find
yourself a glass of claret, and then wait for me in the
hallway." The boy went off. Susannah exchanged the

briefest of glances with Baudin. "My father?" she said.

"Please. Better if you go. I don't want to send that boy to your father's aide and have half Sydney wondering what's happening. Will you ask if I could come and have a few words?"

The words were few and blunt, but easy.

"This place is a damn great jail, Nicolas, for anyone who happens to have got here and happens to be British. The girl's no convict, never was, Susannah won't mind, though she likes her. You say you'll take her, though one girl among a ship's company? . . . Still, that's your business."

"Republicans and gentlemen to a man," said Baudin.

"Well. As governor I can throw her out. I could certainly throw her out for trying to escape, even though she's supposed to be free. I can't lawfully give her safe-conduct to England. God knows what things are coming to. I'm damned if I'll deport her, but what I can't do is simply give her a letter telling whomsoever it concerns that I've just given her permission to go. What I can do is know nothing about it. So I suggest that you have told me nothing. What my daughter tells me oughtn't to be evidence, or if it is I never heard what she said either. Anyway, if it were to happen that two days out you found a stowaway? . . ."

So Mary Bickaith remained on board. Baudin told his lieutenant to return to the ship and do nothing, either way, and say nothing. He and Susannah first returned to the minuet and then slipped outside into the domain.

A Sydney summer midnight can be warm as the Caribbean, and the darkness as deep. When they were not quite away from the house lights an unseen sentry presented arms with a crash and Baudin cursed the man under his breath as he acknowledged the salute. He and Susannah sought the absolute darkness of the farther domain, and the smooth bark of a blue eucalypt for her to rest against. Lovers in Sydney did not lie at night on lawns for fear of snakes. For that matter there were poisonous spiders in trees, but they were less thought of. He led her by the hand until they found the tree familiar to them. It was a massive tree, there for a hundred years. Of all the trees in the world, the trunk of the blue eucalpyt is smoothest to the touch. The bark falls naturally away, leaving a trunk of polished white with only an occasional patch of grey-blue, which gives the tree its name. She leaned back against it and they began the minuet of love-making, a dance as formal as before, with figures and paths, but now for a society of one man and one woman, and in the paths of her body and his. He stood before her. She kissed his lips and his mouth and his eyes. He loosened the tapes which fastened her basque at the back, and rested his face in her warm breasts. She held his head in her hands, and then with her right hand discovered his face. He held her by the hips, and then slid his hands under her skirts to lift them.

"They will think it is surf," she said, and he knew, because she was looking in the direction of the cove at the riding lights of the ships, what she meant. Her skirts lifted with a rustle of paper that must, it seemed to their ears, have carried to the vessels there and been heard by the watch.

She leaned backwards. He always thought the bones of her hips, those two bones which are most prominent as a woman stands, the most elegant of her body. He cupped them in his hands, she pressed back against his palms, and he stroked the concavity of her belly between the hip-bones. Then he parted her legs with his hand, and brushed that hand lightly against her. She was always the most fluid of women. He called it silky. She stood, half-lying, against the tree as he

went so easily into her, penetrating the silkiest of
women, entering the silkiest of girls.

This time she talked to him, as for a while they remained standing still, he inside her, she enclosing
him. "After a week," she said, "my love, a week after
the first night you ever came to my room, you sent me
that signal, SUSANNAH REMEMBER SILKYLININGS, from
the ship, and my father's aide, when he brought it to
me, said he couldn't be sure he had rightly made out
the flags; perhaps it was just some way a French ship
dressed all over. And he was sorry, too, that he had
taken it to my father first, not being certain it was for
me, although it did start with my name. He said my
father read it and smiled and said it was most undoubtedly for me, and to bring it to me, and so he
did."

In the domain, by the tree, Nicolas and Susannah
were as much together as man and woman could
be. As they parted at last, and her skirts fell again
into place with their great rustle, Nicolas was for the
most fleeting of moments taken in his mind out of his
exhilaration and he saw himself, sadly and as if in
a dream, holding in his hands not Susannah but an
instrument of navigation called an astrolabe. That was
a moment and no more, and then his consciousness
returned to the domain, the dark, the warmth, the
present, and Susannah whom he greatly loved. In the
house, the strings still played a minuet.

"We must make an appearance," she said.

"I know."

And so they did, she not even caring to go first to
her room to brush her hair. When they came again
within the lights of the mansion she said, "Just look
and see," and turned round before him, and he smiled
and nodded, to tell her she was assembled. They entered the ballroom together, last toasts were proposed
to Baudin, to his ship, to his officers, and to peace.

Baudin replied, "I bequeath to the French nation the duty of offering to you the deepest thanks for all, for everything, that you have done, but"—and at this he addressed himself directly to King—"it is for me to thank you with my heart for your friendship and love." Then the governor himself, with a boldness neither he nor Baudin nor Susannah gave a jot for, called for a toast to Baudin and Susannah together. That was drunk in the last of the champagne.

It was three in the morning before Nicolas and Susannah lay together in the sandalwood bed. She said, "I did not know about Mary. But she did say, as she dressed me, that she would not undress me tonight." They slept. Of their parting, the next day, nothing shall be said. That was for them to endure alone, and so, after all these years, it shall remain. Captain Philip Gidley King, Royal Navy, captain-general and governor-in-chief of New South Wales, watched the corvettes sail out of the cove, and in his daily log, immediately after a note on the American brig *Fanny,* which had sailed that morning, bound for Batavia and then New England with a cargo of speculative goods, he wrote:

"Ships: *Géographe* and *Naturaliste,* French. Arrived, June 18. Departed, October 17. Whence, Discovery, Whither, Discovery, and, God Willing, France."

Nicolas Baudin, post-captain in the marine of Republican France, sailed away from Susannah, with whom he would, God willing, be in a few months reunited, and away from the continent he and she had named.

10

On July 7, 1803, a Boy, Robert

SUSANNAH STOOD IN THE SUNLIGHT, delighted as a child, while two men, and the wife of one of them, told her the old story of the bishop's cloak, making a play of it for her, enacting it on the patch of grass in front of a cottage in the domain. The two men were George Bryant, who stole the cloak in his youth, and John Easty, who was now pensioned from the army and was the governor's head gardener. Bryant worked as a gardener under him.

"Now Mr. Easty there," said Bryant, "he will be the judge."

Susannah inclined her head to Easty. "My lord," she said.

"No, ma'am," he said, embarrassed at her addressing him in this way even in play.

"Easty," she said, "if you are a judge you are my lordship and you must stand up straight and look lordlike."

Jane Bryant watched. She was the wife of George Bryant. They were the couple who had married not with the fifty-eight other couples of the night of the wiving but discreetly, two months later, as not wishing to be precipitate.

"Well, ma'am," said Bryant, "as you see, Mr. Easty is the judge. And at my trial, while the clerk was writing me down in the court book, a great thing of leather, why, it was the judge's pleasure that the cloak should be placed upon me, as I do place it now on you." And with that, Bryant took the cloak, and draped it with ceremony over Susannah's shoulders. She stood still, stroked the fur collar, turned back the skirt of the cloak to see the blue silk lining, and then smiled at Jane.

"And then," said Bryant, "the whole court of people broke from their reverend silence to applause, and the judge and me talked for ever so long about Dorchester, the which being, as I have said, the city of my birth, and there were such 'Hear, hears' as I never heard. And that is how the cloak came all this way across the world."

The tale had been often told over the years, and gained in the telling.

"And then," said Susannah, "Easty took the silver buckle from it on the boat?"

Bryant said, "As was no more than Mr. Easty's due, seeing it was agreed."

Susannah smiled, took the cloak from her shoulders and gave it back to Bryant, and said, "Very well then, Jane, we too have agreed, on another matter."

Jane curtsied.

It was two weeks after Baudin's departure. The loss had been very great to her, and that afternoon was the first time since then that Susannah had been gay. She needed a maid, Mary Bickaith having sailed with the *Géographe,* and her father said she could do worse than look at Jane Bryant, a steady woman he thought. Because Bryant was a gardener he lived in the cottage in the domain and, if this were agreeable to Susannah,

Jane could perfectly well return to her husband at
night, and come to dress her in the morning. Easty,
whose judgement the governor trusted, had spoken for
Bryant and his wife. The crime for which Jane had
been transported was trivial, the theft of two lengths
of silk, which showed, the governor thought, a superior
taste. Most women stole muslin. So Easty had called at
Government House that afternoon to take Susannah
to the Bryants' cottage. He thought it more proper that
Jane should come to Susannah, but Susannah was less
interested in protocol than in seeing how a woman
who might become her maid lived herself. She had
found Jane a sturdy, soft-spoken Dorset girl, with hazel eyes that were steady. Her cottage was whitewashed inside and out, and smelled sweet, and Jane,
after the first confused curtsies and bobbings, looked
Susannah in the eye, and that settled it. The wage was
not expressed in money. Jane was given to understand,
through Easty, that there would be enough cloth from
the government stores to clothe her, that legs of ham
and the like from the kitchens of Government House
would find their way to the cottage, and that after two
years she might expect a pardon.

The Bryants were delighted.

"Dress the governor's daughter in silk as penance
for lifting your two lengths of felon's silk, Jane," said
her husband, after Susannah left.

Jane said, "I have seen her often, and with the captain from the French ship, and I like the lady."

"She is much liked," said her husband. "But she
knows what she wants."

"I see that."

And Jane settled down to read to her husband from
an old English newspaper. He had never learned to
read himself.

"Fine goings on at Weymouth," she said. She, like
her husband, was from Dorset. "Listen to this then."

She read the Court Circular. " 'Weymouth, August fourteenth. Yesterday morning the King, Princess Augusta, and the Duke of Gloucester bathed. His Majesty, after breakfast, rode out on horseback.' "

"I have been there," said Bryant, "when he did. And walked from Dorchester to see it."

Jane continued: " 'This morning at ten o'clock the royal family, with their usual party of nobility, went on board the *Charlotte* yacht.' "

"And I have seen that party of nobility," said Bryant. "Fine gentlemen and their ladies, and the whole town turned out to wish them well. Often I remember it as a boy."

Jane read and her husband listened, both convicts, both transported beyond the seas, both eager for news of the doings of a king in whose name they had been transported from a country they loved and could hardly hope ever to see again.

A month later it seemed likely to Susannah, and for two weeks before that had seemed a certainty to Jane, who had lived the last three of her twenty-two years in prisons, hulks, transport ships, and the female factory and had seen a great deal of life, that Susannah was carrying Baudin's child. At the first signs Susannah sent word to Jane not to attend her that morning, and then not to come the next, and then not the next. Jane ignored the last message and found Susannah pale and white, already dressed but lying on the sandalwood bed with her face in the pillows.

She said, "I have never been ill before."

"You are not ill now, ma'am. And there is no matter for sadness either, if I see it straight. Nor tears. You will be going home to the captain soon. I beg your pardon, ma'am, but I saw you together, and he is a man who would rejoice."

Susannah sat upright and looked at her maid, seeing

in Jane's eyes the steadiness and sense she had recognized on the afternoon of their first interview in the cottage.

"I know he would, Jane. And I do too. Only, I am so wretched in the mornings. For the rest, I do rejoice."

She told her father later that day, and he came round from behind his desk and kissed her head and rocked her in his arms. He was greatly moved. The instinct for happiness in a man is so great that for long moments he did not think at all, but surrendered himself to a welling-up of his love for his daughter and to a sense of pleasure that, with this coming grandchild, his own posterity was in a small way assured. Then he did think, and came and sat by her on a sofa, and told her what he was afraid she would not have considered, but had to be told.

"My dear," he said, "if this is so, I am a happy man. But, if this is so, then it does mean that you cannot sail as soon as you had hoped. You could have gone with the transport next month, but the passage, at best, is uncertain in length. There are, perhaps, seven more months to your confinement, and seven months might find you still at sea, and you know that is unthinkable."

She had *not* considered that, but she knew her father was right. She suddenly faced the certainty that she would be separated from Nicolas for more than another year, and would have to bear his child in the colony, alone. She was brave with her father, and brave all that day. It was only late at night, with Jane, that she wept bitterly, and the woman wept with her. That night, sleepless and alone, she prayed for the first time since she was a child, for Nicolas, for their unborn child, and for courage.

By the transport on which she should have sailed to Europe, she sent a letter to Baudin, which should reach France three months after his expected arrival.

"My dearest Nicolas," she wrote, "I cannot be certain, but I *know,* which is more than certainty, that our child was conceived the evening you came back to me, and walked up to the cove, and from my room saw the lights of the ships, and then took me to bed. It was the night we named Australia."

Susannah was examined by the best surgeon her father could find. His name was Redmond, a ruined naval surgeon, who, in order to pay gambling debts, had sold forceps, calipers, scalpels, saws, and other instruments of his profession which were unfortunately the property of their lordships of the Admiralty. He had been dismissed his ship and transported, but then, since surgeons of any kind were rare in the colony, had rapidly been pardoned. He was twenty-five. He was not a bad surgeon, but in his naval career he had sawn off more legs than he had delivered children. In truth he had delivered no child at all, though he had watched two delivered at the naval hospital at Portsmouth. It was merciful that Jane, in her career of hulks and prisons, had seen many women delivered, and had delivered two with her own hands. Redmond did have academic advantages. In his days as a surgeon's apprentice he had read the learned treatises of Le Motte, Simpson, Chapman, Gifford, and Gregoire. He also had access in the colony to the article on Midwifery in the *Encyclopaedia Britannica,* a work published in 1771 by a Society of Gentlemen in Scotland, in which the different Sciences and Arts were digested into distinct Treatises. This was in fact not so derisory a resource as would be thought nowadays. The Treatise on Midwifery was long, copiously illustrated, and intended to help and inform those who might need to act on the information.

Redmond had red hair. He was a big man. He attended Susannah in her sitting-room, with Jane as chaperone. He had read the article on midwifery that morning.

"Midwifery, ma'am," he assured her, "is the art of assisting nature in bringing forth a perfect child from the womb of the mother."

"Good," she said. "How big is it now?"

"Big?"

"How big is the perfect child within my womb?" It was unfair to Redmond, and put him at a distinct disadvantage, that Susannah too had read the article on midwifery in the same work that same morning in her father's library, and recognized his definition of midwifery as the first sentence of the article. It was also disconcerting for Redmond that she was prepared to ask bold questions that were not supposed to occur to the delicate minds of ladies of that time.

He hesitated to ask her the date of possible conception, but she conveyed to him that in her opinion the child might be three months old. Then, he replied, after considering gravely, the ovum would at that moment be the size of, let us say, a goose egg. She had read that too.

But she said to herself that she would not mock him anymore. He was trying his best to put her mind at ease, and to explain. There was really nothing else he could do. At three months there was no point in examining her. Those were the days when a doctor, at five months, could not be *certain* that a woman he was attending was pregnant or suffering from a disease producing superficially the same signs. He could be reasonably sure, but not certain. Jane, who knew Susannah more intimately than ever Redmond could have done after a dozen examinations, was more sure than any surgeon. She stood by the sofa on which Susannah reclined, watched Redmond, and never said a word.

Redmond continued his business of putting Susannah at ease.

"A little later on, ma'am," he said, "the child, as it lies in the womb, and is grown—"

"More like a child?"

"When it is grown more like a child, it will recline in nearly a circular, or rather oval, figure, which is calculated to take up as little space as possible."

Susannah waited.

"The chin," said the surgeon, "rests on the breasts, the thighs are pressed along the belly, the face being placed between the knees, while the arms cross each other round the legs. Do I explain myself? Do you see?"

Susannah did see, but what she saw was not the entwining of a child in her womb, but that of herself and Nicolas.

At that moment Baudin was sailing a course due north, one thousand miles from Sydney. He had sailed up the eastern coast of Australia but well away from the coast. No mariner of his day would take the route between the northern tip of Australia and the south of New Guinea. That was a narrow and then uncharted strait. Instead, he would sail far north into the Pacific, thread his way through the Solomon Islands, cross the Equator northwards, then loop down east of Borneo, cross the Equator again, this time southwards, and only then sail west, south of Batavia and the city of Djakarta and across the Indian Ocean to round the Cape of Good Hope. It was the longest possible way round, but the only one known to be safe.

Baudin, with a replenished ship, a rested crew, and the recollection and prospect of Susannah every hour in his mind, was a happy man. His cabin was now possessed by Susannah. He saw her figure as she walked towards him across the quarter-deck, and across the Persian carpets which covered the cabin deck in port but had been stowed once he put to sea. He heard the rustle of her dresses. His voyage of discovery was a success. He had charted the coast of southern New Holland, and part of the east coast. He had on board specimens of emus and kangaroos and countless plants. His charts of Terre Napoléon, which he saw himself presenting to the first consul, were covered by names that made them sound like a French roll of honour. There was Baie Talleyrand, named after Napoléon's foreign minister. There was a Golfe Bonaparte and a Golfe Joséphine. Desert capes and desert places were named for Montaigne, Lafayette, Voltaire, Molière, and even for Rabelais and Jeanne d'Arc. Baudin was going home with hope in his heart and mind. He was too good a navigator not to realize the risks on the passage still before him, but he knew also that, God willing, he would overcome them. He had accomplished what he had been sent to do. He had entirely reasonable hopes and expectations of preferment. Promotion to flag rank on his return was likely, and, though he was not ambitious, what good sailor does not wish to be an admiral? He had made his name, and, though he had named nothing Cap Baudin, he allowed himself the natural and not immodest hope that Napoléon, seizing a pen, would dash down that name on the map and wave away Baudin's protests. Above all, and it *was* above all, he carried in his heart a confident hope of life to be lived with Susannah. His officers, if they thought of their captain's hopes, would have considered that the easiest to be achieved. Susannah had been so whole-heartedly his, whereas flag rank was, they knew, a lottery of preferment determined by a hundred imponderable chances. But to Baudin, because Susannah was the greatest thing he hoped for, it was her—through some mischance and in spite of her glorious wholeness of heart

—that he feared he might lose. As he walked his
quarter-deck he noticed, as he never had done before
Susannah came on board, the scent of the cedar timbers of his ship. One day he summoned the carpenter,
asked if he had any item of sandalwood on board,
and received the man's astonished answer of, "No, sir.
It would be no use." Baudin thought of the sandalwood bed.

When Susannah was six months with child, Redmond
said to her, as if offering essential information, "The
woman is sometimes subject to longings besides."

"Are you offering me strange fruit, Mr. Redmond?"
But the man did not laugh. He never laughed. She
half-expected him to send out for a basket of paw-paw
immediately. Susannah had her longings, but she did
not think them strange. They were to her the most
natural thing. She longed for her lover, and tried to
re-create him in her senses by wandering in the domain, walking the path she had taken across the lawn
when he had walked the parallel path, and going again
and again to the tree against which they had leaned
the night of the masked ball, caressing with her fingers
the texture of its smooth bark. She was still not no-
ticeably pregnant, especially not in the dresses of the
Directory, and she did not need to close her eyes, even
in daylight, to re-create the sounds and scents and
movements, longings and fruitions, of that night. She
did not need to close her eyes. With her eyes open but
not seeing what was at present before them, with her
senses shut to what was there at present but rather
recalling the darkness, and the lights in the cove, and
the watchmen on the ships who must have heard the
rustling of the paper in her gown, like surf, she could
take herself back in mind—and her mind very nearly
took the sensations of the body with it—to the events
of that night. At other times she loved to walk among

the cedars of the domain, and recall the scent of the
corvette's timbers. She wondered occasionally about
Mary Bickaith, who had dressed her that night.

Mary Bickaith was a blessing to the wardroom of the
Géographe, whose officers had adopted her, and a
blessing to the sailors. What she did for the spirit of
those men was very great. By being a woman, and by
being there and talking with them, and asking them,
in the few words of French she had learned, about
Paris, she kept them from the numbness and from
some of the fear of a long passage. The storms of the
Indian Ocean can be terrible, and a corvette is not
built for them. A corvette is a messenger-ship of a
fleet, or a fast raider, too fine in her lines to be a good
sea boat in a gale. A corvette can ride out a gale, but
will be terribly thrown about. Mary was strong and a
good sailor, mercifully never seasick. The crew of the
Géographe had crawled exhausted into Sydney, and a
rest of five months had only apparently restored them.
On the passage home, after four months at sea, they
were nearly worn out again. Once, for five days on
end, the ship was awash, every man was soaked, and
there was no way of keeping dry, and no hot food. No
fire could be lit. A fire was a danger in a pitching,
rolling, yawing corvette. Even if it had been prudent
to light one, it would have been doused in a moment
by the sluicing seas running clean across the decks.
For days they all but drifted in shrouds, keeping only
enough sail to gain steerway. They had long ago lost
touch with the *Naturaliste.* The men shivered in tropical heat. The ship's biscuit was powdered by weevils,
and then moistened by the humid air into a wet dust.
The salt beef stank so that the men could not stomach
it. On their hands sores grew the colour of wine lees.
Their lips shrivelled. Their joints stiffened. When they

emerged from those five days of hell into calm seas, Baudin's first concern was for his men and his second for the animals. The emus and kangaroos had suffered too. His scientists were so incapacitated that Baudin fed the animals himself, and Mary went with him to help. The third lieutenant, Pèlegrin, died. Baudin entered the death in his log, and sat with his head in his hands.

Two hours later his servant entered the cabin and approached him.

"Sir, she is laying him out."

Baudin raised his head.

The dead on men-of-war were not usually laid out, but hustled into weighted hammocks and committed to the deep. Baudin went to see what she had done. He looked at the face of the young man he had known so well, and at the grave face of the English girl. He put a hand on her shoulder and thanked her. They sat in the 'tween decks with a swaying lantern between them shedding its light on their figures and that of the dead man.

"It is so many," he said, "so many."

The captain of a man-of-war feels the full weight of loneliness. At sea he must be separate and aloof. He may talk to his officers, but then only in the line of duty. He may talk to his servant. A perceptive servant, from the carrying in of the captain's breakfast, may very well learn more of him than his first lieutenant. Under the lantern Baudin talked to Mary, and what came to his mind was the list of those who had left Le Havre with him and would never return.

"Stanislas died at sea. He was a botanist. That was two years ago. And Anselm, chief gardener, and Sautier, and Louis, and now Pèlegrin, who was a boy. He came to me that night of the ball, to say you were on board."

"That is what I remembered," she said.

"And so many others, left ill at Timor, left ill God knows where. I knew them."

"We shall come through, sir," she said. Baudin smiled at this innocent assurance. He had sailed the seas of the world, he had been in far worse straits than this before, but he was grateful for this girl's reassurance and for her cheerfulness.

"We shall come to Paris, sir. The men have told me about Paris." Then she dared to come a little closer to his mind, and told him what she knew he wanted to know. Anywhere else, it would not have been her place to tell him, or to say a word, but they were in the vastnesses of the Indian Ocean, and what was her place there?

"Miss Susannah is a constant, loving woman; and I know her well, sir."

"Thank you," he said, and rose and went on deck.

As the watches changed, the first lieutenant brought him a pannikin of water from a cask just broached, and showed it to him, saying nothing. It was the colour of tea.

Baudin nodded. "We shall hold our course to round the Cape," he said. The lieutenant was thinking of Ile de France, an island off the south-east coast of Africa, where they could revictual and obtain good water. But that would take them too far north and lose them weeks. Baudin's orders remained what they had been, to hold course round the Cape.

Back in Sydney, Susannah was asking Redmond a great number of questions. Within a week she would be confined. How many births were difficult?

"In a town of three thousand women . . ." he said.

"Yes, Mr. Redmond?"

"In a town of three thousand, one thousand women may be delivered in a year."

She thought that excessive, but it was a fact that the women of Sydney had been fecund.

"And of those one thousand, in nine hundred and twenty cases the child will be born without any other than common assistance."

"And the other eighty?"

"Require, ah, other assistance."

Of course Susannah was afraid. That was why she showed such bright courage. It was just as well for her that she did not know Mr. Redmond had never delivered a single child, with ordinary or extraordinary assistance. She did guess at his inexperience, but did not ask.

That day, in the middle of the stifling ocean, Baudin was shown the filthy contents of the third bad water cask to be broached in a week. So many of the crew were ill that both watches had to be turned out to execute the simplest manoeuvre. That day it was a fair sea and a fair wind, but he kept reefs in the courses and in all topsails. He did not want to fill the mainsail because it would have been impossible to furl it in the dark, if the squalls of the previous weeks came on them again. He saw the colour of the drinking water held out for him to examine. He saw the eyes of his officers. He saw the eyes of his men on the flush deck. He looked up at the sun. "Lay a course," he said, "for Ile de France." The joy was spontaneous. The men of the watch, knowing this to be their deliverance, cheered in exaltation, and the watch below, either hearing these cheers, or sensing the vessel shift in her course, ran on deck if they could run, or climbed slowly up if they could not run, but every man came on deck and gazed at the new horizon beyond which lay Ile de France. Baudin's servant brought him a glass of a claret he had not intended to open until they first sighted the coast of metropolitan France, having concealed it from his master. Baudin told him to take a glass himself.

Susannah's was a natural and easy labour. Jane was to all intents the midwife. Hers were the hands that helped Susannah when she needed help. Jane also had the prison midwife waiting in the next room, a woman who, though perhaps not belonging at Government House, had delivered a thousand babies. If there was any difficulty Jane had determined to call her in whether Mr. Redmond agreed or not. She rather thought he would have agreed, but in the event it was not necessary. Jane delivered the child, and Redmond supervised. All was proper. Susannah lay on her left side on the sandalwood bed, wearing a linen half-shift, an open linen skirt, and a bedgown. Over the under-sheet were three layers of sheepskins, tied with tapes to each side of the bed. She lay with her knees contracted to the belly, and a pillow between her knees to keep them apart. It was a remarkably easy labour. When she was delivered she was bathed with a soft, warm towel, and then bound around with a broad linen cloth, and the warmed sheets were folded upwards from the foot of the bed and placed over her. In the delirium of her pain before the birth she fiercely held Jane's hands as if they were those of Nicolas, and called out his name.

"You have a son," Jane told her. After the birth Susannah slept. Jane took the child and washed it, wrapped it in linen, and rubbed the head, temples, and breast with spirits. When Susannah awoke the child was placed in her arms, and she named him Robert. It was July 7, 1803.

The prison midwife was given a guinea and sent away. Redmond busied himself forbidding Susannah all nourishment except warm barley water, or chicken water boiled up with cinnamon, to which might be added a third or a fourth part of light wine. Susannah drank with appetite. "Or *less* than a fourth part of wine," said Redmond, "if the patient drinks plentifully." He said firmly that she was to have no solid food for five or six days. After one day, when Redmond was away, Jane gave Susannah boiled breast of chicken.

The governor embraced his daughter with tears of gratitude in his eyes, and took his grandson from her arms with such exaggerated gentleness that she laughed at him. It was a fine boy.

"I am a happy man," said the governor.

"And I am a happy woman," said Susannah. "Nicolas will be happy."

All noise had been banished for the confinement. The wooden floors were laid with druggets, the stairs with cloths, the door hinges oiled, the knockers tied, the bells silenced, and the carriageway strewn with rushes.

"Do away with all that nonsense," said Susannah. "I want to hear the sounds of the house again." On the fourth day—and this was unthinkable in the year 1803—Susannah demanded to move for an hour to a chair by the window so that she could see the trees of the domain and the sails in the cove, and she stayed there all afternoon.

The child was three months old when James Cobb II, master of the *Columbia,* a full-rigged ship out of Boston with a cargo of flour, good salt pork, wine from the Cape, iron tools, and paper, paced up the slope from the cove over the domain to Government House. It was almost a year since Baudin had ascended that same slope, awaited by Susannah. The *Columbia* was the first American vessel to enter Sydney that year. By the autumn, only thirteen vessels of any nation had entered the port. Susannah eagerly sent down to them

all for news of the *Géographe,* though her father told
her it was much too early to know anything. She
missed the entrance of the *Columbia* because she and
Jane and the child had been away the previous two
days at Parramatta, the governor's second residence.
The leisurely ride there and back in the governor's
carriage eased her restlessness. As Captain Cobb
walked up the hill, she was just returning. He saw her
as she got down from the carriage, carrying the child,
a hundred yards ahead of him. He heard Susannah
murmuring to the child, but could not hear what she
said. He saw the woman's white form go indoors,
waited for a minute, gazing round at the eucalypts he
had never seen before, and then continued his walk
up to the house.

A servant ushered him into an ante-room, and returned immediately to take him to the governor.

"Captain Cobb, my compliments. But you have
walked. I sent a carriage for you to the quay."

"I did not think of that," said the American. "The
pilot pointed out the house from the cove and I could
see it was a walk. I came as soon as I put ashore."

The *Columbia* had entered the cove only two hours
before and was immediately noticed by King, who
knew a well-run ship when he saw one. He knew she
was from Boston and then the Cape, but her rigging
seemed intact and even her paint fresh. As she made
in to her moorings as neatly as any man-of-war—
neater, he could not help thinking, than some—he
watched the agility of the men at work in her shrouds,
and the assured easiness of those on deck who, having
for the moment nothing to do, lounged at the rails and
scanned the new coastline. These men had an ease
which might have been mistaken for indolence, but it
was nothing of the sort. The governor had rapidly
learned this from the men of previous American ships.
It was not an indolence, more a complete independ-

ence. King was a sailor who did not need to watch a ship handled for more than a few moments to know something about her officers and crew. He had learned that American officers were often very good, and the seamen, taken at large, far and away the best who ever entered the port. After terrible voyages they were healthy. They could read and write. As seamen they were good enough to be mates in the vessels of most other nations, and some of them made this transition. Having landed at Sydney, they commonly played hell in the waterfront inns, but he let that go. He had fought Yankee ships in the War of Independence. He would have preferred such seamen as allies.

"That is a very fine vessel, Captain," he said. "I watched her put in."

He had also read her signals before they had been relayed to him by his aide. Her captain had asked an immediate interview with the governor.

"We spoke a French corvette in the Indian Ocean."

King had known this was coming.

"She was well off-course for Ile de France. I went on board. We helped provision her. Her water was foul."

King looked sharply at the American, who went on: "It was taken on here, at Sydney. I saw the casks. They were bad casks. I gave her what I could. She will have made Ile de France."

King was in a fury of mind. He wanted to know more, and yet his mind was full of those casks. On account of their blasted rum monopoly, almost all the sound casks in the colony passed through the hands of the New South Wales Corps. Most of the casks with which the *Géographe* was provisioned came from that source. King had seen himself that the water given to the French was sweet. He had watched the casks hoisted, and the casks had been whole, and not rotten. But now he realized that there was a question he had not asked himself: What had those apparently sound casks previously contained? If it was rum then, strangely enough, that was all right. Rum dregs do not much hurt sweet water. But if it was wine, and if the casks had not first been thoroughly charred, then he knew what would happen to that water. Major Johnston knew what would happen to that water. Johnston's men would have supplied those casks, and their monopoly was extending itself into wine.

"Wine casks?" he asked.

"As I guess."

The American placed on the table a package wrapped in oilskin. "Mr. Governor," he said, "I was asked to bring these to you, and I am sorry it is bad news."

"Baudin?"

"The captain's name was Baudin. When I went on board I was told he had not eaten for two days, nor spoken for hours. Their surgeon was dead. An English girl begged me to send for mine. I did, and he found the captain still warm, but dead. The French lieutenant gave me this package." It was a bundle of papers addressed to Susannah. "And he gave me this letter for you. I stayed for the burial of the French captain."

The first lieutenant's letter to King was brief. Post-Captain Nicolas Baudin had died of fever. The lieutenant thought that the last pages of his personal log were intended for Susannah, and enclosed them in a separate package, which he was entrusting to Captain Cobb. Captain Baudin had never ceased to express his gratitude to His Excellency the governor of New South Wales. As for the governor's daughter, the lieutenant believed the journal would speak for itself. He offered the governor and Susannah his deepest sympathy, and for his part could express only sorrow at the death of such a man as Baudin, and commiserate in others a grief he knew they would feel even more keenly than himself.

Captain Cobb looked away as the governor read this, and then turned to see a man quite broken and not attempting to hide the silent tears on his face.

"Mr. Governor," said Cobb, "I am sorry to bring you this news. I will go."

King looked at him. "Oh, no, you must forgive me. But you will need this." He took a sheet of paper and scribbled instructions to his quartermaster-general to supply the *Columbia*'s master with whatever he required, with no exception, and to the provost-marshal of the New South Wales Corps that the master, officers, and men of the *Columbia* were to be allowed free access at all times to the quays and town of Sydney.

The Yankee captain left. In the hallway he passed a dark-haired girl in a white dress, kneeling over a tiny child. She looked up and smiled straight at him. He recognized her as the woman he had seen get down from the carriage. He wondered whose the child was. Susannah thought the visitor very grave and went into her father to ask why. Cobb declined the carriage, which by this time had found him and was waiting outside, and walked down again over the lawns to his cutter waiting at the jetty.

Late that night Susannah read again, as she had been reading over and over all day, the papers her father had given her when she went in so gaily to ask about the American captain in the hallway. There was a painstaking note from Mary Bickaith, which said: "The American surgeon found these papers with Captain Baudin, which the lieutenant says he was writing at his last moment, and they are for you and will send them by the American ship to you. I was with him a lot, with the animals, and it was a fever. I thought the burial was French, but the lieutenant said it was Latin.

The American captain lent me a book in English, and I read the words about the day the dead shall arise from the Sea; and I said the Our Father for his soul, and prayed for you. It was all properly done."

The package also contained Baudin's personal log. On its last page was a letter written to Susannah in his final hours. It was half a farewell to her and half a fevered account of the ship's working. It said:

"Heavy seas all night, pitching, labouring, spraying all over. The emus and kangaroos are seasick. The sea gives them no peace. Morning and the sea is fair. Susannah, you were the greatest gift that was ever made to me. I never hoped for so much. I do not think I shall be able to write any more. May you be loved. May you be cherished in your heart, and in your mind, and in your bed. We made the emus eat by opening their beaks and gave them wine and sugar, and the seasick kangaroos too, though we were very short of these things for ourselves. I had to come to bed but do not find much relief here. I believe we are at latitude 7 degrees 30 minutes S. and longitude 95 degrees 41 minutes E., but I do not know where I am."

These words were his last and were dated July 7, 1803, the day on which Susannah gave birth to their son, a child Nicolas never knew she had conceived.

11

───── ∽৯৫৶ ─────

Bligh's Second Mutiny

LATER THAT YEAR another American ship brought news that after the brief peace England and France were again at war. To Susannah it meant nothing. The world meant nothing to her. In Sydney, a man condemned for burglary was three times suspended from the gallows. The first time the cord separated in the middle and he fell on his face, the second time the rope unravelled at the fastening and he again fell to the ground, and when he was a third time launched the rope snapped short. The lieutenant of the New South Wales Corps in charge of the execution ordered the criminal to be taken back to barracks, and himself petitioned the governor for a pardon, which was instantly granted. The governor congratulated the officer on his humanity, and the pity of the situation took his mind for the first time in many months out of a torpor which had become habitual to him. A small bear of the kind the natives called Koala was found in Sydney, and that was its first discovery by white men. The governor nodded, but did not go to see the beast. An insurrection of Irish was rapidly suppressed, and the governor took reports of it at second hand from the military and questioned none of the Irishmen himself, as he would once have done. In France, Napoléon was proclaimed emperor, but the governor, the day he received the news, did not even speak of it at his dinner table, where he and Susannah now ate in silence and alone. The tremor of a mild earthquake shook the town, but Susannah said nothing even then. She was walking upstairs when the movement was felt. She stopped and watched a chandelier sway and jingle, but then, when it came to rest again, continued upstairs, as if she had seen and heard nothing. Jane Bryant was behind her, carrying the little boy, and it was then that Jane at last spoke sharply to her. It was a year since Susannah had known of Baudin's death, more than a year since Robert's birth, and in that time Jane, not Susannah, had been the child's mother. She said: "I will be straight with you, ma'am. When this child was born, and they strewed rushes, and oiled hinges, and bound up the knockers, you ordered it all undone, so that you could hear the noises of the house going on. Now the ground rocks and you will not notice it. You do not know your child, and all this is not good. It is a year now, ma'am." She put the child in Susannah's arms and went off to her cottage. For the first time in a year, Susannah took her own child onto the lawns and talked and played with him, and then afterwards, at dinner, she did ask her father about the earthquake. There was little damage. For two days she dressed herself briskly, and took the child at times from Jane, but then she relapsed into her long melancholy.

Redmond tried to treat her for this condition. She submitted to tepid baths to drive the blood from the head, and consented to have cold water poured upon her hair to promote the easier diffusion of the humours congested within the head. She swallowed a medicine he prescribed of cephalic and nervine herbs—vervain, sage, plantain, and white maidenhair. He told her the ingredients and their purpose.

"Maidenhair for the loss of a lover?" she said. He did not understand.

It was John Easty who fetched the herbs from the gardens he tended, and he and Jane took Susannah frequently into the domain to divert her mind. They showed her the proper season for planting and transplanting seedling trees. "The roots of a tree," said Easty, "when planted, should spread like a man's open hand."

He placed the seedling in her hand.

"And plant the creature not more than three inches below the ordinary surface of the ground." He dug a shallow hole with his hands, for her to set the tree in.

"And when the hole is filled up," he said, scooping earth around the roots as she held the tree erect, "tread the earth gently round the plant." They planted many trees, and next month he showed her how to dress strawberries, how to cut off the runners, loosen the ground, and place fresh earth between the rows, to make the plants strong and grow large fruit.

Her father, all the while, was as afflicted with grief as she was. John Easty knew this, but less could be done for the governor. He could not be shown how to plant trees. Jane knew it too, and took care to bring the child to him often. He saw what she was doing, and was grateful. The boy was a great consolation to him. One day he called her into his study.

"You have done so much for my daughter," he said, "and so much for me."

"I have done what any woman would."

"No, much more. And I am ashamed that I have not done what I promised when first you came to Susannah. But I have remembered now."

He took a parchment he had prepared, the form of her free pardon, signed it in her presence, and gave it to her. "It is a small thing enough," he said. To the girl it was not a small thing. She embraced him with pure affection, and ran from the room. The governor turned back to his desk and stared at the mass of papers, some signed by him and some still unsigned, but all unread. He was letting the colony go to the dogs, and the dogs were Major Johnston and most of his fellow officers of the Corps. He no longer checked their open monopoly not only of rum but of all trade, so now it went altogether unchecked. The governor was weary. He began to write for the fourth time to London requesting his own recall. The governor's loss was not so great as his daughter's, though his grief for her was great, but he did have to live every day with the knowledge of something she did not know, which he would never tell her. He knew why the water on board the *Géographe* had been foul, though he could prove nothing and do nothing. He took the blame heavily upon himself that he had not thought to ensure that those casks were well charred. It rarely left his consciousness that but for that foul water Baudin might still be alive, and his daughter not bereft.

Back in England, not in London but on a man-of-war off Torbay, Captain William Bligh was defending his honour at a most peculiar court-martial. He was charged with grossly insulting one of his lieutenants on the quarter-deck of the *Warrior* by calling him a rascal and a scoundrel and by shaking a fist in his face, and with at other times acting in a tyrannical, oppressive, and unofficer-like way. It emerged from the evidence that Bligh often called his officers and men damned blackguards, vile and shameful lubbers, Jesuits, and vagrants. He once called the gunner a damned long pelt of a bitch. His defence was original, consisting of a contention that these were expressions commonly used in the navy, and that any officer zealous in his duty was occasionally given to such "ebullition of the mind." He candidly and without reserve admitted that he was not a tame and indifferent observer of the way in which officers placed under his orders conducted themselves in the performance of their duties. He cross-examined witnesses himself, asking one officer: "Is it usual for me, when any duty is carrying on, to use a great deal of action with my hands, without having any particular meaning in it, but being merely a custom, without the least intention of insulting anyone?"

To which the officer replied: "A considerable motion of the hand, frequently swearing at the quartermasters or men of that description who were standing round. A great deal of action with the hands, as if to knock any person down—but I never considered it done with the intention of personally insulting any officer."

Bligh was happy with this answer, as he was with that of the boatswain, who said Bligh had shaken him and torn his shirt, and was very hot and hasty and given to swearing, but that he believed the words no sooner escaped him than his passion ended. For himself, the boatswain never attached any particular interpretation to what was said. He would just as soon sail with Bligh as with any other captain he knew.

The officers of the court were amused to hear so much vilification sworn to in evidence, but found the charges proved and admonished Bligh to be more circumspect in his language. Outside the court he announced to all and sundry that he would get rid of the officers who had spoken against him, as soon as might be, since they had turned out to be the worst of serpents.

In Sydney, King was beginning to use language which if not so inventive was as intemperate as Bligh's, but

with the governor it was not out of natural impatience
of mind but because he was at the end of his tether.
He publicly called the Corps officers damned rascals
and infernal scoundrels, and on one occasion ground
his boot into a basket of eggs. The Corps was estab-
lishing a monopoly in eggs too, and when he learned
this in the market-place he was overtaken by anger.
But the spectators were not to know what the reason
was. Then a woman, unable to pay the price demanded by the rum monopolists, ingenuously came to
the governor himself to ask for rum. He did not understand why she had come, only heard her ask him for
rum, and roughly asked what the hell her name was.

"Bridget, Y'r Excellency."

"Bridget? Bridget? No other name?"

"The men call me Pony, sir."

"Pony? Trot then, you hussy, trot." And he took her
by the shoulders, turned her round, and made her trot.
Susannah saw this.

That evening, when the servants left them, she said,
"That was not like you, Father."

He accepted the rebuke. "I am glad to hear it was
not. I am not inclined to put it so charitably myself.
But, we shall soon be home. At last we are going
home."

"Home?" She had not known.

"My recall came this afternoon. A dispatch from the
Hercules, which has just put in. We go home as soon
as I am relieved by the new governor."

She said softly, "I am sorry, but I will not go."

He did not comprehend her. He did not believe her.
But she would not be moved. She would not go because Sydney, and Government House, and the domain, were the places where she had met Baudin, and
taken him for her first lover, and borne his child. She
did not explain all this. She only said that all the high

moments of her life had been lived in that place, and she would not leave.

"And all the grief?" said her father. "Not that too?"

She shook her head. She did not know how to put it in words, but her grief was deep because her life there, even after she knew of Baudin's death, was spent in a constant recollection and re-creation of those high moments, which made her loss the more painful but still tied her to the place. She had almost forgotten England. Going away meant to her only the going away of Baudin, and he had gone to his death. She would not go, nor would she explain further. Her father began to understand. Would she take time to consider? She said she would consider, but her answer would be the same because her reasons could not change. The governor, staring out of the window on to the darkened domain, said her loss would be very heavy to him. She knew it, and if anything could have changed her mind it would have been that. But she would not change her mind. The governor was too proud to say that the loss of his grandson would be dreadful to him. She knew that, too, and would have done anything not to hurt her father so badly.

That night he did not sleep, and long after midnight, watching at his bedroom window, he saw his daughter walking in the moonlight on the domain. She stepped on to the lawns from the east wing, walked a straight path slowly away from the house, and then stopped and turned as if to face another late-walker across the length of the lawn. He then knew for sure that she would not come with him, but would stay, and he knew why.

When the secretary of state in London looked for a new governor to replace King, he stated that he was seeking a man capable of drawing on his own resources in difficulties without leaning on others for advice, not subject to whimper and whine, an officer of integrity unimpeached, and civil in deportment. This tactful post was offered, two weeks after his court-martial for the use of inventively insulting language, to Captain William Bligh. He was not at first sure that he wanted it. He was not certain even after he was offered £2000 a year, twice the salary of previous governors. He did not wish to be separated from his wife, Betsy, whom he loved, and she could not come with him because she, a sailor's wife, feared the sea and could not face the long voyage. But it was Betsy, who had been his wife for thirty years, who eventually persuaded him to go. Gently, she told him it might be his last chance of high office, and that she wanted it for him. Bligh was fifty-one. He knew it might be his last chance. Reluctantly, he went. In early 1806, less than three months after Nelson won the Battle of Trafalgar, Bligh left England. By August he was in Sydney.

This was Bligh of the *Bounty,* who was already a legend. But the legend was not then what it became. There were certainly those who thought he was a tyrant. Some thought him an outright villain. But it was also remembered that after the mutiny on the *Bounty,* when he and eighteen members of the crew were abandoned in mid-Pacific in an open boat, Bligh navigated the boat for forty days across more than three thousand miles of mountainous seas to Timor, from where he wrote to his wife, "Know then, my own dear Betsy, I have lost the *Bounty.*" It was a feat of courage and navigation. He had never lacked either courage or ability. He had gone with Captain Cook on his last voyage, and was commended by him. He was there on the day in 1779 when Cook was murdered by the natives of Hawaii. He fought at the Battle of Copenhagen and was praised by Nelson. Such was Bligh, a man commended and praised by the two greatest sailors of his day; a man who loved his wife tenderly; but a man given to ebullition of the mind. He was also a friend of Governor King's. They had served together as young men. So King, when at last he admitted to himself that Susannah would not return with him, took his old friend aside, told him everything, and asked him to cherish and protect Susannah and the boy Robert. Bligh gave his word, and invited Susannah to remain at Government House. With his men he was sometimes an undoubted bully, but with women he was gentle.

The day came for King to leave. A governor cannot depart without a ceremony of honour guards and brave music. On the quay, Susannah stood by his side through all this. It was intolerable for both of them. When the last military compliment was paid, and King had saluted the Union flag still flying from the residence in which he and his daughter had lived together for so long, he turned to his daughter and held out one hand to her. He led her a few yards from the drawn-up ranks of the naval establishment. Every man could see and hear, but all looked straight ahead, determined to appear unseeing and unhearing.

"Bligh will look after you," said King.

Susannah could not meet her father's eyes.

He took her head in his hands and raised her eyes to his. "Come with me, Susannah."

"I cannot, but how I wish . . ."

He released his daughter's head, so as not to see her tears.

She saw his hands drop by his sides, and saw that he clenched his fingers into his palms.

She raised her head, faced him again, took both his hands, and threw herself into his arms.

He knew it was hopeless. He held her and rocked her, and then gently released her.

"Good-bye," he said. "Susannah, I am not sure I

can be brave any longer. Good-bye. God be with you."

He walked rapidly to the jetty, where his cutter was waiting, and did not look back as he was rowed out to the transport.

Bligh took Susannah back to Government House, and left her alone as she stood on the lawn, with Robert in her arms, looking out to the cove. She heard the crash of the thirteen-gun salute for her father, and watched his broad pennant disappear round the headland.

Bligh, standing on the veranda behind her, gave her a few minutes after the ship passed out of sight and then walked over to her. "Miss King," he said, "we must begin to teach to your son the art of navigation. One cannot begin too young." She liked the plain way he had called her Miss King since they first met, not fumbling around with a hesitant "Mrs. King"—as many of the officers, and particularly their wives, thought it proper to do. He held out his arms for the child, and she gave it to him. He called out for Easty, and told him to make the boy a small yacht, a foot long, to sail on a pond. Jane made a red ensign to fly at the stern.

Bligh had been sent out with firm instructions to cleanse the colony of corruption and suppress the rum monopoly, and he did this with vigour. He tore up the licences of half the grog shops in Sydney and, when they were re-established elsewhere within a week, sent his sailors to impound the casks of rum. This was his duty, but it did not endear him to the New South Wales Corps, who owned the rum. The Corps officers transferred the ownership of the rum shanties to their mistresses, who set up business afresh. Bligh's sailors called again, and this time stove in the casks with marlin spikes. When the officers protested, Bligh mildly pointed out that their women appeared to be convicts on tickets-of-leave, which was so, and that convicts could not by law traffic in rum. He wished to be clear in his mind. They had themselves informed him that the rum was the property of the women, had they not? The officers withdrew. Bligh pulled down three brothels—walls, roofs, gilded mirrors, and all—but that was more a gesture than anything else. It was, as he well saw, a trade that would thrive however many houses he destroyed, and thereafter he left it alone. But with the rum trade he was merciless and persistent. For a while the Corps officers were reduced to living on their salaries.

"Which," Bligh remarked to Sir Harry Browne Hayes, "they find an outrageous imposition. I say it is they who impose. I would not pay them one-quarter of their salaries. They are the sweepings of the British army, and that is the sweepings of sweepings."

"Ah," said Sir Harry, who had prospered and built himself a house, and came to Bligh's dinners as he had come to King's. "I was once a captain in the Cork militia, and I will not say there was not a keg of French brandy for each man at Christmas, washed up on the shore, unknown to the vigilance of the excisemen, for there was a keg for them, too, but we were not a pestilence to the people."

"Serpents," said Bligh mildly, and this reminded him to ask if Sir Harry's cargo of Irish peat had yet arrived from the bogs.

Sir Harry said it had. He had built his house in snake-infested country, but had seemed unconcerned and done nothing except order his cargo of peat. This had now arrived, and he had encircled his house with a peat moat.

"And since then, not a king-brown snake has been seen, not so much as an adder. It is the property of the peat to charm away the snakes. It is a property well proven in Ireland."

"There are no snakes in Ireland," said Bligh. "Your Saint Patrick is supposed to have chased them off."

"And sure the blessed saint charmed the peat to expel the serpents, so that the very soil repelled them. I have some peat left over, Captain Bligh, which I should be glad for you to have. To repel your own serpents of the Corps."

Bligh declined. He had other ways in mind.

For a week or so Bligh had occupied himself ordering improvements to Government House. He prowled round the house with the government builder, the government mason, the government carpenter, and a foreman of works. At the end of the week he insisted on taking Susannah on a tour to show her what needed to be done.

"Wants new doors," he said, "new windows, window shutters, linings, and frames."

Susannah thought the doors were still good enough. Perhaps if they were just repainted?

"New doors," said Bligh. "New shingling, flooring, whitewashing, plastering."

Susannah made no further objection. She saw he was determined.

"In so rotten a state," said Bligh, "that the whole house wants being new."

But after the repairs were done, Bligh returned to the colony's public affairs. He shot all the stray cur dogs, which was his undoubted duty, but unfortunately he shot Major Johnston's wolf-hound as well, by mistake. But he could also be marvellously bland. He rose at seven and was willing to see anyone before breakfast. When there were protests, he replied that he was doing his duty in upholding the law, as, surely, all officers of the Corps would themselves wish to do?

One day John Macarthur called, and found Bligh in the gardens with Susannah, showing her son how to launch his toy yacht across the newly dug pond.

Macarthur had come a long way in the world since King had sent him home to face court-martial after the affair of the duel. In England delay had followed delay, and, when Macarthur resigned his commission, the impending court-martial was forgotten and never held. Macarthur then turned everything to his advantage, and, presenting examples of undoubtedly fine merino wool from his sheep in New South Wales, he gained the interest of merchants, manufacturers, and the British government. It would be convenient if wool of such quality could be shipped from New South Wales rather than got with difficulty and expense from Spain. The Privy Council in London made him a grant of five thousand acres in the colony, to which he had recently returned.

The morning he appeared at Government House he wanted to talk about sheep, and to ask for fifty convicts as shepherds. It was an entirely reasonable request, but Bligh knew that Major Johnston and his crew, deprived for the moment of the rum trade, were taking to farming and particularly to sheep, manipulating their way to a monopoly in mutton, leaving wool to Macarthur. On this understanding, Johnston and Macarthur were setting up sheep stations together. When Macarthur began to talk of sheep, Bligh found that his blandness had run its course. But at first he showed nothing. He walked on the lawns with his hands behind his back, and still kept his temper with Macarthur.

"You have royal sheep, I understand?"

Macarthur replied that he had been given fifty of the finest sheep from the royal flocks in England, and had brought them out. They were at present grazing his pastures. He asked for the convicts.

"Convicts? You have the king's sheep; why should you have his felons too? What have I to do with your sheep, sir? What have I to do with your cattle, which

you have besides? Are you to have such flocks of
sheep and such herds of cattle as no man ever had
before? No, sir."

Macarthur replied civilly that perhaps the governor
did not know he held his land by direct grant of the
Privy Council. Furthermore he had been promised another five thousand acres if his first venture proved
successful, and he hoped soon to ask the governor for
those extra acres. It was all to the benefit of the colony, which could become rich on wool.

Bligh took his hands from behind his back. "I have
heard of your concerns, sir. You have got five thousand acres of land in the finest situation in the
country"—here he gesticulated violently towards the
horizon where those lands lay—"but you shan't keep
them, let alone have another five thousand for the
asking. By God, sir, you shan't keep them."

Macarthur was still cool. He had his land by direct
grant of the Privy Council, by direct order of the secretary of state, and he presumed his right was indis-
putable.

By then Bligh's arms were flying about in full passion.

"Damn the Privy Council. And damn the secretary
of state, too. What have they to do with me? You
have made a number of false representations respect-
ing your wool, by which you obtained this land."

"I beg you to come and see my sheep, sir. It is the
finest wool. If you will see them, I am sure your opinion will be that of the secretary of state."

"Damn the secretary of state. He commands at
home. I command here. And damn the Privy Council."

Macarthur thanked the governor for his patient understanding, and left.

Susannah could not help hearing all this.

In the afternoon, Bligh asked her to help choose

two brooches to send home to his wife. A jeweller from the town brought a case of brooches to Government House, and it was laid on the walnut table in the ballroom. Together Bligh and Susannah held the brooches in their hands, and up to the light, and when they had found four they liked, two of silver and two of mother-of-pearl, Susannah held them against herself so that Bligh could see.

After a while, she said, "No. My dress is white. Mrs. Bligh, in England, will not often wear white." She sent Jane for a blue silk shawl, and gave it to Bligh. He looked at it.

"Well," she said, "drape it round my shoulders. I will wear it so that you shall see the brooches against it. That will be better."

He put the shawl round her as he would have put it round a daughter, and she pinned on the brooches one by one until they found the two that most pleased Bligh. He had an emu's egg, which he was also sending to his wife, and insisted on packing it himself, so that it should survive the voyage. Susannah watched him as he made up the delicate package.

"Captain Bligh," she said, "in the town they are calling you Caligula."

He finished the package and sat opposite her. "So I have heard. And Major Johnston is putting it about that I propose giving my horse a commission in the New South Wales Corps. He is mistaken. I would not give my dog a commission in that Corps. It is a dangerous militia."

"I do not think all the officers are bad. Major Johnston and Mr. Macarthur did trouble my father very much. In his last year here he aged five years on their account. I have no reason to love them, but—"

"My dear, but what? They are a parcel of damned rogues." Bligh was being very moderate. He would listen to Susannah. If one of his own officers had said

the same, he would have kicked the man down the
steps of Government House.

"Mr. Macarthur—"

"What of Macarthur?"

"He will take your words to him this morning and
spread them all over the town, and use them against
you. And he will write to the secretary of state."

"Damn the secretary of—"

Susannah leaned forward and took his hand. "Those
words will be all over the colony by now. Mr.
Macarthur has a literal mind. But his wool is good. I
have been told his wool is good."

"Oh, I am sure the man is a hero of the fleece. A
hero of the golden fleece. The Spaniards have an order of the golden fleece, a sort of knighthood. I once
met a Spanish admiral at court, Don Faustino Espinosa
de Urquijo y Borbón if you please, who wore its em-
blem, a sheepskin, a sheepskin emblazoned on a
medal. With feet attached."

Susannah smiled at this picture of the decorated
Spanish admiral.

"A sheepskin," said Bligh, "with head and feet attached. I shall have a medal struck for Macarthur,
with head and feet attached."

"Go and see his flocks," said Susannah.

"Some day," said Bligh. "If you will come with
me?"

She nodded.

"Caligula," said Bligh. "If they think I am Caligula
they must delude themselves that this place is Rome."

Two weeks later Macarthur was complaining bitterly
to Johnston of the visit he had received from Bligh.
"When he moves it's like a great planet. Nothing less
than his coach-and-four in waiting, six or eight light
horsemen with a sergeant, three footmen outriders,
and he himself riding in a small sulky with a canvas

awning over him, and the side of this vehicle stuck around with pistols and a blunderbuss, so much is this great man afraid for his beauteous person."

"And I hear old King's daughter was in company with him," said Johnston.

"She was."

"And the Frenchman's boy with her?"

"Also. And Bligh being sweetly civil. He is sometimes civil when she is with him. I cannot bear the man's civilities. He viewed my best merinos and 'Oh,' he says, and 'Ah,' he says, feeling the wool, and he could not have told if I was showing him a goat. And he lifted the boy to ride on a sheep, as if it was a sideshow."

Major Johnston said little. That day Bligh had revoked with contumely no fewer than fifty-one liquor licences, impounded a stallion running loose which belonged to Johnston, and caused two dozen newly landed casks to be stove in. Over many months Bligh continued to be firm. He reprimanded his judge-advocate for passing sentence of death while he was drunk with contraband rum. The governor so frequently acted lawfully, and so persistently hacked at the concerted interests of rum, sheep, and a corrupt militia, that these interests finally found themselves obliged, of course for the greater common good, to go above the law and appeal to natural justice. Which meant that they took matters into their own hands and usurped the power of the governor, persuading themselves that, unless they did so, insurrection and massacre would follow, so great was the people's loathing of Bligh.

This was nonsense, as even Johnston saw.

"God's teeth," he said. "What am I to do, Macarthur? Here are these fellows advising me to arrest the governor."

At which Macarthur sat on the barrel of a cannon

in the square of Hyde Park Barracks and concocted a petition in proper form, stating that the present alarming state of the colony, in which every man's property, life, and liberty were endangered, induced the inhabitants—whose signatures, he assured Johnston, could easily be procured later, when the deed was done —most earnestly to implore Major Johnston, as commander-in-chief of the Corps, instantly to place Governor Bligh under arrest, and to assume command of the colony.

Johnston hesitated. Macarthur took up the petition again, and added this sounding sentence:

"And we, His Majesty's loyal subjects in the colony of New South Wales, pledge ourselves, at a moment of less agitation, to come forward to support with our fortunes and our lives the actions taken in our name."

And so, on January 26, 1808, the twentieth anniversary of the colony's foundation, Major Johnston proclaimed martial law and, asserting that he was acting to protect the civil order which he was in fact about to overthrow, assembled his troops at the barracks and gave them a little rum and then the order to prime and load. The cannon on which Macarthur had sat to draft the unanimous petition of the inhabitants, one of only two field-pieces in the colony which would fire, was trained on Government House.

Bligh, hearing the tumult and learning its cause, came from his study, ordered a man to bring him a decanter of the best Madeira, filled his own glass, and drank a toast to the portraits of George III and Queen Charlotte. As he did so he heard the whole body of troops marching from the barracks with bayonets fixed and colours flying and the band playing "The British Grenadiers." In five minutes, three hundred men surrounded the residence and burst in, kicking down the doors. Bligh fled upstairs. The whole house had been ransacked before he was found crouching under a feather bed, something he always afterwards denied as reflecting on his honour. He was taken to the ballroom, where he faced his accusers with contempt.

"Johnston, I see troops stationed all round this room, like a Robespierrean party, like a Revolutionary tribunal."

Johnston did not reply. Bligh stood facing him. He had put on the full-dress uniform of a naval captain, and was wearing his Copenhagen medal. "This is mutiny," he said. "The world knows there was a mutiny on the *Bounty,* and the world knows the consequences. Johnston, you are a dead man. This is treason." It probably was.

It is generally recorded that Bligh was arrested "in the company of an unnamed lady." That phrase has often been used against him, and very falsely. He may have been intemperate in many things, but he was chaste. The unnamed lady was Susannah, the daughter of his friend, almost his ward, and she stood with her son, Robert, then aged five, in the ballroom with Bligh, surrounded by bayonets.

12

The Generous Heart of the
Comtesse d'Estaing

MADAME LA COMTESSE D'ESTAING HAD NEVER SEEN
the young boy Robert, and, living in Europe, never
could have, but she fervently wished to see him and
had four times written to Susannah, each time asking
that the boy might for a while be entrusted to her so
that she could attend to part of his education, and to
his establishment as a gentleman. To write from London to Sydney was itself an adventure. The letter
could miscarry. The ship bearing it might be wrecked,
or stay revictualling at Cape Town for two months, or
the reply might easily lie six months in Canton on the
homeward passage while the master of the ship in
which it was conveyed waited for a cargo, for to find
a profitable cargo, of tea or silks, he would almost certainly have to sail home from Sydney by way of a
Chinese port.

The countess had been born Françoise Vouvray, in
Rouen, the daughter of a substantial merchant, and it
was she who had for so long lain on the conscience of
Baudin. Hers was the wound that scarred his mind until Susannah, in the last months of his life, brought him
peace, or something very close to peace. In his last

days, feverish, a week out from Batavia and knowing
in his heart that he would never see either woman
again, he wrote not only to Susannah but also to Françoise. The letter to Susannah we have seen. It was
written in the very hours of his dissolution and was of
love and gratitude. His letter to Françoise asked forgiveness from a woman he had not seen for years, and
whom he believed to have greatly wronged him. He
asked her forgiveness for having thought this, and for
having told her—in a violence of despair, loss, and rejection—that she had ruined him. She had been the
occasion of his ruin, but he had brought it upon himself. He had known that for a long time. He also remembered her many acts of love towards him, which
had been recalled to his mind by those of Susannah.
Françoise had betrayed him? What he began to see,
and with certainty, was that he had driven her to it,
and he was ashamed.

He had met Françoise in his twenty-fifth year. She
was a few years younger than he was, a Normandy
woman, some of whose distant ancestors crossed to
Hastings with the Conqueror. She was tall for a
woman, almost Baudin's height. She was fair, and her
eyes were Norman blue. Baudin was an officer of
promise. He adored her. But he was rash. Because he
could bear her absence no longer, simply so that he
could meet and be with her when she returned with
her father from a spring holiday of a month at Baden,
he declined the offer of his first command because it
would have demanded his immediate departure, certainly for many months. It was the offer of an extraordinary command, a first-rate ship of the line of a
hundred guns. He was not an officer of birth, fortune,
or even genius, just high talent. He had been a very
young first lieutenant of a first-rate in the Caribbean,
and his reputation as a navigator was already unques-
tioned. But the command of a first-rate was beyond his

greatest hopes. Still, he did not think for a moment
before doing what he did, though his refusal of so
splendid an offer was tantamount to a resignation from
the service, the more so since the offer came, indirectly, from the throne itself. Bougainville, who was
Baudin's principal mentor, had the ear of the minister,
and the minister had the ear of the king. When Louis
XVI was told of the refusal he shrugged. Here was an
officer whom great merit and greater luck had brought
to his favour, and he chose to throw that favour away.
Baudin was betrothed to Françoise. His rash act ended
that betrothal. At first he made nothing of what he had
done. His brother officers wondered at it, but he told
them nothing. He told Françoise nothing, though she
was distressed at his distraction. "Do not ask me," he
said. "Do *not* ask me." When it became apparent that
there were now no commands for him at all, and that
he would very likely remain unemployed and on half-
pay for the rest of his life, he did tell her, in a passion
of disappointment and rage at himself. When she tried
to comfort him, and to blame herself, he railed at her.
He did not recognize himself. One day, in tears of de-
spondency, she at last defended herself, saying, "I did
not do it. I will not be harried for something I never
wished and would never have asked," and he hit her,
something he had never done, something unthinkable
to him, and disgraceful. When she shook this off, and
still tried to rescue him from his despair, he shunned
her in silence and resentment. They could no longer
marry except on her money, his prospects being quite
gone, and in his pride he railed at this too. She was
faithful for a long time, for a year, but then she did a
deed of self-preservation, and at last accepted the repeated offer of a young nobleman. Françoise still half-
loved Baudin, but she had been pushed too far. No
one could have endured more. She had hoped for
Baudin's children. She became instead the mistress of

M. le comte d'Estaing, a favourite of the king, a man who could open all the society of Paris to her, and of Versailles. At a brilliant court, at the brilliant last burning-out of the last court of the last French king before the Revolution, she shone.

Nevertheless, she was at first uneasy. There was even a time when, having returned from a visit with d'Estaing to the court of Venice—Venice also at the end of its glory and in its last years as a sovereign State—where d'Estaing had been sent by the king on a brief mission to the doge, she wrote a note to Baudin saying simply, "Memories and regrets," and giving a time and place. Baudin came, listened to her oblique account of two months in Venice. She had been fêted. And yet—

"What shall I do?" she said.

It was the moment of all moments which Baudin afterwards regretted. Why should his courage have deserted him? But what courage he had left was defeated by his pride. He could not begin to give her what the count could: he could not offer her Venice. He was angry and humiliated. If he could have brought himself to say, "Please come back," she might have done. There were several times that evening when a single gesture might have changed both their lives, but both were too proud to make it.

The count, who knew of this meeting, was a rational man. He did not want to lose Françoise. He had the sense and tolerance to wait, and to be kind to her. His feeling for her was real, and hers for him. She continued to be his mistress. Baudin took it badly.

And then one day, a year later, a cousin of hers came to him, Jeanne, whom he had met through Françoise. Jeanne knew their whole history. She came ostensibly to inquire about the memoirs of his travels, which she had heard he was writing. She knew a bookseller who published nautical books, and offered

to help with an introduction. Baudin was touched by
this. He had written very little, but he thanked her
and looked strangely at her. She rose to go, and, as
she did, she asked, "You have heard the news of
Françoise?"

"What is it?" he said. Something in the way she
spoke made him afraid. He thought Françoise was ill.

"What is it?" he asked again.

"She married, yesterday."

"D'Estaing?"

Jeanne did not reply. Baudin could only stand and
look down. He never knew what his face showed.

An astrolabe is a representation, a model, of the heavens. The afternoon of the second day after he knew,
Baudin stood in the shop of a marine instrument-
maker near Notre-Dame holding in his hands a plani-
spheric astrolabe of brass engraved with the names of
the days and months, and of the known planets. An
astrolabe makes the grand assumption that the earth is
the centre of a spherical universe, and with it a mariner could, after a fashion, navigate a ship. To hold,
it is a thing of beauty. Its use is as a calculator. Set it
to show the position of the sun, or the stars as they
can be observed, and then make computations com-
prehensible only to a sailor or an astronomer, and it
will reveal the length of day in any latitude. It will
show when the sun will rise over Paris on a given day
of the year, or at Madeira, or in the frozen latitudes of
the North cape. Perhaps the Greeks invented it in the
second century before Christ. Since the fifteenth century the Portuguese used it in more refined form as
an aid on their voyages of discovery. It was never
more than an aid. The instrument Baudin held in his
hands was made in Paris as late as 1700, but it was
even then archaic and by the last decade of the eighteenth century was no longer of any practical value.

Baudin, in all his voyages, had never used one, though he knew its use, but now, in his distraction, he was consoling himself, hardly knowing what he was doing, with a representation of the heavens of which he knew very well neither the earth, nor any man, was the centre. The instrument-maker knew Baudin, to whom in previous years he had sold a sextant and many charts. That afternoon, Baudin held the universe in his hands for two hours. He stood motionless. He was offered wine, which he refused. Then he computed the time the sun rose on 1 December, over Rouen, the day he first met Françoise. He computed the hour of sunset two days later, the evening she became his mistress, and the hour of sunrise the next morning; he had woken before her and watched the day at first reveal and then illuminate her sleeping face. He calculated the position of Saturn in the heavens over Paris on the evening she asked him for the last time, "What shall I do?" And he was overcome.

In the shop, the instrument-maker's boy lit more candles. Baudin looked up to see that it was dusk outside. He gave the astrolabe into the boy's hands and went out into the street. That night he left his lodgings. No one knew where he went. Two months later he found a merchantman at Le Havre which needed a first lieutenant for the Caribbean. From there he drifted into the distant service of Austria, roaming the South Seas for botanical specimens, envious of the better fortune of others, contemptuous of himself for his envy, and loving his lost Françoise with a hopeless love.

So, at the last, it was to her also that he wrote, asking forgiveness, and telling her of Susannah—because, to the mind of the dying man, what had at last eased his soul would, he thought, solace Françoise too. When she received the letter she had a large enough heart to see this. By that time her husband was no longer an envoy of Louis XVI. That king had gone to the guillotine, and so had the count. The countess had fled to exile in London. By the kindness of one of Baudin's brother officers, who commanded the French port where the *Géographe* and *Naturaliste* at last put in, and who knew nothing of Susannah but did know the history of Françoise and Baudin, Baudin's effects, because he had no close family, were transmitted to the countess by a neutral ship. So was a letter from Sydney which some months later came to that same port addressed to Baudin. This was the letter in which Susannah told him that she was carrying their child. The countess made inquiries, and slowly the news came to her that the child was a boy. The countess had no children of her own. When Governor King returned from New South Wales in 1806 she called on him and learned more. He could hardly do other than welcome any interest which might help the son of his daughter, and the countess, though in exile, was still a woman of means. Susannah was petitioned by her father, by the countess, and, through her father, by Bligh, to accede to the countess's request. Would it not be better for the child to go to England for a while; or, better, would she not go there herself, taking the child with her? Susannah declined every proposal. The countess's reply to her denials was always the same—that the offer remained open for her to accept if she should ever wish to do so.

13

~~~~~~~~~~~~~

From a Coalition of Bandits, a New Rome

ON THAT EVENING of the mutiny, in the ballroom of
Government House, Bligh glared at Major Johnston
and then motioned Susannah and her son to take
seats at the long table behind which they had been
standing. He took the governor's chair himself.

"Now, sir"—he addressed Johnston—"you have
your bayonets. I see them. You are a fool who will be
damned. You have your bayonets, and what use are
they to a traitor? To strike at me, sir? You will need
them to strike at me, because you shall have nothing
from me except you take it by massacre and secret
murder. But will you murder a woman? And a boy?"

Johnston nodded to his sergeant that the men should
order arms, so that the bayonets no longer pointed at
Bligh. "In the name of the king—" he began, but got
no further.

"The king?" said Bligh. "You have no king. You
have put the king's protection away. You have a rebellion. You have your rum-rebellion. You will have
your rum again, and your rum-shanties again, and an
intolerable profit from felons whom you will then be

enabled to flog for their intolerable drunkenness. In short, sir, you will soon have all your fortune again."

Bligh looked around, recognizing those officers who were standing with Johnston. "I shall remember you all, gentlemen. But where is the hero of the fleece? Where is Mr. Macarthur? Abiding with his flocks, gentlemen, hiding behind sheepskins, gentlemen, and hiding behind you, gentlemen. Will you all hang for Macarthur's fine fleece?"

Neither Johnston nor any of his officers replied.

Bligh took from the table the Great Seal of the colony which had recently been sent out from England and received with much ceremony. On its face it showed convicts landing at Botany Bay. Their fetters were removed and they were welcomed by a female figure representing Industry sitting on a bale of goods with various attributes arranged around her—a distaff, a beehive, and a pickaxe. She was pointing with her right arm to a vista of ploughing oxen, rising habitations, and a church on a hill.

"There do appear," said Bligh, "to be no rum kegs on it. But take the Great Seal of New South Wales, sir, and hang it round your neck with its cord. You are a traitor and I will see you damned for it. But for the honour of the colony, I beg you to hang yourself first with the Great Seal."

"You and the lady shall remain here," said Johnston. "But"—this to his adjutant—"take the French boy and give him in charge of the orphanage."

Susannah lifted her head and looked in the eyes of the man she had laughed at six years before at her father's table, when, half-drunk, he had railed against the French counterfeiter and insulted Baudin. "No," she said. "Johnston, if you touch my son, I will have your eyes for it." Those were the first words she spoke in the room. No one moved. The adjutant and the other officers knew her. Many of them were in the colony in her father's day. She had many times at Government House received them and their wives, or women not their wives, when the ladies of the naval garrison would not receive them. Some remembered Johnston's old hatred of Baudin. Not one would do anything so wretched as take Baudin's son.

"A rabble," said Bligh, "may make a mutiny and take a colony, and flog all the brutes in it, but it remains a rabble. Johnston, you already perceive the extent of your authority. Get out and govern, and live in fear of every British sail. Put your sentries and spyglasses on the headland, and fear every report and every signal. You have taken the colony. Now you must govern."

Bligh had risen from his chair and was gripping the edge of the table. "Get out. Govern your colony. Govern. Govern." He was shouting.

"Busy yourselves, gentlemen," said Susannah, and it was she who dismissed them.

Johnston did govern, declaring himself lieutenant-governor, an office to which he had no possible title, and posting up a reckless proclamation, which read like something out of the French Revolution. This was foolish since that was an event of which every true Englishman went in loathing and horror. The proclamation read:

SOLDIERS
Your conduct has endeared you to every well-disposed inhabitant in this settlement. Persevere in the same honourable path and you will establish the credit of the New South Wales Corps on a basis not to be shaken.

God Save the King.
By Command of His Honour the Lieutenant-Governor

This was nailed up all over the colony, and was the

first that many well-disposed inhabitants knew of what had been done in their name. Johnston's soldiers, pursuing their honourable path, burned Bligh in effigy in the town and at outlying settlements. The government printer ran off caricatures of Bligh being dragged out from beneath a bed, smothered in feathers. Johnston, coming to a realization of what he had done, was uneasily writing confident dispatches to London. They arrived at a time when the secretary, who was in charge not only of colonies but also of the War Department, had graver things on his mind. Napoléon had invaded Spain. The secretary cursed both Bligh and Johnston.

Bligh veiled the portraits of George III and his queen with dark gauze, so that they should not see the infamy around them in the colony. He wrote copious dispatches, and some of them reached London. When Johnston learned of these smuggled letters he took Bligh's writing paper from him. When Bligh still wrote on scraps of paper, Johnston had the ink removed from Government House. He took Bligh's telescope from him. Dispatches addressed to Bligh were intercepted. Only one letter and one box were allowed to reach him. The box came from his wife and children, who sent him two coats and the material for making another, three pairs of silk stockings, a portrait of his daughter Frances, and some Canton tea. The letter, which came in the early months of the next year, was addressed to Bligh and placed on him the duty of telling Susannah that her father was dead. He had died less than eighteen months after his return, not having received any preferment, pension, or reward. His estate in England had been sold for £7000, which was Susannah's. The letter was from a cousin, who said that, a few days before his death, King had again been approached by the comtesse d'Estaing, and that he had intended once more to ask Susannah, with all the force at his command, to come back herself or, if she would not do that, to send the child for at least a few years to the countess. That had been King's dearest wish, and his last.

Bligh asked Susannah to walk with him on the lawns, to tell her. An escort of two soldiers of the Corps, ordered by Johnston to follow Bligh everywhere at six paces' distance, walked behind them and, when the governor and Susannah sat in an arbour, stood as if mounting guard over them. Susannah knew Bligh well enough to realize he had something to say touching her. She saw him glare at the two men and knew that in a moment he would shout at them to go to hell, and that would be useless. She told him to stay, and went up to the two men herself.

She knew one of them, though not by name. He made a half-gesture of salute. She spoke to him. The man said, "We must keep in sight, ma'am, but we will go farther off."

The two men retired so that they could hear nothing, but only see. They saw that the governor spoke for a moment. Susannah sat up and looked away. Then he spoke to her again. She sat motionless. They saw Bligh take one of her hands in his. Then she lowered her head on to his shoulder and wept. The soldiers looked down at the grass at their feet.

In the arbour, Susannah recovered herself. She had to talk about anything but her father. "Captain Bligh," she said, "I have never asked you. Why did you come here?"

"My daughters," he said. "Harriet, Mary, Elizabeth, Frances, Jane, Ann. Six daughters on the half pay of a captain? Now I shall be able to marry them off well. I was crossing Berkeley Square, on half-pay, with no thought in my mind of the South Seas. And there I met the secretary of the navy, who proposed it to me. But if I had stayed at home that day—you see?"

"Six daughters and no sons?"

"There were two sons, twin sons. We were living in the Lambeth Road. A small house. They would have been fourteen a few days ago. I remember the date. They were christened before they died. William and Henry. It is strange to give a child your own name and know he will die within the hour. I shall have no more sons. The house was near the archbishop's palace, and the church where they are buried lies under the palace walls. The grave is near the tomb of two king's gardeners, father and son, gardeners to Charles I. He was a monarch who lost his head; as I, my dear, may lose mine.

"Though I do not think so," he said, shaking himself out of that fear. "I do not think so."

"And I do not think so," said Susannah.

"After the interment," said Bligh, his mind going back to the churchyard of Saint Mary, Lambeth, fourteen years before, "I had to go to Plymouth, to do with some duty, and could not in any way keep my mind from my two dead boys, until I was desired by Mrs. Netherton, who was a friend of many years, to stay with her and her family—we were eight or ten in the party—at her house on Exmoor. I do not remember exactly where, but it was a very good country house with two good parlours below and a drawing-room upstairs, and good plain furniture, and a hundred and twenty acres around it, and a very good garden which she managed as an amusement, and employed her mind, and kept her health. Our dinner was fish from their ponds, and ducks and green peas and vegetables from their farm. She talked about her daughter who was in London, whom she called a tigress. I preferred it all to any other conversation, and had not laughed since I left home, and before."

Susannah listened. She could no longer remember an English country house.

"My dear," said Bligh, "you must go home. I urge

it. A hundred and twenty acres and a country house make for a cheerful good living. I came here for my daughters. If you will not go home for yourself, you must for your son."

Susannah did not reply, but nor did she forget what he said, or what her father wished.

Robert's sixth birthday was approaching, and Bligh made a great event of it. Susannah was aware of preparations going on but did not inquire, guessing that she too was meant to be surprised. The domain servants had been left undisturbed by Johnston, and she saw Jane and her husband, George Bryant, conferring busily the day before, and knew that Easty and Bligh spent a whole afternoon together in the library, after which Easty emerged with a casual air intended to demonstrate that nothing unusual had been discussed. She noticed that Bligh's full-dress uniform, which he had not worn since the night of the insurrection, was taken out by his servant and vigorously brushed, and the buttons polished.

On the day, Bligh appeared in uniform, Easty in his old regimentals, and Bryant in the borrowed clothes of a coxswain, carrying a great number of tiny ships which he had spent the previous two weeks carving in pinewood. Jane made the sails. Bryant's blue cloak, with its silk lining ruffled to represent the swell of a moderate sea, was spread out on the walnut table and most of the ships arranged upon it. Bligh supervised everything. When he gave the signal, Jane entered the room bringing Robert. He wore the uniform of a midshipman, which Jane had also run up.

"Now," said Bligh to the boy, "you are six, and, since you will one day be a naval officer of the first water, no time can be too early for you to hear the tale of a naval commander who gained the entire admiration of the whole world."

"Was it you, sir?" asked the boy.

"As good a man as me."

And Bligh, with the assistance of Bryant and Easty, then demonstrated not the Battle of Copenhagen, in which he had played a part, nor even the Battle of Trafalgar, which had assured the Royal Navy its mastery of the northern seas, but an action in the Indian Ocean in the year 1804.

"Canton," said Bligh. "And a fleet of East Indiamen are in convoy, sailing for England with a cargo of tea, silk, spices, and other rich merchandise."

The sixteen East Indiamen were arranged on the cloak in line abreast.

"And with them sailed fourteen other merchant ships, and a brig."

These too were put in place behind the Indiamen.

"Now," said Bligh, "there was in Ile de France, across the wide Indian Ocean, far to the west, many weeks sailing, a French fleet of five ships of the line, splendid vessels, under Admiral Linois, a bold Frenchman, who flew his flag in the *Marengo,* seventy-four guns."

The five French vessels were placed on the table, but well over the horizon of the blue cloak.

"The French admiral had notice, how I never knew but he had notice, that the Indiamen would be in that ocean. The fleets converged. The Frenchmen came near."

The French ships of the line were disposed on the cloak, facing the English fleet.

"But there are only five French ships," said the boy.

"But five ships-of-the-line. Any one could destroy those merchantmen one by one. The Indiamen carried cannon, but only against pirates, not against a ship of war. But the French admiral did not attack. He hesitated. He was puzzled."

"Why was he puzzled?"

"Because he had been told to expect sixteen Indiamen, not a fleet of more than thirty craft. And because the commander of the Indiamen was a very great sailor."

"Like you?"

"Well now, the English commander was Captain Dance, and he knew that if he ran, his fleet would be torn to splinters. Or he could strike his flag to the French admiral, and surrender his fleet, and Napoléon would have all that tea, and all those silks, and all that was in those ships. But he did not run, and he did not strike his flag. Before he left Canton the Indiamen had been new-painted with white bands on the black hulls, so that from a distance they could be taken for men-of-war, and Captain Dance had wooden cannon made, and when he saw the French fleet he turned the sixteen Indiamen broadside on to the French, as if to protect the merchantmen behind him, and then ran his wooden cannons up to the gun-ports, and made many signals as if for a battle. And he waited. And the French admiral waited. And Dance ran up the red ensign, the flag of a king's ship, a man-o-war, and waited, and still the French admiral did nothing, but hove to."

On the cloak the French ships hove to.

"And all that night they waited, and Captain Dance lit blue fires on the decks of his Indiamen to keep them plainly in sight of the French all night."

"What happened? What happened?"

"Come the dawn," said Bligh, "and the French admiral in the *Marengo,* ashamed as well he might be of his timidity, slowly approached and fired one bowshot. At which the Indiamen commenced a cannonade with every gun they had. They had nothing that could touch or scratch *Marengo,* nothing that could even reach *Marengo,* and not a shot grazed *Marengo,* but a vast deal of smoke was made and a vast deal of noise, and the Frenchman fled and took his five ships of the line with him, and never did they stop running until they came back to Ile de France."

The French ships ran across the walnut table and fell over the edge.

"And what did the English ships do?"

"Made a good passage to England, and Captain Dance was given a dinner by the lord mayor of London and a knighthood by the king. And Napoléon could hear the laughter floating over from the white cliffs of Dover."

"Will the king knight you too, sir?"

Bligh grunted. "And the great thing, apart from the dinner and the knighthood and Napoléon raging, was this. If the French admiral had attacked he could have taken not only those ships but also, if he chose, the port of Sydney and the whole colony of New South Wales."

At this moment the door of the ballroom opened and the domain blacksmith was conducted in, carrying a miniature sword and scabbard which he handed to Bligh, who drew the sword.

"Hold out your hands flat," he told the boy, "because the steel is sharp." He gave the sword to Robert. It was inscribed, "Robert King, Midshipman, on His Entering the King's Service." Glasses were filled and Susannah, with Bligh and the servants, toasted her son.

That night Susannah lay in bed very troubled. The day Bligh told her of her father's death, he had tried to comfort her by talking about the peace of mind he once found, in a grief of his own, in an English country house. He had urged her to go back. But her father's death had removed the last possible reason for her return. Then she thought of the day just passed, her son's birthday, when she had appeared gay. But she alone in the house that day knew two things which no one else guessed at.

First, her son's birthday was also the anniversary of Baudin's death. Only she and her father had known that. She had never even told Jane, and the others, though they well remembered when news of Baudin's death reached Sydney, had never known the day he died. He had died at sea. That was all they knew. So the day just gone had been, for her, also a day to remember Nicolas more especially than any other day. He had died, six years before, many thousand miles away.

There was a second thing which no one else knew, and the fact that they did not know said a great deal about the nature of the matter. Redmond, the surgeon, had been sometimes with her. The visits of a surgeon to the Government House went unnoticed. Perhaps the child had a cough. Perhaps Bligh had a twinge of gout. Redmond had attracted no attention to himself by expressing opinions for Bligh or against him. He seemed interested only in his own prosperity, and he had prospered. Any competent surgeon would have. Susannah had not noticed his visits, though she supposed, when she came to ask herself, that he had over the past year come at least once a week. On one visit he asked her to marry him.

There had been nothing in their conduct which was intimate, not a word or a touch. He was present at the birth of her son, but that was as a physician. She still thought of him as her physician, not even as a close friend. She was unaware of Redmond as a man. So when he asked, she felt only surprise at a proposal unforeseen and unlooked-for. She did not reply immediately. She was wondering how on earth the words could have been spoken to her. He took her silence to mean that she was considering her answer. Then she said, "No, Mr. Redmond. How could it be?" But as she said this she saw that he thought it could very well be, and that he hoped it might be. So she tried to soften her refusal, which in her mind was complete, by repeating the word "No," but this time more quietly. Then she left him. That was before her father's death. And then, on the morning of Robert's birthday, he brought a gift for the child and proposed again. He could not have chosen a worse time to ask her than the anniversary of Baudin's death, and she said, "Mr. Redmond, never." But she did not speak vehemently. He could not stir her even to an emphatic rejection.

The dispatches Johnston received from London were icily formal. He received no word of commendation for having, as he never ceased to inform the secretary, restored and maintained a perfect order among His Majesty's subjects. He began to doubt, and resolved to get rid of Bligh, whose continued presence in the colony served only as a reminder to the inhabitants of his deposition, which appeared more and more clearly to have been a mutiny. He tried to ship him out on a transport. Bligh refused to go except in command of his own ship, the *Porpoise,* which had brought him out and remained with him at Sydney. Johnston hesitated, but then restored to Bligh the command of the ship, stipulating only that he should sign a paper undertaking to return immediately to England. Bligh signed. Johnston accepted the word of an officer and a gentleman. The ship was Bligh's.

"And will you go?" asked Susannah.

"Finesse, finesse," exclaimed Bligh.

She was no wiser. She was not sure of Bligh's finesse. She did not know what the word meant when it was pronounced in such exultant tones. Then he said that, whatever the appearances to the contrary, he was not deserting her and she would see him again after not many months.

He was animated. He buckled on his sword, kissed her cheek, and stepped briskly into his carriage. "Finesse," he called out once again, and then drove off.

Why did she feel betrayed? She waited until Bligh's cutter put out from the jetty and then walked dejectedly towards the old orangery to watch his ship weigh anchor and depart. It was very hot, and at midday the sun shone directly down. She did not see the ship leave the cove because, for the first time in her life, she fainted.

When she regained consciousness the first thing she saw was the orangery. She had not entered it. It had not been entered for many years, since it had been hers and Baudin's. At first she did not recognize it. When she did, the beginning of a tear formed in her eyes, and she turned her head away. She was lying on a bench in the shade. She saw the figure of Redmond standing watching her. He said, "It is nothing. The sun. You fell on the grass. Bryant brought you here and called me."

He came over, took her pulse, and nodded. Then he withdrew again. He did not comfort her, as any man might have done, by sitting beside her, or brushing her hair from her face. He did not in any way touch her. But he was solicitous towards her. He took off his coat and folded it for a pillow for her head, but motioned Jane, who was hovering, to put it in place. He was distant, and yet she was glad of his presence.

"Captain Bligh?" she said.

Redmond glanced back at the cove. "The ship has gone. Lie back for a few more moments. It is nothing. The sun."

And it was nothing. In an hour she was herself again, but she was not herself again. For the first time in her life she was alone, except for her child. But even a much-loved child does not give that company of an equal spirit which was life to Susannah. She possessed a fierce inner spirit, but on its own it would wither. Baudin had been an equal spirit. Her father

had been an equal spirit, and so, she now saw, was
Bligh, with his extravagancies and tendernesses.
Now there was her son, whom she loved, and Jane,
whom she liked. But she was alone. She was not a
woman who could easily be alone. She could not remain for ever her lover's widow.

A week or so later, Redmond suggested to Susannah
that they should take drives round the settlement. She
first declined, but then agreed. One day was happier
than the others. Redmond took her into town to in-
spect the shop of Mr. Lane, which had recently received, by the arrival of the *Miranda,* out of Boston, a
shipment of clocks and fine watches; an elegant assortment of plain gold, pearl, topaz, and fancy spangled
neck chains, breast pins, and enamelled crosses; and a
variety of children's games and toys. She refused a
topaz for herself, but accepted a child's card game for
Robert, in which the cards bore the likenesses of Bonaparte, George III, Nelson, and the French marshals.
It was a game which, when played out, always ended
in an English victory. Mr. Lane had also received by
the same ship a stock of English cotton prints, calico,
checks, and muslins. She spent half an hour among
the fragrances and textures of the new cloths, and
ordered a length of calico to be delivered to the house.
When they drove back, the wind had got up a little so
that she had to hold on to her hat, and a warm breeze
moved the fabric of her dress against her body. She
could not remember when she had last been conscious
of such a sensation. It had become something she no
longer noticed. Redmond had not once in their
acquaintance called her Susannah, not even so much
as offered to take her hand. That afternoon he asked
her again to be his wife. She shook her head slowly,
but smiled at him. There was a steadiness about Redmond, and this ordinary virtue spoke quietly in his

favour. Had he been more a lover, had there been any instant *rapport* between them, he would have been less acceptable, as resembling Baudin. That would have been unthinkable. He bowed, a formality he still used with her, and said the afternoon was one he would remember.

The nature of Bligh's finesse was not at first clear. He had remained for several days outside the harbour. It became likely that he was not intending to sail for England. Then he made towards Hobart, tried to raise the garrison there against Johnston, and ordered the lieutenant-governor of Tasmania to print a proclamation denouncing the usurping serpents of Sydney. His order was not refused, but, just as the ink had been removed from Government House in Sydney when Bligh began to scatter denunciatory dispatches, so in Hobart, when he demanded the proclamation, all printing ink disappeared from the government printshop. In Sydney, Johnston denounced Bligh as having broken the solemn word of an officer, though he would not say gentleman.

Then, just when Bligh was at his weakest, when he was aimlessly floundering around in the seas off Hobart, pacing his quarter-deck, declaring that he was outlawed, Johnston lost his nerve. He lost it very suddenly, one morning, when he happened to pass The Major Johnston, a grog house named in his honour a week after the mutiny. The publican had erected a flattering sign outside, showing Johnston in full regimentals with a fearsome snake impaled on his sword, and a figure, vaguely resembling Britannia, with her arms raised as if in benediction of the noble saviour of New South Wales. Now the sign had gone. He had the publican brought out and asked him why.

"Blown down in a gale, sir," said the man.

Johnston could recall no recent gale. The truth was

that the publican was a shrewd politician. The inn sign
had been chopped up for firewood. Johnston looked
hard at the man, and ordered his licence to be revoked. It was his last official act in the colony. Next
day Johnston, taking Macarthur with him, sailed for
England. They said it was to vindicate themselves, but
really it was to escape what might be a sharper form
of justice if a British squadron appeared over the horizon and they were obliged to stand trial in the colony.
This was understood by everyone.

Johnston had lost his nerve at a fortunate moment
for him. Only days later, the force from England arrived—an infantry regiment commanded by Lachlan
Macquarie, the oldest lieutenant-colonel in the British
army, who came bringing orders which should have
amused him. But he had been born a Scots laird, and
was a serious man. He anchored in the cove and
waited. There was a scurrying back and forth of cut-
ters as the remaining mutinous officers in Sydney
sent their respects, and informed him, in reply to his
questions, that Governor Bligh was no longer in the
colony, and neither was Johnston. He received their
answers grimly. They smiled uneasily, and set about
arranging a triumphal welcome for him, when he
should come ashore.

At ten o'clock in the morning on the first day of 1810
Macquarie landed with the officers and men of the
Seventy-third of Foot, who stood at attention in drilled
rows, shining and sweating. The ragged troops of the
New South Wales Corps fired three ragged volleys in
salute and then, at the order of their officers, gave
three ragged cheers. Then there was silence. The eyes
of all men of the Corps were on Macquarie, and so
were those of the respectable residents of the colony
who had so lately signed their names to petitions

which now seemed, in the presence of the drawn-up ranks of the Seventy-third of Foot, plain treason.

Macquarie let his glance move over the Corps, the settlers, and the felons assembled to greet him. He nodded to his sergeant-major, and the bugles, trumpets, drums, and pipes of the regimental band played "God Save the King."

Macquarie summoned the senior officer of the New South Wales Corps.

"Is Governor Bligh returned and in residence at Government House?"

"No, sir." .

Macquarie unrolled a paper and in a quiet voice— so that the silence was deeper as they all strained to hear him, and the words carried to every man—began to read a proclamation expressing His Majesty's utmost regret and displeasure at the tumultuous proceedings in the colony and the mutinous conduct of certain persons, appointing Macquarie his representative, and commanding and requiring him to reinstate William Bligh, Esquire, in the office and situation of captain-general and governor-in-chief.

Macquarie paused, as if waiting for Bligh to appear. He did not. The officers of the Corps were at that moment miserably considering the prospect, which now seemed a certainty, of their own courts-martial, and wondering how summary these would be.

Macquarie continued to read: "His Majesty, through his gracious anxiety for the welfare and happiness of his loyal subjects of New South Wales, and for the complete restoration of quiet and harmony, and to remove every motive for future disturbance, has also been graciously pleased to direct me to signify to the said William Bligh, Esquire, that he should at the expiration of twenty-four hours after being so reinstated, receive us, Lachlan Macquarie, in the office and situation of captain-general and governor-in-chief."

His Majesty's loyal subjects there assembled would have laughed if they dared. Bligh restored for one day! One man did laugh, but he was Irish, and he had the Celtic good sense to cut his laughter short.

Macquarie waited for silence, said he lamented extremely that Governor Bligh was not there, and proclaimed himself governor there and then. A tactful sergeant of the New South Wales Corps stirred his men into another ragged cheer, and the gunner lieutenant fired off a salute of fifteen guns, enough for an admiral.

That night there were fireworks. Macquarie barely glanced at them through the library window.

"Miss King," he said, "I had thought you would be returning to England."

"No, Colonel Macquarie."

He was not sure how to treat this extraordinary woman. She had for months been the only occupant of Government House. She had lived there, through the governorships of her father and Bligh, for nine years now. He would anyway have treated her with courtesy as an Englishwoman of his own rank and as the daughter of a predecessor, but there was more than that, which he did not quite understand. When the secretary of state in London gave him his commission as governor he remarked, by the way, that the Prince Regent had signified that he would wish all consideration to be extended to the daughter of the late Governor King. She was believed still to be in residence in the colony and perhaps at Government House. The colonel waited for an explanation, but the secretary said nothing more. This was because he knew nothing more. It was not for either man to question the reasons of the Prince Regent. What neither could know was that the Prince Regent knew nothing either, but was passing on a request of his father, George III, who was now ill and often mad. The old king remembered his conversation of long ago with a young lieutenant whom he afterwards made governor, and he remembered the man had a daughter who had stayed in Sydney. George III was by nature kind. So he said to his son, "I knew the man. I did not know that he died without a pension, almost in want. We talked of Virginia. He had a daughter. If you please, look to the girl."

So when Macquarie met Susannah he was uncertain. He imagined that for some reason she enjoyed the Prince Regent's favour. He discovered she had a son. He assumed she would be going home, and was ready to offer her a return passage in what had been his own quarters aboard the ship that brought him out. It had not crossed his mind that she would stay.

She would have stayed in any case, but there was now one more reason for her to do so. Three days before, after many months of Bligh's absence, and after many months alone, she had at last agreed to marry Redmond. "Yes," she said, "but not yet." She would keep her word. Her pride, if nothing else, would ensure that. She told Macquarie she would remain, and marry. He asked after her fiancé, and she told him.

"But, ma'am, will you form an alliance with a man who came here as a felon?"

"He was soon pardoned, and my father always said that when a man was freed, he became a free man. Colonel Macquarie, most of the men in the colony who know any law, all the police, and the government printer, were convicts. Mr. Redmond has been the governor's surgeon for many years."

Macquarie nevertheless made discreet inquiries. He was told that Redmond was a fair surgeon, but unlikely to achieve any distinction in the colony. His advisers were mistaken. Redmond would achieve great things, and his acquisition of Susannah was only the first of them.

But perhaps Miss King was in Macquarie's mind when he made a speech the following day exhorting the upper ranks of society to hold out a pattern of good conduct to the lower orders. As to those lower orders, he pardoned seventeen convicts, issued to every soldier and felon an extra ration of seven pounds of beef and six ounces of sugar, and recommended regular attendance at divine service. A clergyman, one of those respectable inhabitants who had signed petitions in favour of Johnston, greeted Macquarie with a sermon on the text of Samuel I, chapter 16, verse 12—"Arise, anoint him: for this is he." The remaining officers of the New South Wales Corps were quietly informed that there would be no courts-martial, though their men would be sent home. Peace descended. Then Bligh returned.

"Error, folly, profligacy, irregularity," he expostulated, accompanying his words with much action of the arms.

Macquarie mildly offered him an honour guard of a sergeant, a corporal, and six privates, and ordered that at his appearance all sentinels should present arms and all drums beat a march.

"Infamous mutiny. Outrageous convulsion."

Macquarie offered him an immediate passage home, assuring him that on his departure no single circumstance would be omitted that could convey the respect entertained for him by all ranks of Sydney society.

"Then, sir," raged Bligh, "I see I have no other resource but my patience."

A farewell dinner, which Macquarie had been hoping to arrange for some time, was given for the departing governor. A hundred guests sat down at table.

Sideboards were covered with wine, fruit, and delicacies. Bligh was dispatched with a banquet, fireworks, loyal airs from the band of the Seventy-third, great ceremony, and the greatest relief.

The Attorney-General, in a farewell speech, declared that the polished nations of the world should not look with contempt upon a new colony whose enterprise was not, as was theirs, debilitated by the indolence of apathy and refinement. ("Hear, hear" and applause.) Looking into the future, he beheld the southern continent, superlative in arms as in the arts, giving laws to the world and regarding with proud superiority the effete nations of the northern hemisphere. "In this loyal city of Sydney," he said, addressing a gathering largely composed of lately mutinous officers and magistrates, while the pigs sniffed round in the streets outside, and four thousand convicts in the gaols shifted·in their rags or in their chains, "in this great city I behold arising, from a coalition of bandits, a new Rome."

They danced until three. At noon Bligh sailed for England. Susannah, her son, and the man who would soon be her husband remained in their new-found Rome.

Part Two

14

Robert Goes to Europe

IN EUROPE, after Austerlitz and Jena, there seemed
no battle Napoléon could not win; and after Vienna,
Rome, Madrid, and Warsaw, no city he could not
take. They were grave times, so that in London the
court-martial at Chelsea Barracks of a colonial major
for overthrowing a colonial governor would hardly
have been noticed, except that the governor was Bligh,
and if ever there was a man who could put Napoléon
out of men's minds for a few days it was Bligh. His
evidence against Major Johnston lived up to the expectations of all. He fumed, complained bitterly that
he had been burned in effigy (laughter), vigorously
repudiated the very idea that he had been found lurk-
ing under a feather bed (laughter), and insisted, as
further evidence of the villainy of the usurpers, that
lampoons of him had been published at the government printing office in Sydney (laughter) showing him
in his shirttails (loud laughter). Here the officers of
the court smiled too, but they found Johnston guilty of
mutiny and ordered him to be cashiered, dismissed
the service. The Prince Regent, who as commander-
in-chief had to confirm the sentence, thought it inad-
equate to the enormity of the crime. He considered

Johnston ought to have been tried for treason, and
had to be persuaded that the law would not allow this,
since the events had taken place not in England but in
New South Wales.

"A nonsense," declared the Prince Regent. "Even
New South Wales ought to be subject to the King's
Peace." The lord chancellor of England told him re-
spectfully that, in law, it was not.

"No, neither in law nor in fact," retorted Bligh,
when he was told of this. He felt himself hard done
by, and was appeased only when he was promoted
rear-admiral of the Blue, with the pay of that rank
back-dated six months, the date of his arrival in England. He was surprised to find how distant New
South Wales came to seem even to him. As for the government and its secretaries of state, they were concerned with far greater things, and not only with
Napoléon. The United States, tired of having its ships
stopped at sea and its sailors impressed into the
Royal Navy, declared war on England. "Rebels everywhere," roared Bligh, and wanted to burn New York,
but no one at the Admiralty listened to him and he
was forced to explain his grand strategy at home to his
daughters and to his beloved wife, Betsy. He was exalted when the British did burn the White House at
Washington, but loudly deplored the order sent by the
Admiralty to all English frigates on no account to
engage single-handed the American frigate *Constitution,* which had already sunk two British ships.

Susannah's world, in Sydney, was very remote. Bennelong, not having been seen for many months, crept
back one day from the bush badly beaten and old, and
died in his hut on the domain. She remembered the
first time she saw him, making legs in London when
she was a girl of ten. Susannah's maid and friend Jane
Bryant gave birth to a daughter, Mary, and Susan-

nah rejoiced for her. Susannah herself, after two years of marriage to Redmond, and at about the time Napoléon was at last in retreat, from Moscow, gave birth to a son, John, and Redmond, when he first saw the baby, kissed his wife warmly on the cheek and thanked her. Her son Robert was now nine years old. She was more in his company than in her husband's.

And at about this time the new governor bought 100,000 Spanish dollars and put them into circulation in the colony. To make 200,000 coins of them, he had the middles punched out. The centres were called dump dollars, and the outer rings, with the hole in them, holey dollars. They supplemented, but did not immediately replace, the assortment of Venetian ducats, Indian rupees, South American moidores, French crowns, English guineas, and the odd silver coins brought in by sailors from all the ports of the world which had previously been the colony's only currency. Convicts had been thought not to need coins, and, while they were in the chain gangs, they did not. But by now many were emancipists, having served their sentences. Settlers too were coming, though at first very few. A currency was needed, and apart from the rag-tag of odd coins, that currency had become rum. Now there were dollars. Spanish dollars were thought not to be quite the same thing as pounds sterling, but this coinage of a dying civilization was as internationally accepted as sterling later became. Anyway, in early New South Wales the words *sterling* and *currency* were not generally used in any ordinary sense. Currency was the name given to those children born in the colony, almost all of convict parents, and there was by now a whole new generation of such children. Those free settlers born in England, who had come out of their own accord, called themselves Sterling. The Sterling liked also to be known as Exclusives. These rancorous divisions, between Currency and Sterling, Emancipists and Exclusives, haunted Australia for decades.

Sir Harry Browne Hayes came to visit Susannah after the birth of her son. He picked up the baby, patted it, rocked it, sang to it until it cried, sang to it again until it stopped crying, and then gave it back to Susannah and turned to Robert, with whom he conversed as if with a grown-up. Susannah gave the new baby to his nurse, and then she, Sir Harry, and Robert walked in the gardens.

"My neighbours," he said, "have taken to calling themselves the Ancients. I called on them the other day."

"The ancient what?" asked Robert.

"The Ancient Nobility of Botany Bay."

"How ancient is that?" asked Robert.

"Not really so ancient as me even," he told the boy, and then went on, to Susannah: "Perhaps you know the people. The man ran a day-school in England, never prospered, never made a living; came out here, failed once more at the teaching of children, and turned to raising sheep instead—many sheep, with convicts to do all the work, and so he got a fortune."

Many families had done this. Susannah thought she might have heard of them, but was not sure.

"Their daughter," said Sir Harry, "is getting married. They put a notice in the *Gazette*. . . ."

"Ah." Susannah remembered. It was not then the custom to advertise engagements. The notice had been smiled at.

"Now you remember," said Sir Harry. "And what should the notice say, do you recall, but that a marriage in 'high-life' was soon to take place. Well, they're my neighbours, and out of neighbourly kindness—and I can see you're thinking neighbourly curiosity too, and I won't say you're wrong—well, I called to offer my congratulations. The girl's marrying

an attorney who came out from England a year past.
A fair match, so I offered the family my civil congratulations, and what did the girl's mother reply?
What did she say? 'I assure you,' says she, 'I don't feel
complimented a bit by my daughter's marrying such a
one as an attorney. I endeavour to bring up my family
with different ideas, to give them a proper notion of
their rank and consequence in society here, for I consider my family and a few others to be quite the same
as if you were to speak of the Ancient Nobility of
England, the Dukes of Bedford and Devonshire and
Norfolk and so on.' So she said."

"That," said Susannah, "is a tale improved by you
in the telling."

"Susannah, I improve it very little. A little, but very
little. A natural little. And really, what could I, a poor
knight and an Irish one at that, say to all that Ancient
Nobility? And I do believe she did not wish to receive my congratulations, poor as they might be, nor
to receive me neither."

"Ah," said Susannah, "how can you be received
into high-life, having received a free passage here, at
His Majesty's expense?"

"I was thinking that would be it. I do not," said
Sir Harry, looking down at himself, "appear to belong
to high-life. It must be that I dress too plain." He was
wearing striped trousers, a flared blue jacket with
brass buttons, and two conspicuous watches dangling
at the ends of two chains. The first did not keep time
at all, though it chimed the hours, or mischimed
them, striking twelve several times a day. The second
was set at Cork time, ten and a half hours behind
Sydney time, so that, he said, he should not forget
time past.

"And what," said Susannah, "was *she* wearing?"

"Oh, a gown, a high-life gown, a brocaded gown,
and all in the heat of the day."

He did not tell Susannah that afterwards, in a conversation which he had cut short, the woman asked familiarly about Susannah, whom she did not know at all, and after Robert, calling him the French boy.

Susannah knew some of the more respectable settlers called him that, but she did not care what they thought. Redmond knew too, but he did care. He was becoming a big man in the colony, and minded what was said. He had almost entirely given up his medical practice and taken to sheep-farming, which was one reason why he saw little of Susannah. He spent days at a time on his sheep station. He saw even less of Robert, but always treated the boy well, and tried to play the part of a father. And to Susannah he was a kind husband, in the sense that he was not unkind. They never quarrelled. Now they had a child of their own. Their marriage looked ordinary enough, and ordinary is what it was. It was a marriage which, apart from the new baby, was quite without event. Susannah would not have allowed herself to be seen unhappy, and would not have admitted even to herself that she was. But her days did not flower as they had flowered before. She never spoke of this to anyone, but Jane saw it, Sir Harry saw it, and anyone who knew her at all saw the change in her.

Susannah and Redmond lived in a house on the edge of the domain which Governor Macquarie, remembering the oblique advice offered him before he left England to do all he could for the daughter of Governor King, had given to her for her use, without rent. So the house was Susannah's, held by the governor's grace and favour. Redmond was most conscious that it was her house and not his. The income deriving from her father's estate went to Redmond on their marriage, as was the law, but the house was held by her and not him. This was something difficult for any man's pride to take. It was also difficult that their din-

ner parties were hers. He liked to entertain the more
prosperous settlers, and to please him she asked them.
He did not like to be seen in the company of Harry
Hayes and therefore, again to please her husband,
Susannah rarely asked Sir Harry to dinner, though
they remained fast friends and he often came to see
her in the daytime when Redmond was away. But
Redmond knew that without Susannah he could never
have entertained some of those who did dine at his
table. He could never have presumed to ask the governor and his wife: Susannah could and did. He knew
the officers of the naval garrison came because of
Susannah. He knew that though they were in name
his dinner parties, they were given in her dining-room,
in her house, in her way. She did nothing to make
him feel this: she was loyal to him in that sense as in
any other. But everything was done in her way. She
was not extravagant, though she was to his mind over-
generous and careless of cost, and once or twice he
hinted as much. She replied that she never thought of
it, and that of course was what he meant.

The affair of the candles was a tiny incident. It
was an ordinary dinner party, and, as usual, after the
roast, the servants changed the candles before they
had half burned down, taking the candelabra from the
table and immediately replacing them with others
in which burned tall, new candles.

"What happened to the old candles?" he asked afterwards. She supposed the servants had them. She
never inquired. "But why change them at all?" he
said.

"Shadows," she replied.

"What shadows?"

Susannah was faced with having to explain something that had been second nature for so many years
that to put it into words was not easy.

"Oh, William," she said, "it is just candles. Let me do it as I always have, and leave it at that."

He insisted.

So she explained about shadows. It did not matter to him, she said, and it hardly mattered to her, or to any young woman. But some of their guests were not young, and then it did matter.

"How?"

She walked over to the table, picked up a five-branched candelabrum, and showed him. If the candles were long, then the light fell from above on the forehead and hair and face of a woman sitting down. That was a warmer and softer light, gentler. If the candles burned down as far as half-way, then they were at eye level, which was too direct a light. If the candles burned low, then the light came from below, shadowing and hardening the line of the chin and flickering in the wrinkles of the neck.

"And so," she said, "I shall change the candles."

He was a little graceless about this. She affected not to notice. She continued to entertain his guests and hers. At these gatherings, most of her friends addressed her as Susannah, but Redmond always addressed her as Mrs. Redmond.

Their first real crisis came because Sir Harry Hayes had a fine daughter back in the old country, and because Redmond heard Susannah laugh.

Sir Harry was going home to Ireland at last, and of course he came to tell Susannah and to make farewell gifts to her and to Robert.

"Now my daughter," he said, "is beautiful, and though that is by her own account, by what she has achieved she surely must be so. It was at Carlton House in London, where the Prince Regent was holding a great ball, adding to his own and the national debt, at Carlton House as I say—though it may have

been at his palace at Kensington, but wherever it
was—"

"But you said your daughter wrote and told you?"

"She wrote twice, lest one letter should miscarry,
though both letters came by the same ship. And in
one letter it was Kensington Palace and in the other
Carlton House, the very same ball. When I saw her
last she was a little girl, but even then she had a rich
memory, a various recollection. Not a narrow remembering. She gave a man a choice. A man could select
from what she said, and believe what most pleased
him. So then, at Kensington or London she saw the
prince, danced with the prince, and, being a daughter
of mine, asked permission of the prince to approach
him later; and the prince, I suppose liking the look
of the girl, or being won by the promise that appeared to be wrapped in her dutiful request—for as I
say she had that gift, she always gave a man a choice
to make what he would of what she said—gave his
gracious permission to be approached after the ball,
upstairs, and it was there she told him the sad story
of her father's unfortunate wooing. I can see her
pleading for her father, and the good prince's generous heart touched by her filial words, and I can hear
him saying, 'Let Sir Harry be pardoned. Let the Irishman go free.' And so it was. The pardon is with the
governor now, having come in the same ship with my
daughter's letters, and tomorrow I am promised I
shall have it in my hands, and I shall see the old country again."

Robert said, "And if you go, we shall not see you
again?"

"Only when you come to Cork. And I shall be
sorry to leave you, and to leave my house on the bay
that is as fine as the bay of Cork, or very nearly.
And I shall grieve for my friends here, and most of
all for your dear mother. But I have longed for

Cork, and you know I have kept Cork time on me for the last two years. I suppose it was in hope. Now I shall be there again."

At this the other watch, that kept no time at all, chimed twelve, although it was only four in the afternoon at Sydney, and half past five in the morning at Cork, and Sir Harry unhooked it from its chain and held it out to Robert.

"Will you take this to remember me by? It is no good for time, but it is gold, and I should like something of me to remain with you, as a keepsake."

Robert was delighted. As he took the precious watch in both hands it halfheartedly began to chime again, and Susannah laughed.

"And, my dear Susannah, this is for you." He took from his pocket a silver locket containing, as she very well knew, a tiny likeness of himself on one side and a lock of hair on the other. She had always assumed the lock of hair to be from his abducted love, the girl who was a fine wanton but lacking in the deeper things, the girl who had cost him many years in New South Wales, but now he told her the lock was of his own hair—at which she laughed aloud, and, promising to keep it always, kissed him on both cheeks.

At this moment her husband appeared.

She began to tell him what was happening. "Sir Harry," she said, "is leaving. . . ."

"So I hear," said Redmond.

"Mr. Redmond, sir, I was making my farewells to Susannah and the boy."

Redmond said nothing. His manner did not encourage Sir Harry to continue.

He addressed his last words to Susannah. "Then good-bye, my dear. I do not forget your father. I do not forget . . ."

She knew he was about to say he did not forget Baudin either, but he did not say it.

"Good-bye, Susannah. Good-bye, Robert. Good day, Mr. Redmond." Susannah kissed him again, and he left.

Redmond did not see that she was deeply touched. He had heard her laugh as he approached the house, and it did not please him. She never laughed with him.

"I am not sorry he is going," said Redmond.

"But I am," said Susannah.

"He was a great deal with you."

She lifted her head. "He was, too."

Redmond saw the watch still in Robert's hands.

"What is that?"

"He gave me his watch, sir, to remember him by. It chimes."

"He was altogether too much with the boy," said Redmond. "It was not an influence I liked."

"I am sorry that you did not like it, but I am not sorry in the least that Robert knew Sir Harry."

"To associate with convicts—" he began, but she stopped him.

"William," she said, "that is absurd." And so it was. Redmond himself, though he had been pardoned very early because he was a surgeon and therefore useful, had been a convict. He had chosen to forget it, and had done more than forget it. He had willed it out of his consciousness. It had meant nothing to Susannah, as she had very well shown by marrying him, and she would never have said a word but for his objection to Sir Harry.

Redmond should have left things at that. He was not blind. The nuances might evade him, but he could see Susannah's spirit was up. But when Robert went to show his watch to Jane, Redmond said that his having found Susannah and the boy with Hayes had

brought to mind a matter he had been meaning to
raise for some months. Such influences as Hayes's,
whether Susannah admitted it or not, were not good
for the boy, and Sydney was full of them. Would it
not be better if he were sent to Europe? The countess,
he knew, had renewed her request that the boy should
be sent. Surely, he said, it would be better?

Susannah said, "No. No. No."

He repeated himself. But the reason he gave for
wanting Robert to go, though it had some force, was
not the real one. He really had put it out of his mind
that he was ever a convict. Few people in the town
remembered, and it was a town which connived in
forgetting the past. Redmond was now almost rich.
He was acceptable to the new settler aristocracy.
Susannah, though she did not care, would most
eagerly have been welcomed into that society. But
her son by Baudin was an impediment. Not to her,
because as her father's daughter she could do what
she pleased. But to Redmond, the French boy was
an impediment. Redmond did not see this as a mean
reason, merely a rational one, for wishing Robert in
Europe. All the same, he thought it unwise to tell
Susannah his real reason, and he was right to think it
unwise.

He told her he had returned early to say he would
be away for the night, with his foreman, up-country.

She nodded.

Susannah missed Sir Harry. The older people, who
had known her father, or herself as a girl, were becoming fewer and fewer. She saw less and less of Redmond, but occupied herself with Robert and with her
new son. He had Redmond's eyes. Susannah and the
governor's wife were friends, and took long walks
round the domain. Mrs. Macquarie was a great walker,
and paced out the perimeter of the grounds at three

miles and three hundred and seventy-seven yards. On the eastern side of the domain, down by the inlet known as Farm Cove because there the first furrows in the colony had been ploughed, she sat for hours in the shade of a hanging rock, often in the company of Susannah and Robert.

"He is a fine boy," she said, when Robert had bounded off. "But, my dear, how are you going to educate him in this colony?"

"I teach him myself."

"You can teach a ten- or eleven-year-old boy, but when he becomes older there are some things a woman cannot teach."

"The naval officers teach him as much trigonometry as they know. He already has the beginnings of a competent navigator. He could go to sea. And he handles a dinghy as well as any boy. Easty has taught him that."

"He could go to sea if the colony had a ship in which he could serve, but we have a couple of coasting brigs and a schooner. If the sea is to be his profession, he cannot pursue it here. Susannah, you can bring up a boy, but not a young man. You must send him away for a while."

"Perhaps," said Susannah. She knew the arguments were strong, but she put them out of her mind.

"My dear, you are stubborn," said Mrs. Macquarie. Susannah agreed.

Susannah had many friends, and found a new one in an impetuous young man called Greenway, who came to the colony about a year after Sir Harry left, also as a convict. She concealed this harmless acquaintanceship from her husband. It was the first thing she ever had concealed from him.

Francis Greenway had forged a note of hand to obtain £200 which he contended a man rightly owed

him but refused to pay. He was transported but given
a ticket-of-leave as soon as he arrived, because he
was likely to be useful. Sydney needed buildings. He
was an architect, and an architect who had practised
in the noble cities of Bristol and Bath. He also claimed
a friendship with the great Nash, who was just beginning his grand schemes for Regent Street in London.
Whether or not he knew Nash, Greenway was as
much given to grand designs as that great man. He
was a ruddy West Countryman, very impertinent, who
as a ticket-of-leave man wrote to the governor as an
equal, suggesting grandiose scheme for a new Sydney.
He was lucky, because Macquarie also had such
dreams in his head, for which he needed an audacious architect. Greenway was audacious. Within a
few months of his arrival he was urging plans for a
bridge across the harbour: he was told a bridge there
would inevitably collapse, but this did not discourage
him from bringing forward plans for churches, barracks, forts, courthouses, hospitals, a fountain, and a
stables. It was the stables which above all recommended him to the governor. Macquarie, agreeing in
that one thing with Bligh, considered Government
House a ruin and wished to rebuild. London told him
he could not. But London did not concern itself with
stables. Macquarie therefore welcomed stables which
were far grander than the new house he had been refused for himself. If he could not live decently, then
his horses should. The stables were built—a stone,
castellated, Tudor edifice, among the grand stables of
the world. But Greenway was at heart not a builder in
the Tudor style. He was a neoclassicist, as, coming
from Bath, he would be. Susannah also knew Bath,
having lived there as a girl. She was amused by the
young man's panache. One day, when he had already
been appointed civil architect, he took her and
Robert to the site on which he was building a cathe-

dral. The walls of Sydney sandstone were already rising. Twenty masons were at work, chipping and
smoothing the blocks. The master-mason escorted the
architect and his guests.

"Brush them, ma'am," he told Susannah.

"What?"

"Brush the stone with your hand," said Greenway,
and showed her. She moved her gloved hand across
the block and found that Sydney sandstone, though a
good building stone, will yield a fine dust to the pres-
sure of a hand moved across its face.

The cathedral was building near the Hyde Park
Barracks. It was unlucky that Susannah and Robert
were there the day Tyrone's man was exhibited in the
town.

Flogging was so commonplace in Sydney, so much a
part of ordinary life, that children at play practised on
the trees. They made scourges, drew the strands
through wet, red soil, and left blood-red stripes on
the white bark of the eucalypts. Captain Tyrone was
a quiet-spoken man, who commanded a penal settlement where convicts were sent who had offended
again in the colony. He was a diligent man, concerned
at what he called the diminution in the force of the
cut when the scourge was made of home-grown flax.

"And the use of this flax," he told a missionary,
"creates a great disparity in the punishment, according to the different stages of the use of the scourge."

The missionary did not comprehend, so Tyrone explained that one lash with a new cat was equal to
three when the strands had lost their firmness, which
could happen as early as the twentieth stroke. The
missionary came to the opinion that Tyrone honestly
believed he had a disinterested concern that sup-
posedly equal punishments should fall equally on the
backs of offenders, and that Tyrone considered it an

injustice that one man, receiving fifty strokes with an
old cat, should suffer less than another receiving fifty
with a new instrument. Tyrone liked to call a cat an
"instrument."

"You consider it an inequitable disparity?"

"Yes, to which must be added another cause of disparity which no amelioration in the cut can prevent;
I mean the different qualifications of the scourgers."

"The different strength of the scourgers?"

"Yes." Tyrone had not considered another inevitable disparity, which was the different strengths, of
body and mind, of the men scourged. That difference
would not have occurred to him.

"Furthermore," said Tyrone, "being anxious to do
my duty, I have ensured that fifty lashes under my
superintendence is equal to a thousand under any
other man's before in the colony."

"How is that?"

"Before, the scourgers rarely broke the skin, but
when I have the lash inflicted, I have never seen a
case where I did not break the skin in four lashes."
Tyrone had worked this improvement by making the
handles of his scourges longer, and by ensuring that
there were nine separate strands instead of the five
which the laxness of some officers had allowed, that
along the length of each strand six or seven knots were
tied, and that the scourgers, if they relented in the application of the punishment, or if disparity between
one flogging and another was observed, were themselves flogged. Dogs licked blood from the triangles
where Tyrone's prisoners were tied to be flogged. Ants
carried off the scattered fragments of the flesh of
men's backs. A deep hole was worn in the ground by
the scourger's foot as he pivoted. The most telling result of such diligence was the exhibition in Sydney of
a prisoner who over the previous year had received
two thousand lashes. He was walking quite well be-

cause it was some weeks since he was last chastised
and he was recovering his strength. He was a strong
man who had tolerated well the loss of blood, body
fluid, and the surface skin where repeated lashes had
flayed him. Tyrone made it a rule to offer a man water after the infliction of every fifth stroke. The man
had served out his sentence at the penal settlement
and returned to Sydney, where the soldiers let him remain at the barracks because although he could walk
he could do little else. They fed him and gave him a
blanket. They did this largely out of kindness, but also
because he was a curiosity. It was unusual for a
flogged man to be a curiosity in Sydney, but he was.
The soldiers called him Tyrone's man.

Robert too was discovering how to brush sandstone
when three redcoats marched past, escorting Tyrone's
man to the west end of the town to show him to
the regimental sergeant-major, who disbelieved what
he had been told.

Susannah did not see clearly to begin with, because
she thought that the white glare must be the shimmer
of sun on the man's back. Then she cried out. Tyrone's man had been so flogged that the bones of his
shoulder blades shone through the flesh like polished
ivory horns.

It was not this sight in itself that was most terrible
to her, but rather that Robert did not exclaim, but was
as curious as the soldiers. She saw that her son,
brought up by her, was already at the age of twelve
inured to a violence that revolted her. She remembered Mrs. Macquarie's kindly meant words about
her son's upbringing. How could a young man enter
any sort of gainful profession in the colony? How
could his spirit survive intact the sight of such commonplace brutality? That evening she made up her
mind, and wrote both to Bligh and to the countess.

When eight months later she received replies from

both, she summoned all her courage to send her son away. She did not tell her husband until she told Robert. The boy was delighted at the prospect of a great adventure. He needed to be a little brave to part from her composedly, but only a little. He was old enough to welcome the adventure, but too young to put himself inside his mother's mind and discern the wrench of parting which she concealed from him. Soon after the news came to Sydney that Napoléon had finally been defeated at Waterloo, Robert sailed for England. He was thirteen. Susannah did not watch his ship weigh anchor and make sail. She had watched too many ships leave the cove. She said her good-byes on the quay, where, having embraced her son, she told him—and the words were heard clearly by the sailors in the ship's cutter as it waited— "Robert, wherever you go, and whatever you do, remember who you are, and where you come from."

Then she told Redmond she wanted to be alone for a while and walked from the jetty towards Bennelong Point, where she stood on a high outcrop of sandstone. Her mind was full of her son but she did not look back to the cove but inland, over the growing city. She heard the chip, chip, chip of the masons' chisels as they worked on the stones of the cathedral.

15

~ഗ്ര~

Bedford Square, and the Bois de Boulogne

IT WAS ON A WINTER MORNING IN NOVEMBER, in a
fog so thick that it shrouded the maintops, and the cry
of the lookout that all was well came out of the unseen air, that the ship *Constantia,* bound for London
out of Sydney, brought Robert at last into the Thames
estuary. In Sydney there was mist, but he had never
seen such fog. At Greenwich the fog lay oppressively
in the river. The smoke of one hundred thousand coal
fires of a city Robert had never seen, held low under
the heavy clouds, obscured all but the massive out-
lines of the Greenwich Hospital, the most magnificent
group of buildings in the whole of the kingdom.

On the south bank of the river lay Deptford,
where kings' ships had been built for centuries, and
then, another mile upstream, on the north shore, the
bonded stores and narrow houses of Limehouse and
Wapping, whose foundations rose from the water on
wooden piles. "That house is mine," said the master,
pointing to what was only a dim suffusion of yellow
light floating by a hundred yards away. "They will
know I shall dock this afternoon. Even in this fug, we
shall have been sighted at Gravesend in the estuary,

185

and the post will have ridden to the Pool of London faster than we have sailed."

"Should I know of Deptford?" asked Robert. "I have heard the name."

"I cannot say what you know, sir. But Captain Cook set out from Deptford."

In the flat calm of the fog the *Constantia* was no longer under canvas, but was towed by her own long-boats. The sailors sweated at the oars in the chill. And then, as they came into the Pool, the fog lifted, revealing to starboard the Tower of London, and before them London Bridge. But the sky was still leaden, Robert had never seen such a sky. He had lived all his life in light. Then it snowed, and the master swore, and said this was a freak. It was not a heavy snow, but in the freezing cold it settled where it fell, fringing the rigging of a hundred ships in the Pool, icing the decks, and tracing the bare branches of trees on both banks.

"All the trees are dead?" said the boy.

"Dead?" echoed a sailor. "Dead, sir? No, sir, they have lost their leaves for the winter, and will grow again." Apart from a few fruit trees planted in the domain, Robert had never seen a tree that lost its leaves for half the year. In New South Wales a leafless tree was dead.

When the ship moored, he said good-bye to the master and his mates, gave a guinea to the captain's servant, who had also acted as his on the long voyage, and was greeted on the dock by a liveried steward who removed his hat with a sweep and conducted him to the countess's coach.

"It is four miles to go, milord," said the steward, "and icy for the horses, so we may be some time."

"I am not my lord," said Robert.

The steward bowed as if this were not to be believed, but merely an expression of an eccentric desire he would humour.

They passed by Saint Paul's Cathedral, a gigantic wonder, descended the cruel gradient of Ludgate Hill, where one of the horses fell and had to be heaved to its feet again, continued west along Fleet Street, cut north through narrow and filthy streets, then skirted great squares, and finally entered Bedford Square, where the coach stopped. The steps were lowered, Robert descended, and while his portmanteaux were lifted by four footmen he stood on the stone pavement, wrapped the collar of his greatcoat more closely round him, and gazed in wonder up and around. He had seen wonders. It was a day he would never forget. He had never seen such fog, or felt such cold, or seen trees without leaves. He had never seen so many masts as he had seen at anchor in the Pool. He had never imagined the vastness as Saint Paul's. He had never seen snow. It now lay half an inch thick on the pavement and he bent to touch it, and take a handful. It did not feel like salt. It melted.

"Milord," said the steward, and conducted him to the doorway, by each side of which a blazing torch flared. Before Robert entered he looked up at the five storeys of the stone façade. He had never seen so high a house. He looked back round the square. In Bedford Square alone there were more, grander, and taller houses than he had seen in the whole of his life before. He ascended the three stairs to the porch and was immediately divested of his greatcoat, hat, and gloves. By the hallway fire a glass of hot punch was offered on a silver tray. The steward waited while he first sipped it, and then drank, and then asked if he would care to enter the library. He had never seen so large a room, never gazed at so high a ceiling, never stood on such rich carpets, never felt the warmth of so grand a fire. He was standing facing the fire when

the double doors behind him opened, and he turned
to see, thirty feet away across the room, a woman as
beautiful as his mother but dressed more richly than
he had ever seen a woman dressed. Françoise,
comtesse d'Estaing, was a woman of great elegance.
She was in her late forties. Her hair was very fair,
with strands of grey that she let show. Her gown was
of yellow silk, but in Robert's eyes it was cloth of gold.

She walked to the centre of the room and waited
for him to come to her, but he did not know. So she
crossed to him, extending one hand.

"M'sieu," she said.

He took her fingers, and bent over the hand.

"Madame," he replied.

She smiled, and thought he did that well.

She said, "We will have much to talk about, but
later. You will be shown your rooms. Your clothes
will have been unpacked for you. Then we shall take
supper in an hour's time. But first, your rooms. You
will already have done much for one day."

He said, "I have seen wonders in one day," and
the words so struck her that she raised a hand to her
neck. She rang the bell, and when Robert was taken
upstairs she remained facing the fire, and said, "Oh,
Nicolas."

At supper he sat on her right hand. There were only
the two of them at the long table. "We shall not usually eat alone," she said, "but this is the first evening."
He was bronzed from the voyage across the world. The
Constantia had taken the Great Circle route, south
from Sydney, across the Tasman Sea, south of the
South Island of New Zealand, in the low latitudes
across the Pacific, round Cape Horn, and then north-
east across the Atlantic to Europe, putting in only at
Rio de Janeiro for water and fresh food.

"So you have crossed the world," she said, "like your father."

He said, "My mother has told me that you were a friend of my father's, and that this is why you have been so kind as to—" The boy wanted to know more about his father, whom he knew only from Susannah. He was curious why the countess should, as he put it, be so kind.

"Your father," she said, "was a very great friend. It was in another world. I will tell you about that world later, when you are older, and when you have seen something of Paris."

He was content.

"What shall I do?" he said.

"What will you do now you are in Europe? In a week, you will begin to be taught those things that a young man should be taught. I do not know what they are, but tutors will come who will tell you. That is arranged. After this evening, whenever we are together we shall speak French, and one of your tutors will converse with you in Italian. I did say that I did not know those things that a young man should be taught, but you must forgive me that I have already made a decision on your behalf, which is that a gentleman can perfectly well do without a knowledge of German."

Robert nodded, but did not understand.

"I am French," she said. The Prussians, wherever they touched France, had devastated the country.

He still did not comprehend, but nodded as if he perfectly well did.

"And we shall live half the year in Paris. I am luckier than many. I have lived here for twenty years, and London is my first home. Most of my friends are English now. But my husband, the count, of whom your mother will have told you? . . ."

"Yes."

"After his death, I gave up all hope of a great deal that he possessed in France, and indeed the greater part of it has gone, but his Paris house had the good fortune to be seized at the end of the war by the Duke of Wellington, for his staff. I did not believe it when I was told that the English soldiers had not looted it but had even repaired the depredations of the previous occupants, who were my own countrymen. And then they went to the great trouble of finding me, and restoring it to me, and sending me an inventory they were anxious I should check. It is strange. The French fought for twenty-five years for the dignity of man and succeeded only in stripping away all dignity, but the duke's English soldiers gave me back a house I had forgotten."

"I have heard it said in Sydney," Robert solemnly remarked, "that the French these days are given to an excessive admiration of the English. An Anglomania they call it."

The countess laughed. "That," she said, "is a rebuke I gladly accept."

A few minutes later, after she had said nothing for a while and he had not interrupted her silence, she said, "Will you come by the fire? I have something to show you."

Over the fire was a full-length portrait in oils of a nobleman in court dress.

"The count, my husband," she said. "It was done at about the time I first knew him."

By the side of the fireplace, at eye level, was a framed engraving. It was the head and shoulders, perhaps three inches in height, of a French naval officer, hatless, with the single epaulette of a lieutenant. The eyes and the half-smile took the attention of everyone who looked at it.

"Have you seen that before?" she asked.

"No. But it is my father."

"Yes. In the last year that I knew him."

"Captain Bligh told me he was a good sailor."

"Had he been fortunate, his name would be re-membered with that of Bougainville. He did as much as Bougainville. But now I think you will want to go to your bed."

She stood still looking at the engraving, so he said good night, and went to the door.

"Robert."

He turned in the open doorway and she waited. He did not know what she wanted, and when she saw this, she said, "God bless you and keep you. Good night."

The boy was thirteen. He did not know what was required of him. But he had the divine good sense to realize that some ceremony was expected. He re-turned to her, she put her hand on his head, and it was done. The countess had no children, and had known no children. She had lived in England for twenty years, but she was French. As a child she had always done what any French child did, asked for her parents' benediction before she went to bed. It had not occurred to her that Robert would never have done such a thing. But he had come back to her, and she was grateful. While he was with her, he would be in the place of a son.

The boy slept. Françoise d'Estaing lay awake, see-ing Robert's face and the engraving of his father in the last year she had known him. The eyes were the same, and the brow. His instincts were the same: he could not possibly have known what she wanted, but had returned to her by the fireplace. And most of all, she remembered the boy's reply when she asked if he had not seen many things already in one day. His words were, "I have seen wonders in one day," and those had been, almost to the letter, the words of Nicolas Baudin to the girl Françoise Vouvray, at the end of the first day they spent together, so many years before, in Rouen. As they parted, he said to her, *"J'ai vu, aujourd'hui, de grandes merveilles."*

Next morning they went to see Bligh.

"He remembers you well," she said. "He talks of you very much, and of your mother. How long is it since you saw him?"

"Since he left New South Wales. That is seven years."

"You will find him changed. Try not to show that you do. His wife, Betsy, is dead. He is very ill. I have seen him often. He made me promise to bring you the day you arrived."

Bligh was lying on a sofa in his small house at Lambeth, and did not try to rise. "Françoise, Françoise," he said. "I always know when you come." His sight was almost gone, but he always recognized her.

He did not recognize Robert. All he saw was another figure.

"I have brought you Robert."

"Robert?"

The boy came nearer. "I am Robert King, sir. You gave me a sword when you were governor."

"Susannah's boy?"

"Yes, sir."

"Robert, then. You are Robert?"

Bligh held up a hand, which was emaciated. The countess watched Robert as he hesitated, and then took it.

"I made you a midshipman. Now you are here. You have gone to sea?"

"No, sir, I have come to stay with Madame d'Estaing, and to go to Paris."

"Greek and Latin, and Paris and Rome. I was at sea when I was thirteen. How old are you now?"

"I am thirteen."

"And Susannah? Susannah wrote to me. Was it about you? How is your mother? I never did like Redmond. I told her. How is Susannah?"

"She is well, sir, I believe."

"I never did like Redmond."

The countess said quickly, "And now Robert says there are cathedrals in Sydney."

"Castles? Macquarie is building castles?"

"A cathedral, sir."

Bligh sat up straighter and looked brightly at Robert, as if he were much revived. "It was a Robespierrean party, bayonets all around. And I said a rabble could seize a colony, but could not govern it, and they were all afraid."

"They were all afraid," said the boy.

After that visit, Robert saw Bligh twice more, but was not there with the countess on the day he died. Bligh talked of going to take his first command, which was the *Bounty*. He talked of provisioning the *Bounty* at Tahiti, in Matavai Bay. In his dying hours he sailed to the South Pacific, but he never talked again of New South Wales, except that in his very last hour he called out to the countess by her own name sometimes, but mostly as if she was Betsy, his wife, and twice, very near the end, as Susannah.

He died in the rank of vice-admiral of the White. He was buried in the parish church of Saint Mary, Lambeth, in the same vault with his two sons who had died aged one day, twenty-two years before, and with his beloved wife, Betsy. The inscription described him as vice-admiral of the White, and Fellow of the Royal Society, an honour won for his botany, but there was nothing to show he had been governor of New South Wales. The countess planted round the vault the herb Phlox, commonly known as White Admiral. After the service, Robert took her arm but did not lead her straight to the carriage but a few steps towards Bligh's old house, which was very near.

"What is it?" she said.

Robert could remember Bligh only as a great man. The governor of New South Wales was a great man. To Robert, the rum-rebellion against Bligh was as if it were the whole French Revolution. "I was thinking," he said, "that the men had trouble carrying the coffin out, the stairs were so narrow. It is so small a house for a great man to die in."

"Great men matter," she said. "Houses do not."

After Bligh's death the education of Robert, which was to have been undertaken by the admiral and the countess together, fell wholly on her. The house in Paris, next to the British embassy in the rue du Faubourg-Saint-Honoré, was a palace. The very inside walls were faced with marble. In the suite of drawing-rooms, where the walls had been papered in the zeal of the Revolution with tricolour paper, the scrupulous English had removed this paper and restored the Gobelin tapestries. What they could not replace of the looted Sèvres china they made up with the best of Wedgwood, and offered their apologies for this shortcoming. A boy soon learns to live in a palace, though it was true that it never seemed to him so grand as the house in Bedford Square. That was by comparison an annexe, but he had seen it first.

A defeated Paris insisted on its glory. Robert was taken to view the half-completed immensity of Napoléon's Arc de Triomphe. It was still a dummy, but French pride insisted that the appearance of the arch should be completed with scaffolding and painted canvas. The opera maintained its splendour. Robert often went, in the company of the countess and her friends, and vigorously applauded the new operas of Rossini.

The countess leaned over to him. "Robert, I am inclined to applaud too much, or so I was often told. Perhaps you ought not to follow me in that."

M. le duc de Grisaille, who was often with them, waved this idea away as if it were nonsense, but did say, "There is now such difficulty with applause. There never was."

"Why?" said Robert.

"Because in the old days one knew what to do. One never applauded until the king chose to applaud. There was always silence while one waited for His Majesty. That has gone. Then a man could end an opera quietly, not as this fellow Rossini does, with dominant chord after dominant chord to whip up the claque. But what Italian ever disliked noise?"

They saw a lot of Grisaille, who was often with Françoise.

She said to Robert, "The duke cherishes old ways, although he half mocks them. The Revolution fell very unequally. He was a duke when I was the daughter of a merchant in Rouen. Now I have all this, and he has lost everything. I know he does not appear to you to have lost everything, but he has very little. Some people, when they look back over those twenty-five years, notice only that nowadays the men dance with their hats off at a ball, whereas before they kept them on. To so many others, those years were the end of everything."

By the time he was seventeen Robert, when he was in London, was an English gentleman. When he was in Paris he could pass, in speech, dress, and manners, for a Frenchman. He was more than competent in five languages, two of them dead, but that was then expected. He rode. He hunted. He was a handsome young man. When he was seventeen he was introduced at a levée to Jacqueline Brie, an actress at the Comédie-Française, by the way a courtesan, and above all a woman of agreeable warmth and wit. She was an indiscreet gossip but was still received everywhere because of her vivacity and because her indiscretions were on the whole without malice.

She took to Robert. She taught him, in one evening, how to flirt. She showed him how to offer her little flowers of courtesy and compliment.

"Perhaps we shall meet?" she said. "Do you ride in the Bois?"

He said he did.

She called to Grisaille, who was playing écarté with the countess and another couple. "Duke, will you lend me one of your mares tomorrow, for the afternoon? I mean to show Robert the Bois."

Everyone heard.

They rode out along the avenue de Neuilly, then south into the Bois de Boulogne, skirting the oak woods which had been stripped for firewood by the occupying armies of England and Prussia in 1815, through the newly planted chestnuts, sycamores, and acacias, with their lighter foliage, and southwards for another mile. They began at a walk, broke into a trot, then cantered along the ridings until she reined up sharply, letting him canter past. He circled her at a gallop while she waited.

"Bravo," she said softly, and turned her horse's head into the dark wood of mature, spreading oaks, until she reined the mare in again.

Robert would have been insensible if he did not feel that a woman sitting side-saddle in a black riding habit on a summer afternoon in the Bois, and now holding out her arms to him, was one of the more splendid sights of life. He flicked the reins of his own horse over a bough, walked to her, and put his head in her lap. He had forgotten, or he did not know, that a woman sitting side-saddle conceals beneath her skirts the pommel she sits astride, and so his ardent head encountered this leather pommel and not the softness he had expected. She laughed, and took his head and moved it a little to the side, finding him the softness he wanted.

"Take me down."

He did, and they stood facing each other.

"Do not let the mare stray."

He secured it.

"Now let me down again." She took his hands and, as if curtsying, lowered herself to the bed of leaves. She let her hair fall back.

"Come here then."

"So," she said, half an hour later that afternoon, as she lay lazily back, gazing upwards at the sky between the oak branches, and watching Robert as, ten yards away, he leaped upwards trying to catch a low oak bough, to swing on it in great high spirits. "I see a young man greatly pleased with himself."

He was abashed and came back to her. "Jacqueline, I did not mean that."

"But why not? I am happy to have pleased you. It is some years, I tell you, since I saw a man frisk so happily."

He sat beside her and helped her retrieve dry leaves from her petticoats.

"They are everywhere," he said.

"Then take them from everywhere." She pressed his hand to her waist beneath the riding habit and the petticoats.

They hunted leaves.

"I have heard," he said, "that you knew Napoléon."

"Say what you mean. You have heard that I was his mistress."

"And that the Duke of Wellington, when he was in Paris . . ."

"You are a proud boy, and put yourself in exalted company."

"Yes, and that is insufferable, isn't it?"

"No, not from you. It is a tale often told, but none the less true. To sleep with Napoléon, oh, you slept with the conqueror of the world. But Wellington was far and away more of a man."

The boy stroked her hair.

"And now," she said, "you are thinking how to inquire about yourself. Yes?"

"Yes."

"Well, I have never known anyone else try to swing on a tree. Thank you for that. And you were not ungentle. And that is enough for any man to be told."

He took her in his arms and said, "I would do anything for you. Anything."

She released herself. "I am afraid that you might. You might take after your father in that. But, Robert, you shall not, because I shall not let you. I shall not let you begin. I will tell you this now, while we are both happy, but we shall not come here again. I shall not seek you out again, and I forbid you, and I ask you, not to try to see me. I have made you a little gift, because I wanted to. Of course we shall meet occasionally, in company with others. Let us be affectionate friends. You will find other women."

"They will not be the same."

"You cannot conceivably know that. And I tell you that you are wrong. Now, we shall ride back, and we shall ride back happily."

"What did you mean about my father?"

"Nothing. Now, help me up."

When he returned, the steward handed him a note

which said, "When you have changed, come to my sitting-room." He found the countess reading. "There was no point in telling you before," she said, "but I will tell you now. Last night Mademoiselle Brie asked the duke if he would lend her a horse to go riding with you this afternoon. He did once have many horses but that was many years ago. Now he has none. This morning he borrowed money to buy a horse to lend to her this afternoon. Tomorrow he will sell the horse at a loss he cannot afford."

"I did not know that."

"How could you—though I did once tell you he had little. But it would be kind of you to accept no further invitations, and to offer none yourself. I say nothing against Mademoiselle Brie. She ought very well to have known, but she is thoughtless."

"I give you my word."

The countess had not expected matters to be resolved so easily. She was gratified, but she looked sharply at Robert, and asked herself in what intangible way had he changed so suddenly. He had changed. The evening before a woman had taught him how to woo. That day she had given him, in an afternoon, the beginnings of an understanding of the nature and quality of the relationship between a man and a woman, of longings and fruitions, which he had never begun to guess at. Above all, by forbidding him the desperations that often follow, she had opened to him a comprehension of much that had before only dimly entered his consciousness. Her reference to his father had opened the door of this comprehension further still. He began to see for the first time the power a man and a woman had over each other.

"May we speak?" he asked.

She assented.

"When I first came to you in London, you said you

would tell me, when I was older, about what you called almost another world."

"Yes."

"I have been told you were presented to the doge."

If the countess had been a woman of artifice she could have smiled away the inconsequentiality of this question. But it was not inconsequential. It went to the heart of the matter.

She was back in the great Venetian palace, at the banquet, which she had attended as mistress of the emissary of Louis XVI. She was a young, supple girl curtsying so low that her high wig touched the red steps before the throne. She had murmured "Serenissimo," as she had been told, and the old doge told her in careful French that she was a beautiful woman. She had been so surprised that he should acknowledge her at all, let alone say such words, that she stumbled over the hem of a petticoat, which tore. Probably only she felt it tear, but it was something she had never forgotten. That visit had been golden, and yet unhappy.

"I was presented to the doge," she said.

"And you were at Versailles too?"

"After my marriage. I was presented to the queen, but not to the king. The ball was always on a Sunday. You will think of it as very grand. It was very grand. My court dress cost what my father earned in a year when I was a girl. He was a woollen merchant. Do you know, it was not the magnificence that most awed me. D'Estaing was very kind. I was touched by his gifts, not magnificent gifts, but silver. You see, before the Revolution, as a bourgeoise, I could by custom wear nothing made of silver, and no plumes in my hat."

Robert looked past the countess at the two likenesses which were taken from England to France and back again whenever the household moved—the life-size oil of d'Estaing and the tiny engraving of Nicolas Baudin.

"Why am I here? What was my father to you?"

"Your father and I were to be married."

"He loved you?"

"And I loved him with my whole soul."

"But you married d'Estaing."

"I married d'Estaing."

"This afternoon, in the Bois, I told Jacqueline I would do anything for her. She said she was afraid I might. She said I very well might, like my father. She forbade me to see her again. What was it that my father did?"

She told him the whole story of the declined command, the broken engagement, and Baudin's broken career.

Robert asked, "And that is why I am here?"

"Yes."

"You and my father were all that to each other," said Robert, "but you married d'Estaing. Forgive me, but you once told me that men mattered and houses did not."

Françoise looked at the boy. "Robert, we brought out the best in each other and the worst in each other. We tore each other apart. Why is it that those things inspired at the start with the greatest generosity and love, end so often in havoc?"

There was a long silence.

"My mother does not know?" he asked.

"Not unless Nicolas told her, and I do not think he would."

Robert embraced Françoise as he never had before. There had never been any constraint between them, but now it was as if they were at the same time mother and son, and the dearest of old friends. When they returned to London, Robert enrolled at Gray's

Inn and began to eat the twelve dinners a term which
was the only preparation then required of a man who
proposed to make a career in the practice of English
law. He and the countess never again alluded to the
conversation of that evening in the house in the rue du
Faubourg-Saint-Honoré.

16

❦

The Lemon Tree

THIRTEEN THOUSAND MILES away from Bedford
Square and the Bois de Boulogne, the criminal court of
Sydney was working routinely through its business of
theft and murder. Robert Duncan stood charged with
the murder of Abel Hughes in the penal colony at
Newcastle, seventy miles north, where both had been
serving sentences of one year's hard labour for the
joint theft of a pig in Sydney. Before that theft, both
were ticket-of-leave men. They were originally transported from Norwich eight years before, also for the
theft of a pig.

Duncan did not deny the capital charge. He neither
defended himself nor was he in any way defiant. He
stood awaiting the inevitable sentence.

But the judge-advocate was new from England and
was not satisfied to write down, "Death," and see the
man taken away.

"Was there a quarrel?" he asked. "It was revenge?"

"Revenge, sir? He was my friend."

"Let me be clear. If there is any defence it is my
duty to hear it. So let me be clear. You and the man
Hughes were felling a tree together?"

"Yes, sir."

"And so that it should fall in the direction you wished, you had on one side undermined the roots. There was a large hole, so large as a man could climb into?"

"Yes, sir."

"And when this man got into the hole, to look at the roots, to determine how much more work remained to be done before the tree fell, you struck him on the head with a hatchet. And yet you say he was your friend?"

"He was very weary of his condition. I too was weary of my life. He dropped like a log of wood. Oh, sir, if people knew how easy it was to take a man's life, things of this kind would happen oftener."

The judge-advocate was a very young man, in his twenties, and he was a Christian. He was badly troubled because, in spite of the enormity of the act, he did not think he saw evil in the wretch before him.

"You say you were both weary of your life. Had you been much flogged?"

Duncan had been speaking indifferently, almost inaudibly, but now he raised his voice and cried, "Let a man be what he will, when he goes *there* he is soon as bad as the rest. A man's heart is taken from him, and he is given the heart of a beast. Sir, if I have been bad, what has been done to make me good?"

The young judge-advocate, and all those in court, were abashed by this outcry. For the first time the murderer met his judge's eye.

"No, sir," he said, speaking again in the voice of indifference, "we was not flogged. That has lately been given over a little. There was the box, sir. That was enough."

"What box?"

"It is a dark box in which a man is put. He is given water but no food. He cannot properly stand, nor properly sit, and he cannot see the air. Men do not dread it for a day or two perhaps, but after three days a man is not in his mind."

Duncan was a Roman Catholic. Father Massey, the priest who shrived him before his execution three weeks later, was the same missionary who some years before had listened while Captain Tyrone quietly explained the methods by which he would ensure that fifty lashes inflicted under his superintendence should be the equal of a thousand under any other man's. After the display of Tyrone's man in Sydney, that officer had been admonished that no man ever again was to receive at his orders more than twenty-five lashes without the written approval of the governor. Because he was an officer who loved his duty, he obeyed, and had instead devised the box. In this he was only a little ahead of penal fashions. Solitary confinement, often in the dark, was soon to be the guiding principle of the Philadelphia system of imprisonment, which was thought to be marvellously reformative and would spread throughout the larger cities of the United States. Tyrone's diligent ingenuity was, however, entirely responsible for making it impossible for the prisoner either to stand or sit.

The priest who shrived Duncan very much wished to see Tyrone's penal colony, and first approached the judge-advocate, who declined to give his authority because, although he was a Christian, he was also a Protestant and did not wish a Romanist to circulate in a settlement where many of the inmates were Irish. The English fear of Irish insurrection was always great, and priests were considered to provoke rebellion. Having been refused in that quarter, the priest then considered whom else to approach.

At that time the new governor, Sir Thomas Brisbane, moved from old Government House in the cove to his much larger country residence at Parramatta, fifteen

miles upstream from Sydney. He came into town once
a week to discharge his duties, but spent much of the
rest of his time cataloguing the 7385 stars visible in the
southern skies, which he plotted from a new observatory he built at Parramatta. It was the most complete
study ever made of the southern sky, and won Brisbane the Gold Medal of the Astronomical Society of
London. He was an amiable man, who had got the gov-
ernorship because he was a friend of the Duke of
Wellington. Brisbane thought to make Parramatta the
Richmond or Versailles of Sydney; was pleased that
the approach road was wider than Pall Mall; liked the
house, whose portico had been erected by Greenway;
liked horse-racing, of which he became a great patron
in the colony; and was the only man who ever called
Susannah Sue.

"Sue," he would say, and he told her this tale often,
forgetting he had told it before, "the duke said, when
there was first talk of my being sent here, that the
secretary of state demurred, objecting that he wanted
someone to govern not the stars but the earth of New
South Wales. But they appointed me all the same."

That afternoon he had sent for her to see the effects
of an electric fireball which in the morning, between
nine and ten, after an immense burst of thunder, had
struck the Parramatta house. He met her carriage in
the driveway, waving his arms and exclaiming, "Sue,
Sue, the observatory is safe, untouched. Praise be."
His wife and son were also safe. They had all been
taking breakfast in the only room in the house that
was unscathed. He showed her the wreckage with the
enthusiasm of scientific detachment. He had never
before seen the results of such a visitation. He scrambled around with his foreman and Susannah tracing
the path of the fireball. "You observe," he said, pointing at the solid wall of his office, "that it made its exit
there, making a hole rather larger than a musket ball."

The celestial and terrestrial globes on either side of his fireplace were unharmed, but the papers on his desk were singed. He showed her the skylight in the roof through which the ball had entered; the ruined ceiling of his and his wife's bedroom through which it had passed; and the lobby where the doors had been wrenched from their hinges and hurled across the flagstones, and the fanlights over the doors shattered into a thousand glass fragments. There had been no fire, though the smell of sulphur hung everywhere. But his observatory was safe, and Brisbane rejoiced. His wife and child were safe, and he rejoiced. He was already measuring the exact calibre of the cavity through which the electric fireball made its exit. He showed no apprehension of the danger in which he had stood. He was, after all, a man who had served in the carnage of India, Canada, and the Peninsular Wars.

Into this sulphurous mess, with the carpenters and glaziers already scurrying around measuring up for repairs, with Brisbane absorbed in his own observations, and Susannah awed by the nearness of the escape, came Father Massey. His visit was unannounced. He came to ask access to the penal settlement, where he knew thirty-one convicted men were awaiting execution. On the face of it, he could not have chosen a less likely moment to get what he wanted. But God was with him. The signed papers on the desk were the death-warrants of those thirty-one men. At first Brisbane listened to Massey as the priest followed him around. Then he sat at his desk, motioned Susannah to the sofa, and heard Massey out. He picked up the singed papers and glanced through them. Five were for murder. He signed these. The rest were for theft or forgery. He rang for his secretary and directed him to draft pardons for those twenty-six men, and a *laissez-passer* for the priest to see whatever he wished at the settlement.

The priest fell on his knees and gave thanks. The governor affected not to notice this, and the secretary got the man to his feet.

"I wish to go too," said Susannah.

"No," said Brisbane.

"I very much wish to go."

"Sue, Sue, Sue, it is just no place for a woman."

"Since I was a girl, I have repeatedly been told this entire colony is no place for a woman."

"But what for?"

"I once saw an example of Captain Tyrone's work and have never forgotten it." She told Brisbane about the man flogged to the bone.

"But, Sue, I have never even seen the place myself."

She did not reply to this, but let the obvious retort go unspoken.

"Very well." He directed another pass to be made out, and later, after Susannah left, gave orders to his secretary to make sure that if she insisted on going—and he heartily hoped she would not—she was to be accompanied by an ensign and six troopers, whether she liked it or not. Then, before he retired to bed, the governor, who could not bear to see a man kneel, because one's inner emotions were not something to be shown outwardly, confided this to his journal: "Sunday. Had inexpressible satisfaction in sparing the lives of twenty-six fellow creatures condemned to death. If I may have been the instrument of saving one soul from death, may I have that soul for my reward."

Susannah did insist on going. Two weeks later she and the priest set out. Redmond was as usual up-country, and she merely sent word to inform him that she would be going to Newcastle for a few days. It was a desolate place, with huts only for the guards. The three hundred convicts had only rotted canvas for protection from the heat of the day and the cold of the night. They had not a blanket between them. They fed at dawn and at dusk, from troughs, and worked through the day without break and with only muddy water from a foul well to sustain them. They worked chained together in gangs of six.

"Assemble the felonry," ordered Tyrone. When they were paraded by his guards, who were themselves mostly convicts utterly dependent on Tyrone's good will, and the more savage therefore to their fellows who were still in chains, he told them that a Romish priest and a lady would be coming to amuse themselves inspecting the sweepings of the colony, and (very quietly) that if one man so much as uttered a whisper that he was discontented with his lot, which would of course be a calumnious lie, he (Tyrone) would have to ensure that such a lie was properly punished.

This was received by the convicts with a broken smile, because these were men with whom life had gone so wrong that even the common words of speech, and the word *life* itself, had taken on new and perverse meanings. Life signified to them the various cheats and deceptions practised to sustain existence: life to them had been theft, beatings, waylayings, and the seizure by the stronger of the weaker man's share, even of water.

"Christ," said one, "a Judy and a Milestone come to taste the Steel."

"Maybe they're right Go-alongers," said a second. "Work 'em up to the arm-pits. Gammon the coves."

A Judy was any woman, and a cove any man. A Milestone was any fool, and therefore any clergyman, country bumpkin, or other gullible creature. The Steel was prison, from the Bastille. A Go-alonger was anyone simple-hearted enough to swallow a line, any hard-luck story. Such a Go-alonger could be worked up to the arm-pits, that is to say taken for all he was worth before he woke up to the fact that he was being taken for a ride. To gammon was to deceive. Most of the inmates had manifestly failed to gammon the twelve; that is, they had failed to deceive a jury into finding them innocent. To croak was to die. To be done was to be convicted. Bunce was money, and a bit was a small coin. To be cleaned out was to lose everything. With these people it was a language of despair. Almost all had been chanted, that is to say had rewards offered for their arrest. Almost all had been bridged, betrayed. Almost all had been unpalled, that is deprived of pals or friends, by the gallows. Most terrible of all, a bad man was called a good man and a good man bad. It was as if they had to adapt their words to the complete subversion of their hearts, and could not bear to speak anything outright.

Tyrone received his visitors with courtesy. He let the priest stand, but for Susannah found a chair, an awning, and some tea. He was surprised to see the escort. For the day he had released from chains those men who would not instantly murder him if they had the chance. But their debility spoke for itself, and so did the weals and sores where the fetters had only that morning been removed from their ankles. Not a man among them dared lift his eyes to the visitors.

"The condemned men are in there," said Tyrone, indicating a windowless shack with barred doors. "Perhaps," he said to the priest, taking the pardons from his pocket as he spoke, "you would care to reveal to them their fates before you console them?"

"You have had those reprieves for a week," said Susannah, "and you have not told those men who is to live and who is to die?"

Tyrone shrugged. "They will know soon enough." The priest said, "And those who are to die?"

"Will be taken to Sydney and there hanged," said Tyrone.

"And those who are reprieved?"

"Will remain here as my guests."

Susannah got up and began to walk towards the prison shack, but Tyrone touched her arm. "It is dark inside," he said, "and in spite of all care, the felonry stink." So thirty-one pale wretches were led chained into the light. The sun blinded them. They could not easily see to walk, and as one man stumbled he brought down two others, who cried with pain as the chains cut into their shrivelled flesh. The ensign escorting Susannah glanced at her. She showed nothing.

"Gentlemen," said Tyrone, addressing the bones and rags assembled before him, "here is a priest who will comfort your immortal souls, after first telling you what is to become of your mortal bodies."

The priest loathed Tyrone. He took the paper from the man's hands. On it were written the names of all thirty-one men, in alphabetical order. The priest looked rapidly over it, crossed himself, and said: "I see most of you are Irish, and of my faith. Some of you are not. Your own priest is not here. I will read this list, with joy for some and sorrow for others. I will first say 'Our Father,' in which all may join, because I shall say it in no spirit of faction."

He said the Lord's Prayer, putting into English, in his own words, the Latin of the Roman missal.

Most of the men mumbled some of the words. Tyrone briskly joined in, only his words were those of the English prayer book. Susannah thought he made the words a mockery.

Then the priest unrolled the list and began to read:

"John Andrew. Your sentence is commuted to five years in this settlement."

The man, who had been weeping, continued to weep.

"You are reprieved," said the priest.

The man still wept.

"Patrick Barford. You are reprieved and your sentence likewise commuted." The man bowed his head.

"John Connell." The man looked the priest square in the face.

"John Connell, you are to suffer the full punishment of the law, and may God have mercy on your soul."

Connell laughed. He fell on his knees, embraced the fettered ankles of the man next to him, and laughed, and gave thanks.

The priest thought him distraught, but then saw that he was elated, and rebuked him for the blasphemy of thanking God for his death.

"No, Father," said Connell, "I know I shall not be in Heaven, but I shall no longer be here."

And throughout the calling of the thirty-one names, this was the pattern. Those condemned to be hanged rejoiced to be free of their earthly oppression, and those reprieved wept. The priest was a brave man, but needed all his courage to carry through the grotesque litany of welcomed death and lamented reprieve. The ensign, who had seen enough service to be familiar with the pain and torment of mortally wounded men, swore to himself and thought he had never witnessed anything so horrible. Susannah stood motionless and a tear ran down each cheek. As the naming ended, and after the priest said a blessing, at which the soldiers of the escort spontaneously knelt, Tyrone came over to Susannah and bowed. The man was of course quite mad. She saw through her tears that he was smiling. He was carrying a rattan swagger-stick with which he flicked at one of the condemned men who was half-lying on the ground at her feet. Susannah did not know what she then did. She held out both gloved hands, palm upwards. Tyrone, still smiling, placed his rattan in her hands, where she let it lie, and then with a rapid upward sweep slashed him across the forehead.

Tyrone fell dazed. The ensign half-drew his sword and kept his eye on the assembled prisoners, but not a word came from them and not a movement. The privates of the escort rose slowly to their feet, lest any sudden movement should precipitate the riot they all expected, but no convict moved. The ensign glanced at Tyrone, left him where he had fallen, and, taking Susannah's arm, led her briskly away. As he held open the carriage door for her, she found she was still grasping the rattan. She gave it to the priest.

Though it was only seventy miles by sea from Sydney to Newcastle, the chances of wind and weather and the difficulties of the short journey inland made it six days there and back, and by the time Susannah returned it was to find Jane overtaken by disaster.

Jane's husband, George, had a friend, Thomas Daley, also an emancipist, who had borrowed money, obtained a small grant of land, and started a market garden and orchard on the north shore. He grew peaches, oranges, pomegranates, and apples. He had no lemon trees, but his neighbour, a settler arrived from England three years before, had many. One day Daley stole a single lemon tree, which was conspicuous because in his orchard it was alone. The settler's bailiff saw the lemon tree, recognized it by a grafting mark as his master's, and went to fetch a constable. Daley saw the bailiff inspecting the tree, and, while he was gone, uprooted the tree, which was only three feet tall, and smoothed back the soil into the spot where it had been planted. Then he threw the tree into the harbour, so that when the bailiff reappeared with the policeman there was no lemon tree. It then became Daley's word against the bailiff's, and there the matter would have ended. Except for one thing. The constable was going through the formality of questioning Daley when by an evil chance Bryant appeared, having taken the ferry across the narrow channel from the cove to north Sydney. Thinking to help his friend, he told the constable that on each of the three previous days he had visited Daley and had on no occasion seen a lemon tree. Therefore a lemon tree could not have been there. This was a foolish lie, kindly meant, but disastrous. It took the constable an hour to discover that no ferryman remembered carrying Bryant on any of the previous three days. It took him another hour to visit the domain, where Bryant's fellow gardeners, thinking in turn to help him, insisted innocently that Bryant had been at work in the domain at all times in the preceding days. There was now enough suspicion to create at least a case to answer. Daley was summoned before the magistrates. Bryant was unaware what his own friends and the ferrymen had said, and took his oath that he had visited Daley on three separate days and seen no lemon tree. Daley was acquitted of the charge of theft for lack of evidence. Bryant, after the unwilling evidence of the ferrymen and his fellow gardeners, was convicted of perjury. The magistrates, wishing to be lenient and not caring to flog a man of fifty-two, but unable to overlook a perjury, sentenced Bryant to one month in a penal settlement. Short of letting him go it was the lightest sentence they could have imposed. They did not stipulate which settlement he was to be sent to. A clerk, filling in the committal form, wrote in "Newcastle." It was all very summary, and by the time Susannah returned Bryant was on his way northward and Jane was beside herself with fear. Susannah found herself implored for help at a time when she was least able to offer any assistance at all.

She had already received a brief note from the governor asking if she would like to explain herself. She went to see him, part contrite and part defiant, contrite that she had abused his trust and embarrassed him, ashamed that she should so have lost command of herself, but not at all regretting the results of that lack of control. Tyrone deserved to be struck as contemptuously as she had struck him. The governor kept her waiting for twenty minutes, and when she was summoned to his room she passed in a corridor the ensign who had accompanied her to Newcastle. He was just leaving after a long interview. "I am sorry for this, ma'am," he said. "I had no alternative, and I could not stop my men talking. It is all over Sydney."

"You were kind," she said, "and I did not make things easy for you."

He bowed. He was a boy of nineteen.

"Well," said Brisbane, not sitting or asking her to sit.

"Nothing excuses what I did," she said.

"No, it does not. And here," he said, tossing a folded paper on to the desk, "is a demand from Captain Tyrone for an apology, which I imagine you will not make."

"Never. Though I do to you."

"And what was that damned young officer doing, the one I sent with you, that he should let this happen?"

"I think you have just seen him, and if he would not tell you himself, then I will: he could not have behaved more properly, and he could not conceivably have foreseen what I did. I did not know myself until the cane was in my hands. I did not know what I did until it was done."

"That does not help."

"The man is mad, sir."

Brisbane nodded. "That was the opinion of that young man, too. He spoke up for you with some courage."

"I would not wish this to hurt him."

"It shan't. But I take all this very badly from you, Sue."

"The man is mad."

"That is now my concern. I will tell you this. I have a letter from my judge-advocate, which concerns some box. I have that young officer's report. I have a letter from that priest. Tyrone has no commission to run a Hell-on-earth. I will bring the man here and he shall answer to me, but this is no concern of yours and you will not meddle further."

She did not reply.

"Look, damn your eloquent silence, Sue. It is nothing to do with you, and you will leave it alone."

"How long will it take to bring Tyrone to Sydney?"

Brisbane showed a flash of anger and struck the desk with his fist.

Susannah said, "Sir Thomas . . ." He looked round. She never called him that. And her voice had changed.

She said, "I know I have disgraced myself. I am not proud to have made such use of the kindness you have always showed me. But now there is something I must ask you, if you will hear me."

There were times when Susannah's heart was in her voice.

Brisbane was angry, but when she spoke as she did then he could in no way refuse to hear her.

"Tell me."

She began, "There is a man . . ." and she told him briefly the long story of George Bryant.

"And he is gone to Newcastle?" said the governor.

"He will be there now."

"Sue, I will do what I can for him. I am sorry it is perjury. A month is very light, you know. But I am sorry it is Newcastle. I will recall Tyrone as soon as I can replace him, which will be a week. In the meantime I will send orders, today, that no unusual punishment shall be inflicted on Bryant. He shall not be flogged. You can reassure your maid."

"She is my friend too."

"Very well, Sue. I will do what I said. But I would do the same for any man, because it ought to be done; you understand that?"

"I know you would. Thank you." She left him.

By then George Bryant was at Newcastle, and Tyrone was overseeing his labours. The committal papers that came with all prisoners, young and old, said that they were to be put to hard labour, and Tyrone carried out his orders. The work for a man of Bryant's age was terrible. Twelve hours a day, under a sun that seemed to remain for most of the day vertical, these three hundred men felled timber and dragged the logs to the river to float them downstream. Bryant worked with five others. The six were joined at the ankles with light chains. Bryant had worked in the fields, or in the gardens of the domain, all his life. He was as strong as the others, and after a few days would in spite of his age have toughened and become stronger than them, because he had been for so long better nourished. They were half-starved. But Bryant was one of two men in that gang of six who were desperate. The first was David Hirst, who was desperate because he was ill. He said he had a cold, but a low fever had been with him for months, his soft cough was that of tuberculosis, and he was very weak. He was not desperate from the knowledge that he would very likely die within the year, because he did not have that knowledge. He was desperate because he could not keep up with the others, and went in fear that this would be seen and he would be punished for his idleness by being thrown into the box where a man could neither sit nor stand. His mates knew he was weak, and they concealed this by taking an added burden on their own backs. Among three hundred men, Hirst had so far escaped notice but knew he would be found out one day soon. The other desperate

man was Bryant. His torment was that of the mind.
He did not think himself unfairly punished. He did not
regret his spontaneous and useless lies to help a
friend, but his false oath sworn upon the Bible bit
deeply into him. He was harsher on his own perjury
than the bench of magistrates had been. They saw
perjury every day. But Bryant had never before sworn
a false oath. And the separation from Jane was nearly
unbearable. Theirs was the steadiest and closest of
marriages, having none of the fire and lustre that had
been life to Susannah and Baudin and would have
sustained their marriage, but possessing a firmness of
comfort, faith, and love. They had never been separated until a few days before when—all between
morning and evening—Bryant was seized, sentenced,
hustled to the quay, and thrown on the transport to
Newcastle. He would have left with no possessions
at all except that one of the ferrymen went to the domain cottage and gathered up two shirts, a Bible, and
some bread and fruit, and tied them all in the blue
cloak, loosely knotting the ends. He used the cloak
because he could see no bag in the cottage. Besides,
the nights at Newcastle would be cold, and the cloak
was warm. The ferryman hesitated to take these things
because Jane was not at home. She was scouring the
town looking for her husband in the wrong places and
not finding him. The ferryman paid a sailor a dump
dollar to give the bundle to Bryant, which he did. When
he arrived with his bundle at Newcastle, Bryant had
more than any other man there. The guards took the
apples but tossed him back the stale bread, the Bible,
the shirts, and the cloak. Tyrone ruled by the book.
He made a felon's life a misery, but a felon's property was sacrosanct and God help any guard who stole
it. The guards had been thieves themselves. There is
no honour among thieves, particularly not among
thieves who have risen to be guards, but they feared

Tyrone, and, besides, had no use for a tatty cloak. One of them knew its story, and amused himself by giving Bryant the nickname of Bishop.

"Here y'are, Bishop. Take your cloak of office, Bishop." For three days Bryant worked to exhaustion in his chain gang, from dawn to dusk. When night came the men, still in their chains, fell into exhausted sleep, except Hirst, who coughed and could not sleep.

Tyrone had not become more savage after Susannah's assault on him. He knew she had harmed herself more than him. To strike an officer in front of convicts was an outrageous affront, but he took comfort from the sure knowledge that condign punishment would be visited upon her. He had written the governor a reasonable letter—and its tone *was* one of sweet reason—requesting an apology. When he received an order to present himself before the governor, he assumed that it was to receive this apology. He had the assurance of madness. He never doubted.

So on the morning he received the governor's letter, which was Bryant's fourth day in the settlement, Tyrone was in good humour. He harboured no unusual vindictiveness in his mind when he left his hut to deal with a gang that had downed tools and refused to continue.

"See to it yourself," he first told the corporal who came to him with the news.

"I have seen to it all I know, sir." The corporal meant that he had kicked three of the men as they lay, and promised one a flogging, but the fellow had not seemed to care and had answered nothing at all. "They are taking their ease on the ground, and will not work."

Hirst had collapsed, and the others, also very weary, refused to go on. Bryant was one of them. The six men sprawled on the sandy scrub, waiting for Tyrone. They had no doubt they would work again. They had

no doubt they would be punished. They were of two
minds towards Hirst. They would continue to support
him until he was beyond support, but they knew
that could not be much longer now, and they would be
relieved when he died.

Tyrone appeared and the guards kicked the men to
their feet. Hirst found the strength to stand, and to
Tyrone's glance looked no worse than the others. Tyrone also saw Bryant. "And the Bishop?" he said.
"Are you leading your colleagues out of the paths of
righteousness?" He did not know this was Susannah's
man. He had no especial animus against him.

Hirst found his tongue, "No, sir. The Bishop does
not lead. There are no leaders."

Tyrone was even disposed to be generous. "I lead,"
he said. "Get back to work and there's an end to it."

The men stood with lowered eyes. Another moment and they would have turned listlessly back to
the timber they were dragging, and carried on. But
from Hirst there came an unearthly croak.

"Never no more. We will destroy ourselves first."

"And then," said Tyrone, all affable and tapping
the sides of his breeches with his rattan, "you will be
in Hell."

"What is Hell?"

The gang was twenty feet from a canal dug to float
the smaller pieces of timber to the river. Tyrone
tapped the sides of his breeches again. "Have these
men double-chained," he said to the corporal. It was
done.

"March them to the canal."

It was done. They stood on the edge.

"To the very brink," said Tyrone.

They were edged up to the brink. The bank was
sheer.

"Gentlemen felons," said Tyrone, "how could I
wish to stand between you and your desires? If you

are disposed to destroy yourselves, here is the opportunity. The canal is deep, and the chains heavy. You are on the brink. You would undoubtedly sink immediately."

He walked behind them, flicking his rattan. It was a show. The corporal, seeing this, whispered to a guard who fetched Bryant's blue cloak.

"What is this?" said Tyrone. He was told.

Tyrone smiled. "Well then, life is barren enough without its trappings. Let us be cautious therefore how we strip these trappings away. Give the Bishop his cloak. Put it on."

"Put it on." Bryant heard the words of the judge of so many years before, and felt the cloak placed round his shoulders.

"Well?" said Tyrone.

Hirst jumped. The corporal and two guards leapt to prevent him, but they were too late. The six men were on the brink, and Hirst dragged them in. All the other men but Bryant were weary of life, but only Hirst had wanted death. They struggled. Bryant was the last in the line of chained men. He clung to a root in the side of the bank. The two guards frantically supported his shoulders. The corporal fumbled in panic for the iron key that would unlock the fetters, but it was useless because the chains were not at the wrists but at the ankles. When the guards could no longer hold him, and when he could no longer cling to the root, he drowned in terror.

"They are not dead," said Tyrone when the bodies were dredged up fifteen minutes later. He was active in their resuscitation. He laid the men in the scorching sun, for the heat to revive them. He caused the bearded ends of feathers to be introduced into the aesophagus. He wrapped the men in canvas, and ordered that their heads should be kept in constant motion by being tilted side to side at the hands of fellow convicts. "Put the solid parts of each man in motion," he cried. The dead men's arms were rotated vigorously. He proceeded through each certain remedy. He ordered rum to be forced into the men's mouths, and while the guards ran for this he made do with warm urine, which he had read to be efficacious. He ordered his own snuff to be blown through quills into their nostrils, and tobacco smoke to be blown through long reeds into their stomachs and, as he imagined, into the intestines. Finally, to drain the fluids from the men and restore their vital functions, he hung them upside down by the ankles. "They are not dead," he said. But the six men had drowned in chains. As they hung downwards in Tyrone's last certain remedy their ankles were still chained. In the panic no one had thought to remove the fetters.

Tyrone went to his hut. "They are not dead," he said. "Tell me when they stir." Half an hour later, on his own initiative, the corporal had the six men taken down, and covered the bodies with the canvas which had unaccountably failed to revive them.

After the men sank, the blue cloak still floated over the spot where Bryant was dragged down. To Tyrone, property was sacred. He had the sodden cloak retrieved, and that too was laid out in the sun to dry. He intended to restore it to Bryant when he revived. He did later ensure that it was returned to the widow.

17

───~∞∞~───

Manly Cove

IN SYDNEY, Susannah's striking of Tyrone with his own
rattan had for several days been a fable, but the death
of the six men in chains was still unknown. One morning, when it was ninety in the shade, but the heat was
tempered by a southerly breeze, Susannah, her son
John, and Jane's daughter, Mary, took a walk down to
Bennelong Point to view the harbour and talk to the
governor's waterman. Now that Governor Brisbane
spent so much of his time at Parramatta, the man had
little to do in Sydney and was ready to earn a few dollars on the side. Susannah taught John as she had once
taught Robert, preferring her own judgement to that of
the various pedagogues who, having failed in London, came to Sydney and put advertisements in the
newspapers offering to teach Latin, Greek, French,
Mathematics, Physiognomy, Trigonometry, the Ele-
ments of Calculus, and, in short, to give a thorough
grounding in all the knowledge thought necessary to
prepare a young gentleman for the Professions, Commerce, etc., all to be taught by new and improved
methods. Susannah was a thorough and determined
instructress, but that day she had promised John that

if the weather was favourable she would see if the
waterman could take them to Manly, a fine beach
reached by crossing the open waters of the harbour,
sailing through the heads, and then bearing north. It
was six miles from the town, too far to row, and the
trip therefore depended on the wind and on the waterman's judgment of how it would hold throughout the
day.

The waterman came out of his hut to greet them.
"Good morning, ma'am. Good morning, sir. Good
morning, Mary."

"So, Mr. Smith, do you think we have a fine day for
it?"

Susannah knew the winds and currents of the bay
almost as well as Smith, but he sailed those waters
every day.

He surveyed the cove, and the harbour beyond, and
the sky—as he had already done twenty times that
morning—and said they could have a worse day for it
if there were no change, and he foresaw no change.

"And you, ma'am, were of the same opinion?" he
said, looking at the picnic hamper she carried. "Or
you'd not have brought that."

They set off in the governor's fifteen-foot cutter, and
just over an hour's easy sailing in light airs brought
them to Manly. It is a beach of magnificence. The bay
encloses a semicircular sweep of sand. Apart from one
stone cottage, there was no building in sight. Sydney
could have been a thousand miles away. As they went
ashore, Smith scanned the beach for signs of tracks but
there were none. He scanned the brush for signs of
dead fires, but saw none. He helped Susannah and
the boy ashore.

"We shall be alone, ma'am," said Smith, "except
that if I know Wilkinson, he'll be here by this afternoon."

"Who is Wilkinson?" said John.

"You will see," said Susannah. Then she turned to Smith and told him to give Wilkinson her compliments, and to say that if he wished to come he would be welcome but that any demonstration he wished to give she would rather he kept within his pen.

"And my voice goes with that too," said Smith, and off he went to tell the man. He returned to say that nothing would keep Wilkinson away, but that he promised to keep within the pen.

"What pen?" asked Mary.

"You'll see, young miss."

"And Smith," said the boy, "when we landed, why did you look around? Are there savages?"

"Here?" said Smith. "Not anymore, sir. Years ago, yes. But all you see now, and I've seen two or three in, oh, the last five year now, is a poor outcast. Once in a while."

"Why are they cast out?"

"There was a man called Bennelong, who died about the time you were born. He was a famous black, and they gave his name to that far western point of Sydney Cove that you know. He was a famous black that went to Europe and bowed to the king."

John looked to his mother for confirmation.

"I saw him," said Susannah. "I knew him."

"But when he came back, sir," said Smith, "why, he was cast out. He drank liquor, and put his women in petticoats, and forgot how to hunt, and when they cast him out he died."

"Did you not give him food, Mother?"

"Most of the time he hid," said Susannah. "And no one knew where to find him. It was pitiful."

"It *was* pitiful," said Smith. "I have seen men leave food for him that he would not eat."

"Why would he not eat?"

"He would not eat what he did not catch himself,

and in the end he could catch nothing, and so he ate nothing. Then the soldiers gave him rum to see him drunk. They meant well. I gave him rum. I did not mean badly. But he died."

"Will all the blacks die?" John asked.

"I don't know about die. But it is true they have mostly gone, no man knows where."

"I shall help them," said Mary.

Smith looked at the girl. "No, Mary. Best helped by being left alone. They were not always pitiful creatures. Take this beach. Why was this beach so named?"

"After the man who found it?" John suggested.

"No. No more than Lord Sydney came to find Sydney for himself. I do believe that noble lord's name was given as a compliment to the city, but, since he is long dead and longer forgotten, the city instead will be an everlasting compliment to the family. Which is an irong, Master John, since that lord's son has never yet been heard of, or nothing that he ever did anyway; and that lord's father was member of Parliament for as rotten a borough as ever existed, a borough with two members and four men to elect them. Winchelsea it was, and I know Winchelsea because my father came from there."

"Was he a waterman too, like you?"

"He was not. There was no being a waterman at Winchelsea, because by the time my father lived that fine port was so silted up it had no more sea in it. As I remember, sir, it was a mile's walk from Winchelsea to anywhere near the sea. So, as I say, to call so fine a port as Sydney after them, does the family too great honour."

"But what about Manly?"

"I had forgotten that was the story I started with. Why, it was the first governor that ever came here, who saw some blacks on the shore, and they did not run, as they often ran, or crouch and gibber and throw spears and then run; but they all approached him like men, and spoke to him, it was said, as if they were the owners of a great estate welcoming a chance visitor and offering to show him the grounds. So he gave the leader a hatchet, at which he bowed and offered the governor in return a throwing stick—which he showed him the use of as if it was something beyond the wit of a white man, but showed him very civilly, and when the governor failed to throw it at first, retrieved it civilly and showed him again. And they were gentle to their womenfolk, which the blacks are often not, and so the governor said, 'Seeing you are so manly, I shall call this Manly Cove.' "

"But perhaps the blacks already had a name for it before that?"

"If they did, they were too polite to disappoint the governor out of his intended generosity, and took the name as a gift."

Susannah opened the lunch hamper.

"Join us, Mr. Smith," she said, but he made excuses not to, saying he needed to remain near the cutter. He accepted a leg of chicken and ate that, propped up against the side of the boat, with the bread and cheese he had brought with him in a handkerchief.

After midday, a figure left the cottage a quarter of a mile away, crossed the dunes, and walked along the shore towards them. As he came nearer they could see he wore trousers of thick dun-coloured canvas, a shirt of the same thickness buttoned down to his wrists, gloves, and, what showed the man not to be the beachcomber he might have been taken for, a stout pair of much-patched leather boots reaching to his knees. His face was burned mahogany by the sun. He nodded to Smith and then approached Susannah, making as if to remove his hat.

"Wilkinson," she said, when he was still ten feet off, "stand where you are a moment."

He stood grinning. This was a request he was used to receiving.

"If your hat contains what I think it does, then do me and Mary the courtesy of *not* removing it."

"I did promise there should be nothing but in the pen, ma'am, and so it shall be. But I see you remember the hat. Lord, ma'am, there nothing there but so familiar a creature as would be lost if I did not bring her."

"What creature?" asked John, and would have run to the man, except that he slowly put up a hand to halt him.

"Watch then, young man. Watch, young miss."

The hat stirred on the man's head, as if the headband were tightening of its own accord, and from the broad brim a tail emerged to curl over his brow like a love-lock. The child did not see what it was. There were four spectators, all with their eyes on the man's brow and his hat. Susannah sat very still. The boy innocently gazed with open curiosity. Smith sat apparently as he had been, but his right hand was on his belt, at his knife handle.

Then John saw. "Snake," he whispered. A boy not an Australian would have shouted in fear. John was afraid, but he remembered what he had been told, again and again—that if ever a man saw a snake he must kill it, but if the snake was within striking distance of another man, then he must whisper a warning, *never* shout. Mary held her breath.

"Oh, snake is it?" said Wilkinson, and he gave the tail a good pinch, at which it retired to join the rest of the animal in the brim.

"Well done, boy," said Wilkinson, "and well done those who taught you. It's not every boy that remembers not to shout."

"He might have hurt you?" said the boy.

"Might, but he wouldn't. He's no king-brown, boy,

because I'm no hero. A king-brown I would not allow, leastwise not on my head."

"And as for you, Smith," said the man, "how many's the time you've seen this, and never a time yet when your hand did not go to your knife."

"And always will," said Smith.

"Ah. That's fair. Each man to his trade. I dare say I'd be a poor man to be with in a squall."

They followed Wilkinson across the beach to a spot near his house where a pen stood, ten feet square, made of wattle. In each corner rested a metal rod three feet long, with a hooked end. In the center were a sack and a smaller bag. Wilkinson smoothed back the gauntlets of his gloves so that they protected his wrists, and then removed his hat and twirled it round. As it twirled, a yellow snake untwirled from its brim, and, finding itself on the ground, came straight for the man. He deflected it with a flick of his leather boot, caught it by the tail, and fed it into the mouth of the small bag, all in a second. Then taking up one of the metal rods with one hand, he picked up the sack with the other, loosened the knot at its mouth with a motion of his thumb, and tipped onto the earth around him three snakes, two only a foot each in length and the third six feet long. The large snake slid lazily to a corner and he did not watch it at all. The two smaller ones came at him rapidly from two directions at once, each biting a boot. John heard the impact of each snake against the leather, and saw what he had not known before, that a snake bites with open jaws, and does not softly penetrate, as he had imagined, with its forked tongue. As the snakes came at him again, Wilkinson leaned down and picked each out of the air with his leather gauntlets as they struck and tossed them one after the other into the neck of the sack which he held open with the rod. This was barely accomplished when the large snake launched itself from its corner at

Wilkinson. This time John did shout, and so did Mary, but the man knew it was coming and, as it struck at him, not at his boot but higher than that, he deflected its head away with the hooked rod, catching it at the throat and flicking it by its own momentum to the corner of the pen farthest from which it had come. It attacked again. Once again Wilkinson deflected its drive in the same way, but this time flicked it high in the air, and, as it passed him, he caught its tail and slipped it, again by its own momentum, into the mouth of the sack, which with a quick twist he knotted.

Susannah and the waterman had seen all this before. John and Mary had not. They now knew snakes did not move up and down like sea-serpents or like woodcut illustrations from the story of Adam and Eve. Snakes propel themselves with a sideways undulation. They bite with open jaws. And they are very fast. John would have said as fast as a galloping horse, but that was an illusion because the pen was small; but as fast as a cantering horse.

Wilkinson earned his living from those snakes, giving sideshows on holidays, existing on the pennies thrown into the ring. For the past few years a renaissance of Christianity had hurt his business. Holidays were almost all Sundays or saints' days, at any rate holy days, and the clergy of Sydney had forbidden him to perform in town on the days when he was most likely to draw crowds. Besides, one clergyman had been bitten, and though he had recovered, and the snake had died, that had been enough to make the clergyman's colleagues thunder out from their pulpits that the serpent was the symbol of the anti-Christ, and so on. Now Wilkinson lived as best he could by giving sideshows at villages outside the city, and by entertaining the few visitors to Manly.

"Are they all poisonous snakes?" asked John.

"All."

"And you left the poison in them all?" said Mary.

"Ah," said Wilkinson. "There you have me." They had already given him a dollar, and he felt it unfair to withhold a secret of the trade from them, though one secret he did not tell was that he had to train the snakes to attack. So he said: "There are four snakes which all run at me. Never at the same time, as you saw. But there is no saying they might not. Now, they do say, and I have never seen it shown otherwise, that to confine several in a sack together, as I do before I release them, lessens their appetite for biting. But all the same, four is too many, and I have drawn the venom of three."

"Which one is still poisonous?" asked John.

"The big one. The king-brown. He is a certain killer."

"But why," said Mary, "have you not drawn his venom?"

"Because my father once tried, and did not live to tell me why he failed."

It was only two o'clock, but Smith was watching the sky and the way the sand blew. They must be getting back. It was a placid passage. Even the water between the heads was calm. But Smith kept the lugsail half-furled, and watched the tops of the trees on the north head for any sign of movement, though there was none. They were well into the shelter of the harbour, within half a mile of the Sydney Cove, and within sight of any watcher in Farm Cove or on Bennelong Point, when they were struck by what Smith had known might strike—a sudden squall known as a southerly buster. It was as well that the canvas of the cutter was of Australian flax, and therefore frail, and that the sail, half-furled though it was, split from end to end with the force of the gust, otherwise the cutter might have been dismasted and capsized. As it was, the boat shipped

water before Smith recovered it, and then, again in the
most deceptive of calms, rowed it to the domain jetty.
Redmond, from the grounds of Susannah's house, saw
the useless canvas flapping as the cutter made fast,
and the sodden skirts of his wife as she stepped onto
the jetty. The boy and girl were drenched too. He
waited for them.

As Susannah and the children left the jetty they
passed a gang of fifteen convicts building a wall under
the easy superintendence of a sergeant and three private soldiers.

"That's her," said one.

"Who?"

"That's the one that gave Tyrone what for."

The word ran along the line of men, and they waved
their trowels and cheered the woman. It was not a
ragged three cheers, not a matter of hip, hip, hip,
hooray, but a roar of cheering gratitude. Men in faded-
yellow prison uniforms jumped up, waved their arms,
and cheered. And what could Susannah do? The sergeant yelled at the men to keep a respectful silence,
but they did not hear him, or took no notice. The three
soldiers, who had been leaning on the wall smoking,
roused themselves and stood to a sort of attention, and
the sergeant, seeing that order was not to be preserved,
and moreover heartily sympathizing for the first time in
his life with the rabble he could not restrain from cheering, saluted Susannah. He would have saluted her anyway, but the convicts took his salute as approval of
their cheering and cheered the more loudly. Susannah
nodded to the sergeant and walked on towards the
house, where at the open door Redmond stood in silent
anger. Mary bobbed to him, and ran off to her mother's cottage. Redmond took no notice of her, but stared
at John's clothes.

"Go and get out of those things, and leave your
mother and me."

John glanced at Susannah, who motioned him to do as he was told.

"And now, madam," Redmond started, "I come home to find—"

"William," said Susannah, "I too am wet. I see you have something to say, but it will wait until I am dry." And she went to her room.

Throughout dinner he said nothing. John went to bed, and still Redmond said nothing. He went to his room across the hallway, and for half an hour she heard nothing. She read in her sitting-room. Then he called her. He had left the door of his room open. But he called out, "Come here."

"I am here," she replied, and continued to read.

He called again. This time it was almost a shout, but she waited. After ten minutes he appeared in the doorway of her room with a glass of brandy in his hand. He was not drunk. Redmond did not get drunk.

He said evenly from the doorway, "I came home this afternoon to find the house empty. When I went to look for you I was in time to see you and my son, and your maid's daughter, whom you seem to like to take as well, very nearly overturned into the harbour, by a squall a child could have foreseen, let alone Smith, who should have had more sense."

"You can thank Smith's sense that we are safe. He knows those waters better than any man."

"What were you doing?"

"I took them to Manly."

"And after I arrive, in time to see you and my son coming ashore from the adventure—"

"John is my son as well as yours."

"That is something you should remember. I arrive back, and what do I see? As you come ashore, you are cheered by a gang of convicts, and you acknowledge

those cheers graciously." Redmond's voice had little
animation, and therefore he could not be said to sneer,
but the word "graciously" was not intended to please.

"I acknowledged the sergeant's salute. I know him.
And whether I knew him or not, I should have done
the same."

"And John waved."

"Boys do wave."

"The matter is, Mrs. Redmond, as you very well
know, that during my absence you have made yourself,
and me, the talk of Sydney by interfering where you
had no business to interfere, in the administration of
this colony, and by striking an officer, so that convicts
cheer you."

"What I did, I think I would very likely do again. I
have accounted to the governor for what I did. He is
bringing the officer back from Newcastle. I suppose
there will be an inquiry. I will account to him but not,
William, to you."

"You discredit me, Mrs. Redmond, by what you do
in my absence."

Susannah was not at that moment going to tell him to
call her by her Christian name, but once again it struck
her as absurd that the man could not bring himself to
do this, but called her Mrs. Redmond as if to emphasize
that she was no more than an appendage to him.

"Anything I do," she said, "whether it pleases you or
not, is likely to be done in your absence, because you
are never here."

"I have work to do," he said. The work was increas-
ingly that of his sheep station.

Redmond was still standing in the doorway, as he
had been throughout this conversation.

"Please sit down," she said.

He remained where he was.

"Well," she said. "What is that black armband you
have been wearing today?"

"For Johnston."

"Major Johnston?"

"He died three days ago." Johnston the insurrectionist, having been cashiered, had been allowed to return to New South Wales on condition he took no part in the politics of the colony. He had given his word, and kept it. He returned and flourished on sheep. He had been one of Redmond's intimates. Susannah had not seen him for years. He had kept very much in the company of sheepmen. One of them was Macarthur, who had also been allowed back, though not until nine years after the mutiny he had encouraged. He was now the biggest of the graziers.

"I am sorry about Johnston," said Susannah.

"Hypocrisy," said Redmond. "You hated the man."

Johnston brought back to her mind so much that was vivid in her past—her father, Bligh, the mutiny, her defiance of the man across the ballroom, and Baudin.

"You hated the man," Redmond repeated.

"No. I think my father did, and I never knew why. I never knew him to hate anyone else. But I did not hate him, though I very much disliked him. And when I say I am sorry, I am sorry, at least for the death of a friend of yours."

"He was one of the great sheepmen," said Redmond.

"And, William, I suppose you are very nearly one of those great sheepmen now?"

"And if I am, then you will see why I cannot have my wife meddling in affairs which will upset the colony, or reflect on my credit. This must not happen again, and if it does, I shall go and I shall take John with me."

He had previously been so content to leave the child to her that she had never thought of this. No one had ever threatened Susannah since Major Johnston in the ballroom. She rose and met her husband's eyes with as much defiance as she had faced Johnston. But Redmond left her standing there, and went back to his room. He was the father of the child, and in an infinitely stronger position than any insurrectionary major. He was beyond her power.

18

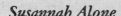

Susannah Alone

At ELEVEN the next morning the governor drove into the carriage drive of Susannah's house, descended alone, ordered his escort to dismount and wait, and was received by Redmond himself, who expressed delight at the unexpected visit.

"Good morning, Redmond. I'm afraid my business is with your wife. Could she be told?"

Would the governor take some refreshment first?

He shook his head and waited silently, which Redmond took for displeasure, and expressed the hope that Mrs. Redmond's recent conduct had not been such as . . .

"No, man. But let me see her."

This sounded more peremptory than the governor intended, but he hated what he had to do and was in no mood for niceties with Redmond.

Susannah appeared.

"Alone, Sue," said Brisbane, but then thought this discourteous and turned to her husband. "I'm sorry, Redmond, to ride rough-shod into your house like this, and then demand to take your wife off on her own. I beg your pardon, and I hope you'll understand."

Redmond withdrew. The governor and Susannah were left alone in her sitting-room. She saw this was no visit of ceremony. There was no ceremony in Brisbane's face.

He said, "What I have to tell you is the worst news, Sue."

"Bryant?"

"Where is his wife?"

"At her cottage, with her two children. You are telling me he is dead?"

"He is dead." He told her that Captain Tyrone had presented himself at Parramatta the previous evening with a fantastic story which placed great emphasis on the methods untiringly applied to revive the dead men.

"Sue, I would not have believed him, but he came with a corporal. It was impossible to see the two of them together without coming to the conclusion that the corporal practically had charge of Captain Tyrone. Certainly he was the more rational of the two. And his story was the same as far as the story mattered, which was how those poor men died."

"Which men? How many? How?"

Brisbane told her. She covered her face with her hands, and repeated, "Jane, Jane, Jane, Jane."

"Sue, I do not think she should be told exactly how."

"Oh yes she shall."

"That would help no one. I was thinking to keep a little pain from her."

"It will come out. It was seen by too many. Where is that corporal now, and where is Tyrone, and what of his trial?"

"The corporal is on his way back to Newcastle. Tyrone is under close arrest, and if I could shoot the man I would. But he is mad. You told me that, and now I have seen for myself. The corporal will say nothing. The two guards who saw it will say nothing. Tyrone will never see the outside of a madhouse again.

The six men are dead. Bryant is dead. My only concern now is with his widow, and I have come to you because you first came to me. I am proposing what in my judgement is right; or, perhaps, what is kinder to the only creature to whom any kindness in this wretched matter is now possible, and that's Bryant's widow."

"I never thought you meant otherwise," Susannah said at last.

"Then, will you take a moment for thought, and tell me if you think what I suggest is right? I do not know the woman. I do not know her needs."

"She had a husband. She has two young daughters, one aged ten, and one two years old. And what of the other five men? Had they five wives?"

Brisbane opened his hands helplessly.

"What of them?" Susannah demanded.

"Of the six men," said the governor, "the corporal tells me that even the names of four were uncertain, and that the fifth, who was dying, was unmarried. The sixth was Bryant."

"God have mercy upon us."

"Sue, if you will show me to Mrs. Bryant, I will myself tell her that her husband died. I shall lie, and may God forgive me for that, and tell her he fell into the canal. There shall be no chains."

"No. Go home. When was the widow of a man who died in a prison last told by the governor himself? That would not help. Your presence would show you were lying. But," she said, touching his shoulder, offering some consolation, "few men would offer to do it. It is good-hearted of you. But let me tell her. Then, God help me, it will be believed."

Brisbane thanked her. Then he explained the matter of the cloak, which Tyrone had returned to Parramatta dried, pressed, and neatly packed. He had brought it with him, and would place it in the front hall.

He left. Susannah prayed, and then went to tell Jane.
Jane told her elder daughter, Mary, that her father was
dead, and her younger daughter, Elizabeth, that her
father would not be coming back ever. She fetched the
blue cloak from the hallway where Brisbane left it.
Carrying it still in her arms, she walked slowly over the
domain lawns down to the water's edge. She gazed
across the cove towards the north shore, facing the
plantation from which the single lemon tree was stolen. Then she turned her eyes towards the open harbour. She stood for five minutes, hugging the folded
cloak to her breast. Then she walked rapidly into the
town and visited four friends. She had formed an intention of great heroism, which she carried through to its
uttermost.

Jane called on Smith, the waterman. She met Andrew
Lilley and David Allen, who worked as fishermen in
Rushcutter's Bay and sold the fish in the town. She
talked long into the night with William Moatham, who
had once been master's mate aboard a frigate. Jane
was a free woman. Governor King had signed her
pardon many years before. Her two daughters were
born free. Smith, the same waterman who had taken
Susannah and the children to Manly Cove, was a
ticket-of-leave man. He was the governor's man, and
his position, among that community of felons, was one
of great privilege. Lilley and Allen were convicts, but
worked for an easy master who left them very much
alone and even let them keep a tenth of the proceeds
of any fish they sold on his behalf. Moatham was the
only man whose situation was in any way hard. He was
a convict, who could not expect a ticket-of-leave for
another two years, and he was made to dig ditches. Of
all the group he had suffered the greatest fall in being
sent to New South Wales. He was born in the southern
Cornish fishing village of Mousehole, which its natives

pronounce Mowzell, had gone to sea at ten, by fourteen
knew the English Channel, on its French and English
shores, as well as any man could, and in 1800, when
there was a real fear that Napoléon might invade Britain, was taken into the Royal Navy straight away as
master's mate. The sailing master is not to be confused
with the captain of a ship of the Royal Navy. The
master has no command and no commission. He is
responsible to the captain or commander of the vessel
for its handling and navigation. He may advise the
captain how to manage the sailing of his vessel, but the
decision is the captain's. An exceptional master, or a
master in time of war, may reach commissioned rank,
and then the way up is open to him. Captain Cook
served many years as a master and did not receive his
lieutenant's commission until he was a few months
short of forty. Bligh, in his turn, once served as master
under Cook. But those men were exceptional. A
master is a sort of maritime sergeant-major, and likely
to remain so, but it is an honourable rank, as is that
of master's mate. A master's mate is likely to be promoted master after a few years. At the age of nineteen
Moatham, because of his intimate knowledge of the
coasts of Normandy and Brittany, was guiding sloops
and frigates through the inlets of northern and western
France by night, searching for craft which might mount
the invasion that never came. Master's mate, of all
ranks, is perilous, poised between up and down. Once
a man is master, he will not be broken thoughtlessly.
But while a man is master's mate, it needs only one
slip and he is back to ordinary seaman. A bad commander, an irascible commander, an uncharted rock,
and he is back in the fo'c'sle. In the running aground
of the frigate *Hecate* in 1801, Moatham saw two of
his friends swept overboard and perish, and he swore
at the incompetence of the lieutenant of the watch who
had disregarded his urgent advice. Next day he was

back in the fo'c'sle, and from the day of that injustice
the fall of a capable and brave man could almost have
been foreseen. He sank to transportation.

Moatham, Smith, Lilley, and Allen listened to Jane
Bryant. All had known her husband. She had the ready
sympathy and fellow-feeling of all. The only man to
hesitate was Smith, perhaps because he had the most
to lose, or perhaps because he was the most level-
headed of them all and saw the risks more clearly. But
he also saw that he was essential to the whole enterprise, and that without him it would fail before it
started. So he consented.

Next day, Moatham visited Nathaniel Charles, the
skipper of an American schooner out of New Bedford
who had put into Sydney with the usual speculative
cargo of cloth, canvas, spirits, and New England manufactured goods. Trading between British colonies and
the United States had barely been interrupted by the
War of 1812, and several governors of New South
Wales, such was their need, turned blind eyes to Navigation Acts which restricted trade with foreign, and
therefore American, vessels. If a cargo was needed, it
was bought. This gave the Americans the raffishness of
habitually successful freebooters. The Americans had
also never forgotten 1812. In that war their seamanship was superior. Free men made better sailors than
pressed men. Not that life on board an American
vessel was really any more free than on board a ship
of any other nation. An American captain, like any
other, was, at sea, second only to God, and that was
only because of a technical matter of seniority. But the
Americans were honestly infected with the idea of freedom. There is no better place in the world than a ship
to demonstrate with conclusiveness, and within an
hour, that no two men are created equal, but the power
of an idea survives all demonstration that it is nonsense. The Americans believed, and their belief made

them strong. American skippers personally got on very well with their Royal Navy counterparts in Sydney, but this did not lessen their contempt of a colony that was no more than a gaol. It did not lessen their contempt for what they saw as a hard slavery of the greater part of the people there. The French thought the same, but the Americans were more vigorous, and had a missionary zeal and a missionary good faith. Captain Charles listened to Moatham, agreed to what was proposed, and sold him a compass, a quadrant, and the necessary charts. He then waved away further money, and gave enough good Yankee canvas to replace twice over the split lug-sail of the governor's cutter in which the escape was to begin. Everything was agreed, and Captain Charles was a man who would keep his promise.

They gathered at Jane's cottage. Lilley and Allen, the two fishermen, brought two seines to fish with and a gaff to spear larger fish, and eight gallons of fresh water in leather bottles. Moatham brought the instruments he had purchased, two makeshift spears, and a handsaw. Smith had from nowhere found two ancient blunderbusses, and powder for them. Jane bought and begged fourteen pounds of salt pork in a barrel, a hundredweight of rice, and the same amount of flour. There was also some sugar, tea, and coffee. The waterman had two lanterns in the cutter, a barrel of tar, and a cask of rum. For warmth they had the clothes they wore, four blankets, and the blue cloak. It was nine in the evening, twenty minutes after a summer sunset, and they would leave at nightfall. A dozen souls who had helped them to collect supplies must have known what they intended, but no whisper of it got out. Jane wrestled hard with herself and then was unable to face Susannah. It hurt her to leave for ever without saying good-bye to a woman she loved. She asked the advice of the others. Smith was for telling, but the others would on no account trust Susannah. So it was settled.

It was an uneasy evening for Susannah. That morning she had been to see how Jane was. Jane had thanked her again and again, and at their parting was in tears. Susannah thought the tears those of grief for a dead husband, and that the thanks were offered for what she had so lamentably failed to achieve. She found such thanks hard to bear. Next to Jane, Susannah felt the death of George Bryant more than any human being. That evening Susannah twice put on her shawl to go to Jane, but twice thought it more merciful to leave her in peace. The next day she would suggest that Jane should come to live in the house and leave the cottage.

But still, she was so uneasy that at half past ten she did go to the cottage. There was no answer, and she entered. The cottage was dark and empty. Where were the children? On the kitchen table, she found a note Jane had left. Susannah read it, and hurried down the path to Smith's jetty. The cutter was gone. On the path back, she found a scattering of rice where one of the bags had leaked as it was carried to the boat. She returned slowly to the house and to her room, where she again unfolded the note. It was in pencil, on grocer's paper, and it said:

Dearest Susannah—who next to my George and children I always loved as My Life, and Shall never forget the goodness of you. We are gone without Farewells because the Others were fearefull and would not tell any Person, though I spoke against their Feare and would have told You before any one. We are Gone to America, having plenty to carry us there, where Mary and Elizabeth will Prosper, and the Others be Free Men. God be with you for All you Did, and We shall surely meet one Day in the Lands of Promise.

Susannah sat and thought fiercely. Jane was a free woman, and had Susannah known she wished to go home, or to America, she would have paid the passage for her and the children. And who were the "others"? Jane was free but if she was assisting convicts to escape she was again a criminal. They had plenty to carry them there? Spilt grains of rice did not suggest plenty. To what vessel had Smith's cutter carried them? She might still be able to help. If she could find them aboard any ship in the harbour she could at least make their passage easier. She knew there were only two American vessels in port. She knew the captains of both. She harnessed the sulky herself, and, near midnight, observed by the sentries, called on both. Neither had passengers. Captain Charles did say to her, in parting, "If I see your people, I will do my best for them."

When she returned to the house Redmond was waiting, demanding an account. "There is nothing," she said. "It is nothing."

Next day, when the hue and cry was up, Redmond kept silence, not for Susannah but for the sake of his own reputation. When the port-officer came to ask why Susannah had visited two American vessels the night before, she told enough of the truth. She was looking for her maid, Jane Bryant, who was missing. She pointed out that Jane was a free woman. The port-officer remarked that three convicts and the governor's waterman were also missing, and so was the governor's cutter. He said every vessel in the harbour had been searched. They could only have escaped in the cutter.

"The cutter?" she exclaimed. It was the cockleshell that had nearly overturned bringing her back from Manly. "And Jane has her children with her?"

The port-officer concluded that Susannah knew

nothing, and he was very nearly right. She said nothing of the letter. She feared terribly.

In the carriage drive, boxes were loaded onto Redmond's travelling coach. Susannah ran to his room and found he had taken nearly all his possessions. Through the window she could hear John and Redmond's chief stockman talking about the sheep station they would reach in two days' travelling. Redmond met her as she ran down the stairs. He said, "I am doing what I said I would do. The port-officer may believe you had no part in this escape, and I suppose the governor will believe you, but I will not. I am taking the boy. I have taken him for visits before, and I suggest you allow him to believe this is another. I shall allow you enough to keep the house up."

"I had nothing to do with this escape," she said.

"But I do not believe you. Now, will you say goodbye to John? You will need to be cheerful."

Susannah lifted her head, walked slowly into the yard, and made conversation with her son while he instructed the coachman how to secure the cases containing the sporting guns Redmond had just bought for him. They said good-bye as if it were for a week or so, kissing each other on the cheek. The escape had evidently been kept from him, because he called back, as the coach began to move off, "Tell Jane next time she shall come to see the station. And tell Mary, too. She thinks she is too young for the journey, but she is almost the same age as me." They waved while the coach was in sight.

Susannah walked into the empty house, and through the empty rooms, and was alone.

19

————•◦◦◦•————

The Escape Around the World

FOR TWO DAYS AND TWO NIGHTS, in mercifully fair weather, the four men, the woman, and the two children, sailed northwards, passing on the second night the lights of Newcastle. They were not pursued. On the orders of Sydney, a look-out was kept to the south-west, but not to the north. To the north there was, except Newcastle, nothing. To the east stretched the Pacific as far as Cape Horn. The day after the disappearance of the cutter, the American schooner slipped out of the cove, bound for Tahiti and Valparaiso. The port-officer, feeling uneasily that he was acting irrationally, searched her again before she weighed anchor, found nothing, and took a farewell drink with Captain Charles.

"Would they steal the governor's cutter to come aboard my vessel?" asked the captain.

The port-officer said he thought not. "God help them wherever they are, and those children."

"Amen to that," said the captain.

Susannah watched the port-officer's boat return, and by the pilot sent a last message to the captain of the schooner. She remembered Jane's assertion in her letter

that they were going to America. Susannah's note to
Captain Charles said, "I have no reason to suppose
that you may, but if you should be at any charge on
account of Jane Bryant, her children, or the others, I
will repay it when you next call at Sydney." As far as
the coast-guard could keep her in sight, the schooner
sailed due east, for the Society Islands, Tahiti, and
Valparaiso.

On the third night north the seven fugitives slept
ashore, in the lee of a sandbank. The two fishermen
caught enough fish to enable them all to eat well. Jane
cooked some rice. They found no water, but allowed
themselves a plentiful ration from the supply they had
brought. North of Newcastle they found enough coal,
in an outcrop, to keep them warm, which was as well
because there was little scrub-wood to make a fire. The
men kept watch two hours turn and turn about through
the night. All the ammunition they had for the blunderbusses was a mixture of shrapnel, grit, and old nails, but
they hoped that this far north the blacks would be so
unfamiliar with firearms that the noise of the powder
alone would be enough to ward them off. No blacks
were seen.

The cutter sailed well. On the fourth day, when the
wind dropped, they rowed easily. They had six oars, but
men for only four. They sang. No one watching these
seven creatures on that ocean could have said they were
desperate. No one would have said, watching them, that
their water was reduced to six gallons. No one could
have thought Jane a recent widow; but that was her
courage. When, two nights before, they had left Newcastle astern, she gazed after the last few lights, and
this was all that could have told anyone that there lay
buried the man because of whose death she, her daughters, and these men were making this voyage.

On the fifth day they came to a cove, and Moatham
nodded. The breakers at the mouth were deceptively

rough, and they made an easy passage into calm waters, beached the cutter, collected brush, and made a fire. The wood was green. "Smoky Cove," said Moatham, "taken possession of in the name of us." They made a meal of more rice and fish, and even a little salt pork. They brewed coffee. A sane observer would have said it was mad. They could not stay there. There was no water. Their provisions must be running out. If the weather broke, there would be no shelter. No one knew where hostile blacks might be. And yet the fugitives lit a fire. All that night they kept the fire blazing. At dawn they all went to the farthest point of the cove, looked out to sea, and returned, and all that day and the next night kept the fire burning. It was at dawn the next day that Jane and the men looked hard at each other and said what they had at first not given one thought to say, and then, for the last day, had been afraid to say.

"He has left us," said Moatham.

"No," said Smith, "we do not know that."

Lilley and Allen mended their fishing nets. Lilley said to Moatham, "It was you who dealt with him. Why do you say he has left us? You were sure of him?"

"I say it because he knows these shores. And because any vessel must have seen our smoke. If he were here, he must have seen it." Jane said nothing. Smith resolved to search farther north.

"But if he should come when we have gone?" said Jane.

Moatham knew that was impossible. The American schooner, whose captain had promised to meet them in this cove and then take them across the Pacific and round Cape Horn to America, would have made better time than a cutter, even leaving a day later. If he had not come already, he would not come at all. And yet, said Jane, he might have been delayed at Sydney. That was indeed their only hope. So they left in plain view

on the headland a cross six feet high, and another in
the cove, and messages at the foot of each, and then
they sailed slowly north, examining each cove. The ration of water was halved.

Only Moatham was sure they had been deserted.
The others hoped. Moatham was wrong, but it did not
matter. Two days later, after they prospected first
north and then south again, they found the schooner
wrecked and broken-backed on a headland they had
previously passed in the night. She had been there before them, and been driven ashore in a storm that
blew itself out before they arrived. Some of her crew
had the good fortune to drown. The dismembered
carcasses of the others were scattered over the beach.
Here the blacks were cannibals. Moatham recognized
the features of Captain Charles.

They salvaged four floating barrels, one of rum,
two empty, and one, priceless, half-full of fresh water.
Smith and Moatham also dragged two spars from the
surf. To approach the wreck more closely was dangerous. The seas that were smashing her to pieces
would smash any man. If they stayed, more casks
might wash ashore, but they could not wait for fear of
the blacks. They could not bury the bodies, but heaped
them over with sand. Then they sailed the cutter
north again, back to Smoky Cove, but lit no more fires.

The men were then generous. They knew that to go
back was almost certainly to hang. But they knew
that if the children went on they would probably die.
They offered to return, and Jane declined their offer.
They had to go on. If they remained where they were
they would undoubtedly starve. Only Moatham knew
what lay north and west, and he told them. He had
never sailed those waters. The chart he had from the
American captain took him no farther north than the
rendezvous the schooner had never kept. But Moatham
had seen the old Dutch charts, the charts of Cook, and

the charts of Flinders the Australian. A chart and its features remain long in the memory of a man who was once a master's mate. He said that to the north was the Great Barrier Reef, the greatest coral reef known to man, stretching for twelve hundred miles up to the northernmost point of New South Wales at Cape York. He did not know this reef. No navigator did know it well. They would have to negotiate the channel between the reef and the shore. They would have to sail by daylight and beach the cutter by night. He knew nothing of the natives. He knew there were harbours. Captain Cook had once repaired the *Endeavour* in one of them. The climate was tropical, and the rains those of a monsoon. Farther north lay New Guinea, where no white man would survive. They could not go there. Once at Cape York, they would set course west across the Gulf of Carpentaria, and then across the Timor Sea to the Dutch East Indies. Their destination, said Moatham, was Kupang on the island of Timor. It was agreed. Moatham spoke with authority. Only Smith, the governor's waterman, comprehended the magnitude of what was proposed.

They sailed northwards across the Tropic of Capricorn. The monsoon set in. The rain came. For eight days they had no hot food. But they caught the rainwater in the sail, and filled the casks they had salvaged and the leather bottles they had started out with. In turbulent seas, no fish were caught. They chewed the rice grain by grain. When two fish were washed aboard, Lilley gutted them with his thumb and made the children eat them raw. "Suck them if you can," he said. To encourage them, he did so himself. The children stomached them. The children were not seasick, and the men not severely. Jane was badly seasick, and could not take food or rum. To be wet to the skin was the natural condition of them all. They shivered themselves warm. They never lost account of days, which

Smith notched in the gunwale with his sea-knife. Then the rains ceased, and water ran low. When they came to the barrier reef they had to find a landfall each day before dusk, and one night, in exhaustion, were all but murdered. None of the men saw the blacks. A child screamed, and Smith fired a blunderbuss into the air. In the powder-flash they saw a hundred faces within ten yards. The savages did not attack again that night. Next morning the footprints of seventy or more could be seen in the sand, and the cask of rum was gone from the cutter.

They were saved many times—by luck, by courage, by a change of wind, and, later, by rain which fell when they were down to their last pint of water. They were saved so often that after a while they never thought of it. They only knew they survived. On one occasion they were undoubtedly saved by an island. It was a coral island in the barrier reef. They had ample water, because it had again rained incessantly, but they were exhausted. They knew they could not make the mainland before darkness fell. Providence was with them. They ran through the small reef surrounding the island, though if they had been dashed to either side it would have been their death on the coral. Then, when they were safely through the reef, they saw breakers only two hundred yards ahead. The breakers were too severe, and they all knew it. And then, through the breakers, a way through the surf appeared, and the breakers did not smash the cutter, but drove it safely up a fine beach of black sand. If the breakers had not driven it so far they would not have had the strength to drag it themselves to a safe distance from the shore. Then the rain stopped and there was an hour's hot sun to dry their clothes and the blankets. Two blacks appeared, an old man and a woman, the first natives who had been friendly. They carried a firestick. For the first time since any of them could remember, they lit a fire. They accepted the fish the blacks offered, ate, made coffee, and all slept. That was the only time they ever slept on land knowing there were blacks but keeping no guard. They were too exhausted to care. Next day the blacks returned with another, younger man and his woman, who made signs with a stick in the sand. It was the children who understood that they were drawing a turtle. The two fishermen followed the blacks. Smith and Moatham, now recovered enough to stand guard again, remained with the cutter and Jane and the children. An hour later the fishermen returned, each with a turtle, enough to last for a week. They cooked turtle flesh, and drank turtle soup. Apart from the fish, this was their first hot meal since they left Sydney, and the first ample meal since they knew the schooner was wrecked.

For three days they rested.

Then Smith came to Jane. "We must go, and you must tell them."

"*I* must tell them?"

"They will do for you and the children what they will not do for themselves. Jane, they would die here."

She glanced at the two fishermen sprawled on the beach, and thought perhaps they might. But then she looked at Moatham, who was gazing out to sea as if laying a course.

"Him?" she said. "I believe he could navigate us to Portsmouth."

"I believe he could. And I believe if any man can get us to Timor, he will. If you tell him. But I have watched him for two hours, and what I see is the reef-stare. Listen to me, Jane. I have spent my life among sailors, and I have heard tell of it. When a man is driven as far as he can go for the moment, when he is at the end of his resources, he goes into himself. Many good sailors rot on coral islands. A man, when he is weary, gazes at the surf breaking on the reef, and hears the sound, and if there is drink to drink, he drinks, and then gazes at the reef, and drinks, and gazes again, and his spirit is so lulled that he loses all activity. Men lose their will that way. If he should lose his, we are all dead, Jane."

"Then," she said, "take the children along the shore."

Jane went over to the man staring at the reef. "Good morning, Mr. Moatham."

He nodded without looking at her.

"Mr. Moatham," she said, "I have wondered. What is coral?"

He spoke almost straight into the air. "There is noble coral, so-called, and that is richly red. And then there is your rose coral, and your mushroom coral. I have heard it is nothing but the old skeletons of the smallest sea creatures, which when alive are like tiny anemones. But when it is coral it is dead, and I have never seen it alive."

"I had a coral necklace, that was given me in England," she said.

He smiled. "Those reefs are the dead necklaces of many sailors. We were fortunate to come through that as we did, so easily."

"And we shall get out easily enough?"

He did not reply.

"Walk a little with me," she said. She took his arm, and led him away from the two fishermen, who were too apathetic to glance up, and away from the children, whom Smith was engaging in a hunt for fire-wood.

"It is warm," she said. "Shall we sit?" They sat on the beach. Again he sat facing the reef, a little in front of her, not speaking. At the nape of his neck his grey hair was long. She put out a hand and stroked it, and continued to stroke it. He turned his head and she feared that his eyes were hostile, but they were not. They were red with long gazing at horizons in hot sun, and they were helpless. She held out her arms to him and he put his head on her breast. Then he talked. Over many years, Moatham had receded into himself. When he talked it was not so much to her as to himself, saying aloud what he had over and over again said silently in his thoughts. His words were incoherent. Only Moatham and any God in whom he confided knew that he was reliving the capital moments of his life. He spoke the names of Marazion, Truro, Mousehole, and Bodmin—the geography of his life as a boy. Then there was Plymouth, and the *Hecate*, and two names Jane could not catch but which were those of the two men lost when the *Hecate* struck. That was the running aground of one of Her Majesty's frigates, which had floated clear with the tide, but the wreck of Moatham's life, which had never since found a tide to float it. Then there was one joyful recollection, none the less incoherent. To Jane's ears came the date of February 28, repeatedly, and the words, "I am back." She thought they were the words of a woman, to Moatham, perhaps written as the only three words of a letter, on some long-gone February 28. She did not know, and she did not ask, and Moatham never spoke the woman's name. When he stopped for a moment she held him tight in her arms, and then let him speak again, and then once again held him, until he wept openly and bitterly. She rocked his head like a child's. It must have been two hours. Then he raised his head, and shook himself.

"That I should let myself go so," he said. "It is very weak."

Jane said, "You are as strong a man as I know. And if you wept, do you not think a woman is proud to hear a man weep for good reasons?"

By early afternoon they set sail, making only for the mainland that evening. They had left the island that had saved them but which, to save themselves, they had to leave. They had eaten. They had rested.

They had salted down a cask of turtle flesh and filled
another with turtle oil.

They were in peril of their lives every day, but on
two occasions in particular came very near to death.
Once, in the Gulf of Carpentaria, they were chased by
blacks of a kind and of a ferocity they had never seen
before, not the blacks of the south-east coast of New
South Wales who never went to sea at all and took to
water only in bark canoes, but by warriors in canoes
of thirty oars. By then they had been six weeks on the
passage, they had reached a weariness they did not
realize until they tried to pull at the four oars and
found they were too feeble to keep in unison, and they
were saved only by a change in the wind. The governor's cutter, flying before the wind with her lug-sail,
outran two canoes of thirty oars. Beyond the gulf they
found the estuary of a river, rowed upstream to replenish their fresh water, and were working their way out
when they were hit by squalls and all but swamped.
The cutter began to leak so badly they had to throw
two barrels and their blankets overboard to lighten her.
Jane wrapped Elizabeth in the blue cloak and refused
to part with that. They beached the cutter at last and
spent two days paying the seams with the barrel of
pitch they had brought from Sydney. And then, after
ten weeks, they came to Timor and the Dutch port of
Kupang.

They were Europeans. They were in distress. They
did not need to recount their much-rehearsed tale of a
shipwreck, because they were evidently shipwrecked.
The barrels they had on board, and two spars, were
plainly from a Yankee schooner. They were those recovered from the wreck of Captain Charles's vessel.
They were fed, clothed, and housed without the least
suspicion. The Dutch governor promised them a passage to the Cape of Good Hope on the next East India-
man. After a week there was an incident which they

feared might give them away. The governor asked them to sign an order on the British government to repay him for the provisions he had supplied. The four men and Jane were in the room with him, and he asked the senior to sign.

They hesitated, as no sailors ever would. There is a hierarchy on board any ship which is very plain. Moatham, who was known to have navigated the cutter, would have been the obvious man. The governor pushed the paper towards him. But Moatham, having done all he had done, hesitated to commit what he thought of as a forgery. Smith hastily signed. When the men were together later, they were apprehensive, and for a day feared arrest. They need not have worried. The governor had noticed, but thought either that Moatham could barely write, or that they were simply confused after an exhausting passage. He could not have suspected that they were. The truth would have been the wildest and more unlikely of all speculations.

Then they were unlucky. The first vessel to put in was not a Dutchman, but a British frigate. This was the foulest and most unlikely chance. Commander Danvers was told of the English survivors and asked to take them to Cape Town. He interviewed them, guessed not that they had come from Sydney but that they were convicts on their way there, and put the men and Jane in irons. On the expostulation of the Dutch women of the colony he released Jane from fetters, so that she could look after her daughters. Then he set course for the Cape. The first weeks of that passage were through the filthiest of tropical climates. The sailors, seeing the vapour rise from jungles of the islands of the Java Sea, said the whole land gave off a poisonous miasma. Four weeks out, the elder child, Mary, died not from any miasma but from exhaustion assisted by scurvy. The men of the lower watch committed her decently to the sea, though the commander would not heave to for the burial. Jane was permitted to be present, but the four men, who begged for this indulgence, were not. The commander gave as his reason that he did not dare to risk mutiny. The five, seeing no point in further deception, told the sailors they were from Sydney. Danvers was told with some awe by his sailing master that Moatham had navigated the cutter from Sydney to Timor by means of a quadrant and compass. The commander immediately confiscated these instruments. He was an unusual officer, and at Cape Town received his deserts at the hands of the port-admiral.

Commander Danvers submitted a formal report, and next day was summoned to the flagship. Admiral Sir Julian Cunningham, Knight of the Thistle, was a very senior and undistinguished admiral, whose last command this was. He was returning home to farm in Scotland. He had spent all his life at sea. In many wars it had been his misfortune never to be where the battle was, and scarcely to fire a shot at an enemy. He had borne this with patience, and was loved by almost all the officers who served under him, one of whom had been Nelson. He was a man of honour. He also had a reputation as a mild man.

"Danvers," he said, "I have your report."

"Sir."

"You kept these people in irons from Timor?"

"I thought it necessary."

"So that four skeletons should not rouse a mutiny among your own crew of, what, one hundred and eighty men?"

"I judged them likely to be seditious, sir, from their previous conduct."

"You discovered they had navigated from Sydney to Timor, in a fifteen-foot cutter, in an open boat?"

"Yes, sir, they stole the governor's cutter, which I took on board."

"Danvers, I am a sailor, and that is your profession too. Let us consider. Of what length would you estimate the passage to be from Sydney to Timor?"

"Of three thousand miles, sir. And above."

"Rather above. That is, shall we say, comparable in distance to a passage from Portsmouth to Boston? Forgive me, I was familiar with that second port in my youth. You will not be; but you know its position?"

Danvers said he did, but really he did not yet follow the drift of the admiral's remarks.

"That," said the admiral, "is a feat of courage and seamanship which I have never in my life approached, and which perhaps you have not. At a quick computation I would say they sailed farther in an open boat than Captain Bligh when his mutineers put him off the *Bounty,* and Captain Bligh, you will recall, had a crew of eighteen seamen, not two fishermen, a waterman, a woman, and two little girls."

"I think so, sir."

"Then, man, you are beyond praying for. Have you no admiration for excellence in your own calling? Can you not understand what those people have done? I see you cannot. Very well. I say nothing, Danvers, of the death of the girl on the passage here from Timor. There is enough death in those waters. But to keep those men in chains was unconscionable, and not to see what they had achieved was insensible. Put them aboard my flagship by this evening. They will return to England with me. Restore to that man his quadrant and compass. Good day."

Moatham was brought to the admiral's stateroom with a guard of two marines.

"What are you?" said the admiral.

"Moatham, sir, a convict."

"And before you were a convict?"

"Master's mate, sir. *Hecate,* thirty-four guns."

"Ah. Moatham, did you bring that cutter from Sydney to Kupang?"

"It was a fortunate passage, sir."

Cunningham told one marine to fetch the master of his own flagship, and charts of those waters. The master's name was Robert Strong. When he appeared, the admiral dismissed the second marine too.

Cunningham rose, walked round to the chart table, waved the two men near him, and said to Moatham, "Show me how." Cunningham and Strong listened for half an hour.

Then Cunningham said, "Moatham, for what crime were you transported?"

"Theft, sir."

"You do not hedge, do you?" said the admiral. "Then tell me, were you an habitual thief?"

"It was only once, sir."

The admiral left the two men at the chart table and gazed out of the stern quarterlights. "Moatham, what I can do for you when we return to England I have no means of knowing. It may be very little. But you have my word I will do what I can."

He swung round. "Mr. Moatham, on the passage home it is my pleasure, as I feel it will also be Mr. Strong's, that you should mess with him and the other warrant-officers."

"Sir?" said Moatham, utterly confused.

Cunningham repeated himself, and said that Mr. Strong would see to it.

"Sir, there is one thing I must say."

"Say it."

"God knew more about that passage than I did, sir."

"I fancy God needed your assistance at times."

"And, sir, without Smith, we would be dead. And without Jane Bryant we would never have started, nor continued, nor ever finished. It was she that did it, sir."

No one who knew Sir Julian Cunningham was surprised at this act of generosity. It was part of the man. He was a good sailor, who throughout his life encouraged in others an excellence he did not see in himself. He was a man who never in his life did a cowardly act, but was never called on to do a greatly courageous one. Therefore he valued and rewarded in others a courage which had never been demanded of him, and which he could never be sure he possessed. He was also a kind man. This is not to say that his act of generosity towards Moatham did not give the admiral pleasure, but he did not do it to gratify himself. What that act meant to Moatham was not to be calculated. His bitterness departed. He messed with his equals, whose admiration was not so openly expressed as the admiral's, but was still evident. His equals thought Moatham a good and modest man. The generosity, kindness, and above all justness of an admiral made up, as much as any action could, for the bloody-minded injustice of a careless lieutenant that night on the *Hecate.*

Sir Julian's flotilla was three months at the Cape before it sailed. News of the arrest of the seven at Timor and of their being sent to England had reached Sydney. Susannah was astonished and delighted at their survival. The news of the death of the older girl had not yet arrived. Susannah and Robert often corresponded. She knew he had taken to the law, and now wrote asking him to do all he could for the prisoners when they arrived.

Three months in the Mediterranean climate of the Cape was a splendid restorative for all of them, and the passage home, which from the Cape can be easy, was on that occasion miraculously smooth. It was Sir Julian's last passage home, and the sailors said the South Atlantic was showing its respects to a well-loved

sailor. Only the Channel was rough. Sir Julian's ship
paid off at Gravesend, he was piped ashore, and then
he did a last quixotic thing. He ordered his own barge
to take the prisoners downstream to London Bridge,
flying his broad pennant. The flotilla had dispersed in
the Channel, some ships to Plymouth, some to Portsmouth. The news of the Botany Bay people was in
London days before them. When they landed at London Bridge a thousand men and women waited to
greet them at the Monument, the Doric column two
hundred feet high erected to commemorate the Great
Fire of London. The tipstaff met them, and from there
they were conducted to Newgate. It is a mile to walk,
and it became a procession. Jane came ashore first,
with Elizabeth wrapped in the blue cloak; then Moatham, in a suit of broadcloth, the gift of his fellow
warrant-officers and made by the ship's tailor; then
Smith; and then Lilley and Allen. There was no cheering, everywhere a silence, but when the procession began, the men with one movement doffed their hats.
Billingsgate fish-porters, cabmen, clerks, and the brok-
ers of City banking houses, all uncovered.

It was the duty of the sheriff of London to be there.

"This," he said to his tipstaff, "is a strangely silent
demonstration."

"And a very firm one, sir," said the tipstaff. "The
firmest I ever saw."

Next day at Bow Street the five adults were arraigned before the metropolitan magistrate. The charge
against the four men was that of escaping from
a sentence of transportation, and that against Jane
Bryant of aiding the escape. Jane was allowed to carry
Elizabeth in her arms. The court was full. The magistrate, old Bond, addressed the prisoners.

"Will you listen to me? In a moment my clerk will
read the indictment aloud, so that you may know with
what you are charged. But before we do that I will tell

you as simply as I can what course these proceedings may take. When the indictments are read you may deny the charges, or you may say nothing. I am not your judge. Whatever happens today, it will be my formal duty to return you to Newgate, and you may later, if the Crown so decides, be brought to face a judge and a jury at your trial."

The court reporters and hangers-on, who knew very well how this stuff was commonly rattled through, to the near-incomprehension of the prisoners, looked at each other and grinned.

"Now," said the magistrate, "at this or at any subsequent proceedings, you may say nothing, or you may speak for yourselves, or you may address the court through counsel who has already communicated to me an offer to represent you, without expense to yourselves. You might think yourselves wise to accept his services, but the decision is yours."

The prisoners looked at each other, and, seeing their confusion, the magistrate said, "If it helps, my advice to you would be to accept the gentleman's offer."

They nodded.

"All of you?" said the magistrate.

They all nodded again.

The magistrate turned to the barristers' benches. "Mr. King, you have seen the indictments and do not demur at their form?"

Counsel stood to say he did not. Jane Bryant looked in the face of the young man she knew and yet did not know. He knew her. The indictments were read, the magistrate recited the formal committal to Newgate, and, before handing the prisoners over to the sheriff's officers, gave them a purse of forty guineas subscribed by some gentlemen known to him. The magistrate called King to him. "Mr. Attorney has been in court, as you may have noticed." Robert had not, but glanced up in time to see the Attorney-General leave through the side door. "He will see you in my chambers."

Robert bowed. Old Bond, a good lawyer, a man who spent forty years as an advocate before he accepted the stipendiary magistracy at Bow Street once held by Sir John Fielding, said, "King, you won't mind if I suggest you listen to the Attorney and say as little as possible beyond 'How d'you do?' and 'Good morning'? I've known Sir Charles for many years. He listens well to silence."

Sir Charles Bankes, Attorney-General of Great Britain, after the lord chancellor the principal law officer of the realm, head of the legal profession to whose members he was known simply as "Mr. Attorney," surveyed Robert King.

"How d'you do, King? Your people are guilty, you know."

"How d'you do, sir?" said Robert. He did not really know where he stood. He had seen the Attorney-General only once before, in court, when as a student he had watched him prosecuting two men for treason. They had hanged. He knew very well that the Attorney would himself prosecute in only the gravest of cases, and beyond that he knew little more. It was only two months since Robert had been called to the Bar at Gray's Inn, and in those two months he had appeared in court once, as junior counsel to a much more senior man, and he had said not one word in court, having been called on only to watch.

The Attorney-General kept silence and considered. King's people were plainly guilty as could be. Very well. But transportation was hated. The escape had been heroic. Three of the prisoners, the woman, Moatham, and Smith, had a natural dignity which would distinguish them anywhere. And if the woman was going to stand in the dock carrying that child of two years' old . . . Then there was that silent demonstration when they landed. The sheriff had plainly told the Attorney that he had seldom seen anything like it. There also lay before the Attorney, on the table, a letter from Admiral Sir Julian Cunningham, in which he wrote, "I confess that I never looked at these people, without pity and astonishment. After having combated every hardship, and conquered every difficulty, they had miscarried in an heroic struggle for liberty." He had no doubt the admiral would say that in court if given the opportunity. The admiral also offered to employ on his Scottish estates all the prisoners, should they be acquitted. The admiral did not say, but Mr. Attorney very well knew, that he owned, at a rough guess, a tenth of the more arable parts of Scotland, which gave him a certain influence even in London. The admiral also returned, from all those Scottish acres, sixteen members of Parliament, a number useful to the government of which the Attorney was a member. Then Mr. Attorney looked at King. No barrister ever has his wig cleaned, so the length of a barrister's experience can readily be determined from the state of his wig. King's was the whitest he had lately seen. A new man would have the jury's sympathy. He might be competent. Or, which from the Crown's point of view would be much worse, he might be useless, in which case the judge would by tradition help him in every conceivable way, perhaps to the extent of conducting the defence himself. These were the thoughts that ran through the Attorney's mind. Robert had only the faintest glimmer of all this, though to get that glimmer from the impassivity of the Attorney showed the beginnings of a legal instinct.

"Who will pay for the defence?"

That was none of the Attorney's business, but Robert replied, "There are sufficient funds, sir." It was a lucky answer, because the Attorney's mind went to those Scottish acres, and assumed a connection between them and the young barrister which did not in fact exist.

The Attorney leaned back. The young man said nothing.

"King, the prisoner Jane Bryant seemed to know you in court, and you to know her?"

"My grandfather was governor of New South Wales, sir, and Jane Bryant was the midwife at my birth."

The Attorney covered his face with his hands, and for the first time in legal memory laughed, and laughed. He already knew what sort of a case he had, but now there was this too. All it needed was for this piece of information to be volunteered in court, and the jury would be in tears and the prosecution in rags, if it weren't in rags already.

Robert stood silent.

"Beg your pardon, King. A man's birth is no laughing matter to him, eh?"

The Attorney picked up the indictment, took a pen, and scrawled across it, *Nolle prosequi*. The Crown was stating, in the person of Mr. Attorney, that it did not wish to pursue the indictment. It was all done with. The prisoners would go free. That was that. He passed the endorsed paper to Robert, who read the two words.

"Good morning, sir," said Robert.

The Attorney called him back. "King, if that was the first case you have ever argued, and I think it was, you did it uncommonly well."

Robert said it was only fair of him to admit that his conduct of the case had been exactly that advised by Mr. Bond the magistrate.

"I knew that. But you see, King, you managed to carry out his advice, which few men do. It says a lot for you. You will do well. Good day."

20

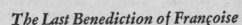

The Last Benediction of Françoise

ROBERT TOOK JANE, her daughter, and the four men
to Bedford Square. The four men had accepted the
admiral's offer and would be going soon to his estates
in Scotland. Jane did not yet know what she would do.
They were all bewildered. Their release seemed more
a miracle to them than their magnificent passage.
They looked on Robert as a saviour. It was useless for
him to protest that he had done almost nothing, and
that any man could have done as much for them. It
was useless for him to explain that, had they not
been represented at all, the result would have been the
same. It would have taken a couple of weeks rather
than a couple of days, but that was all the difference
his presence could possibly have made. They did not
believe him. It seemed insulting to tell them the truth,
which was that their release was a simple matter of
policy. He did tell them that the interest of Sir Julian
had mattered a great deal more than his advocacy.
The most they were prepared to believe was that the
two men had played an equal part.

Their release became an event of the Season. Members of both Houses of Parliament, various duchesses,
and idlers of other descriptions left cards at Bedford
Square. The countess looked at the second afternoon's

collection, heaped in a silver tray, and told Robert it might be simpler to give a once-for-all reception. "Will it be all right for your people if we do?" she asked. "It will be given for them."

"I'll see that it will be all right for them," he said.

He asked Jane to come to see him in the library.

She curtsied.

"Jane," he said, "there are some proprieties to be observed, and the first is that you will never curtsy to me again. Now, you have seen the newspapers? You, and Elizabeth, and Moatham, and Smith, and the others are famous people. In London, fame may last for several weeks. The countess is going to give a reception, and we shall ask those people who've already called and left cards, and some others. And anyone you would like to ask as well."

"We do not know anyone in London, Mr. Robert."

"Very well. But this is a reception in your honour, the five of you, and the little girl. You must all be there. The countess will receive the guests, and so will you, Jane. That is the way we will do it."

"I don't rightly know how, Mr. Robert."

"When they come into the great room the steward will call out their names, and they will come up to the countess, and then to you, and you both say 'How d'you do?' or some such thing, and that's it. The countess will tell people who you are, they will say a few words to you, and you smile. You've seen it many times at my mother's house."

"But it's not for me to do. I can't do it."

"Yes you can, Jane. I will stand the other side of you. You do exactly what the countess does. If she curtsies, as she will to anyone who's very great or very old, or both, you do the same, but to nobody else. If she shakes hands, you do the same. And I'll be next to you and be doing the same as well, except that since I'm a man I mostly just nod and say 'Good evening.'

Jane, if the king comes, which he won't, do what the countess does, which will be to curtsy and say 'Good evening, sir.' "

"What about Moatham and the others, sir?"

"The others will be at the end of the room, and after a while I'll break away and look after them. Now, will you do this for me?"

Jane considered, and then saw he was smiling, and smiled broadly back at him. "I will."

At the party, Jane received with a dignity which charmed everyone who came to see her. Afterwards the countess kissed her on both cheeks and hugged her. The greatest man to appear was Viscount Castlereagh, His Majesty's secretary of state for foreign affairs, an old Tory, who looked at her and said, "More than I could have done, Mrs. Bryant. You know, ma'am, when I was at the Colonies I used to write dispatches to New South Wales, or put my name to 'em anyway. Was reminded of New South Wales the other day in Cabinet. Blacks massacring convicts; well, six or seven convicts."

"It is true, sir, but white men have killed the blacks too, and more than six or seven."

"I dare say, ma'am. I dare say. Yes, I remember it well, dispatch after dispatch to New South Wales. In my day, the trouble wasn't the blacks or the convicts; always the military. Officers always getting above themselves. Yes, dispatch after dispatch to Sydney. Signed them all."

"I'm sorry I never saw any of them, sir."

"That's the thing, ma'am. You put your name to dispatches, and send them off, and nobody ever does see them. And suppose they do reply? Ma'am, I'm still putting my name to dispatches, and I shan't be still in office to see the replies, even if they ever come. You're a brave woman." And he wandered off into the crush where Robert presented Moatham, who was told he was a good fellow. A few minutes before, Moatham had been accosted by Jeremy Bentham, who now accosted Castlereagh.

"I know you as a tyrant, sir," Bentham began civilly.

"Very likely, very likely," replied the statesman. "Nobody has a good word to say for anyone these days. I know of you as a political economist. Good evening to you." Castlereagh mellowed wonderfully in the last months before he cut his own throat. To the countess, when she found him again, he remarked, "Fellow Bentham, much more entertaining than I'd thought. I'd always heard he was a great man except that he would talk constantly about happiness, as if he were an American. He's said to believe any action's good if it produces happiness. Rot. Suppose a pickpocket were to make himself happy by picking Mr. Bentham's pocket?"

Castlereagh had come because he was an old friend of the countess's, and also out of curiosity because his had been one of the voices which had told Mr. Attorney it might be politic to be generous with the Botany Bay people. Bentham had invited himself.

"I once met that man Jefferson," said Castlereagh. "The American. Can't remember where. Can't remember what we were talking about. Perhaps we'd stopped a few American ships. Can't remember. Decent fellow. Knew where to draw the line. Didn't go on too long about life, liberty, and the pursuit of happiness; but I tell you, Countess, for a while there we were batting inalienable rights back and forth, across the dinner table. And all it was about was a few ships. I remember now. It was ships."

"I once met him," said Françoise. She had been a girl, with d'Estaing. Thomas Jefferson was American minister in Paris. It must have been seventeen eighty-eight or eighty-nine, a world away.

"I was a girl," she said, "and he was kind."

"Even American ministers are kind to girls, my dear. What'd he have to say for himself, though? That's another matter."

"All I had to talk about was inalienable rights too. It was all I knew about him. It was at the Tuileries. He said he'd changed the words. It was originally life, liberty, and the pursuit of property, and he changed property to happiness in his Declaration of Independency, and either nobody noticed or nobody dared to object to happiness."

"They wouldn't, would they?"

"He sent me a lace shawl the next day."

"What's sending a girl a lace shawl but the pursuit of pleasure? I've done that, Countess. Often. In Ireland."

"I remember he said another thing. That you ought not to confuse the pursuit of happiness with the pursuit of pleasure."

"That, my dear, is evidence of an agile mind."

The steward came over to the countess, who nodded. He gave three raps on the table. "My lords, ladies, and gentlemen, I ask your silence for Mr. Moatham."

In a quiet voice, at times almost inaudibly, and encouraged by Smith, Moatham got it out that from the purse presented to them at Bow Street they had purchased two watches, which they had had inscribed, and which, with the permission of those gentlemen, they wished to present to Admiral Sir Julian Cunningham, and to Mr. Robert King, as thanks for doing more than any men in the world could have done.

It was a surprise to both men. The admiral was never so gratified by anything as by this unlooked-for gesture. Robert remembered the watch given to him many years ago by Sir Harry Browne Hayes, and told that story, and said he would treasure them both.

When the chatter began again, Jeremy Bentham sought out Jane Bryant.

"Think of me as one of His Majesty's judges," said Bentham. "Think of me as that. And a poor man is before me for what—the theft of turnips, invaluable turnips, priceless turnips. And what is my sentence? I say, 'I sentence you to transportation, but to just what I know not. Perhaps to storm and shipwreck, perhaps to infectious disorders, perhaps to famine, perhaps to be massacred by savages, perhaps to be devoured by wild beasts. Away with you, take your chance, perish or prosper.' "

"There are no wild beasts, sir," said Jane.

"And when a man has endured the length of his sentence," said Bentham, "as it may be seven or fourteen years, tell me, is he a free man?"

Jane said, "Mr. Robert's grandfather, the governor, always said that New South Wales was a free land, and that in a free land there could be no slavery, and therefore no slaves."

"But is a man free, after his sentence has been served? Is he as free as a man who comes out free from England?"

The whole assembly was now listening.

"No," said Jane, "he is not."

Thus was the central issue of a whole continent put in a few words by Jane Bryant in a drawing-room in Bedford Square. Her adventures, known to everyone in that room, and the way her words were spoken, heard by everyone, and the nature of that gathering, because the men in that room possessed among them a great deal of power, ensured that Jane's words were infinitely better heard than if they had been addressed by any member of Parliament to a House of Commons in its natural state—that is to say with a bare quorum present, and half of that quorum asleep.

"And," said Bentham, "if such men are not free, then by whose authority are they not free? Not by the authority of the secretary of state or by Lord Castlereagh's, even though I do call him a tyrant, because he will recognize that word for what it is, a mere offer to exchange political compliments. He would not say such men were not free.

"If I were a young man," Bentham continued to Robert, "a young man starting in the law, I would say that there was my great issue, and I would return to the country of my birth and seize that issue. If I were you I should return to New South Wales. And," he said, addressing Jane, "if I were younger and a woman of your courage and plainness of speaking, I would take myself also back to New South Wales. You have work to do there."

At which he bowed in rapid sequence to Jane, Robert, Castlereagh, and the countess, and left in a silence that lasted until he disappeared through the doorway. The old radical knew how to make the most of an exit. The *Times,* the *Morning Post,* the *Edinburgh Review,* and a hundred other newspapers, reviews, and pamphlets were full of it all.

Three days later Françoise said, out of the air, out of a conversation which had nothing to do with return or parting, "Dear Robert, you are going back, aren't you?"

"Yes. I was in any case."

"And Jane and her daughter?"

"Yes. She told me yesterday. I asked her why. I said it was a long way to come in order to go back. I said she ought not to be swayed so soon by Mr. Bentham. I said he was an habitual swayer of minds."

"I think he might be pleased that you should think that."

"She said that, with respect to Mr. Bentham, it was not he who had done the swaying. She had swayed herself by what she heard herself say out loud, which she knew was true but had never thought to say before. Then she said a strange thing. She said when they escaped they started out first for America, which I'd forgotten. And she told me about a letter she left for my mother. She had never expected to meet her again on this earth, but had said they would meet in the Lands of Promise."

"And now she thinks New South Wales may be the Lands of Promise?"

"Françoise, I think she may now believe that people can have a hand in creating their own Lands of Promise. But I think that is a reason that must take its turn with others. I think Sydney is home to her, which she sees the more clearly now she is away from it. She now knows no one here. I think she also loves my mother, which she feels more clearly now she is away from her."

"So you will take her?"

It was arranged. Jane wanted first to see again the Dorset villages where she had lived as a girl. An older sister, an old aunt, and a grandmother were still living, and Jane herself was aunt to children she had never seen. Robert reckoned with the possibility that once she was in Dorset she might want to stay there, and, if she did, he would wait a while to see that she was settled in her determination, and then leave. Otherwise, they would go on to Weymouth, take passage along the coast to Plymouth, and take ship there for New South Wales. Within two weeks the others had gone to Scotland and Jane and Robert were ready to leave too. The countess's coach would take them to the West Country. While the boxes were loaded, on the pavement in Bedford Square, where he had first arrived years before, Françoise d'Estaing and Robert stood facing each other in the same room where they had first set eyes on each other that evening.

She smiled and once again extended one hand.

"M'sieu," she said.

He took her fingers and bowed over them.

"Madame."

So they laughed, and went out to the coach. The countess kissed Jane, and held Elizabeth tightly and kissed her too. Then there was no getting away from the good-bye to be said. The others were already in the coach. Robert stood and looked into the blue, Norman eyes of Françoise d'Estaing, Françoise Vouvray, whom his father had loved, and who had become to him as much a mother as his own mother. She held herself very straight. It was he who cracked, holding out his arms to her, and she ran into them. They separated. It was still unbearable. He was an Englishman in an English square, watched by passers-by who were English, but he went quickly down on one knee, and she said the familiar words of the benediction she had spoken to him every night since he arrived in her house. Then it was all right.

21

◦◦◦◦◦◦

In the Morning, It Was Leah

IN THREE DAYS' easy driving they reached the Dorset
of Jane Bryant's ancestors and of her husband's. They
came to the country of the villages near Dorchester
which all begin or end in "puddle." There are Puddletown, Tolpuddle, and Affpuddle, and Jane's remaining family lived in and around them.

Robert left Jane with her aunt at Tolpuddle, and
went the few miles to Dorchester, where he took a
room at the King's Arms. His was a very grand equip-
age for Dorchester, and it was assumed he would take
the grandest room, which was on the first storey at the
front, a room with a fine bow window, generously
glazed. It was an old posting inn where coaches
changed horses on the way west to Exeter and Plymouth, but the porch with its Tuscan façade, and the
rooms at the front, were new. While his two coach-
men and the inn servant lugged the baggage, a girl
from the inn bobbed at him in the lobby, flew up the
stairway in front of him, waited for him on the landing, and chattered round him as she showed him his
room. She was dark and lithe, with the brown face of a
country girl. She spoke a soft Dorset dialect that he

could at times hardly understand. Would he come and
look out of the window? Now see, there to the left,
as far as a man could see, that was Grey's Bridge.
He must have crossed that coming into the town.
Didn't he recall that, sir? And there to the right as
far as a man could see—and she stretched herself
as far out as she could, leaning forward from the waist
with her bare arms on the windowsill, urging him
to do the same—at the top of the hill was where the
soldiers were in barracks. And then swiftly she was
gone, all life, leaving Robert smiling at the brief remembrance of her. She was both chambermaid and
kitchen-girl. At dinner she appeared briefly, standing
in an apron holding the dishes of meat, carrots, and
peas from which the waiter served Robert. He looked
up at her. She would not catch his eye, but knew very
well she pleased him. After dinner he smoked for a
while, and then went to his room. He was sitting in the
bow window, doing nothing in particular but observing the High Street, when, with a light knock, in she
came, bobbing again and asking if she should turn
the bed back. She chatted again. The men said his
horses were too fine for Dorset roads, good turnpike
roads though they were, and she thought the men
were right. Not shod for those roads either.

"What is your name?" said Robert.

"Leah, sir, because—"

"Leah? But surely that's a Hebrew name, and
you're from Dorchester?"

"I'm not from Dorchester. I'm not a town girl, sir.
I'm from Puddletown. And as for me being Leah, sir,
we're all named from the Scriptures, my brothers and
sisters and me, and Scripture names aren't Hebrew,
are they, sir?"

Robert reflected that the only Leahs he had known
were Jewish, the daughters of City bankers and merchants in London.

"In London," he said, "there are plenty of Rebeccas and Ruths, but I don't think they are named from the Scriptures. The custom is going out in London."

"If that's so, sir, then folk lose the chance of naming children right."

"How's that?"

"Well, sir, I was expected at night, and was to be called Rachel. But I was delayed, sir, and was not born till morning."

"Ah. Yes?"

" 'In the morning, behold it was Leah.' Genesis, sir."

"You know your Bible better than I do," he said.

"You're an educated gentleman, sir." That put it so exactly that Robert smiled.

"But that wasn't the end on it, sir."

"No?"

"My father was so set on calling me Rachel that he gave me that name too, even though I did come in the morning. So he called me Leah Rachel, and when at the christening the parson asked him why, he spoke up at the font and said he never had thought the Scripture story was fair dealing, and that him giving me both names made amends for it. The parson said if a learned man said that, it would be blasphemy, but seeing as it was my father, it wouldn't be counted against him."

The girl stood watching Robert, put her hands on her hips, and said, "You don't rightly follow it all, do you, sir?"

"I'm afraid I don't."

"Well 'twas an old swizz, sir. I always thought that story was an old swindle soon as ever I could read it. You know Jacob, the one that had the dream where there was a ladder with angels going up and down it, and at the top was God and he said to Jacob that he and his tribes after him should have all the land they could see? The Promised Lands, see?"

"The Promised Lands," said Robert. "Go on."

"See, Jacob went on a journey and came to a well, and there were flocks of sheep belonging to his uncle, and one of the girls tending the sheep was Rachel, and she was his uncle's daughter. Jacob took to Rachel and said to his uncle he'd work seven year for him if he could have Rachel to marry. So they struck the bargain, like a hiring fair on Lady Day. Well, after seven year he asked for her, and they had a wedding feast, and I dare say he took a bit of drink, and they sent Rachel to him when it was dark, leastwise they said it was Rachel, but in the morning he sees her's not Rachel at all. 'In the morning, behold it was Leah.' Leah's her older sister. Well, there's an old swizz if ever I saw one, and Jacob tells his uncle so, and the uncle says he can have Rachel too if he works another seven year, and so he does, and has them both, but he should rightly have had Rachel in the first place. There's more to it than that, but that's what matters. Anyways, my father speaks up at the font, and he says there won't be no short-changing when he gives me in marriage—as he hopes, God willing, he'll live to do— seeing that he'll be giving away Leah and Rachel both at one time to the same man. So I 'spose when it comes to the wedding, Parson will say, 'Leah Rachel, do you take this man?' But nobody calls me anything but Leah in the ordinary way of things, nor ever has."

She chatted on. She said she couldn't help hearing him talk with Mr. Brigges, the waiter, and asking about Puddletown, and the church there, and the monuments of old knights lying there.

"I shall go there tomorrow," he said.

"I come from there, sir. I always say the stone creatures in the transept are my monkeys, only they aren't monkeys, they're apes. Shall I show you, sir? It's my free day tomorrow. I could tomorrow."

"Show me, Leah."

She bobbed and was gone. Robert slept very well.

After breakfast he walked into the High Street and she was there.

"I'll rest the horses today," he said, "so tell me where I can hire a gig."

"Lord, sir," she said, "it's no more than a walk."

"How far is it?" he asked.

"A mile or two, sir."

It was six. After one or two it became plain she was much more used to walking than Robert. He was no better shod than his horses for the Dorset roads, but he covered the six miles in two hours. She got him some ale, and then showed him the church, unaffectedly holding out her warm hand to him as he climbed the gallery stairs behind her. It was the gallery where the fiddles and serpents played for hymns, and the choir sang. For nearly two centuries, fiddlers and choristers had carved their initials in the wood of the gallery. The oldest date was 1635. The gallery was one of the newer parts of a medieval church. "There's mine," said Leah, showing Robert the carved characters, "L.M. 1636."

"Sixteen thirty-six?" he said.

"Well, sir, I reckon any letters ought to be old or they'm not worth the carving, but I didn't want to be first, because 'twouldn't be believed, so I carved mine a good year after the first."

She showed him the Norman font, where her father had said Genesis was a swizz.

In the transept they saw the knights, the old knight and his lady lying side by side in stone, and the brasses of Christopher Martyn, died 1524, and Nicholas Martyn, 1595. Then there was the fine Martyn monument with canopy and carved creatures.

"My monkeys," she said. "Only they're apes."

They could have been either.

"No," she said, "Parson says they're the Martyn

apes, since apes are that family's creatures, only they look like dogs because the man that carved them never saw either ape nor monkey. I've seen a monkey, at the fair, so I call them monkeys."

"You carved your name L.M.," said Robert. "What is the M?"

"Martin. But all the real Martyns, the old ones, went from hereabouts centuries ago to the Crusades, and never came back save as monuments. Parson says so. All the Martins now living never owned so much as a field, or a stone in a field. I'm no knight's lady, sir. I'll never lie by the side of a stone knight."

It was her church. She was at home in it. She was not awed, but she was not irreverent. She led him by the hand to the three-decker pulpit. She would not go to the top deck, from which the parson preached, but on the second storey a heavy folio Bible lay open on a lectern, and she mounted the stairs and faced it, with her eyes closed.

"I must point the Book," she said, "to see what it says for you."

Still with her eyes closed, she touched the open Bible with her forefinger, and then looked to see where she had touched.

"It don't matter," she said. Robert could have sworn there was a tear in her eye, and that this happy girl had become unhappy.

"What is it?"

" 'Tis nothing but the old Apocrypha."

"What does it say?"

She answered bravely. "It is Ecclesiasticus. 'Put not thy faith in a light woman.' "

She came down. This time it was he who took her hand. *"That,"* he said, "is *not* you."

But it had taken the sun out of the day for a while. She did not chatter to him now. He insisted on hiring a fly to take them back to Dorchester, and at Yellow-

ham Wood on the way back, when she asked him, he
pulled up, and she got down and gathered a posy of
primroses, which she gave to him.

"Leah," he said, "I should have done that for you."

"It is for what you said."

The ride back restored her spirits, and when he
handed the fly to the groom at the King's Arms he
jumped down, bobbed at Robert, and ran away into
the inn and upstairs. Half an hour later, long before
dinner, when he was sitting in his bow window writing, she knocked softly, came in, and did not chatter,
or ask to turn down the bed, or make any pretext for
her presence, but stood with her back to the closed
door.

Robert was nineteen. Since the day with Jacqueline
in the Bois de Boulogne he had met, and pursued, and
been pursued by, many women—all of them older
than himself, all without exception worldly, all of his
own rank. As a result he was an assured young man.
He had felt affection for all of them. But none of them
had been vulnerable, none of them younger than himself. This girl, he thought, was perhaps only sixteen.
She was in fact fifteen. He would be gone in two days.
He had seen her face in the pulpit that afternoon. He
owed it to her to care for her. Yet how was he, without bruising her, to tell her to go? Besides, he did not
want her to go.

What passed between them was the most solemn
of regards.

He said, "Would you consent if I were to ask you
to come to me this evening?"

She shook her head stubbornly. "No. Now."

He walked across to her. But it was she who, without looking, bolted the door behind her. It was she
who threw back the bedclothes with one sweep. She
stretched up to kiss his face. She drew his face down
to her breast. She gave to him a warmth which, when

she saw with what affection he received it, she re-
doubled. No woman had ever been so sweet to
him. And she was as assured as he was. She embraced
him with her warmth and encircled him with her
brown legs.

Then she talked. Then she chattered. And Robert,
from the candid generosity of Jacqueline Brie in the
Bois, and the ingenuous warmth of Leah Martin at the
King's Arms, formed an early expectation of the goodness of women, which is one of the most fortunate be-
liefs a man can hold.

That afternoon Jane came back from seeing her sister, her grandmother, her aged aunt, and her nephews
and nieces. Elizabeth, who was a sweet child, had
been made much of. But Jane had been away for
nearly twenty-five years. She was recognized by no
one, and those who did remember her when their
memories were stirred were themselves so changed by
age that she did not recognize them. Not one. Not her
sister. Now that she had come home to Dorset, it was
New South Wales that seemed home to her. In Dorchester she walked up High East Street, and then up
High West Street, asking after anyone who remembered
George Bryant, but her husband was forgotten too.
She went to Robert and said, "I will be coming home."
He told her they would set out the next day.

That evening she wanted to see one last part of the
town, the West Walks, where she would remember the
avenues of trees if they did not remember her. Robert
went with her. They walked in silence.

On the way back in the dusk she pointed out Yallop
Bros. in High West Street, the shop where as a girl she
stole those two lengths of silk, and, opposite, the
court where she was transported for that high crime.

"What is a wedding dress made of?" asked Robert.

"Whatever a girl can afford, sir. Cotton. Muslin. Satin. Silk."

That night Leah tapped on his door very late, when he was already in bed, and slipped in beside him, curling round him. As the clock of Saint Peter's struck two, he watched her asleep. Once she stirred and made little noises as if dreaming. Then he fell asleep himself and when he awoke, at eight, she was gone. On her pillow was a note, in pencil:

> *You nead more sleap than I do I shall be gone to*
> *market today Remember my monkees as I shall al-*
> *ways remember what you said—*
> *Yr affectnte Leah*

At eleven o'clock Robert went to Yallop Bros., Drapers to the Nobility, Gentry, and Citizenry, and commanded two lengths of silk to make two wedding gowns.

How much was required, asked the shopman. Of what height were the ladies?

Robert held up a hand to show him.

"Both ladies the same height, sir."

"Both."

What quality silk did he require? Silk of Italy or of the Levant, or the silk of Piedmont?

"Such as a knight's lady might wear."

The shopman was used to humouring the nobility and gentry, and bowed gravely.

Robert carried away from the shop two lengths of the finest Piedmont, and left them for Leah. "Here," he wrote to her, "is one wedding gown for Leah and another for Rachel, whose husbands will be fortunate in them both. I shall remember your monkeys. What I said was true."

They left for Weymouth at noon, and a week later embarked from Plymouth for New South Wales.

Part Three

22

Susannah Recovers Her Dreaming

JANE BRYANT, her daughter Elizabeth, and Robert returned as heroes. London newspapers had reached Sydney before them. The magistrates, the free settlers, and the principal sheep-owners, Redmond among them, made representations to the governor that to preserve the peace and prevent any tumultuous gathering the three should be made to land discreetly at a cove a few miles west of Sydney. Governor Brisbane was by instinct sympathetic to the settler interest, but put aside these suggestions. First, he had no power to do what he was asked. Second, he could think of no better way of provoking a tumultuous assembly than to forbid it. The woman Bryant would be welcomed as a heroine because everyone knew she had acted heroically. He felt so himself. Though he could hardly congratulate a woman who had led an escape from the colony, he knew it would be idiocy to try to prevent a triumphal return. He proposed to do nothing. He would rely on the good sense of Jane Bryant and Robert King. Dispatches from London said they had behaved there with good sense, and he trusted they would again. So no extra guards were mounted, and the police were told to turn a blind eye to a reasonably festive drunkenness.

Jane was received with bunting, drums, a string band, a brass band, and the cheers and exultation of more than a thousand emancipists and ticket-of-leave convicts. She was chaired to her old cottage, which had been prepared for her, and Elizabeth was carried head-high by her side. Robert appeared with Jane on the quay, but when she was chaired away he slipped back on board ship and in the rejoicing was not missed. Hundreds accompanied Jane to her cottage. Her friends went inside with her. The others sang and cheered around the cottage, until they were told that rum would flow freely at the Black Dog and the Sheer Hulk, public houses in the district known as The Rocks, the other side of the cove from the domain. The rum was supplied by Robert, who made a brief speech and then left others to make longer speeches. It was reported next day that some of the drinkers became so saturated with rum that when they lit their pipes a blue flame came from their lips, and that became a legend. But it all went off very well.

Susannah did not go to the quay, but after the roisterers had left Jane to go off to The Rocks she went to the cottage herself and the two women embraced. Above all, Susannah and Jane were happy to be together again. There were other things to be talked of, but they could wait till the next day.

"And where is Robert?" said Susannah. Jane told her of the plan to supply rum in convenient places, a plan contrived between Robert and the port-officer when his cutter met the ship at the headlands, and that Robert would soon be back.

When Susannah returned to her house he was there waiting for her.

There were practical matters to be settled. Jane was to

leave her cottage, with its memories of her husband, and live with Susannah, though certainly not, Susannah insisted, as her maid. Jane suggested that a housekeeper was needed, and that is what she became. She insisted that one duty should remain hers and not the maid's. She should dress Susannah in the evening, and brush her hair at night. These were the times when they talked most closely together. This was understood by them both. It went without saying that Elizabeth would come with her mother. It was then that Jane asked after John, and was told that Susannah had not seen her second son or her husband since the day after she last saw Jane. They were prospering greatly up-country. Redmond came occasionally to Sydney and was sometimes accompanied by John, but never brought the boy to Susannah. She had asked to see him, and this had been denied her. She asked again, and received the reply that her insistence could only hurt the boy. She did not ask again.

The affinity between Susannah and Robert was strong and deep. It always had been, but now it was different. They parted as mother and son, and as mother and son they were reunited. But the parting was six years before, when Robert was a boy. Now he was a man. Susannah saw him as a man, and he saw her as a woman. Like the countess, she saw Nicolas again in him. Father and son were very alike. Robert was taller and broader, but his features were his father's. His eyes were the same. But in her son, Susannah saw not only Nicolas but herself.

There were gestures of the hands which had not been there before in the young boy, but were there now, and they were hers. He could not have imitated them from being in her company. It was heredity showing itself in like gestures expressing like feelings. For instance, they were discussing where he should live. She naturally said her house was his. He said he

would soon be starting to practise law, and would engage his own chambers in the town. She understood.
There was no contention between them but both
mother and son, making a point, said at the same moment, "You see . . ." and found themselves accompanying the words with identical gestures. Both sat
resting their elbows on the arms of wooden chairs.
Both were leaning forward with both hands raised so
that each saw the other's palms, with the fingers half-
apart and half-curved. Both saw the same gesture at
the same moment, both held it for a second, and both
smiled.

Susannah looked at the hands. "It is as if we were
two heraldic lions in conversation," she said.

And they held their heads in the same way. He had
her directness, whereas Nicolas always had a diffident
look. Susannah wondered if her son had her own
sudden wilfulness.

Robert asked about Redmond and John. Why had
she not written to tell him, if not straightaway, then
after a while? She was not sure. Perhaps it was because she had continued unconsciously to think of
Robert as the boy he had been when he went away.
She said she could not realize, from such a distance
and after such a time, how much he would have
changed. Robert understood this. Did he not see his
mother in a completely new way? A boy of thirteen or
fourteen knows that his mother is beautiful. But Robert at nineteen saw for the first time that Susannah
was a woman of rare vividness and life and wondered
how she lived alone, if she lived alone. It seemed she
did. Robert lived in the house for a month or so while
he found chambers. Susannah presented him to Brisbane, and they got on well. Brisbane took his duties
in the leisurely way Robert had seen in the men he
met at the countess's in London, who seemed to run
the British Empire from Whitehall, or from their clubs,

with the same urbane ease with which they ran their country estates. Those were the days when young gentlemen in the Civil Service—the Home Office, the Foreign Office, the Colonial Office, or whatever department—drifted into their offices at ten, drifted off to their clubs for a leisurely lunch at noon, and then, having drifted back to Whitehall, stayed there until four and no later. Their masters, the secretaries of state, demanded no more of themselves. The House of Commons sat half the year, if that, and the Lords a great deal less. It was assumed that if a man did not have the capacity to bear the burden of high office with ease, he did not have the capacity to bear it at all.

Soon after Robert's return it became known in Sydney that Mr. Commissioner Wyndham was coming out from London with full powers to summon witnesses, enforce their attendance, take their evidence, and to inquire in any manner he considered necessary into the late outrages committed by and against the natives of New South Wales, and thereafter to advise His Majesty's secretary of state in any way he thought fit; and the governor was requested and required by His Majesty to give all aid and assistance to James Wyndham, Esq., in the performance of his duties. Governors do not like commissioners sent out to watch them governing.

"You don't know the man, do you?" the governor asked Robert. "Not at the Bar, is he? Not a barrister? With respect, my boy, a prying barrister is the curse of the governing classes."

"I don't know him. I've heard of him. Well liked. The last thing he did was on Irish workhouses, much thought of. Much reported in *The Times,* as I remember. He said something about awful consequences if the potato crop should ever fail, but it was dismissed as too fantastic. Far-seeing, they said, far-seeing and fantastic."

"What's potatoes got to do with workhouses?"

"That's what he was asked at the time. He said a quarter of the whole population of Ireland was in workhouses, that even in workhouses they had to be fed, that in Irish workhouses nobody was ever fed anything but potatoes, so it was very much his business to inquire what would happen if one year there were no potatoes."

"What came of it?"

"Nothing," said Robert. "But it was highly thought of."

"Not at the Bar, is he?" asked the governor, returning to his first anxiety.

"No, not a barrister. A good classicist. His edition of Horace's *Odes* is much admired."

The governor thought the man was altogether excessively admired, but was relieved he was not a barrister. A good classicist he could take. Excellence in dead languages was universally thought to be a quality that fitted a man to play his part in the government of Empire, and perhaps it did. Wyndham was in fact at the beginning of a long and brilliant career in the Civil Service, though moving from the Irish poor law to New South Wales was, as the governor put it, no more than moving from one workhouse to another. He was glad the man was not at the Bar, but would rather he was not coming at all.

At first meeting the governor was gruff and the commissioner cautious. Wyndham formally presented his commission, which the governor formally accepted, and then, with the document lying on a low table between them, the two men made what can only be described as small talk, which neither knew how to bring to an end. Eventually the governor said, "You know, Wyndham, Mrs. Redmond's got some paintings of blacks. Might help you."

"Indeed."

"Done by her father. Her father was governor here, you know."

Wyndham did not know, nor did he think there was much to be learned from the paintings of a former governor, but he could not say so. The governor, for his part, was anxious to bring to an end this interview at which neither man wished to commit himself by saying anything, and so he seized a pen, dashed off a note to Mrs. Redmond, and placed it affably in the hands of the commissioner. This gave Wyndham a pretext to express his thanks and take his leave.

The governor brushed away the thanks, "Not at all, not at all," and Wyndham departed, relieved to get away but knowing that, little use as he felt the introduction would be to him, he could not fail to present the letter since it had been the first accommodating gesture of the governor. Commissioners are as uneasy about governors as governors about commissioners.

So he called to present the letter to Mrs. Redmond, and both were utterly surprised. The governor had sent word to her that Mr. Commissioner Wyndham might be calling, but she had expected, as far as she expected anything at all, a brief conversation with a man of whose presence in the colony she knew her friend the governor to be nervous. She had not expected a man so young. Wyndham was thirty, younger than she was. But that was a triviality. What was not trivial was that the instant she saw him she knew that for too long her days had been deserts, and would no longer be. Wyndham had expected a Mrs. Redmond, and saw instead Susannah. Both, at the moment of meeting, thanked the gods.

They stood facing each other for only a few seconds before Susannah collected herself, asked him if he would sit down, and said she would show him the watercolours she had.

"There are only three," she said. "My father sent the others to London as he did them." The first showed a naked aborigine full-face in an attitude of dance, with both arms extended, the right hand clenched and the left held with the open palm displayed. The second showed a group of three blacks, a woman cooking fish over an open fire, a man eating a fish, and another man standing, waiting. The third showed a family going walkabout, the man leading, the woman following with spears and fish in her hands and a child on her back, and a boy bringing up the rear carrying more spears and a glowing firestick.

"The third sketch was always thought the best," said Susannah, "but I prefer the second. I have seen them eat fish like that, holding the head and tail and eating the middle out, nibbling along the bone. They eat with delicacy, and pick the bones clean."

"I like that one too," he said, "but I have seen the third, the one with the family, or something very like it."

"You may have done. There was a set painted of that family, and Mr. Blake the poet had an engraving done from one of them. I do not possess a copy of the engraving, but I think he made them very noble savages indeed, and lost a great deal of the life. Or so I thought."

She was right. The Blake engraving is not so revealing as the original, done in his spare time by a governor making a record of what he saw to send to his superiors in London.

"They are very living," said Wyndham, "and done with love."

"He would have been surprised to hear you say that, but it is true. Everything he did, he did with love."

She put the watercolours back on the table, sat facing Wyndham, smoothed her gown over her lap, and smiled at the man.

"Thank you," he said; and then, "I was awed by your king and queen in the hallway."

So he might have been. George III and his queen, eight feet high in vast gilt frames, confronted the visitor from either side of the entrance to the drawing-room.

She said, "There is no room for them anywhere else. They are too big. Captain Bligh gave them to me, intending them I think as a parting gift, though in truth I believe they were not his but my father's. I know he had them brought from England. But they are the portraits which Captain Bligh loyally toasted the night he was deposed."

"You were there?"

"Yes, I was."

She said no more about that, but went on: "So, you have come to see about the blacks. They do not often come into the town any more, so perhaps you have not seen a single one yet?"

"I have seen two," he said, "and one was dying. It was the afternoon after I came off the ship. As soon as I went to my quarters I was told there were these two natives, under a tree very near the house, and I went to see them. There was an old man and his son. The son had lain under the tree for three days, and was dying. No one knew of what. Every few moments the old man spread himself on the boy's body, trying to revive him with his warmth. Or else he would have him in his arms, rocking him. He lifted up the lids of his eyes, so that he could see the day. But the young man died."

Susannah leaned back in her deep chair and regarded Wyndham, and he, not looking into her eyes, which would have been too direct a communication,

but at her hands, which lay in her lap, thought her
grave and lovely. Each had said something which confirmed to the other the instant *rapport* both had felt.
His compassionate observation of the black and his son
touched her, as her statement that all her father had
done, he had done with love, had struck Wyndham as
a shining and splendid thing for a daughter to say.

"Mr. Wyndham," she said, "if you care to come, I
think I can take you closer to some of the natives than
you might otherwise get at first acquaintance."

"I think you know them well?"

"No. No one knows them well. But I know some of
them, through my father. Bligh treated them well, too.
They have long memories. They will still receive me.
In a few days' time there is to be a corroboree, and, if
you wish, we could attend. It will be within a few
miles' drive."

He would have gone anywhere with her. He said
that if she would send word when, he would send his
carriage, and left with a greater sense of hope, and of
delight to come in her society, than he had ever known
before.

The corroboree began at sunset. The clouds on the
western horizon changed from white to gold, and then
to orange and to deeper and deeper reds. In the eastern sky the heavens became at first, by an illusion,
more blue, and then sank through gradations of blue
into greens and greys. Susannah and Wyndham
watched from a place of honour, on a knoll. As the
stars rose the blacks gathered in greater numbers, appearing unseen from the outback until there were
many hundreds. All were men. No woman of their
own race was there. To say that they danced is too
feeble a word. Fires were lit, and as the men swayed
they flickered with light, out of the light of one fire into darkness and then into the light of another fire.

Then they enacted the hunt, and their spears and throwing sticks glistened in the air and in and out of the light. Susannah and Wyndham followed the flight of one spear which rose high in the sky out of the light and into the stars, and then fell out of the stars.

"It came out of the Southern Cross," she said. "Look, follow those two pointing stars upwards." She took his hand, raised it, and moved it so as to demonstrate to him the pattern of the constellation. "Trace them with your hand. After the two pointing stars, there are the four stars of the Cross. I knew some of my father's sailors, who needed no more than to glance at the sky, who still did this. They called it touching the stars."

She released his hand.

"The blacks say that those two brightest stars in the Cross were two brothers who went hunting, and were trapped by a bushfire, and escaped to the sky."

In front of Susannah and Wyndham the men leaped like silhouettes across the glowing red of an outcrop of sandstone illuminated by the fires. The long yellow grass showed gold in the light. The men's skin glistened. They were anointed with seed oil and painted with charcoal, red ochre, and blue clay. Men became lizards, kangaroos, and trees. Other men, the hunters, sang a chant.

Wyndham said, "I have heard a corroboree called a speaking pantomime. Whoever said that had seen and heard nothing."

"When I was a girl," said Susannah, "when I first came to the colony, my father's gardener, John Easty, who is still gardener in the domain, was taking me into town one day when we met two blacks who knew him. He had given them an axe head. He said to me, 'I will show you two things, one now and one later,' and he moistened his finger with his tongue, and then, while the black man stood still, not at all minding, he rubbed his finger on the man's shoulder so that I could see that he was covered in a caking of dirt, a crust. Then Easty told me to do the same, and I did. I felt the caked dirt, and then, after a lot of rubbing, the skin beneath it. The man submitted, making no protest. Easty said, 'Remember by that, that these men are savages; but I will show you another thing too.' Then he took me to a corroboree, like this, and I felt probably as you now feel, and Easty said to me, as we watched, 'They are savages, and it is foolish for learned philosophers who have never encountered them to say that they are not; but you must also see, as you watch this, that they have souls; and even if not Christian souls, souls as good as ours.' "

"I think you do know them well," said Wyndham.

"No. But in this country I have felt in myself something which I think they feel, and if this is so, then I have something of the beginnings of an understanding. These fables of theirs, peopled with lizards and stars and memories of ancient events, may seem nonsense, but my own world has been peopled with stars, and with the memory of events that were once events but have become so changed in my mind that they are now as much myths as any myths of these men. They are the legends of my own history. I think legends are the spiritual side of events, events changed by long remembering. I could never explain the spirit of the cove, where I have lived since I was a girl, but I know I would never for long leave that place."

"I would have asked you why you stayed."

"I do not *know,* but I feel that the place, because I have lived there, and because others I knew lived there, is now part of my consciousness of everything. And that *is,* to me, everything. The spirit of that place is as real to me as my present consciousness of this moment."

"As real as what you see now?"

"As real as what I feel and hear and see now. And part of what I feel is what I think you may feel. The presence of others is part of ourselves."

"That," said Wyndham, seeing her side-face in the flickering fire, "has been demonstrated to me undeniably this evening."

"I know."

While they were talking, the black women had come into the light, joining the men.

"Oh," said Susannah. "Mr. Wyndham, you may want to leave."

He took her meaning. "Or I may feel later that I ought to have left?"

"Yes."

"Do you wish me to take you away?"

"Stay," she said.

The women too were painted, but differently. A broad charcoal line encircled each breast. Vertical lines were drawn between and above the breasts. On the back of each woman, curved lines represented the boomerang of her lover, and between the maidenhair and navel of each was painted the phallus of her lover.

A woman called Kunnunurra stepped forward, and the man Toongabbe with her. She sank to the earth as if in a faint, and he knelt by her, seeming to whisper in her ear, and then to breathe in her ear, and then to whisper to her breasts.

"Do you know what he says?" Wyndham asked out of the dark.

"He is invoking the spirit, which will become a child."

"His child and hers?"

"We would say so. They would not."

"Tell me."

"For them, a child does not come from the joining of a man and a woman. The man does not beget a child with his body. They see no connection between the joining of a man and a woman and the birth of a child."

"How can they not see?"

"It is not a creation, but an incarnation, or a reincarnation. The spirit has always existed, and always will exist, but does not at this moment live in the embryo form of a human being. They do not get the child. They prepare the way for it. If a spirit enters the woman with the man, that is fortunate, but incidental. If a child is born, it will be the incarnation of a spirit that was waiting to be freed."

"And when a spirit dies, it passes into another?"

"It will continue to exist until it is freed again, and embodied. The blacks are very good at time. Everyone will tell you they are very bad at time, but that is not true. If they say they will come on a given day, or even in a certain month, they may not. They are careless in that sense. They will say, 'I did this tomorrow,' or 'I shall do this yesterday,' because the past and the future are all included in the present."

Wyndham said, "They say that if nothing exists but what a man perceives, then at any given moment, for any man or woman, his past and his future must exist in the present?"

"That is it. They call it the Dreaming. There is a continuity of existence. Sometimes, if they are driven from all the places they have known or their tribe has known, then they lose their sense of the knowledge of the past, and their sense of the place around them, and then they are lost souls. They can will themselves to die. The Dreaming is everything."

The woman and the man were now standing, facing each other, swaying with a slow rhythm.

Susannah said, "The woman is 'singing the man.' That is what they call it, though she does not sing, or utter any sound. If she fixes her gaze upon the man's brow, she is said to be singing his brow, and whatever she sings becomes hers. If she sings his hands, they become hers. Whatever she sings, becomes hers."

The other blacks, who were watching, began a slow chant.

"What do they say?"

"They are describing what is happening. I think it will become evident."

Susannah did not translate, but this was the sense of the chant.

> *Man's prick,*
> *Long one,*
> *Grow long,*
> *Think of her, come into her,*
> *Grow long, open the legs of the woman on the*
> *   bed of leaves,*
> *And having grown long,*
> *Quicken,*
> *Let the quick semen enter her,*
> *Making a way*
> *For the spirit*
> *That will enter her.*
> *Prick, grow long, grow long.*

All the spectators were chanting. The standing, moving couple alone remained silent.

"You see, she is singing the man," said Susannah again.

But that had become, as she said, evident. It was at first a simulation, not an enactment. That was part of the ritual. Kunnunurra and Toongabbe did not at any moment touch.

The eyes of the woman were upon the man who, as she sang him, did grow long, and erect, and did in spirit enter her, thrusting with rhythm into the air until, to a sigh from those who watched, the spirit left him and ejaculated into the air, rising shining, rising among the stars, falling in flickering ribbons against the firelight, and then falling to the earth.

So far as that is plain, it is a true account of what happened: so far as it is exalted, it reflects the exaltation of the participants and of the watchers.

The members of the corroboree slipped away into the darkness to perform the enactment, of which this was the simulation. In the dark Susannah gave Wyndham her hand and said, "Shall we return?"

On the way back in the carriage she broke the silence only once, and said, "They say that the man who loses his Dreaming, or the woman who loses hers, is lost."

Susannah had not known what they were to see, until the women appeared. The men usually danced alone, enacting the hunt. The women rarely appeared too. But when Susannah had known what was going to happen, she said "Stay." She found, on the way back, that she had lost her shawl. She did not say so, but Wyndham understood from her quick glances around. He said nothing either. When the carriage stopped at her door she said, "Good night, Mr. Wyndham," and he handed her down.

Jane undressed her.

"Mr. Wyndham will be here again, ma'am?"

"Yes," said Susannah. "Yes."

Wyndham spent much of that night and the next morning fighting against Susannah. She had taken him utterly outside his experience, and beyond. He ached to go back to Susannah, but he knew that if he did he would not be in command of himself. For a man who, since he was a boy, had been sure of the sovereignty of intellect, this was an extraordinary realization.

His servant shaved him.

"Richardson," he said, "the lady lost her shawl last night."

"Yes, sir," said the man. Richardson had accompanied his master the night before, sitting in front with the driver. While Wyndham and Susannah watched the corroboree, Richardson stayed with the driver who, being a ticket-of-leave convict who had spent many years in the colony, told him a great deal more about Susannah than Wyndham knew. The story, as the driver told it, was in the main true, though enhanced. Baudin had never been an admiral. It would have been incorrect to call Redmond a bloody wife-destroying villain. But the story of the French admiral and the French admiral's boy was essential to any understanding of Susannah, and so Richardson, for the moment, understood her better than his master did. The servant was much older than Wyndham. This was his second generation in service with the family. He had been with Wyndham's father twenty years before, when that gentleman was a cavalry colonel in India. The older Wyndham was now dead, but Richardson had seen him made very happy by a woman, unexpectedly met in Simla, who had showered him with love throughout one last summer before he returned to England, his estates, and his family. Richardson had never told the son, because to do so would have been a breach of confidence, even though the father was many years dead; but he remembered that summer.

So when Wyndham said, "Richardson, the lady lost her shawl last night," the scenes of that Simla summer passed across his mind in the few moments before he replied, "Shall I attempt to recover it, sir?" It was a considered reply, and when Wyndham signified that he might if he wished, he did.

In the afternoon Richardson appeared with the shawl. "I had it from a black, sir."

A nod.

"To whom I thought fit to give a half-guinea, sir."

"Which you shall be reimbursed," said Wyndham.

He understood very well that Richardson had given perhaps a shilling to the ticket-of-leave driver who took him back to the place of the corroboree, and tuppence to the black who had the shawl. But Richardson, although he was prepared to accept a reasonable profit on his enterprise, would have taken good care not to find the shawl unless he thought the finding of it might be to his master's advantage. And Richardson did not suggest, as he might have done, "Shall I see that it is returned, sir?" because he knew that if he had, Wyndham would have felt bound to say, "Of course," and left himself without the means to see Susannah again.

Wyndham was a scholar and a man of the greatest probity, but does it follow that the impulse of life may not run strongly in such a man? At that moment it ran strongly in him, telling him, "Go to her again." Even so, it was three hours before he wrote a short note to Susannah saying he had the shawl and asking if he might take occasion to return it.

She said she would be grateful if he did. He called on her again. For an hour they talked about the colony, his childhood in Camberley, hers in Bath (where he had also briefly lived), his preferences in foxhounds, and her preference for China over India teas, before at last he got up and began the phrases of leave-taking. He supposed she must have other business to attend to. He was glad to have seen her again. Was it not strange they both knew Bath? She listened to these phrases with the smile with which they are customarily received. He had retained the shawl, and now held it out to her. She looked him directly in the eyes; he failed to meet hers, which told her again what she already knew.

As soon as she received Wyndham's note, Susannah had decided she would, if necessary, herself make more than the first move. She thought it unreasonable

that the man should always have to run the risk of re-
buff. It was not that she thought Wyndham lacked the
courage to say what had to be said, but rather that he
might not know how to say it. She was right. When he
failed to meet her eyes she got up. When he did look
at her again and, as if remembering himself, offered
her the shawl, she took one end of it and no more.
They were left standing, each holding one end of a
silken, Indian shawl.

"Mr. Wyndham, say candidly what you wish to
say."

He looked up, and then she said the words which
gave him nothing to lose.

She said, "I think I shall very much regret it if you
do not."

But she was not really asking him to say anything,
only telling him that she knew there were things he
wished he had the words to say, and so she kissed
him swiftly and, taking his hand, put it to her cheek.
At which he put his hand on her shoulder, and then
held her by the waist, and everything was very plain.

Susannah crossed from the bed to the windows. There
was only a crescent moon. She looked back at the bed.
His voice said, "I think you are amused?"

"I am happy," she said. "I am fortunate."

Susannah, while Redmond continued to live with
her, even when he was indifferent to her and more often away than at home, remained faithful to him. After he went, taking John with him, and she was alone,
she could no longer live without lovers. There were
two. But she was a woman of a lovely whole-
heartedness. For her, unless there was wholeness of
heart, there was nothing, and with those two men she
found that there was nothing. The affairs were brief.
But with Wyndham, she knew from the instant she saw

him that they would be worlds to each other. So she said, "I am happy, I am fortunate."

So was he. He was a great deal more fortunate than her. Wyndham had never known well any women but his sisters. He had never before found himself in a woman's bedroom. He was fortunate that Susannah rapidly discovered this without showing she discovered it, and then led him without showing that she led. He did not know he had found a woman who was both bold and gentle. By the laws of any reasonable expectation he should at that moment have felt a remorse born of a conviction that he had sinned. He did feel this later, when he was alone. But because she had led him so assuredly to a contentment of body and mind, he felt no remorse at the time. Beyond anything he ought to have been grateful for that. He would have been, had he known.

She came back to the bed. "I read in this morning's *Gazette*," she said, "that Mr. James Wyndham was due to dine at the barracks tonight with the colonel and his officers."

"Will it seem too terrible, and presumptuous, and tell you too much about my hopes, if I say that I sent my apologies this afternoon?"

She laughed.

"But," he said, "there is something which greatly worries me. I do not know your Christian name."

Of course, he would not. He knew her only as Mrs. William Redmond.

Susannah told him her name.

23

Waltzing Matilda

BEYOND THE WESTERN FOOTHILLS of the Blue Mountains, which divide Sydney from the inland continent, mountains which for twenty years defied all attempts to cross them, lay fine pasturage and most excellent sheep country. There were few gulleys and no swamps, but healthy hills on a gravelly soil. At times it was like a gentleman's park in England, for carriages could be driven over the fine sward between the trees. In other places there was more and lusher grass than in an English meadow, grass two and three feet high. In this country, Redmond had acquired by successive grants and by purchase a sheep station of fine grazing land, as large as an English county. If an observer had been able to survey the whole of that kingdom, on an early evening in late autumn of the year that Jane Bryant and Robert King returned to Sydney—on the evening in fact that James Wyndham discovered Susannah's name—he would have seen at the farthest eastern extent of the land the new mansion of William Redmond; at almost its farthest western extent, at Tongala, the rum-shanty known as the Abandon Hope; and, ten miles to the north of this shanty, a solitary man on the plain preparing to eat a solitary supper.

The man had tramped forty miles that day. He camped near a creek which irrigated the meadows that stretched as far as he could see. On one side of the creek a bank rose, and the man was making camp there on a patch of sandy gravel between two euca-lypts. He filled his billy-can from the creek, and brewed tea over a fire built from the bark and twigs of the eucalypts. He sipped the tea from a tin mug which held a quart, and then returned to the creek to refill the billy, in which he boiled his supper—bacon of the coarsest and saltiest kind. He ate it with a tasteless, hard, ship's biscuit. He was on the tramp. He knew he would find a week's work the next day at the station to the south, and then he would be on the tramp again. That was how he had spent his life since his emancipation two years before. Since his last work he had tramped for seven days, and had seen no human soul except two blacks, whom he would not have counted as human souls. He had not seen a white man for a week, or a white woman for three. A man be-comes used to solitude, but never to the sudden loneli-ness that comes upon him at times from out of that solitude. He threw more bark on his camp fire. Then he removed his neckerchief, put it on the ground, took the pistol from his belt, and placed it on the necker-chief to prevent sand getting into it. A man on the tramp carried all his possessions in a kit-bag tied at the neck. The bag was called his matilda. A man on the tramp, carrying his bag, was said to be waltzing his matilda. That was the plain meaning, but there was another.

When he had eaten, the solitary man on the plain took up his matilda, held it as if it were a woman, and danced silently round the fire he had built. When a lonely man did this, in the outback at the end of the day, then in another sense he was waltzing his matilda.

This was long before the words of the song were written, though the haunting tune was already known and played. It was an old Scots air which Gordon Burns knew because he was a Scot, from Perth. He would have no trouble finding work the next day because in the old days in Perthshire he had been a shepherd, and such men were rare. As would later become well known, Burns was a man of ruddy complexion, five feet eight inches tall, well-built, bearing on his left cheek a small scar in the shape of a star, and speaking with a Scots accent.

At the other extreme of this sheep kingdom, at the same time as Burns found the creek by which he camped, a quarter of an hour before sunset, William Redmond was bringing to an end the hour which he devoted every day to the instruction of his son, John, in the art of shooting. Sunset is very late in the day for that kind of instruction, but Redmond was thorough. He told his son that a man, when it came to it, would not be able to choose the time of day or the state of the light. So he taught John to shoot in full light and half-light, in true light and treacherous light. The boy was eleven years old, and already a good shot with a carbine. In the fading light he had just hit four bottles out of five at thirty yards. His father then hit the fifth with a pistol shot, which was much applauded by the boy.

"Father, why won't you let me use pistols?"

"Because your wrist and your arm are not strong enough. Another year. You will soon handle a carbine as well as I do. Pistols later. Now, in."

They gave the weapons to a bearer, and walked across the lawns to the house. It was a two-storeyed Georgian house, grander than all but two or three in Sydney, and grander than the governor's at Parramatta. Redmond had been lucky. The small grants made to him by Macquarie prospered. Very early he sank two wells and struck water, which saved him in the drought of 1815. He sold fine crops of wool while his neighbours had to slaughter their flocks for mutton. Redmond bought out three neighbours. His prosperity then qualified him for yet larger grants, which he had received in time to enable him to thrive by satisfying an altogether new demand from England after the war. Redmond benefited indirectly from Napoléon who, as part of his plan for One Europe, shipped Spanish merinos to France and Germany. By the 1820s England was unable to compete with the woollen products of those two countries. The only other wool so fine came from New South Wales. Redmond was shipping thousands of bales to Hull and Liverpool. He was a rich man, and his mansion was grand. Of all the sheepmen, probably only Macarthur was richer, but he was showing early signs of madness.

As Redmond entered the hall he glanced at the table, with inserts of Sèvres porcelain, on which his letters were placed. There was a note from his foreman about the next day's journey. He and the boy stretched out in leather chairs in the drawing-room. The mantelpiece was of marble from Italy. Over it was a portrait of the boy done six months before by a Frenchman in Sydney who had introduced himself as formerly of the court of Louis XVI, and, whether or not that was true, had produced a good likeness of John in European hunting dress holding aloft by the legs a pair of dead quail. On a pedestal rested a bust of Redmond by a German sculptor, also resident in Sydney. For dinner, Redmond and his son ate not quail, because there were none in New South Wales, but trout bred in the fish ponds and lamb raised on the station. Redmond's house, like that of a few other big sheepmen, had its own vineyards and made its own wine. It even made its own drinkable champagne, of which the boy was allowed two glasses.

"Father," said the boy, "what is a half brother?"

Redmond answered slowly. "Why?"

"Because I have been told that Jane has come back, and I should like to see her again. And that Mary is dead. I am sorry, because we once went to Manly together, with Mother. Mary was my age, almost. And I have heard that Robert King is back, only they say he is my half brother."

"Yes," said Redmond. He had told the boy nothing himself, but knew that it would all reach him sooner or later through the servants.

"I do not know what a half brother is," said John. "I have never heard him called my half brother before."

"It means that I am your father, but I am not Robert's."

"I do not remember Robert. I remember Mother talked about him. He went to England. But she called him her son too, as well as me."

"Yes."

"So both Robert King and I are her sons, but only I am your son?"

"Yes."

The boy did not pursue this, and by not making things clear to him there and then Redmond ensured that he would learn about Baudin from gossip too. But John did say, "When shall I see Mother? We do go to Sydney sometimes."

"Do you wish to see your mother?"

"When we go to Sydney."

They were not going to Sydney the next day but to visit the overseer of the Tongala Section, five hours' ride away. And in that section, at the same time as Redmond and his son were dining, the residents for the time being of the rum-shanty known as the Abandon Hope were just settling down to mutton and damper.

There were ten of them in a hut ten feet by six. The walls were made of raw sheets of bark stripped from trees, and so was the roof. Mud was piled on top of the roof, making it almost waterproof when it rained, but for weeks at a time there was no rain, and then the mud dried and cracked so that in the day-time those inside could see the sky through the roof, and at night a man approaching the shanty would see light shining up from within. The table was a plank of eucalypt. It had been made when the wood was still green, and the heat of the cabin had curled and warped it so badly that a man had to be careful where he placed his mug of tea, or it would slide off. The chairs were tree-stumps sawn off eighteen inches high. At the hearth, which ran the whole length of one of the shorter sides of the shanty, Joseph Halloran was kneading the damper. He took flour and water, kneaded it, flattened it out, placed the flat cake on hot embers, and then covered it with more embers. After half an hour it was uncovered and eaten straightaway, hot. Cold damper is as soft as brick. The mutton was stewed, as always, and the whole washed down with quarts of tea.

Four men slapped down coins, which Halloran accepted, nodding. They were paying for a week's food. Four others offered nothing, and he made no remark. The last, a raw young man who had started work only three days before, fumbled uneasily in his empty pockets and then offered a handful of tobacco. Halloran shook his head. The customs and courtesies of being on the tramp were new to the young hand. Halloran made his profit on rum. You paid for rum. But if you worked in that section, or if you were passing by and came in for the night, nothing was asked or expected for food and shelter. If a man was known to be flush,

as four of the men in that shanty were flush, then
what he slapped down would be accepted. But if a
man had nothing, nothing was required of him. There
were shanties where even to offer was an insult, but
most keepers would take money from those who could
pay.

"Time to pig down," said Halloran, and he and two
others who were old residents rolled into bunks that
lined the wall opposite the fire. Then sheepskins were
flung on the floor, and the other seven men lay the
length of the hut with their bare feet towards the fire,
and the rest of their bodies covered in any clothes,
blankets, or other skins they had, which they shared
between them.

For a while they smoked.

All were Redmond's men. Two were convicts assigned to him. Six were convicts on ticket-of-leave,
whom he paid. Halloran and the new young man were
emancipists.

"I saw his kitchen in his mansion," said Halloran.
"The vista from that man's kitchen."

The kitchen, though Redmond never saw it, was the
marvel of his house. The drawing-room, the library,
the reception rooms, and the ballroom were opulent.
But the kitchen was a beautiful room and Halloran, a
shanty-keeper, knew this. It was the largest room in
the house. The builder had given it space, width,
height, and light from a clerestory of windows in the
high walls and from a skylight too, and all this light
reflected off whitewashed walls and white scrubbed
flagstones. An iron spit which could roast an ox turned
in a fireplace twelve feet wide and ten feet high.

"And there is a battery," said Halloran, "of copper
saucepans, and broiling pans, and pans to fry in, and
moulds for water-ices, and great ladles, and stirring
spoons four feet long. I counted them as they hung on

the walls, and there were one hundred and eighty-four, all copper, all shining.

"And the vista . . ." Halloran had seen great houses in Ireland, and knew a vista when he saw one. From one end of the kitchen, with the whole room glowing in light reflected from white walls and from that battery of copper things, you could see across the flagstones, through the open door into the courtyard, across raked gravel paths, to the open door of the lobby at the other end, and in the lobby was a floor laid diagonally with squares of black and white Italian marble.

The fug in the shanty was by then very agreeable. It was the warmth induced by the wood fire, tobacco smoke, and rum.

"And the champagne cellar," said Halloran.

None of them had ever tasted champagne.

"There is a shaking table for the champagne," said Halloran.

"What of it?" asked a shepherd.

"It is not a table at all. It's an affair like a great revolving drum which is turned each day. Turned slightly. Every day."

"And why's that?"

"So that the sediment, which is in champagne, gathers on the cork, and leaves the wine sparkling and clear."

"You ever tasted it, sediment or not?" asked the sceptical one.

"I never did."

"Nor ever will. We raise his sheep, and shear his sheep, and bale his wool, and that Redmond, because he's a free object, has his champagne, and all the country he can ride over in one day."

Redmond was considered a free object. Not one of his men knew he too had been a convict. It was something by then unknown in the colony. Redmond was thought to be so aristocratically free an object that he had a nickname, which had stuck: he was known as Pure Merino.

At dawn the next morning Gordon Burns scraped the previous day's mud from his boots, slung his matilda and his billy over his shoulder, and began to walk south by the sun to the Tongala Section. Two hours later, Redmond, having breakfasted on chops, steak, claret, and coffee, set out with his foreman and John to ride there also. His visits of inspection were never announced. He liked his overseers and men to be uncertain when they would see him next. Redmond was a tolerable master. He did not flog his assigned convicts for every loss of a sheep, as one of his insolvent neighbours had. One servant of that man, maddened by constant beatings, loosed a whole flock into the bush, and only half were ever recovered. The loss of two hundred head hastened that man's bankruptcy and the sale of his land to Redmond. For himself, Redmond found it enough to threaten the return of a convict to Sydney, which generally meant an appearance before a magistrate who was a friend of Redmond's, and then the chain gang. He had sent three men back in the previous year and was feared for it. But he did not flog his men, and in that way was a great deal better than many. But he was not a man who was admired, only envied.

Burns reached Tongala before noon. The overseer, who knew him from the year before, took him on. Redmond's party arrived by mid-afternoon. The overseer conducted a tour of sheep-pens, fences, barns, wool sheds, bullocks and bullock-drays, tools and tackle. Redmond inspected the wages' books. He looked round the overseer's office, at the horse-hobbles, tin dishes, pannikins, stock-whips, guns, powder canisters, and a collection of pharmacist's bottles containing cure-alls for the diseases of sheep, who are delicate animals, for ever ailing. He glanced at the overseer's room, where he and John would sleep that night before returning the next day. The overseer and the foreman would sleep in the bullock stables.

"Any new hands?" asked Redmond.

"Two, sir. One I've had four days now. Ticket-of-leave man from the town."

"Not much use with sheep?"

"I keep him at fence-mending. If he stays, he'll learn."

"And the other?"

"Came in today, just ahead of you, sir. A good man."

"Seen him before then?"

"Last season, sir."

"Why do you never keep good men?"

"It's always the best that are restless. Always the best that go off on the tramp, sir. This man's a shepherd."

"We'll see the shanty."

This was unwise. The shanty was Redmond's, like everything else on that land. Halloran was his hut-keeper, paid by him, though also allowed to take a cut of rum profits. But the men's shanty was their territory, and a wiser master than Redmond would have left it alone.

The overseer waited, hoping by his silence to encourage Redmond not to go to the Abandon Hope.

"At sundown," said Redmond.

So at sundown they went to the shanty. The overseer, carefully preceding Redmond, knocked on the open door. Nobody ever knocked on the bark door of the shanty. Halloran, who was bending over a spit by the fire, did not look round but shouted, "Whoever that is that knocks, the door's open."

Redmond stepped into the fug of tobacco and roast-

ing meat. No one stirred. The talk stopped. Halloran,
half-looking round, saw the high leather boots in the
doorway, and straightened up.

"Good day, Mr. Redmond. Would you be taking a
drink with us?"

Redmond looked round at the ten men sitting on
the tree-stumps which did for chairs, or else lounging
on the ground. No one stood up for him, not even his
assigned convicts.

"And is that your fine son with you, sir?" asked
Halloran.

Redmond said, "This is my son. Which are the two
new men?"

The very raw young man who had been four days
at the station did get up. "Me, sir."

Redmond glanced at him. He evidently was not the
shepherd.

"The man who is a shepherd," he said.

"Here," said Burns, from the floor.

"Name?"

"Burns."

"Shepherd, Burns?"

"Aye."

"Then," said Redmond, "you know a lamb from a
ewe."

The overseer caught Halloran's eye. The bolder men
in the hut looked steadily at Redmond and said nothing. The less bold looked at the dirt floor. What the
overseer had known within ten yards of the shanty,
and what Redmond noticed as soon as he stepped inside, was that tonight the men were not eating old
mutton. Ewes will bear lambs until they are old and
stringy, and it was only then, when the flesh was tough
and tasteless, that they were killed to feed the station-
hands. For weeks the men had eaten old stewed mutton. That night of all nights there was not mutton but
lamb, which was forbidden. Two lambs were roasting

over the fire, and the aroma was not that of stewing mutton.

"Aye," said Burns, "I know a lamb from a ewe, mister."

It was in part due to Burns that there was roast lamb that night. The year before, when he had passed that way, working his week or two weeks before going on, he and Halloran had become mates. When he had appeared that day, it was in the nature of a celebration that he and Halloran had gone and picked out two lambs.

Redmond surveyed Burns. "Crawler?" he asked.

Crawler was a term of offence. A crawler was an assigned convict who absconded from his master and lived how he could, by petty theft if possible, by work if he had to. Burns, who was an emancipist, held his peace.

"Crawler?" said Redmond again.

Burns had got the scar on his cheek in a brawl in a Perthshire tavern. The other man had come off worse, and the assault had brought Burns to the other side of the world. By the time Redmond came to the shanty, Burns had drunk his share of rum and water. He got to his feet.

"No crawler, mister. I crawl to no man, though that man be Pure Merino."

Redmond put his hand to his pistol.

"The boy, sir," said the overseer, putting himself between Burns and Redmond.

Redmond pushed his overseer aside, drew the pistol, and held it loosely, with the barrel pointing down.

"Out," he said to Burns.

It had begun to rain. Inside, first drops and then rivulets fell from the roof bark, and spattered and hissed as they fell on the fire. Outside it was pelting.

"Out," said Redmond.

Burns looked at the pistol, at Redmond, at the boy,

at the overseer, and then round the shanty. He raised
a hand in farewell to Halloran.

Redmond stepped aside. Burns stooped down,
swung his matilda over his shoulder, put on his hat,
and walked past Redmond into the rain. Six feet
from the shanty he stopped, looked back at Redmond,
and said, "Purer Merino I never saw, mister."

Redmond raised the pistol and fired over the man's
head. Burns considered, spat on the ground, and
walked away. Then, while Redmond remained fifteen
minutes in the shanty to shelter from the rain, Burns
walked to the stables and saddled the finest horse,
which was Redmond's bay, and rode into the outback.
He rode for three hours before the rain stopped. He
rode on until he came to country where rain had not
fallen at all and the ground was dry. Then he hobbled
his mare, lit a fire, and stood by it in his soaking
clothes, from which the steam rose. First he dried one
side, and then turned and dried the other. His boots
remained sodden. He brewed tea, drank the last of the
rum with which he had filled his flask at the Abandon
Hope, and then, huddled in an opossum rug that he
took from his matilda, rode on. By taking the horse he
had become an outlaw. Sun-up, which found him still
riding, was the dawn of Gordon Burns's first day as a
bushranger.

24

—∽◦∾—

Woman in a Lighted Doorway

"WE, Jorgen Jorgensen," said Jorgen Jorgensen in Susannah's sitting-room, "thereupon proclaimed that we
did not hesitate to announce [laughter from Susan-
nah] that the people of Iceland had thrown off the
intolerable yoke of the Danish oppressor and had
unanimously called Us to be Monarch and Head of
State."

Mr. Jorgensen was a Dane who had once upon a
time seized the throne of Iceland. It was a fact. It was
for this and other matters of State—principally fraud
and the amassing in London of most imaginative debts
with no means or intent to repay—that he found himself a convict in New South Wales, in transit, on his
way to the newer convict colony of Tasmania. In Sydney, since he was harmless, he was allowed ashore to
pay social calls, the captain of the convict transport
requiring only a written assurance, given on his word
as a gentleman, that he would return. This he gave,
signing the document "Jorgen, R."

He was good company, took it very well when
others found it impossible not to smile or even laugh
at his adventures as he related them, and laughed

320

himself. Without any doubt he had proclaimed himself king of Iceland and maintained himself in great state until the Danish government requested his removal and the British sent a frigate to take him under arrest to London.

"How," said Susannah, "was your unanimous call to the throne achieved?"

"By Ourselves," said Jorgensen, "with twelve men and a brace of pistols. We took the governor's residence with ease. The Danish governor, Count Tramp [a smile from Susannah, but that was the man's name], was resting on a sofa with a Danish lady."

And how had King Jorgen maintained the government?

"In Iceland, ma'am, there are only the common people and the priests. I halved the taxes of the common people, and doubled the stipends of the priests."

Jorgensen accepted more tea, and gave the briefest sketch of a career in which he had gambled in London, Lisbon, and the Cape of Good Hope, taken part in several revolutions, captained two ships, offered his services as a spy against the Americans to the British Foreign Office, and also—which was his reason for calling on Susannah—met the late Governor King in a London coffee house after his return from the colony. Jorgensen was a famous liar, but it seemed from the details of his narrative that the meeting with King was genuine. They had played chess. Jorgensen recalled a game his opponent won with a strategy known as the Queen's Walk, which Susannah knew was typical of her father's play. She was touched to hear him remembered.

Then followed more European escapades of Jorgensen's, the account of which he ended with this sentence: "I will not attempt," he said, "to describe the amazing panorama of the field of Waterloo." At which Susannah dissolved into laughter and Wyndham, who

was just that moment entering the room, leaned on
the doorpost and tried unsuccessfully to hide his.

Susannah introduced Mr. Commissioner Wyndham
to Mr. Jorgensen, king of Iceland.

"Iceland?" said Wyndham.

Jorgensen inclined his head. "We have," he said,
"found Ourselves pushed to the front of affairs at both
ends of the earth. But, Mr. Commissioner, I would not
mislead you into thinking Our career was all kingship.
Monarch We have been, but also naval captain, revo-
lutionist, British diplomatic agent, dramatist, preacher,
political prisoner, gambler, hospital pharmacist, explorer, and commercial traveller; and the most demanding of these professions, We may say, was that
of hospital pharmacist. An error by a monarch is
generally retrievable, but one by a pharmacist sometimes not."

"If," said Wyndham, "you are a competent pharmacist, I could give you a note to the government surgeon
in Tasmania which might get you a ticket-of-leave and
employment."

Jorgensen graciously accepted the offer and took
his leave.

Wyndham asked Susannah, "Shall we go out?"

She picked up a sketching block and pencils, and
they left the house, walking in the direction of Farm
Cove and Woolloomooloo Bay, half a mile to the east.
She never walked with him on the lawns down to
Sydney Cove. On the eastern shore of Farm Cove,
very near the point where the waters of the cove met
those of the harbour, she sat on a sandstone shelf in
the shade of a hanging rock. Skirts were now much
fuller, waists were at the waist, sleeves were long,
necks high, and hats wide-brimmed. Susannah gave
Wyndham the sketching block, arranged the skirts
around her so that the folds of white muslin fell either
side of her on the sandstone, waited while he sat on

the grass and took up his pencil, and then turned her
face towards the harbour. The place and the situation
were familiar to them. Wyndham was more than a
competent artist with the pencil. He had not done the
Grand Tour, as he would have done but for the war,
but the galleries and museums and great houses of
England contained between them, in objects that had
been bought or looted from all over the world, as
much as a man could see in many Italian cities.
Wyndham was familiar with the etchings of Rem-
brandt and the drawings of Fragonard and Watteau.
He knew life in a drawing when he saw it, which was
why he had seen it in Governor King's watercolours
of aborigines.

Susannah did not pose for Wyndham. She just sat
there, leaning back on her hands. She took off her hat
and let down her hair, taking out the pins and then
shaking out the hair with a toss of her head. When the
sun fell lower in the west, the overhanging rock no
longer gave shade, and her face was lit by the full
rays. After a while she replaced the hat and shaded
herself again.

Wyndham sketched quickly. He was not making
one careful portrait but creating several figures on the
same large sheet, and he was drawing her not only as
she appeared before him, but as she appeared in his
recollection and his imagination. It had begun a few
weeks before, when he sketched her head and shoulders, caught almost a likeness, and was encouraged by
this to draw her standing, sitting, and then lying. He
had always drawn her in this place, and yet the first
sketch in which he caught her to the life was one of
Susannah full-face, with grave eyes and half-smiling
mouth which, when he showed her, she instantly
recognized for what it was. He had drawn only her
features, nothing else, but what she recognized was
the moment and the place, which was not at the rock.

It was herself looking up at him as she lay in her bed, and what was also present in that sketch was the woman's consciousness of the man looking down at her.

Wyndham had first drawn her reclining, dressed, and alone. Then reclining, dressed, while the figure of a man stood looking down at her. Then he drew the courtly pose of the man helping the woman to her feet. Then the man holding the woman by the hands as she lowered herself to the ground. The two figures then went through the progressions of a man with a woman. Susannah sitting upright on a sofa with Wyndham standing before her, as if talking. Susannah reclining on a sofa with his head in her lap. Susannah lying on that sofa half-dressed, holding out her arms to her lover. Then there was Susannah lying with her lover beside her. Then there was Susannah entered and embraced by him. In all these scenes, the face of the man was never seen, but hers always. Over the weeks, as he drew, Wyndham showed her the sketches sheet by sheet.

She once asked, "But don't you separate yourself from me, don't you stand apart as it were, when you see and draw yourself and me like that?"

"I do not separate myself. I could not. I am there with you. But I am also an observer. I suppose that is why I can never draw my own face."

The best of the drawings without any doubt was that of Susannah's head alone, as she looked up half-smiling. It was the best until that afternoon.

After half an hour she said, "Now you must let me see."

He had drawn her head and shoulders, with her hair up, and with her hair shaken out. He had drawn her hatless and with the wide-brimmed hat. Then he had achieved two small masterpieces. The first showed Susannah lying on the bed by now so familiar to them, entered by her lover. What Wyndham had achieved for the first time was the absorption of the man as it showed in the lines of his back, and the intentness of the woman in the clasp of her arms round the man's shoulders, and in the raptness of her face. That was the first sketch. The second was an ideal—two lovers locked together, supported by nothing, lying on nothing, floating as if in air. It was all essence, and, for what it mattered, was technically the better of the two drawings. But the first had life and substance. Susannah passed the backs of her fingers lightly across the lines of the first drawing, and then, stopping her fingers at the representation of her own face, said, "I love you for that. It is not as I have ever seen myself, but I know it is how I feel."

Late that night they lay in bed talking. She lay with her back to him, and his right hand rested lightly on her hip. They had known each other for a few months, yet the gesture seemed as accustomed as that of a man to his wife, married many years and well beloved.

"Then the report on the blacks is done?" she said.

"Written and dispatched."

James Wyndham had sent to London a report which would, like his report on Irish workhouses, be very much noticed. He wrote that he doubted if more than a few of the white population of New South Wales understood the blacks, and had met no single black who understood the whites. Their conception of the soul, life, work, and property was in every fundamental feature different from that of an English Christian. The state of being a Christian was almost enough in itself to disable a man from an understanding of the blacks, but all Christian benevolence was necessary if those blacks were not to die, and the race become extinct. Yet if anything could more than

Christianity disable a man from an understanding of these poor savages, it was an adherence to Rousseau's doctrine of the Noble Savage. The blacks did show manliness and generosity in some circumstances, but nobility was an attribute of plenty—of a plenty of sustenance for both spirit and body. As to bodily sustenance, the blacks around Sydney were being driven from the richest of their traditional hunting and fishing grounds. As to the spirit, they were losing their Dreaming. He explained the concept of the Dreaming. The older and weaker civilization of the blacks would not withstand the impact of the newer and more vigorous civilization of the whites. Furthermore, the whites had resorted, sometimes in fear and sometimes from cupidity, to massacre; and the blacks, bewildered at every turn, had been guilty of treachery and cannibalism. Wyndham then made a recommendation which was condemned as impractically radical. A mixture of the races was impossible. Even an association was difficult and full of dangers for both black and white. He advised His Majesty's government to segregate the two races, and to protect the homelands of the blacks. The alternative was a drift to disaster, and probable extermination. He was, with respect, His Majesty's humble servant, James Wyndham, Commissioner.

There was not a word in that report which was not written by Wyndham, or which did not express the convictions formed by his own mind, but the formation had been assisted by Susannah. In London the report would be debated in the Lords, Wyndham marked down once again as a man whose rise would be rapid, and nothing would be done.

In bed, Susannah said, "And now I have something more to be grateful to Jane for." She had. Wyndham would normally have returned with his report. But the escape of Jane and the others, and the reports in the

London press of the reception at Bedford Square, had created a demand for an inquiry into the whole business of transportation, to which the government thought it prudent to accede.

"Wyndham's there," said the secretary of state. "Get him to do it." The prime minister assumed this expressed the consensus of Cabinet? Very well.

"If he'll stay there," said the Irish secretary. "It's asking a lot of a chap to swallow one dose of Ireland and now two of New South Wales."

Consensus of Cabinet was that Wyndham was a good fellow who would do what he was asked. So he might have done, but he did not think about reasons. He stayed for Susannah.

So, that night, lying by Susannah's side, Wyndham said, "I am grateful to Jane too. You know, when I start on transportation in a week's time, I shall have Jane as witness and Robert appearing before me as advocate for the emancipists."

"That is proper?" asked Susannah.

"To hear Jane as a witness is proper. To hear Robert as counsel: I have thought about that. He knows how things are between us?"

"Of course. He has seen us together."

"If this were London, I should recuse myself. But it is Sydney, and there is no one to take my place, and precious few to take Robert's if he were to withdraw. Anyway, I shall not hear him as your son, but as counsel for his clients, and that will be understood by us both."

Susannah said, "But, James, you must be prudent. You are commissioner. I must not compromise you. It did not matter with the blacks. But an inquiry into transportation will touch Redmond. Without transportation, what will he do for shepherds? I am still his wife, and if he knew of us, he could make a great deal of it."

"I shall hear him as I would anyone else."

"But be prudent. Do not be seen with me too much."

But how far could Susannah herself be prudent? It is one of the graces of whole-heartedness that it is sometimes incapable of prudence. They had been so far secure because they were seen together only by those on whose loyalty they could depend. To prepare his report on the blacks, Wyndham had to travel. He was naturally away from his town lodgings for two or three nights at a time. He did not often stay the night with Susannah. There were the afternoons. But when he did stay, when he would not go or she would not let him go, this was known only to his man, Richardson, and to Jane; and Richardson was as loyal to Wyndham as Jane to Susannah. Susannah's new maid had met Wyndham early some mornings, but she stood aside and said not a word. Jane was sure of her. They were safe.

In the first week of his inquiry into transportation, Wyndham went to hear witnesses at Newcastle, and to see for himself how the penal settlement there was conducted. It was now reformed. He was to return on the Saturday, but on Friday received a message from the governor asking him to come to Parramatta at the week-end if he possibly could, on a matter of urgency. He wrote to the governor saying he would come, and to Susannah that he would not now be back until Sunday or even Monday.

"Wyndham," said the governor, and the two men, after their first apprehension of each other, were now friends, "you have received or you will receive an application from a man called Tyrone to give evidence before you."

"Tyrone?"

"He is in the madhouse here."

Wyndham, who had not remembered the name, did remember a letter from the madhouse.

"Wyndham, I don't know what that letter said. The superintendent would normally read any letter sent by an inmate, but thought it would be improper to intercept a letter addressed to you as commissioner. That was my opinion too."

"I do not remember that it was more than a simple application to give evidence."

"Now," said the governor, "it would be improper for me to make any request to you in respect of that application, so I shan't. I'm not sure it isn't improper for me as governor to say anything at all to you in the matter, so if you stop me, there's an end to it. But I'd like to offer you some information which might save a lot of distress. I'll say nothing about the application, which is up to you, but I want to tell you about an event of two years ago."

Wyndham nodded. The governor told him the story of the six men drowned in chains. Wyndham understood that if Tyrone, formerly a captain and now a lunatic, were to appear, he would probably tell the whole story, thinking in his mad way to exonerate himself. The colony would be inflamed, the whole affair of the escape would once again be opened up, and, most of all, Jane Bryant would know for the first time how her husband died.

Wyndham accepted some whisky. He began to see how the closeness of the colony led to corruption, the smallest of corruptions at first, but leading to who knew what? In London he would not have heard Robert as counsel: here he would. Now, in the graver matter of Tyrone, he knew that his judgement was swayed, and he knew that his mind was already made up, by consideration for Jane Bryant, a woman he knew. He fell back on a device of procedure, and

prayed that he might be doing right. His commission
gave him wide discretions.

He said, "An insane man might by reason of that
insanity be incapacitated from giving evidence. That's
one thing. Another is that there's nothing in my commission which says where I shall hear evidence. The
man need not come before me. I may go to the man
and hear him at the madhouse."

Nothing more was said. What Wyndham proposed
to do was in every way proper. Only he knew that his
reasons for acting in that way were those of policy.
And there he was hard on himself. In humanity to any
woman whose husband had died as Jane's had, he
would have heard such evidence in private, had he
known what it was likely to be. He would visit Tyrone
in the madhouse.

He dined with the governor. At nine o'clock, when
they were smoking and talking, a servant brought a
note. Wyndham broke the seal carelessly. Not until he
opened it did he realize it was from Susannah. Just
as he had once not known her Christian name, he still
did not know her handwriting. She had never written
to him before. There had been no occasion. But that
night she could hardly bear his longer absence, and
she wrote. The note said, "Darling, please come back
tonight if you conceivably can. Please come back."
She signed herself with the single initial "S."

The servant said the messenger was waiting for a
reply.

"Is there anything? . . ." asked the governor.

"If I may," said Wyndham.

The governor waved him to the study. Wyndham
took up a pen and wrote, "Susannah—I so much want
to come, but it would mean complicated excuses, and
I don't see how I can. I'll be back early tomorrow."
He sealed the note and sent it out to the messenger.

He returned to the governor, and they did not retire

until eleven, a late hour in a colony which rose with the sun. Wyndham always slept well, but now he did not sleep. Just past midnight he dressed, roused his clerk, and said he was returning to Sydney. He would take the clerk's mare. The carriage and the clerk could stay at Parramatta until Monday, when he would return to see the man Tyrone. Wyndham left a note for the governor saying he had after all decided that he should have returned in response to the message he had received, and offering apologies. Then he saddled the horse himself and rode to Sydney.

It was only fifteen miles on a dry, warm, moonlit night, but even so it was extraordinary to travel that road alone, so late. He was challenged by sentries as he left Parramatta, three times along the road, and twice in Sydney, once as he entered the town and the second time as he approached the domain. Each time he answered with the single word, "Officer"—the response required from any gentleman, whether he was ensign or governor. The truth of this response was never doubted. It was two o'clock before he arrived at Susannah's. He led the mare into the stables, unsaddled her, threw a blanket over her, and fed and watered her. You cannot enter a stables silently. The other horses were roused, and by the time Wyndham walked across the courtyard to the house there was already a light in the hallway and in one of the upper rooms. He was seen. The door opened before he could ring, and there was Susannah.

She stood at the open door, barefoot and in her night-dress. He had seen her like that a hundred times before; and yet he had never once seen her like that. Susannah, in that night-dress, in her bedroom, he had seen many times. But now the time and the place changed the nature of everything. Susannah in that night-dress in the doorway open to the domain, and at night, was something else, and quite different. Su-

sannah in her bare feet, there, was something else and
different. Her appearing there expressed in that scene
and in that moment all the hope, anxiety, longing,
fear, warmth, and love that was in her.

She said, "Oh, I did not think you would come."

He enclosed her in his arms. Over her shoulder he
saw a figure with a candle at the top of the staircase.
It was Jane. She recognized who it was at the door,
and vanished. Susannah held Wyndham. "I did not
think you would come."

Of course the sentinels at the domain recognized that
it was Wyndham who answered their challenge, and
saw to whose house he rode, and they talked among
themselves. But they thought it nothing to Wyndham's
discredit. It showed that even commissioners were human, and he was considered a lucky devil. Wyndham
and Susannah were also seen by another observer as
they embraced in the lighted doorway, but there was
no talk of that at all, at present. The governor, when
he received Wyndham's note next morning, thought it
no part of his duty to surmise, but, having nevertheless surmised, hoped for Wyndham's sake that he
would be circumspect. Wyndham returned to Parramatta to see Tyrone in the madhouse alone, and heard
again the story he already knew from the governor.
Tyrone was pleased that the commissioner should
come to him rather than summon him, thinking this
showed the importance attached to the evidence he
had to give. For a year Wyndham toured the colony,
and heard anyone who wished to be heard. He heard
Redmond as spokesman for the wool interest, and
Redmond departed satisfied that he had convinced
Wyndham of the importance to New South Wales of
the wool trade, which he had, and that convicts were
essential to the well-being of the colony.

Then it was time for Wyndham to go. He would

write his report on the ship on the passage to England. He had been in the colony eighteen months. He had to leave Susannah. He did not ask her to come with him, not because he did not want to, but because he knew he could not, and that her reply in any case would be a refusal. It would be an impossible proposal. For him to ask her, for them to discuss it, and then for her to decline, would have done nothing but cause pain. She was still married to Redmond. Only kings and great dukes divorced. Each single divorce required a separate Act of Parliament. Susannah knew she could never be Wyndham's wife. So, even between themselves, they never thought of returning together. Everything made it hopeless. For Wyndham to return with the wife of a man who was principal spokesman for the colony's wool interest would also have vitiated large parts of his report. They had to part, and they knew this and faced it.

Wyndham was completely changed by Susannah. In eighteen months she had done for his instinct and spirit what his tutors, schoolmasters, the university, and the practice of politics had done, over nearly thirty years, for his intellect. Not that instinct and intellect can be divided. That is the point. In Wyndham they no longer were.

They walked together. He said, "It will be spring now, in England."

She said, "You have missed the spring? Englishmen do here, for several years. You have missed the trees coming into leaf all at once, and the flowers coming into bloom, and the sudden greenness?"

"I suppose I have. You put it more vividly than I have felt it. But I have felt it."

She stopped, and took a leaf from a young eucalypt. "Oh, we have brought in fruit trees from Europe. Some I planted are now quite grown. And in the town there are plane trees, which were brought in,

and they lose their leaves in the winter, and then
come into leaf and give shade in the summer. But
their foliage now seems bright to me. I am used to the
tints of greys and greens that are everywhere here."
She turned over the eucalypt leaf in her fingers, a narrow leaf, olive-green above, grey beneath, without
gloss. "It is subtle," she said. "The tints are very gentle."

She had told him something about Baudin, though
never his name. It had aroused in him a twinge of that
most absurd and destructive of emotions, a jealousy of
past things, which he felt and then dismissed. She had
told Wyndham what she did only to explain that, if
she could, she would not grieve for him as she had
for Baudin. Not because she did not love Wyndham,
but because grief destroyed the spirit.

"And if you wish to please me," she said, "you will
not grieve for me, but remember me with happiness.
I shall remember you with happiness. You gave me
back my Dreaming, and I shall not lose it again."

A few days before his departure, when they went
to the hanging rock for the last time, she asked him to
give her the drawing which had first caught her to the
life—only a head and shoulders, but the one that
showed her consciousness of him in her eyes.

Wyndham took the other sketches back to England
with him, and, at his death, which was many years
after this story ends, they passed with his other papers
to his Cambridge college. His career had been a brilliant one. He had ended by accepting an earldom but
declining the viceroyalty of India in order to become
instead Regius Professor of Classics at Cambridge, a
sacrifice which, since the Chair was not even at Ox-
ford but only at Cambridge, was thought to be excessive. The Fellows of his old college gathered one
evening to consider a portfolio, found among his state
papers, and marked "New South Wales, Susannah."

As the first drawings were taken from the portfolio, a
eucalypt leaf fluttered loose and dropped on to the
table. None of the Fellows recognized it. They gazed
at the sketches in silence. All the Fellows were bach-
elors, many of them clergymen, and most of them
celibate. It was by then two-thirds of the way through
Victoria's reign, and the instincts of these gentlemen
should have been to destroy the portfolio. Not one of
them made such a suggestion. The Master of the college, an aged man, looked long at one drawing and
with a movement of his hand followed the lines of it
almost as Susannah did when she first saw it the afternoon Wyndham drew it. Then there was another,
which moved them all, which showed a woman in a
lighted doorway, at night. The drawings were depos-
ited in the college library along with the rest of the
Wyndham papers, and the portfolio marked "New
South Wales, Susannah," took its place with others
marked "Soudan," "Jamaica," "British Columbia,"
"Bengal," and with the names of other parts of the
Empire where Wyndham became commissioner or,
later in his long career, governor.

Susannah framed the drawing she kept, and hung it in
her sitting-room. It was only a head-and-shoulders but
visitors often looked at it, and then returned to it,
sensing that there was more to it than they could see.

25

———————⟨ঞ⟩———————

Great Oaks, and the Wild Colonial Boy

IN THE SEVEN YEARS after Gordon Burns was driven
out, and outlawed himself by the theft of Redmond's
mare, the Tongala Section greatly prospered. Where
there were once ten shepherds and a hut-keeper, there
were now thirty shepherds, each with eight hundred
sheep. Halloran was still hut-keeper, but his shanty
grew to be three times the size it was, and he had two
men under him to serve up mutton and damper, and
more mutton and damper, washed down with quarts
of tea.

"Listen to this," said Halloran, one supper-time,
holding up a copy of a Sydney newspaper three weeks
old. "Pure Merino has been lecturing the assembly
again about Great Oaks." Halloran was one of only
two men of the thirty gathered in the shanty who
could read, and his reading aloud was a large part of
their entertainment. Redmond had become a member
of the colony's legislative assembly which, though it
could legislate for practically nothing, certainly assembled and thundered away on mighty matters.

Redmond was reported at length. As the colony
grew and prospered, he said, and as the day grew

closer when they would inevitably govern their own
affairs, when the assembly would be responsible not
to the governor in Sydney but directly to His Sovereign
Majesty the King, it behoved them to consider what
form the government of the newly independent colony
should take. There would of course be an elected
Lower House, for was theirs not a country of free
men? ("Hear, hear.") Though the extent of the franchise was a matter to be decided. ("Hear, hear.") But
there should also, as in the Mother Country, be preserved an ordered society, an hierarchy, the pinnacle
of which should be an aristocracy. Aristocracy was
that Great Oak (here the honourable member was interrupted by cries of "Hear, hear" from those members who thought of themselves likewise as Great
Oaks, and by howls of laughter from those other members who had been harangued once too often about
Great Oaks on pinnacles). Aristocracy, as the honourable member was saying, was that Great Oak which
gave shelter to, and under whose shading foliage
thrived, the honest commerce of their fledgling continent. (Cries of "Baa, baa," from certain members.)
Honourable members, said Redmond, might bleat if
they wished. The assembly would notice that those
members who went "Baa" were merchants whose fortunes were based on the shipment of commodities
other than wool, who had grown rich on whale oil,
who had prospered on the provision of whalebone stays
for ladies' corsets. He might call them the members
for blubber-and-stays. ("Order, order.") An aristocracy could be created only by His Britannic Majesty, whose loyal servants they all were, but he would
dare to say that no finer candidates for a new House
of Peers could have arisen than had done so from the
sheepmen of this colony. (Cries of "Squatter" and
"Sheep king.") Mr. Redmond said he had been called
both these things, and proudly accepted both titles.

What were hurled at him as gibes he accepted, with humility, as compliments. (Laughter.) They might laugh, but had not the fortune of the colony been made from the world's finest fleece, and had he not advised settlers for years, many members among them, to put their money into four legs? The wool trade itself had indeed proved a Great Oak. (Laughter and further cries of "Baa.")

What the newspapers did not say, because the reporters were ordered not to mention it, was that at this point the blubber-and-stays interest began to sing "The Four-Legged Oak," to the hymn tune of "The Old Rugged Cross." But in the shanty, the thirty men were already bawling the song. Redmond was repetitious in his speeches, and the response of the blubber-and-stays men was well known.

It was in the middle of this uproar that Shaw, the driver of a bullock wagon, ran into the shanty and silenced them all by shouting, "Johnny's shot. The poor sod's shot bad." They brought him in and laid him on sheepskins. He was a shepherd, and still clasped the silver-headed crook he had brought with him from the old country. They took it from his hands. He was dying. One ball from a carbine had pierced his throat, making a neat wound as it entered, and a larger, ragged wound as it went out at the back of his neck.

"Bushranger," said the driver. "We was ambushed two miles out. A horseman. But when he rode up to us, after he shot Johnny, he never came close, but looked and turned away. He did it for nothing." The driver was his mate, and stood with tears of anger in his eyes as Johnny died. He lived ten minutes and, though he gasped and tried to speak, the blood bubbled in his throat and he could not say a word.

Halloran left the cooking to his two assistants, and with Shaw and two others carried the body of John

Erskine to an outhouse and laid it out. "He was a good man," said Halloran. "He was a careful shepherd. You could tell that by the way he walked among his animals, without disturbing them. They never feared him or ran from him. It is a sure sign."

The four men stood round the body.

Halloran told Shaw, "Go back to the shanty and get some rum for yourself. We will come afterwards."

After he went, Halloran looked at his two companions and said, "Now, boys."

Erskine had been an unusual man. He understood sheep. That was a gift possessed by perhaps six of the thirty men on that section. He had also been determined to have a sheep run of his own one day, and that was a determination shared by no one else. The odds against an emancipist were so great they were impossible. An honest emancipist could hardly thrive. An ex-convict who made money generally did so at the expense of his former fellows, selling them high meat at high prices, or sozzling them with rum until they were too drunk to know he charged them for three times what they consumed. An emancipist who thrived, most often did so by taking the week's pay of a man in one drunken night. Erskine had wanted to be a sheepman. If he had been a settler, he could have a grant of three thousand acres for the asking. An emancipist could hope for only one hundred acres, useless for sheep. But Erskine had saved for five years and possessed £396 sterling. Although the currency was the dollar still, accounts were made up and wages reckoned in sterling and the equivalent paid in dollars, which, when paid into a bank, were again converted back to sterling. By each conversion the wage-earner lost a percentage, but Erskine had sterling in the bank. He had meant to take up his grant of one hundred acres, buy another two hundred acres, borrow enough for four hundred sheep, and then take his chance. It

was not much of a chance. He would have had to buy
newly shorn sheep. It would have been a year before
he could shear them again, and then six months before he got paid for the wool by the Sydney merchant.
In that time, a single drought, or a pack of dingoes,
or an ordinary epidemic of disease could ruin him.
Sheep were a rich man's game. A rich man could
wisely put all he had in four legs. If he had capital, he
would survive. If he survived, he could not help becoming richer. A poor man had one chance in a hundred. But Erskine had meant to try. Now he was dead,
and his money was in a Sydney bank. He had no
known family. He had made no will. His £396 would
be forfeit to the colony.

"Well, boys," said Halloran, "it is up to us to find
Erskine's will. Shaw was his mate, and I know he left
it all to him."

"Bang to rights," said the second man. The third
nodded.

Halloran wrote a will. He had done this for men before, though before their deaths. He had once been
an attorney's clerk in Dublin and knew a form of
words. Then the dead man had to sign.

"While there is still life in him," said Halloran; and
then, so that he could, if it came to it, swear that the
man signed while there was still life in him, he caught
a fly in his cupped hands and put it into the dead
man's mouth, which he closed. Then, taking the stiff-
ening fingers, he placed the pen in them, and guided
the hand so that by the side of the words, "John
Erskine, His Mark," the hand of Erskine made a cross.

"Now you must witness," said Halloran. He had
asked these two men because he knew one could write
and the other, though he could not properly write,
could copy the characters which represented his name
if they were written out for him to copy. The will was
made, signed, and witnessed. The fly was released

from the dead man's mouth. Halloran took the paper and folded and refolded it back and forth until it frayed, and then put it in Erskine's pocket to be found the next day. Then they covered the dead man and left him.

Once a year for the previous seven years, Redmond had suffered a raid from a bushranger who was one of many celebrated in ballads of the time as the Wild Colonial Boy. He broke into Redmond's Sydney office and did not crack the safe but carried safe and all away. In two successive years he held up wagons carrying payrolls to the sections of Redmond's station, and took the money, amounting to £3000 in all, each time taking the draught-horses with him as well, and, before he rode away, ordering the driver and guard to remove all four wheels from the wagons and smash the spokes. Twice he broke into Redmond's mansion, once taking all the silver plate and a packhorse to carry it, and the second time drawing the bungs of all the wine casks in the cellar, so that two years' vintages spilled into the cellar and flooded it. Each time, wherever the robbery took place, Redmond found next morning the skin of a newly slaughtered lamb nailed to the main door of his mansion.

The lambskin left Redmond in no doubt who nailed it there, and so the description of Gordon Burns, alias John Henryson, alias Robert Dunbar, alias the Perthshire Shepherd, alias the Wild Colonial Boy, of ruddy complexion, five feet eight inches tall, well-built, bearing on his left cheek the mark of a small scar in the shape of a star, and speaking with a Scots accent, became famous. Rewards first of £50, then of £100, and finally of £200 were offered on posters tacked to a thousand trees. The Wild Colonial Boy had killed two men. The first was a servant of Redmond's who levelled a gun at him while he was escaping with packhorse and silver, but was himself shot before he could fire. The second was one of the horse-police who pursued the bushranger for five days, and was killed by a shot from a carbine. When Redmond was told of the murder of the shepherd at Tongala he resolved to get the man himself this time. He took five armed men with him. Four were policemen, whose services Redmond could command because he was now a magistrate, and the fifth was his son John, aged eighteen, the best shot of them all. Redmond was preparing to depart at dawn the next day when he received a note from Robert King asking if they could meet soon on a matter of business. Redmond replied that it would have to be later that day, or else when he returned. Robert came in the evening.

Redmond and Robert King had never spoken since Robert's return. They had seen each other a few times in the streets of Sydney, acknowledged each other, and passed on. There was no enmity between them. There was a certain estrangement. Robert felt that Redmond had treated his mother badly. But if the two men had moved in the same circles they would at least have been civil. They did not, however, move in the same circles. Redmond was almost always up-country. Robert rarely left Sydney.

But there was no enmity. When Robert came, the older man offered his hand, which Robert accepted. They sat, and Redmond waited.

Robert explained that this was a difficult thing for him to do. He had received news of the death of the comtesse d'Estaing, with whom he had spent several years in Europe. For those years she had been a second mother to him. Redmond said he was sorry. Of course he remembered the lady who had often written to his wife. He had never met the lady, but he offered his condolences. But, further than that, he did not see? ...

Robert said, "The countess appointed me as executor of her will in New South Wales."

"Yes?"

"There are two bequests to persons in the colony. One is to me. The other is to my mother."

"I see. To my wife?"

"Yes."

"And what is the effect of this bequest?"

"The countess states plainly in the will her intention to create trusts in favour of my mother, so that the income of her residual estate, after bequests to me and others, should accrue to my mother."

"Yes?"

"I am the executor in New South Wales of those trusts. I have consulted three other members of the Bar, and the opinion of them all is the same as mine, which I have communicated to my mother."

Redmond waited.

"The will," said Robert, "was made in Paris according to French law. According to English law, which is the law by which the will must be construed in the colony, the trusts fail."

"I see," said Redmond.

"My mother instructed me to tell you this. If you will ask your solicitors here to approach mine, they will tell you how the will affects you."

Robert got up.

"This has been awkward for you," said Redmond. "If I understand you, the effect of what you have been obliged to tell me is that because the trusts fail, the property goes as a simple bequest to your mother; and then, because she is my wife, the property falls entirely to me?"

Robert said, "That is broadly the effect."

"What is the amount?"

"About a hundred and fifty thousand pounds."

This was a very great fortune, much greater than

Redmond had thought. He was one of the richest men in the colony, but it was more than he possessed.

At this moment John entered the room to ask about the next day.

He and Robert shook hands as strangers. What else could they do? For reasons known to himself, Redmond never permitted John to see his mother, even when the boy asked. Robert and John were half brothers who had not spoken since Robert was thirteen and John four. They were sons of the same mother, and did not know each other.

Redmond said, "I go up-country tomorrow. When I return, I will attend to this matter. I do not envy you what you have had to do this evening. Will you tell Mrs. Redmond—will you tell your mother—that she will be hearing from me? And will you give her my regards?"

Robert passed on this message to Susannah, who nodded. The loss of money did not distress her. She did not think of it as the loss of a great fortune, because what could a fortune buy? It could buy more land and sheep. That is what Redmond would do with it. Since she came to New South Wales she had always had the leisure and independence to do as she wished. She had the house. She had enough. While her father was alive and governor she did not think of money at all; nor had she since. A governor's daughter does not need to think about money, and it is difficult to get into the habit afterwards.

In the week since the news had come, she was much more bothered about Robert. The countess's death was a blow to him. They had written often. She had not told him she was ill. Now, a week later, he had done his duty as executor. The evening, after he came back from Redmond, he told Susannah, "That part of it is done."

Susannah said, "You loved her, didn't you?"

"Yes. She was generous beyond words to me." He had never told his mother about the first evening he saw the countess, the meeting in the drawing-room, and the benediction before he went to bed, but he did now. He had never told her about the two portraits. Now he took a small package from his pocket and gave it to Susannah.

"It came to me," he said. "I prize it, but it will be much more to you."

It was the engraving of Nicolas Baudin, with the one epaulette of a lieutenant.

She said, "Nicolas."

Susannah held the framed engraving cupped in both hands. She felt the sting of tears, and did not let Robert see her face. She went to the window. Nicolas was younger in the engraving than she had known him, but what came first to her mind was that the eyes were as she had remembered them throughout the many years when she had possessed no likeness of him. She had remembered well.

"I will go," said Robert. He was opening the door when Susannah said, "Stay with me."

It was a long time before she managed to ask her question. Why had the countess, whom she had never seen, tried to leave so much to her? By the will Robert received a bequest of £50,000. That made him rich. Susannah could understand that bequest. But why should three times that amount have been left to her? Robert explained that if the trusts had been valid in the colony, the property would have been hers for life, and would then have passed to her heirs.

"That is not it," said Susannah. "Why a life interest to me? Why anything to me? Why so much to me?"

"I think it was a way of leaving it first to Nicolas and then to me. I think perhaps she saw you as Nicolas's heir. You see, she and Nicolas . . ." He had never told his mother or anyone about the conversation in the rue du Faubourg-Saint-Honoré, and nor would he now, more than to say that.

Susannah said, "I know. He never told me. But I should have been insensible not to know when she wrote asking for you. I have never admitted this before, but that was one reason why I would not let you go for so long. Then I thought that was ungenerous of me, as it was. I am glad you went. You never saw your father. But in seeing her, you must have seen something of him."

She came away from the window and put the engraving on the table. She smiled at Robert. "Although," she said, "seeing him that way, you must have seen him as a younger man than I did."

Halloran knew very well in his heart who had shot Erskine, but he could not understand why. At Tongala the career of the Wild Colonial Boy had been followed eagerly. The horse-police had ridden as far as that farthest section of the station, nailed "Wanted" posters to a few trees, and asked questions which were always answered in the same way. No one knew Burns, or had ever known him, or seen him, or heard of him. The reports in old Sydney newspapers of his raids on Redmond's property were read aloud in the shanty. The spilling of Redmond's claret, so that two vintages slopped knee-high on the flagstones of his cellars, had them howling with laughter. When Burns's career went from robbery to killing, well, the killings of a guard and a policeman were fair game. They all knew the meaning of the lambskin pinned to Redmond's door after each attack, because Halloran had told them about the evening Burns met Redmond, and of Burns's fine contempt for Pure Merino. But only Halloran of all the men in the section had stayed seven years in the one place, and only he had ever seen, met, and talked to Burns, and been his mate. Halloran had never seen him again, but he knew Burns had been around Tongala on several occasions. He found the remains of camp fires, and the tracks of a hobbled horse round the fires. Not all the sheep that were lost fell prey to dingoes. Dingoes maul a carcass. They do not gut it and leave the innards. He knew Burns had taken sheep. He had a fair idea that the tea, coffee, and sugar missing from his stores were taken by Burns. He said nothing. Burns had been his mate, and he knew how he was driven out. But to kill Erskine was not fair game. It was murder.

Redmond, his son, and the four policemen came at noon. Redmond's inspection was cursory this time. He had other things on his mind. Now it was John who demanded curtly to know why a flock had been let to graze too long in one place. Who was the shepherd? When the man appeared, John asked why the ground was paddled in one spot, why it was churned up by the feet of the sheep, showing they had been there all day. If they stayed still too long they crowded each other, and the weaker were lamed. If it had rained, then their feet took the wet rot from too long standing. The man plainly had been neglecting his work. And why was that dog kept? He was too old to be useful. The shepherd answered that, though the dog might be old, he was wise; but he thought to himself he would take good care to keep that dog from John's sight on the next visit.

Redmond rested the night and then took off the next morning, breaking his force into three groups and sending them in three directions, fanning out over the section. He took one policeman with him and rode to the west. Two other policemen rode east. A third party composed of John, a policeman, and Halloran, rode north. Halloran did not wish to go, particularly not in a party with John in charge, but he could not refuse.

He undoubtedly knew the section better than any other man there.

It was to the north, near the old camp where he had passed the night before walking to Tongala the day before he first became a bushranger, that they first found traces of Burns.

"Do you know the blacks hereabouts?" asked the policeman.

Halloran denied that he did, but John did not believe him. He ordered a fire to be lit, and they waited. The fire was not for warmth. It was a summer's afternoon. After three hours two blacks approached cautiously, their heads and the tips of their throwing spears showing over the crest of the shallow rise. They did not attack. In that section they would not attack, since they knew there were many white men and retribution would be bloody. They could also see that the three white men by the fire were well armed.

"Walk towards them," said John. "They will know you, I think."

Halloran did as he was told. He knew the men would know him, and they did.

John looked coldly at Halloran. "Now tell them we want them to track a man."

Halloran told them in signs and a pidgin mixture of Tongala dialect and English. John gave the blacks tobacco, and promised them two lambs if they found the man.

To track a man on horseback over meadowland is so easy that the whites could have done it for themselves, but after the meadowland there would be scrub, and then, if the trail led that far, mountains. That night they found a camp fire. To a white man the ashes seemed cold. The blacks held the ashes in their hands and to their lips, and said they were two days' warm. Since the fire would have burned all night, the man was a day and a night ahead of his pursuers. Then they came to the bush. There a horse's tracks are still plain. At one point they lost the trail in a creek, which was now almost dry but perhaps had not been the day before. A man would water his horse at a creek. He would fill his own water flasks at a creek. But Burns had not stopped there. They could find no trodden ground, and no fire. The horse was being ridden at a walk, but the rider was not stopping. Furthermore, he had ridden along the bed of that creek for a mile. It took the blacks two hours to find the track again. The rider had doubled back on himself. He was expecting to be followed. This became a certainty when, an hour further on, they found tracks carefully obliterated. For the whites, that would have been the end of the trail. They waited in a group, unable to do more than look for the most obvious signs, like crows circling. No crows circled, but after a quarter of an hour two crows did appear, flying steadily westwards into the unexplored interior.

The policeman said, "Even the crows have lost their way."

"But we have not," said John.

Halloran waited for the blacks to reappear, as he knew they would, with a fresh trail to follow. They did. It began a quarter of a mile away, in a gulley, in what were now granite foothills. The blacks proceeded steadily, calling softly to each other when a new scratch was found which betrayed the passage of a horse. Once they called up John, whom they had readily recognized as the leader, and excitedly pointed to two scratches he could barely make out for himself. John asked Halloran what they were saying. It was that the man was now leading his horse. "How far ahead?" asked John. The blacks could not say. But soon there were signs which did enable them to say.

There was a squashed ant, but the body was not yet dry. The man was less than a day ahead. Then a broken twig, but the point where it was broken was still perceptibly moist to the blacks, though it had lain in the hot sun. The man was four hours ahead. Then, in a sparse patch of grass, a few blades were trodden. Three hours ahead. Then there were salt marks on the granite. These were drops of sweat from a man, which had dried. He was less than two hours ahead. Then they found salt drops not yet quite dry.

John, Halloran, and the policeman rode up onto a ridge, and there before them they saw the man. He was three hundred yards off, on a plateau, walking his spent horse. The policeman looked at John, who estimated the range, and nodded. It was a long shot, and it would betray their presence, but then so would one glance back by the fugitive. The policeman drew his carbine, aimed carefully, and fired one shot. It cracked the silence of the mountains, echoed among the rocks, and missed. The startled man looked back, mounted, raised his horse to a trot, and tried to make off. John and the policeman led their horses two hundred yards out of the gulley until they reached the dusty plateau and could mount. Halloran hung behind. John cursed him and shouted at him to follow. The policeman's mount and John's were not fresh, but they were not exhausted, and they bore down on Burns. The dust rose from the dirt. In the confusion Burns doubled back into the dust. John was a good enough horseman to wheel and pursue, but he was impeded by the policeman, whose horse carried him headlong on. The policeman reined in, and at a hundred yards hit Burns's horse with one shot from the carbine. It fell. With a second shot he thought he hit Burns, but the man staggered into a gulley, and in the melée the policeman and John somehow lost sight of him. They could now take their time. Burns was finished. They walked their horses slowly up to Burns's horse, which John recognized as his father's old bay mare. The policeman went up to shoot the struggling animal, but John stopped him. "You may need all you have for Burns yet." The dust was settling and the two men moved to cover, and waited. They had time. The first move, if there was to be a rapid move, could be Burns's. If not, they would go slowly after him, in their own time.

Burns at that moment was lying in his own blood under a scrub half-way up a gulley. His left arm was smashed where the policeman's second shot had hit him, but in his right he still held his carbine. He was looking dully at Halloran, who was standing ten feet away.

"Well," said Halloran. "Old mate."

Burns looked down in hopelessness at his arm, and at the stones on which he lay, and then up at Halloran.

Halloran came closer and sat on his heels. "Why did you kill Erskine, the man back at Tongala? Why did it come to murder?"

"I was coming to pay you a visit, mate; anyway, to visit your stores."

"But you shot the man. What for?"

"Who was he?"

"A shepherd, as you were."

"I was riding in. Then there was the bullock cart. And in the sun, there was this guard, and the sun glinted on his musket. I thought he raised it, meaning to aim at me. I saw the sun glint on a barrel."

"It was no gun barrel," said Halloran. "It was a glint on a shepherd's crook he always had with him. He brought it out with him. It had a silver head."

Burns said nothing. Then he said, "A man gets too

quick, too afraid. Then he shoots too easily. Because he is afraid."

Quietly John and the policeman came up from behind. Halloran saw them. Burns saw Halloran's eyes move, and turned his head. It was true Burns had a carbine still in his right hand. It was also true that he could not have fired it, not having the strength to lift it. It was true he did turn towards John, but he only turned his head. Whether or not John realized that the man was helpless only he knew. The fact was— and this was much talked over in the shanty later— the fact was that the policeman made no move to shoot, and did not even raise his carbine as he approached. But John shot Burns twice. The first pistol shot killed Burns, entering at the temple. A death mask was later sold in the streets and shops of Sydney. Like all death masks it was serene, and like most death masks it lied in being serene. As it happens, the mask was not of Burns at all, but of a hanged convict. Burns's head was too badly shattered by the pistol ball to allow any recognizable mask to be made. But the mask that was sold went into folk history, and then into scholarly history, as the death mask of the Wild Colonial Boy.

Redmond congratulated John. Back in Sydney he took legal advice on the countess's bequest to Susannah, and was told, in an opinion which took an hour and a half to express, that because he was Susannah's husband the income from the amount bequeathed was certainly his for life, though after that it was a question whether the property would revert to his or to Susannah's heirs. His solicitor mentioned to him, dryly enough, that as husband he was also liable to provide for the maintenance of his wife, according to the reasonable expectations of her station and his, even though they were separated.

But there was no doubt the countess's money was his for life.

Susannah and Robert no longer stood in Redmond's way to social advancement. He was the very personification of the Ancient Nobility. He had known of her attachment to Wyndham, and the commissioner's report on transportation had not pleased him. It fairly summarized the evidence of Redmond and the arguments for the sheep interest, and said plainly that the large sheep-owners and graziers relied on convict and ex-convict labour, but it ended with the thundering words that transportation, though chiefly dreaded as an exile, was undoubtedly much more than exile; it was slavery as well. And with slavery, Great Britain, as a Christian nation, should no longer defile itself. Transportation should cease. But it did not cease. Wyndham's report was much noticed, and nothing was done. So, Redmond wished to be just. In matters of money he was hard but just. He wrote to Susannah offering her one-third of the bequest. She replied thanking him, but saying she did not need it. Redmond, who understood the uses of money, could not comprehend such an answer. He wrote a second time, offering at least an annuity. She replied, again thanking him, again saying she had no need. The house was hers, and, for the rest, she had enough. But she thanked him. Redmond remembered very well that the house was hers, by grace and favour and apparently in perpetuity. He still wished to be a reasonable man, and made a third offer, this time to Robert. Redmond said his enterprises would now be greatly increasing, asked Robert to work with him, and offered him an equal partnership in the sheep station with himself and John. Robert told Susannah. "This is generous of him," she said. Robert agreed, but he knew he had other work to do. He too declined, again with thanks. Redmond did not try again.

The will of Françoise, comtesse d'Estaing, leaving in effect the bulk of her estate to William Redmond, Esq., grazier, was admitted to probate in Sydney in the same court and on the same day as the will of John Erskine, shepherd, of Tongala, which left to Arthur Shaw, station-hand, his entire estate of £396 sterling.

26

───────⁃∽૭∾⁃───────

The Tolpuddle Martyrs

ONE DAY IN FEBRUARY 1834, Viscount Melbourne,
His Majesty's secretary of state for Home Affairs, the
man after whom the city was later named, found
on his desk two letters which caused him grave concern. The first was from the Duke of Wellington, who
informed Melbourne that half the agricultural labourers of Hampshire, the county in which the duke
had his country seat, were members of those dangerous bodies, the trade unions. This was untrue. The
duke was misinformed. But, nevertheless, the duke
said so, and the duke was a national hero and a gentleman. The second letter was from William Ponsonby,
a member of Parliament for the neighbouring county
of Dorset, who reported that in the village of Tolpuddle discontented field-hands had been kneeling in
white robes before a death's-head and reciting oaths
of secrecy which ended with the words, "Remember
thy end." This was also untrue. Ponsonby was mistaken. But Ponsonby was Melbourne's brother-in-law.

Thus it was that a new, reforming, radical government found itself engaged in rigging a state trial.
A state trial it was, though it was held not in Westmin-

ster Hall but in the courtroom in High West Street, Dorchester. And it was certainly rigged. It has the honour of being probably the last trial to be so openly rigged by a British government. Successive administrations had feared insurrection ever since the French Revolution of 1789 set a bad example. The European revolutions of 1830 were tiny affairs, but the British government went sniffing round for sedition. Rioters burned Nottingham Castle and Derby Prison, and, in the countryside, a few hundred haystacks blazed. So death's-head oaths in Puddletown were to be made an example of. But what was the crime?

Miners had been imprisoned for illegal conspiracy when they threatened to strike, and shoemakers for "leaving work unfinished," but the Tolpuddle men had done neither of these things. Posters were plastered on the walls of Dorsetshire cottages threatening with transportation any man who joined a union, but they had not done that either. But they had formed what they called a Friendly Society. Six men were arrested and taken to Dorchester gaol. Their heads were shorn. The foreman of the Grand Jury was the same Ponsonby who was Melbourne's brother-in-law. The judge was Mr. Justice Williams, on his first assize. The Lord Chancellor, who on the government's instructions appointed him one morning, was asked in the afternoon by his clerk to sign some trivial papers; he declined, saying that no man could be asked to do more in one day than make Williams a judge. On the day of the trial in Dorchester there was still some doubt what the indictment would be. The judge, knowing that all the evidence the Crown had pertained to the taking of this death's-head oath, directed the Grand Jury, to find that a true indictment could be brought under the Act of 37, Geo. III, cap. 123, the one hundred and twenty-third Act of the thirty-seventh year of the reign of George III, 1797.

Counsel asked for that volume of the statutes. "But, m'lud, if I have the Act to which y'r lordship was referring, it is one for the suppression of mutiny among seamen of the Royal Navy, at the mutiny of the Nore. We are not at the Nore, there is no mutiny, and there are no seamen. And anyway, if y'r lordship pleases, the Act's as dead as mutton."

The judge replied that, as to mutton, Dorchester was dairy country.

"And that is the substance of y'r lordship's reply to my submission?"

It was. The six men were tried under that Act. The chief witness of the oath-taking was a son of a man who worked as gardener for a Dorchester magistrate, and even he was uncertain.

"Can not you remember?" asked the judge. "I will give you a moment to remember." The man remembered.

"Now," said the judge to one of the accused, "what is the secret sign or signal by which the unions know when to meet all over England?" The man replied that there was no union that he knew of, and therefore no sign. He asked to read a statement of defence to the jury. The judge said it could be read for him, and a clerk took the paper and muttered away to the jury.

"My lord," protested the prisoner, "it is so mumbled over, in such an incomprehensible manner, that although I know what is there, having written it, I cannot follow it."

James and George Loveless, John and Thomas Stanfield, James Baine, and James Hammett were sentenced to seven years' transportation, and heard their sentences pronounced in the same high, classical, austere courtroom, and beneath the same royal coat

of arms as Jane Bryant had heard hers pronounced
more than a generation before. And that is how the
Tolpuddle Martyrs came to New South Wales.

In Dorset, family ties are close. The two Stanfields
were both cousins of Jane's. Thomas Stanfield was
nearly fifty at the time of his trial, and well remembered Jane's visit of many years before. The visit had
been brief, but Puddletown is small, and the tale of
Jane's sudden appearance was told and retold. Stanfield's son John, now in his mid-twenties, recalled the
day the lady from London came in a great carriage.
Those were the days when a Puddletown man could go
all his life without seeing Weymouth, thirteen miles
away, let alone London, and Jane Bryant was therefore remembered as a woman who came from London,
and went to Weymouth, and then to the even more
distant city of Sydney. John Stanfield particularly
remembered the countess's coach and its four horses.
So when the six Tolpuddle men were sentenced,
letters were written ahead to Jane in Sydney. Robert
had not the easy intimacy with Bourke, the new governor, that he had enjoyed with Brisbane, but Bourke
was approachable. He was said to be distantly related to Edmund Burke. The slight difference in
spelling of the names did not diminish his belief in his
relationship to the great statesman. So Bourke was
amenable, and when Robert made representations on
behalf of the Tolpuddle men the governor was neither
surprised nor ill-disposed. He knew Robert had represented many emancipists and convicts. Robert told
the governor that he ought perhaps to declare an interest, in that Jane Bryant, his mother's housekeeper,
was cousin to two of the men.

"I see," said the governor. He knew Jane Bryant
too. She had also appeared at many emancipist meetings. Nothing very much was said between the two

men. The furthest the governor went was to say that he would naturally consider any request from Mr. King, and that so long as the Tolpuddle men behaved well he was sure their stay would not be arduous. As Robert was leaving the governor called him back and told him the name of the transport on which the men had been shipped, and her probable date of arrival, and Robert saw that things were not going to be difficult at all. They were not. The governor had already received dispatches from London expressing the secretary of state's conviction that the governor would treat the men with proper humanity. The secretary for the colonies, like some other members of the government, had been surprised at the flimsiness of the indictment. To get rid of dangerous unionists was one thing. To do so on such an empty pretext, and on a pretext which looked as empty as it was, was another. The rigour of the sentence should be mitigated if this could be discreetly done.

Jane and the older Stanfield recognized each other on the quay when the transport came in. The men were released on Jane's recognizance for their good behaviour, which the governor had told her he would accept. She found the men lodgings, where on the second evening they all ate supper together. They invited Robert, who, as Jane told them, had already acted on their behalf. She said he was the man who had miraculously secured her own release in London. At Jane's suggestion, Susannah was also asked. So was Jane's daughter Elizabeth. The men were surprised to find themselves looked after and provided for, and forgot for the moment the misery of their imprisonment, exile, and the sordid voyage in the 'tween decks with two hundred other convicts. They had all conducted themselves at first with dignity, suffering their heads to be shorn in Dorchester gaol without protest, and holding themselves proudly when they were taken

to Portsmouth in unnecessary chains. But the voyage
exhausted them all. When they reached Sydney they
were surprised to be greeted not with more chains but
with kindness.

There were only five of them at supper, not six.
George Loveless, who had acted as spokesman for
them all in England, had been separated. They
thought he was coming out on another ship. Over
supper, drinking beer which, though not Dorchester ale,
was better than any they had tasted for many months,
they told the story of their adventure from the first.
How, when they first saw the posters threatening
transportation, they had walked the five miles from
Tolpuddle to the great house at Kingston Maurward
and asked the lord of the manor for his advice, which
helped them little. They remembered not knowing
how to approach the Palladian mansion, not wishing to
go directly up the carriageway to the main portico, but
also not wishing to tread on the lawns which would
take them to a side door. They remembered how the
lord of the manor told them they had no recourse but
to accept the wages the farmers offered. They told him
wages had fallen from ten shillings a week to nine, then
to eight, then seven, and finally to six. They could not
live on it. He said he could do nothing. It was this recollection that made them at first hesitant when Jane
suggested they should ask Susannah to supper. They
imagined her as lady of the manor of Kingston
Maurward.

"And if she were," Jane retorted, "do you think she
would have sent you away with such words?"

Susannah was the only one at table who had never
seen Dorset. It was as well she had not, because the
men were able to tell her, and in telling her they talked
about home, recalling to themselves the only countryside they had ever known. It was very dear to them.
They talked of meadows and rivers, of gorse and tall

ferns and heaths, of lanes and hedges, and of pine and birch woods, and forgot their exile.

Until James Baine said, "When we were coming in yesterday morning, a seaman on the ship asked me what I thought of the bay. And I told him it was the finest sheet of water I ever saw in my life, only we were at the wrong end of the world."

There was a silence which lasted too long, and Robert ended it. "I have often thought of Dorset," he said. "I have often thought of Dorchester." He had. That evening, meeting these Dorset men, he had remembered the King's Arms, and Leah.

His interjection succeeded in taking them back to Dorset, and away from the sadness of Baine's remark. They were all drinking again, and Robert said, "I once gave a girl in Dorchester two lengths of silk, for two wedding gowns . . ." He was going to continue, when Jane caught his eye. She was telling him to stop, but he did not take her meaning, and would have gone on except that she interrupted, saying, "It was for two lengths of silk I came here first."

The men laughed at that, but then John Stanfield leaned easily back in his chair and asked Robert, "She was a Dorchester girl, then?"

"Puddletown."

"Pretty girl?"

"A delightful girl," said Robert. "A *good* woman."

Stanfield said, "I have three sons back home, and a daughter. Reuben, Simeon, Joseph, and Dinah."

"Ah," said Robert.

"Genesis, sir," said Stanfield.

There was an echo in Robert's mind. He was perplexed for a second, and then it came back to him, and he knew.

Stanfield said, "I'll put you out of your misery, sir. Reuben, Simeon, and Dinah—the children of Leah. Joseph the son of Rachel."

Around the table everyone except Susannah and
Elizabeth understood. Jane had known, having been
with Robert in Dorset. The rest knew because the story
was a famous one in the villages of Puddletown and
Tolpuddle.

Robert looked round at the faces of the men, and at
Stanfield, and was about to offer whatever apology he
could to the man for having inadvertently spoken of
Leah, when Stanfield smiled widely and held out his
hand across the table and shook Robert's.

"Lord, sir," he said, "she told me. How do you
think a girl like her'd come by two lengths of silk,
Piedmont silk she always said it was? Except"—this
with a glance towards Jane—"by lifting them from
Yallop's shop. How'd she come by them? She had to
tell. And why should I grieve for her good fortune? It
was before I came along. And I tell you. You called
her a good woman just now. When she first told me
about you, she said you were a kind man. And she
said you promised to remember her monkeys in Puddletown church."

"I do remember them," said Robert.

"She's a good wife," said Stanfield, "and a beautiful
woman." He glanced at Elizabeth, who was trying to
ask Susannah what the story was, and said, "That little
girl there, Jane's daughter, she'll be like Leah."

Robert looked at Elizabeth and said yes, she might;
so she might.

"And I'll tell you something, sir. That silk is still
dancing in Dorchester. Or 'twas when I came away, and
'twill again when I go home. 'Twasn't worn just the
once, on the wedding day, like the gentry do. A
Dorset girl keeps the gown she marries in and dances
in it when she's a woman. At balls, and harvest sup-
pers. And on holidays. And Leah's got two of 'em. So
you see, you did well by her, sir, giving her the silk.

For it will last all her dancing days, and then go to Dinah."

"Dinah?"

"Dinah the daughter of Leah. Genesis, sir."

They parted in marvellous good humour. Robert could not remember when he last liked a man so for his generosity of spirit, and wished him and Leah all the joy in the world.

"Which I will tell her, sir, when next we meet."

Robert went back to his mother's house that night. "Silk?" said Susannah. "Two lengths of silk? Leah? Rachel? Genesis? Monkeys?" He explained, and she was pleased.

"You said she was delightful."

"She was."

"Are you glad that your silk is still dancing?"

"I can see her dancing," he said.

The five Dorset labourers remained in Sydney as ticket-of-leave men. The governor thought it most unlikely that they would serve out their seven years or anything like it, and told Robert so, adding, "You realize, of course, King, that I have no authority whatever to tell you anything of the sort?" Robert told the five men all this, but one thing on which they most required reassurance was the well-being of the elder Loveless, George, who, as they now knew, had been sent to Tasmania. This was six hundred sea-miles away, and by reputation had become an even grimmer penal colony than Sydney had ever been.

"Your man is there," said Governor Bourke. "But I had a dispatch from my lieutenant-governor there the other day, saying he'd offered to let him bring out his wife if he liked, so it seems it doesn't go too hard with him."

But this suggestion that George Loveless should

bring out his wife caused no end of trouble. The lieutenant-governor meant it to be a humane offer, and was astonished by Loveless's reply.

"But, sir, I should be a monster to send for my wife to come out here to misery."

These words were not spoken contumaciously, but after consideration, and thoughtfully, as if their truth were self-evident. It brought the lieutenant-governor up short that any man should tell him he was presiding over misery. Still, he told Loveless to reconsider, and after some months he accepted, and wrote to England asking his wife to come out. He did this before he knew, by way of a letter from Robert, that his stay at the wrong end of the world was not likely to be as long as he thought. He replied, saying Robert could now imagine his plight. His wife might already be on her way out to Tasmania. Robert went to Hobart town to see him. It was a passage of three days.

By the time he arrived the situation was even worse. Dispatches from London arrived one day before Robert. The prime minister, wanting to be rid of the whole affair, had told the Commons that the Dorchester labourers would be set free and sent home free of expense and with all comfort. The lieutenant-governor promptly put down Loveless's name to go home on the next ship.

Robert made a formal application for himself and his client Loveless to see the lieutenant-governor.

"Damn it, King, every convict who's been put on short rations for a week will soon be knocking on my door accompanied by counsel."

Robert reminded him that Loveless was now a free man. Loveless was brought in, and spoke eloquently for himself, "Your Excellency knows that you persuaded me to send for my wife. And for aught I know she may now be on the water, it being nine months since the invitation left this colony. It would be a dreadful thing for me to leave before I have heard from my wife. You offer me the next ship or none, and I speak against that. Sir, it is not just."

Loveless had been a lay-preacher in Dorset. Having pronounced this sounding speech, he stood with his burning eyes fixed on the lieutenant-governor as if on a sinful congregation. Robert saw that the man could have made a fortune at the Bar.

A pause. The lieutenant-governor said he had done what he had done out of humanity.

Another pause. Loveless said nothing, but did not take his eyes from the man's face.

Robert stood apart from them, looking out of the window, remembering the first case he ever argued, and the only one he ever argued in England, before the Attorney-General. He remembered how he had argued that case, with silence; with "How d'you do?" and silence, and then one sentence.

So he maintained silence, and then allowed himself his one sentence. He remarked that the lieutenant-governor now had it in his power to resolve matters easily, by acting again with the same humanity he had shown when he let Loveless send for his wife: and he could do that by permitting Loveless to remain until it were known whether his wife was coming or not.

A pause.

"So be it," said the lieutenant-governor.

27

Don't Tread on Me

ON THE PASSAGE back to Sydney they ran into Iago. Iago was a pirate, whose name was shortened from that of the city of Santiago in Chile, from where he had come to New South Wales twenty years before. He was Spanish. He began his career as a privateer, preying on the coastal shipping of western South America, and making plundering excursions to Tahiti and Fiji. On one voyage he was driven by gales as far south and west as New South Wales, where, having to careen his vessel to repair storm damage, he chose an obscure island in the Bass Strait, between the mainland and Tasmania, and found seals. The islands were alive with seals. They were an even easier prey than coastal shipping. For many years he made a living not principally from piracy but from clubbing these seals to death as they lay on the beach and bartering the skins with the shady traders, themselves little better than cutthroats, who visited the islands in luggers twice a year. He and his crew lived on kangaroo meat, and on the salt pork, biscuits, and rum for which they traded their sealskins. They slaughtered or enslaved the blacks of the neighbouring islands. At first, out of instinct, they ravished and killed the black women, called gins, but soon found it wiser to keep them alive. A gin was better than no woman at all. A gin could also do all the work, allowing Iago and his companions to live a life of ease, from which they had to rouse themselves only to slaughter seals. Over the years most of Iago's Chilean seamen died, and were replaced by convicts who escaped from the penal settlements on Tasmania. Iago never quite forgot his original vocation, and attacked any vessel sufficiently small or helpless. He left alone the whaling ships owned by the men of the Sydney blubber-and-stays interest. The whalers were too well-manned and well-found, and the chance of reprisal too great. But he would attack anything helpless. There were half a dozen other privateers like Iago up and down that coast.

Robert was taking passage back to Sydney in the colonial schooner *Australis*, a forty-footer, new-built and a fast sailer. These are often turbulent waters. Twelve hours out of Hobart town she ran into heavy seas which carried away her jib-boom. By daybreak the storm had blown itself out, and *Australis* was lying hove-to while her hands made good the damage. In this state she was found by Iago's brig, the *Vallarta*. The *Vallarta* was probably fifty years old, having been built in Barcelona before the wars with France. She was a ruin of old age. Her hull was leaky and her canvas fragile. Even if her canvas had been sound, her masts could never have carried a full set of sails. But she had been built for life as a privateer, and carried six four-pounder cannons. She was still quite capable of taking a crippled schooner one quarter of her size.

The *Australis* saw her early, but too late. Her only hope was to run, but the wind at dawn had dropped to light airs, and was in the wrong quarter too. The *Australis* was armed. But all she had was a tiny two-

pounder, a swivel-gun, and five muskets, one for each
of her crew. The privateer brig was undermanned,
but still carried a crew of twenty. Trevelyan, the skipper of the *Australis,* recognized the brig. He had
never met her, or thought to meet her. He had never
seen a vessel so old. He knew Iago's reputation. The
skipper had been a boatswain in the Royal Navy. He
knew what hope they had. He could not run. If he
hoisted a white flag, Iago would murder them anyway.
If they fought, they would have the slenderest chance,
and that chance would depend on Iago showing an
incompetence which was not likely.

At that moment the *Vallarta* put a ball across the
schooner's bows. They were already within range of
the four-pounders. The brig could stand off and
pound the schooner to pieces, and they would all be
dead. But Iago would not want to do that; he wanted
the schooner, not a foundering wreck. So he would
approach and board, and then they would be dead too.
There was only one hope. It was a chance in a hundred, but the best they had. Trevelyan saw the state
of the *Vallarta*'s canvas, then guessed that her crew
was unseamanlike, and knew that the schooner, crippled as she was, could outmanoeuvre her. If he ran
the schooner before the wind, sailing her straight towards the *Vallarta,* he could approach her bow-on so
that he would, with luck, be out of reach of her cannon, which were mounted broadside. Once the
schooner was beneath the brig's bow, he could use his
swivel. A swivel-gun fires canister, metal cans which
scatter a rain of jagged bits of rusty metal. It is shrapnel. At close range a lucky shot could kill a dozen
men, twenty men, cutting them to pieces. But that
would be a brilliant action. The skipper knew he
needed a hundred things to go right, and not one thing
to go wrong. If the *Vallarta*'s crew had muskets, he

was beaten. If they had canister, he was beaten. If they boarded him in the scuffle, he was beaten.

And before he could do anything he had to bring the schooner about, and for too long he would be broadside to the brig. He prayed they could not shoot. But he knew that at that range they could hardly miss.

They could not shoot straight, but one ball struck home.

If a cannon ball hits a man it will tear him in two. Even if it only glances a man, it may disembowel him. But to kill one man is the least damage one cannon ball can do in a sea-battle. If it strikes a mast squarely it will bring it down, and that would sink the *Australis,* capsizing her. And a ball, striking so small a vessel, carries with it such an impact that her timbers shiver, and her seams open. The ball that struck *Australis* took her high in the starboard bow. It shook her whole frame. But worse than that were the splinters. Most seamen who die in battle are not sheared straight in two, but pierced by flying splinters from the timbers of their own vessel. The schooner was built largely of ironbark, much harder than English oak, and most seaworthy. But its flying splinters are the more deadly for their hardness. When the ball struck, splinters killed two of the crew outright, piercing the head of one and the breast of the other, and wounded a third man in the arm. But still the schooner, having come about, made straight for the brig. Robert could not keep his eyes from the man who had fallen not two feet away from him. The splinter that entered his brain killed him, but twenty other, smaller splinters, had laid open his face and bare shoulders. Two feet away, Robert was untouched, but he was deathly afraid. He took the dead man's musket and crouched, like the other men, for shelter, though if another ball struck there would be no shelter from splinters anywhere on board the schooner. They ran straight for the brig as if to ram her. Iago was astonished. The seamanship of his crew of seal-killers was as incompetent as the schooner skipper could have hoped. The brig could not manoeuvre. As the schooner ran under her bows, the skipper jerked the lanyard to trigger the swivel, and six men died on the brig's foredeck, torn apart by jagged bits of metal.

But as the two vessels slid past each other, almost hull to hull, the jury rigging of the schooner's jib-boom fouled the brig's main chains. The schooner's crew hacked her free. As they did, one man was killed by a musket shot. When they did push free, they had lost all way, and were drifting in the brig's lee. As soon as the brig could turn, however sluggishly, and train her cannon, the schooner was lost.

And then, a mile away, from behind an island which had been shielding her from view, came the vision of a full-rigged ship, under full canvas. They did not know what she was, but Iago knew what she might be. A full-rigged ship of that size, for she looked to be all of eight hundred tons, carrying that much sail, was very likely a frigate. She was too deep-hulled for an English frigate, but certainly she was frigate-rigged. It did not matter to Iago of which nation she was. A man-of-war of any flag would take his brig and hang him. He ran before the wind, with as much sail as he dared, leaving the schooner floundering. But he had no chance. The frigate gave pursuit, hailing the schooner as she passed, and then, coming up to the *Vallarta* two miles ahead, put a broadside of four balls into her at the waterline. It was enough. Her timbers were rotten. She listed. The frigate put two shots into her rigging, and her foremast toppled. As it did, she foundered. The *Vallarta* had fired one shot in return, and that missed. The ship circled the brig as she settled. Those of her crew who survived scrambled for floating spars. The frigate left them and beat back to windward to the drifting schooner.

Only, she was not a frigate. She was built by the same yard on the Charles River that had built famous frigates, and frigate-rigged was a fair description for even a seaman to use of her. She flew the Stars and Stripes, with the twenty-five stars of twenty-five States in 1836, and, as a battle ensign, the former American Navy Jack, with its red and white horizontal stripes, the yellow snake sliding diagonally across them, and the motto "Don't Tread On Me." It was a battle flag she was not formally entitled to fly. She was the *America,* 850 tons, Captain Cobb, out of Boston, bound for Sydney with a speculative cargo.

On the deck of the listing schooner, Robert and Trevelyan watched as the *America* approached. Both were exhausted.

"Oh, God be praised," said Trevelyan. "Oh, God be praised." He tried to rise to his feet to acknowledge the *America*'s signals as she closed the schooner, but lacked the strength and fell back.

Robert said, utterly bewildered, "A Yankee frigate in these waters?"

But Trevelyan by then knew what she was. "No frigate, sir. I did take her for a frigate. With that rigging, sir, any man might, but no frigate ever carried that much sail."

By then the *America* was almost up to them, and Robert and Trevelyan gazed at the ascending tiers of mainsails, topsails, topgallants, royal-topgallants, and sky-sails. Her crew were furling her main courses as she made to heave to.

"A merchantman, sir," said Trevelyan. "I've heard tell of them, but never thought to see one. Not in these waters."

But there she was. Like any ship in those waters,

she was armed. With that rig she was fast as any frigate. Like any ship that could, she would, by a sort of
freemasonry of the sea, destroy a pirate so that it
should not survive to harry others. She was a beautiful
American merchantman at a time when American
sailing ships were beyond question the finest in the
world. Even Englishmen admitted that. She was the
first of a line which ended with the Atlantic packets
and the tea clippers. She was an astonishing ship.

The *America* hove to, keeping the schooner in her lee,
and launched a boat with the first mate and six sailors.
The *Australis* was awash and listing. As the mate
climbed aboard he slipped on the tilting deck. It was
slippery with blood. Three men were dead. The other
three were hurt, one badly. Trevelyan and Robert
had come off most lightly. Robert, who felt himself
earlier to be unscathed, later found that his left shoulder was full of a hundred splinters of shivered wood.
His shirt and coat were bloody and he was badly
shaken. The American mate said very little. He made
a rapid survey of the schooner. He kept two seamen
with him, and told four others to take the three survivors to the *America,* and then to return for the dead.
Trevelyan wished to remain with his schooner, but
the mate shook his head. "I'll see to her, mister. We'll
get her back to Sydney."

On board the American ship, Trevelyan collapsed.
Robert was conscious, but utterly weary, and shivering.
He thanked the captain.

"You saved our lives; those that could be saved."

He did not know what the captain replied. Two men
carried him to a cabin and placed him on his side on a
bunk. They looked at his shoulder.

He recalled one of the men saying, "Sorry, mister.
Hold on," and then the man began to take out the
hardwood splinters, one by one. After an hour Robert

half sat up. A man tried to give him some coffee, but suddenly he was sick. The man cleared up the mess, laid him down on the bed again, and then a hand held his head and made him sip some liquid. It was a solution of opium, and he slept for fifteen hours.

It was night when he awoke, and his first consciousness was that he was looking upwards through a skylight at a clear sky full of stars. His eyes rested on the stars, and then he recognized a constellation. The stars of Aquarius winked above him and to his right, high in the sky. Still lying on his back, he shifted his eyes to the other side of the skylight, and there low on the horizon as he looked left was the Southern Cross. He was not a sailor, but a man in a continent of empty spaces gets to know the stars. Besides, Susannah had taught him. So before he raised his head from the pillow, and before he knew why he was lying where he was or what had brought him there, Robert knew that he was moving eastward. Then the movement of the vessel as she cut easily through tranquil seas told him he was on board ship. Then his mind recalled the schooner, and the morning. He tried to raise himself.

A voice said, "Why not lie still for a while yet?"

It was a woman's voice. She must have been sitting near the cabin door. Now she moved across and he saw her standing above him. Then she sat beside him. "Talk some, if you like."

Her voice was American.

"The schooner," he said.

"We are towing her."

His comprehension was still slow. He said, "You are the American ship?"

She nodded.

"Then thank you." He tried to raise his hand, but could hardly move it. She took it in hers.

"I have been sleeping."

"Yes."

"The men?"

"There are three of you," she said.

He put his face into the pillow. Three other men, alive that morning, were now dead. He remembered that he had expected to die. He held on to the hand that held his. Then he slept again.

Next morning early a man came to him, gave him coffee, which this time he could drink, dressed his shoulder, and told him he would live a while yet. Robert drank more coffee, ate a bit, and was told to stay in bed. The captain would come to see him.

At mid-morning he did. They introduced themselves. The captain was James Cobb. He told Robert briefly how things stood. Trevelyan and the other survivor were mending. They had buried the three dead men at sea the day before, as decently as they could. The schooner was in tow. He hoped they would make Sydney with her, but her timbers were sprung, and she was leaking badly. He had two men aboard her, bailing her out. If the weather held, she might make it. Another thirty-six hours should see them in Sydney Cove. Cobb was a strong, solid, bearded man. He suggested Robert should not attempt to get up before next morning.

In the evening the woman came to him again. He was sitting up when she knocked, and found himself staring at her as she entered. She noticed it.

"I am sorry," he said. "But, you see, we have spoken twice before, but I never really saw you."

It *was* the first time he had seen her. She was tall, very tall for a woman. She was unbelievably slender. In profile she looked Persian, or as he imagined a Persian woman might look. He had never seen a Persian.

There is little space in a ship's cabin to show natural energy in movement, but whatever she did, she did with a flexuous activity. Her very movement across the eight feet of cabin from the door to his side was all activity, and yet when she sat beside him she was composed. Her eyes, of so dark a blue as he had never seen before, looked steadily at him.

He admired the ship. She said the captain was half-owner of the *America* and of her sister ship, which should now be in the China seas. She talked about Boston. He told her about Sydney, which she had never seen.

At a break in their conversation he asked, "Whose bunk have I taken for the last two days?"

"Oh, the bed is mine," she said. "No, no, no, do not thank me too much. I have slept in the saloon."

"You saved me," he said, "and I have not even told you my name."

"The captain told me," she said. "And I am Anna Cobb."

"Oh, his sister?"

"His wife."

Of course she was his wife. Why, Robert asked himself after she went, had he said, "His sister?" Captain Cobb was a Boston man, and as plainly of English stock as a man could be. Trace him back three generations and you would come to Devon. Anna was not in the least English. In nothing was she English. She could not be Cobb's sister, only his wife.

The *America* came into Sydney harbour gently because of the schooner she was still towing. As they hit the swell between the north and south heads the schooner shipped more water. Cobb sent his second mate across to the two men aboard the *Australis,* to beach her if they could, or, if she foundered, to take to her jolly boat, which was still sound. The *America* hove to for fifteen minutes while the mate rigged a gaff sail and cast off from the ship. In that time the *America* signalled the gist of the encounter with the *Vallarta* to the semaphore station on the head, which passed the signal to the cove. Robert was by now on deck with Cobb and Anna. As they entered the harbour slowly, under royals to catch the light breeze, Cobb flew the American Navy Jack as his ensign at the stern. The only ship of the Royal Navy in the harbour was the twenty-gun sloop *Naiad*. Her young commander watched the three American sailors beach the half-foundering schooner in Farm Cove, which was a feat of seamanship. Then he took the telescope from his first lieutenant, recognized the battle flag the *America* was flying, and smiled. The engagements of the War of Independence and that of 1812 figured in the education of any English naval officer. As the *America* came to anchor, the *Naiad* gave her a salute of thirteen guns.

At government wharf, Captain Cobb, his wife, his first mate, Robert, and Trevelyan were welcomed by a crowd of hundreds, with the port-officer and Susannah among them. The port-officer was an old, superannuated captain, who had seen action in the War of 1812. He received Cobb, congratulating and thanking him on behalf of the governor.

"Your ensign, sir," said the port-captain. "I fancy *Naiad* recognized it, and I remember it."

"Well," said Cobb, "you thank the *Naiad* for me, will you, sir. I don't rightly think your Admiralty would approve of thirteen-gun salutes for a Yankee any more than the Navy Department back home would approve of me flying the Battle Jack. But I'm James Cobb III. I had it from my father, who was James Cobb II, and he had it from his, who was James Cobb I and fought under it in seventy-eight."

Susannah, who had caught some of this conversation, left Robert for a moment and came over. "Captain Cobb?"

"Yes, ma'am."

"A Captain James Cobb put into this port in eighteen-oh-three, master of the *Columbia*."

"My father," said Cobb. "But you couldn't have known him, ma'am?"

Susannah had never known him. She had seen him once, when he walked out of her father's study and passed her in the hallway as she was kneeling over Robert, who was a child of a few months. She asked her father who the visitor was, and he told her, and told her also what the stranger's business was. It was Captain Cobb who had spoken the French corvette and brought the news of Baudin's death. Now Cobb's son had saved Robert.

28

*The American Woman, and Map-Given
Fear*

CAPTAIN AND MRS. COBB, Robert, and Trevelyan were
entertained everywhere in Sydney. The governor
gave a banquet in their honour, to convey to Captain
Cobb the colony's thanks for saving the schooner
and three of the souls aboard her, and for ridding the
colony of a pirate. The sheep kings gave an even more
magnificent banquet to welcome the largest American
ship yet seen there, a ship, moreover, which was going
to take a cargo of wool to Baltimore and might open an
American market. At this banquet Redmond was the
host and Robert introduced him to the Americans.
Again Robert got on well enough with Redmond. They
were more than civil. But between Robert and John
there was a coldness that Robert tried to overcome but
could not. John, who was now in his early twenties, was
more aggressive than his father in defence of the wool
interest. The sheepmen presented Captain Cobb with a
medal, bearing on its face the arms of New South Wales
with extra sheep added round the circumference, and on
the obverse a representation of the *America,* correct
in its glorious rigging, which very much pleased him.
The third banquet was given by the emancipists.

Robert had represented their cause for years, and they
wished to show gratitude for his rescue. And, such
was the spirit of faction, it was impossible for the
emancipists not to give a grander banquet than the
sheep kings. They presented Cobb with a ship's clock
inscribed: "From the Grateful Citizens of Sydney."

Sydney was a drinking city. The graziers drank
deeply at their banquet, but this only made their
speeches more self-congratulatory, which did not
matter. But at the emancipists' banquet one incident
struck Anna. They were well into the speeches when a
Dr. Malone rose to propose yet another vote of thanks
and was immediately challenged by one of the three
hundred diners. The doctor was not one of them, said
the challenger: neither he nor his forebears had ever
seen the inside of a gaol. To which the doctor eloquently replied that his maternal grandfather had
been transported for no less noble a feat than highway
robbery. The doctor was cheered and his challenger
roundly booed.

"It was not highway robbery they were cheering,"
said Robert later. "They were cheering themselves if
you like. Four out of five men here were once convicts themselves or are the sons or grandsons of convicts, and that is absurdly held against them by the
new settlers. It is unjust, and they feel it."

"I have seen it," she said. "It is a caste system. It
is worse than that." Her very first day in Sydney, she
had seen chain gangs of men emerging from the
barracks and shuffling dispiritedly along the dirt roads.
The broken spirit of the men, and the way it was
broken, angered her. The chains, the yellow convict
rags with broad arrows, and the public humiliation
of their having to walk through the streets chained
and dressed like that, deeply offended her. Robert
had seen it almost all his life. She saw it with new
eyes.

He took her to meet the Tolpuddle men, and she admired their independence. "But they are quite different," she said.

"Because they are from the English countryside and not from the squalor of a city," said Robert. "Because they know their cause is just. Because they know they were unjustly sent here, and know that is the opinion of most men. Because they have not been broken by privation while they have been here. Because they know they are going home." So they were. They were waiting for the next transport, and would go as free men. George Loveless's wife had heard in time of the men's release and had written to Tasmania to say she would wait for her husband in Dorset, so he was going home too. It was a happy issue.

Captain Cobb was often up-country with the graziers discussing cargoes of wool, and freightage, and at those times it was natural that Anna should see a lot of Susannah and Robert, particularly of Robert. He showed her Sydney and Parramatta, and one day they crossed to Manly. They walked together on the beach.

"You are very American," he said. "And yet the first time I saw you on the ship, the first time I was able to look at you, not just hear your voice as you told me to drink something, I thought you were Persian."

"Not so long ago," she said, "every American was something else." They walked on.

Then she said, "Persian is not far wrong. I am Armenian. My grandparents were born there. It is all a legend to me. My grandfather used to talk of home. He called it home. It seemed to me, as a child, that all the history of the world happened in that country. He talked about the Tigris and Euphrates, and Mount Ararat, and Aleppo, and Isfahan. He was not from Isfahan, but my grandmother was. Isfahan is in Persia, so you see you were near."

"But I have never seen a Persian," said Robert. "Except in paintings on vases."

"Then there are two legends. Your legend, from vases. And mine, from my grandfather. It seemed to me, as I listened to him, that Armenia had been overrun by every army in the world at one time or another. But they all went away afterwards, and we stayed. There were Greeks, Phrygians, Arabs, Tamburlaine himself. Did Tamburlaine have blue eyes? Maybe I have Tamburlaine's blue eyes. Or the eyes of some ancient Greek."

They walked along the beach. Robert was quiet, wanting to hear her talk. She said Armenians were supposed to be the first Christian nation.

"Are you still a Christian?" he asked.

"Yes, that remains. I think much more remains, too. I am probably more Armenian than I know."

She stopped and looked out into the harbour with her back to him. "All that water. I spend my life at sea. You know, the first Armenian king is supposed to be descended from Noah."

Robert could not afterwards have said why it was at that moment, but he took her lightly by the shoulders, turned her round, and kissed her on the mouth. When they talked about it later—the lovers' endless question, "Why that moment?"—she told him she was suprised and pleased. She openly kissed him back. Then they walked to the boat, and he took her back to Sydney Cove.

It was in the best room of Edward Hargraves, hotelkeeper, that Robert and Anna became lovers. He did not wish to compromise her by suggesting his own chambers, which were too well known.

Hargraves was an Englishman who had come out

from Hampshire not as a convict but as a settler, though settler was the wrong word for Hargraves, who never in his life settled at anything but was always trying something new. At fourteen he went to sea. At eighteen he left the sea and became a runner for a lodging-house in Liverpool, at a time when that port was the second city of England and the Empire. It was his business to approach newly arrived passengers on the quays and persuade them that the lodging-house represented by him was the newest, cleanest, best appointed, and most reasonable; where a man could eat good food, sleep between clean sheets, and probably not be robbed. This persuasion had to be carried on in competition with twenty other runners for twenty other lodging-houses. Hargraves was not dishonest, but he learned to be sharp. He reasoned that once he had a man's baggage he had the man. He worked on a percentage from the lodging-house. From this percentage he paid two strong men to assist with the baggage of the passengers he was persuading; that is, to carry it off rapidly in the direction of the lodging-house. The baggage was not taken by force. It was merely picked up smartly. It was done to help the traveller. No theft was intended. But Hargraves had discovered that a traveller infallibly followed his baggage. His career as a runner came to an end the day he failed to realize that a gentleman whose baggage he seized was a magistrate on the Liverpool bench. He went to sea again, and after one China voyage found himself at Sydney, where he saw that honest lodging-houses were badly needed. He founded one and called it Hargraves' Hotel. Robert conveyanced the land and property for him. Hargraves was anxious, from previous experience, to maintain an amiable acquaintance with a man who knew the law. He was always civil to Robert, and happy to let him his best bedroom, which had a dressing-room adjoining. He showed the room to

Robert, asked no questions, suggested a price lower than the going rate, and gave him the key. He mentioned that there was also a side entrance that Mr. King might find convenient, since it led to a street away from the quayside, which was often jammed with horses and drays.

"Just so," said Robert.

The *America* was moored a quarter of a mile away, and Anna could easily come into the town unobserved. She came in a day dress of green silk, carrying a small bag. Robert took her to the rooms. It was afternoon. They were cool rooms, but full of light.

She asked him, "Will you leave me for a while, and come back?"

He waited for ten minutes and then returned, knocked, and went in. He had been walking on the quay in the bright sun, and at first could hardly see her in the room. She had closed the shutters. She was standing in the doorway of the dressing-room, in white. As his eyes became accustomed to the darkness he saw that she was in a nightdress with long sleeves, and had brushed her hair out. Her eyes were lowered and she did not raise them. She did not speak.

He locked the door behind him and went to her. She seemed even slighter than he had imagined, but, though she was in her bare feet, at the same time taller than he had thought. She seemed as tall as him. He held out his arms to her. She took one hand briefly, no more than a touch, and then slipped into the open bed. He saw that she had folded the sheets back ready. She lay with her face away from him, though with her eyes open. He leaned across to touch her hair, and then went into the dressing-room. She had closed the shutters there, too, but he could just see that her dress was laid out on the sofa as neatly as if left by a maid ready for her mistress to put on. Her other clothes were folded on a chair. The three rings she

wore, which had been her mother's, were laid in a
row on the dressing table. He threw off his clothes,
leaving them where they fell, went out, and lay beside
her. He held her shoulders through the linen night-
dress. He was naked, and she was warm as he lay
against her. He could feel that she was covered down
to the ankles by the night-dress. He kissed her
mouth, and she kissed him back, though not as she
had at Manly, but much less openly. He raised his
head to look at her and she made her first movement
since she lay down, lifting her hand to his face and
running her fingers across his cheek. He kissed the
fingers. He caressed her and parted her legs, but only
through the linen, letting his hand rest there. Then he
found her ankles, and raised the night-dress to her
waist. When he went to enter her she murmured
something. He did not catch what she said, but something in the tone told him to wait, so he waited, penetrating her only a little, stroking her hair and lying
still. Then he entered her a little more, but not fully,
careful not to hurt her. She had kept her eyes closed,
but now she opened them and looked into his. In her
eyes was something he had not seen there before. He
had almost always seen her active, but what he saw
now was quiescence, and as their eyes met he ejaculated into her, sharply taking in his breath as if he
were saying, "Oh." She enfolded him in her arms.

They lay in this way for some minutes, until he
moved away and lay beside her. He loved her closing
of the shutters, her undressing alone, the night-dress
that covered her, her silence, her whole chaste reti-
cence.

After that they met often. One day she said, "Is it always so easy?"

"Hush, sweet," he said. She had no idea how delightful she was. No one had told her before. She
still closed the shutters. She was always to do that. She

had always been the sweetest, but now she was also the most pliant of lovers. She was, as he never ceased to wonder, so lightly made. She arched her back like the figures he had seen of Cretan dancers, raising her hips from the bed for him to enter her as he knelt before her. He held her to support her, but soon found she was no weight on his hands, and did not need it. She was tall, but so supple that the arching of the back came instinctively to her. He never knew a woman who gave herself so naturally. But in her most arched and supple moments she retained a decorousness pleasing beyond words. It said, without words, that she was a woman who would never give herself lightly, and that is a great thing for a lover to know.

She rarely spoke as they embraced. But she once said, "This is abandoned and entire, and you have done that."

"That is a huge thing to say."

"I mean it to be."

He never knew a woman so entire, or so decorous with it.

And she had a sweet gaiety too. Afterwards, she would put on his Indian-silk dressing-gown and sit cross-legged on the bed, and her eyes shone as he told her preposterous stories.

"There was a tiger," he said, "in Madras."

She nodded, sitting very upright, listening.

"When I came out from England we touched at Madras. And at Madras there is an English club, a club for English gentlemen."

"I too have put in at Madras," she said. "I found many English entrepreneurs and many English makers of good fortunes."

"Those are English gentlemen. Well, in this club——"

"With punkah wallahs to pull great fans back and forth, to cool the air?"

"At any rate to move the hot air round the club

rooms. Well, there was a billiard table, with wooden cues brought out from England, and ivory billiard balls brought out from England, made of ivory shipped to England from Africa—which is the point of having an Empire—and billiard tables of green baize. And gentlemen played billiards in the cool of the evening."

"You said there was a tiger."

"He came in and wanted to play billiards. He was a large tiger. Man-eating. Striped."

"All tigers are striped."

"Wide stripes. The tiger came in, out of the jungle perhaps. . . ."

"Of course," said Anna.

"And sat under the billiard table to wait his turn. At which the two men who were playing said, 'By Jove, there's a tiger,' and one went for a gun to shoot it. There were guns on the walls. But the other man said, 'Not cricket to shoot a sitting tiger. Not done.' They paused to consider. 'The fellow can't be a member,' said the man with the gun, regarding the tiger. 'No,' said the other, 'can't be, can he, seeing he's not English. Aren't any English tigers. Wouldn't say he was a member, would you?' So, with reluctance, they shot him, though, since he looked a decent sort of tiger, not before they asked him to leave and he declined. There's a stuffed tiger's head on the wall now. They use it for the billiards' trophy."

Anna, still sitting up, spread out her slim fingers on the bed. "We are like children," she said. "We play, like children. We talk about tigers with wide stripes."

Anna insisted, after the first times, that she should bring food. There were cheeses and *pâtés* and fruit which she brought in a basket from the ship and laid out on napkins on the bed. She brought silver fruit knives from the ship, hall-marked with the crest of a

Boston silversmith. It was as if it were a picnic, and their bed were a lawn.

"It is natural for me to wish you to eat," she said. "I would cook for you. I am an Armenian woman still." Sometimes, on saints' days, she burned incense. She told him the Armenian Church was very like the Greek Orthodox in its observances.

"My dear Anna," he said. He loved her for it all.

"I told you my name was Anna," she said. "That is my American name. The name I was given by my parents was Anahita."

"What does it mean?" he said.

She shook her head.

"What does it mean?"

"Love and fertility," she said.

He kissed her hands. He had never before wanted children as he did from her.

She wrote her name for him in the Pahlavi script, and taught him to read the characters. He said they were quite like Greek.

Robert and Anna were lovers, and she was the wife of a man who had saved his life. It had just happened, but he knew it was indefensible and tried to forget it. With Anna he could forget it. They were happy lovers.

Sometimes they met Hargraves and he asked Anna about America. Was it a good place for a man? Could a man like him flourish there? "I think you would thrive anywhere," she said. She told him he would undoubtedly do well in Boston or New York. "Though," she said, "there are other men there who possess get-up-and-go. You would find plenty of others like yourself."

"I shall go then."

"Sydney could become another Boston," she said.

"No. I shall go to America."

Anna conducted the business of the ship. She dealt

with the chandlers to replenish the *America's* stocks
of food and tackle. She dealt with the shipwrights to
arrange the refitting of the 'tween decks, to take wool.
It was she who paid the crew. Robert learned that
this business had always been hers. She took to bringing the ship's ledgers to their meetings. When they fell
asleep it was most often she who woke first, and he
would find her reading, or writing, or adding figures.
At first he was amused. Then he was puzzled. Then
he was irritated. He thought to himself that the only
time she let in the light was to see the ship's books.
He told himself he must never say so bitter a thing
to her, and then immediately said it. He said it more
than once. One day he took a book from her hands
and closed it. He could not explain it even to himself, but it seemed wrong. So soon after their most extraordinary moments together, which he knew were as
much to her as to him, she wanted to be at work
again, while he only wanted to lie and talk with her,
or do nothing at all.

"It is not easy for me to do nothing," she said. She
said it was in her nature to work, that it had been in
her parents' nature, and was in the nature of the
Yankees among whom she lived and one of whom she
had married.

"It is what you call American get-up-and-go?" he
asked.

They laughed. They should not have laughed so
easily.

Robert and Anna grew closer as lovers but drifted
apart in other ways. Anna observed this. Robert did
not, because he did not see what his heart did not
wish to see. But the differences grew. Once when
Cobb travelled inland, Anna stayed the night with
Robert, which she had not done before. They lay in
bed all evening, and Robert awoke after midnight to

find her leafing through bills of lading by the light of an oil lamp. He took the papers from her hands and threw them across the room. She looked at him with coolness in her eyes, got up, walked in his dressing-gown across the room, and picked up the papers. He had acted more impetuously than he meant, but her coolness drove him to another foolishness. He dressed rapidly, saying nothing and not looking at her, and left her. As soon as he walked through the door he knew he should go back, but he walked for an hour on the deserted quay. When he did return she was dressed and about to leave, even at that hour of night. She appeared composed, though if he had come back five minutes earlier he would have found her crying.

"Robert, what did I do to deserve that?"

He said, "I too have my work. But I should insult you if I brought a brief to bed with you, to work through some miserable claim for damages after you had fallen asleep."

He was very unhappy. The differences between them, which had previously delighted him, were now dangerous. She was American, and he had loved her activity of mind. She was Armenian, and he had admired her reverence for her ancestors and her dead parents, and her sureness in her faith. But Robert had come to see that Anna's certainty of faith carried with it an intellectual certainty which worried the liberal tolerance that had been educated into him. Still, and in spite of everything, he assumed Anna would remain with him when the *America* sailed. From their early days as lovers he had assumed this. They both had. They reached this conclusion rapidly. She had promised to leave Cobb. But now Robert did ask himself how this could be when she was still absorbed in the ship, its refitting, its taking on of cargo, and its everlasting ledgers.

Susannah had seen very early what Anna meant to her son. She was apprehensive. She saw in Anna a woman as strong as herself, but profoundly different both from herself and from Robert. She did not say anything until one day when he came again and talked about Anna.

"I have never known anyone so single-minded," he said.

"And you are like your father, single-hearted."

"If I am, so is she. And I trust her."

"Robert, first of all she is the wife of the man who saved you. That is something you will never forget. But, if you could put that aside—and I know there are times when anything can be put aside—ask yourself how well you know her. You say you trust her. You trust her because you see, rightly, that she has a conscience. It is a conscience which will make her do what she believes to be right, whatever it costs her, or you. I think it is an American spirit. They will try to change the world. You do not understand her. She will never be feckless, but her good conscience will hurt you more than fecklessness, because you will have expected more."

Susannah was perhaps right. Robert never found a more likely explanation.

Anna acted suddenly. One afternoon she and Robert walked in the grounds of the domain, on the lawns and among the trees. She illuminated everything with her presence. He told her so. He admired and prized her, and thought her beautiful. When he looked back afterwards, he thought there had never been a time when he was so conscious of her, of her movement, of the way her clothes sat lightly on her, of her scent, of her eyes, of the delicacy of her hands. He was very much in love with her. She discovered him looking at her with love. She led him to a high point where they could see the cove beneath them, and the *America* lying among the other vessels.

"Sit down," she said. And still it was to come as a surprise to him.

She sat by him.

"Robert, I am going."

He looked at her, and then down at the *America*. "For him?"

"For him, partly. I am his wife."

"You have always been his wife. Why do you discover that now?"

"For him, partly. But also because, even if I were not his wife, you and I are too different. We have seen that."

Robert reasoned with her until he knew it was useless, and then he said nothing.

She too was silent.

"And what of everything else?" he said. "Was that nothing?"

"You know it was a great thing to me."

"You said it was abandoned and entire."

"It was. It has changed. Other things have changed it. I could not say it was entire now."

"I was sure you would be constant. I see I deceived myself."

She tried to explain. "Dear Robert," she said, "we are different. You expect too little."

"I evidently expected much too much."

"I mean that out here, in the colony, you expect too little. I am going because I know it is right to go, and I must. But there is also this—there is such a great difference. You do expect so little. You are afraid."

"Of *what?*"

"When we came into Sydney harbour for the first time, do you remember I said this could be another Boston? You have heard me tell Hargraves that too. And do you remember, as we came in, I said there was a magic about the place? There is. But you have only to stay here a few months to hear nothing but sniping between those whose parents were once convicts, and those whose parents were not. Bickering will achieve nothing."

"And what has this to do with us?"

"You are angry when I work."

That was not an answer, but it was the essence of everything. And Robert was so lacking in perception of this woman who meant so much to him that he said, "That is a big thing?"

"Yes. I once said something was a huge thing, and it was. This is another huge thing."

"And if it is, what on earth has it to do with fear? You said fear. Fear of what?"

"You are afraid of distance. You do not know it, but it shapes your mind. I think you are all afraid of distance. You see that you are the farthest, most distant, most lonely. The distance is nothing. It is a few weeks' sailing, and what is that in a lifetime? It is a fear that comes from maps. It is a map-given fear. Whenever you look at a map, you are underneath. The maps were drawn by Europeans. If I lived in Sydney, I would draw maps on a new projection, so that Australia was the centre of the world. London and Paris are still the centres of the world to you, and so long as you think that, so long will it remain true. You expect too little. You demand too little of the Cosmos."

With that immense assertion she left him. If she had considered, she might have realized that, to him, a large part of the Cosmos was herself.

The next day she sailed. She left a letter which was not unkind, or unloving. "It was entire," she wrote, "as I have never known it before." She wished him long life, and signed her name, Anahita, in Pahlavi characters.

Next morning, when the *America* rounded the headlands and disappeared from sight, Robert walked back to Hargraves'.

"She will be coming back?" asked the man.

"No."

Robert went to their rooms. He picked up the silk dressing-gown, and a forgotten silver fruit knife that she had brought from the *America,* and he remembered the afternoons when their bed was a lawn and she had said, "We play, like children."

Her loss was very great to him. He had wanted children by her. Her name of Anahita, love and fertility, was now an irony.

Then there was her display of the power of will, which fascinated him. The Enlightenment, exalting Reason and proclaiming that it is up to Man to shape his own world, came from Europe, yet Robert, whose education was European, took it to promise so much less than Anna did. Their understanding of the idea was wholly different. Robert had observed how little Man could achieve in the shaping of his own world. This did not surprise him, or cast him down. It did not mean that a man might not attempt great things, though to *expect* too much was hubris. Robert's reasonable European mind accepted that Man was only Man. Anna as a reasonable American could not swallow that word *only.* Man was Man, and there was nothing, given the will, and work, he could not achieve.

On the late evening of the second day Robert took the knife Anna had left and walked out across the domain to Bennelong Point. It was an hour past sunset. A half-moon sat high in the sky. To his right, in Farm Cove, he could just make out the hulk of the schooner, which had lain there since the *America*'s sailors beached her. Her timbers were too badly strained to be repaired, and she had been stripped and left to rot. Robert turned back to Sydney Cove and to the lights of the twenty vessels lying at anchor there. He took the knife with the hallmark of the Boston silversmith and hurled it high and far. As he watched its flight his mood changed. He was no longer remembering what had been, but thinking of what might be. As the knife described its parabola against the sky, and then dropped towards the waters of the cove, it flew sometimes in darkness and sometimes in flashes of reflected light, caught by the moonlight or by the rays of the ships' lanterns as they rode, and it entered the waters of the cove with a long flash of light.

29

A Marriage Blessed with Grace

THE YEARS THAT FOLLOWED were a time of marriage, death, and, in public affairs, what was politely termed a fretfulness of society.

Sydney had the distinction of being regularly described—by visiting missionaries or by lady writers, generally of obscurely noble birth—as the most dissolute city on earth. Since the great ports of Liverpool and New York were also regularly condemned in the same words, this meant that Sydney was thriving. The city was building. Wide avenues were laid out. The Countess Ominskova—whose nationality was variously stated to be French, Polish, or Russian—was only one of the lady travel writers who was accosted by a dockside tout who offered, for the price of a drink, to show her the one street in Sydney where no house had ever been broken into. This offer was always accepted, and the tout then conducted the lady to a length of avenue recently laid out by a speculative builder, a road on which, as the visitor would then discover, no single house had been broken into because no single house had yet been built. But the avenue had been built, by road gangs of con-

victs. Sydney was the only great city in the world
where white men were still slaves. As the visitor
leafed through his morning paper he noticed rewards
offered for information leading to the return of stolen
horses and absconded bondsmen. The usual reward
for a horse was seven pounds, but for a man only
two. It was easier to get another convict than another
horse. But the refinements of life were there for the
prosperous. One Saturday, John Redmond came into
town to be fitted for his new overcoat of llama cloth at
the establishment of Hayes and Co., late of Savile
Row, London, and, while he was at the tailor's, his
wife bought toys for their two young children, a
humming-top for the boy and a doll for the girl.

Mrs. John Redmond was the daughter of a grazier
whose kingdom was not quite so large as the older
Redmond's, but still a kingdom. The sheep kings' families were already intermarrying to strengthen their
dynasties. John's was as political a marriage in its way
as that of a Tudor prince to a princess of Aragon. The
sheep kingdoms now stretched in a boomerang
around south-eastern Australia, covering a territory
that extended as far as from Boston to New Orleans.
And Redmond's was the most powerful kingdom. Since
Macarthur's recent death, after years of madness,
Redmond was the emperor of the sheep kings.

He had become milder with age, success, and
riches. He was not a man to whom women, or any
woman, had ever intensely mattered. His passion had
been to create a kingdom, and he had done it. So he
did not see that, because of him, many years had lain
fallow for Susannah. It was not in his nature to comprehend the depth of her distress when he took her
son John away. But he was now sorry that he had
acted unjustly towards her in never allowing her to see
John again. He would have done, but for Wyndham.
The night Wyndham returned from Parramatta and

was embraced by Susannah in her night-dress in the lighted doorway, they were seen from the domain by a groom who was woken by the sounds of the disturbed horses as Wyndham stabled his mare. The groom received a sovereign now and then from Redmond in return for such information. Redmond had not been envious or jealous of the scene in the lighted door which the groom described to him. But he had been very much in fear of anything that reflected on his good name. He did not wish it to be known that his wife had a lover. That is why he would not allow John to see Susannah. He would not let his son see a mother whose actions might bring the name of Redmond into disrepute. But that was all past. Redmond now thought he had been hard, and would have made amends if he could. But by the time he was assured enough of his own success and name to relent towards Susannah, and no longer to fear her, John had hardened. As a young man he would not visit his mother. They had seen each other only twice, both times in public places. He had raised his hat, and that was all. When he married he did not ask his mother to the wedding, and replied formally to her letter of congratulation. When the children were born he told his wife they were not to see their grandmother. Susannah bore this. She was used to the estrangement from John, and expected no more.

But she was more delighted than she could have imagined by the events of the late summer of 1838. Young women in Sydney could not "come out" in quite the style of London. There was no Eton and Harrow match at Lord's cricket ground, no Royal Ascot at which one watched not the horses but the society gathered in the royal enclosure. There was no queen whose gracious nod in response to a girl's ceremonial curtsy signified that young lady's formal entrance into society. But in Sydney there was a gov-

ernor to curtsy to, and balls to dance at thereafter.
When Jane's daughter Elizabeth was seventeen,
Susannah presented her to the governor. She had come
out. She was escorted to balls by the young men of
the colony, and sometimes, at his mother's request,
by Robert. It was expressly at his mother's request. He
would not have thought of it himself. He liked Elizabeth, but did not particularly notice her. She was
younger. When his mother asked him, of course he
took Elizabeth to this ball or that. Then it became a
pleasure to him. He was surprised. He had thought of
her as the little dark girl, two years old, whom he first
saw on the landing stage at London Bridge, and then
next day in the dock at Bow Street, wrapped in a blue
cloak and held in Jane's arms. She was the little girl
who had crossed the world. He remembered her at
supper with the Tolpuddle men when they arrived in
Sydney. He saw her frequently around his mother's
house, but that was all. He still thought of her as the
little girl wrapped in a cloak.

He was supposed to entertain her. He soon became
aware that it was she who entertained him. After
Anna, looking for too much, he had found nothing.
Now he looked forward to calling to collect Elizabeth,
listening to her excited talk on the brief drive to this
house or that, and then dancing with her, or watching
her dance with other men. He saw that others thought
her beautiful. He looked at her again, and saw that
she was. She took such joy in whatever she did. She
made life sweet for him again. Afterwards, when he
brought her home, if it was not too late and if the night
was warm, they walked for ten minutes on the lawns
of the domain. She took his arm and chatted. She
asked him about Paris and London. It was fifteen
years since he had seen either city, but he told her
what he remembered.

"More than *twenty* times the size of Sydney?" she said.

He assured her London was. And Paris.

Elizabeth had been brought up in Susannah's house very much as Robert had in the countess's. She had become pretty well the daughter of the house. Susannah opened the society of Sydney to her as Françoise d'Estaing had opened that of Paris and London to the young Robert.

Jane was pleased to see her daughter so happy. She said, "She thinks the world of you, Mr. Robert."

"And she is a great pleasure to me," he said.

One night they returned from a ball given by James McDonald to celebrate the coming out of his daughter, Margaret. It was a grand house, almost as grand as the sheep kings', overlooking the harbour from the heights of Vaucluse. The drive back took forty minutes. It was past midnight. Elizabeth was in high spirits, it was still warm, and they walked a little before going in.

"Margaret says her father has more ships than anyone in the colony."

Robert thought he probably had. He had five coasting schooners, a brig, and a three-masted barque, that made voyages to India and China.

"She says that because she has no brothers, she will run the whole fleet when it comes to her." Margaret was seventeen, the same age as Elizabeth, but young for her age. It was not that she did not love her father, but she still had the child's matter-of-fact acceptance of her parents' eventual death and her own sure survival. Once a few years before she had written a prize essay at school which began "When Mummy and Daddy died, Dr. Smithson came downstairs and gave me thirty pounds." From this beginning the narrator went on very successfully to run the family's fleet. She received full marks for imagination. And imagination

it was. Women in Australia did not run sheep stations
or ships. There were still fewer women than men in
the colony, and no tradition, as there was in America,
of the pioneering woman overcoming all odds to run
her dead husband's ranch or sheep station, call it what
you will.

But Miss Margaret McDonald's imagined ambitions
took Robert's mind back to Anna's real ones. He
was looking out at the bay. The skeleton of the abandoned schooner was still beached in Farm Cove. He
could see it. He fell silent. Elizabeth, who had been
holding his arm, released it and walked a few steps
away. That season, fabric rosebuds were worn everywhere—in the hair, as a corsage, at the hem of a
dress. Earlier in the day, before the ball, Robert had
given Elizabeth a silken violet to wear at her throat.
She was dark-skinned and the violet looked better
than a rose. It was the first gift he ever made her, except for the birthday and Christmas presents he had
given to the child Elizabeth, to the Elizabeth who
had been a child to him until so recently.

She preserved the silence. This was new too. The
child he had known was always chatting. The young
woman he had come to know in the previous two
months also talked easily and happily. He loved to
let her talk. But now she held the silence, and then she
said, "Robert, what is it that you want most?" It was
not a child's question, not an offer of three wishes. She
wanted to know his mind.

"Robert, what do you want most of all?"

He answered in one word, "Children." How he had
wanted Anna's children.

Elizabeth said, "And I should love to give them to
you."

It is not possible for a woman to say more. He
looked at her, and she met his serious eyes. She was
no longer the girl he had been escorting to a few

dances. She was at that moment Leah in Dorset, years before, looking at him across the room with the bow window, the time she came in and stood by the closed door after they came back from Puddletown. He saw Leah in her for the first time, though as soon as he did, it seemed obvious. She was very like. Dorset families are close. She was a Bryant. Leah was a Martin. The Bryants and Martins had intermarried for years. She was Leah, but more than Leah. She was a girl whom until so recently he had seen almost every day, and yet not seen at all. And now she said such words to him.

"Elizabeth," he said, "dear Elizabeth."

He saw her to his mother's door. They said good night. Then he went to his own rooms in town. He thought of her all night.

Three days afterwards Robert was called in by the governor and offered a judgeship of the Supreme Court of New South Wales, which he declined. That evening he told Susannah, who was not surprised.

"I said it was very good of him, but I was an advocate. Certainly I saw my work for the next few years as that of an advocate. He was decent about it, just nodded, said he'd rather see me a judge, but then, on the other hand, supposed he should be grateful for any reasonably moderate advocacy of the cause I seemed to have adopted. I said I was much obliged."

The governor was a believer in hierarchy, in order, in the keeping of one's station in life. It was the fashion of the times to believe in the virtues of the free settler. The governor's masters in London believed in it, and so did the governor. This did not mean that he was anti-emancipist. A British subject was a British subject, whatever his rank, whatever his parents might have been, and whatever his previous crimes might have been. The governor believed in an English free-

dom under the law, even in an English equality before
the law. He wished some of his judges showed a
greater understanding of the principle, which was
one reason why he had offered Robert the judgeship.
The legal rights of the emancipists he would respect
and even enforce. In a way he was a man of divided
mind. Though he would ensure their rights, if he
could, he was apprehensive that a too sudden acquisition and exercise of new freedom by the emancipists
might lead to their too sudden political power. He
was a man of his generation, and anything like democracy was anathema to him. Democracy meant the
French Revolution and the mob, or, at least, the
American War of Independence and rebellion.

It came down to this. The governor disliked excess.
Democracy was excess. Though he believed profoundly in the virtues of the settlers, he rebuked their
excesses too, and even those of the sheep kings. He
had recently declared null and void a deed—sealed
and delivered, and signed by the marks of three undoubted aboriginal chiefs—by which the younger Redmond had acquired about ten miles of land in exchange
for the following valuable and legal consideration, to
wit: eighteen Birmingham knives, three colanders, one
hundredweight of flour, three coloured statues of the
Virgin Mary, three tomahawks, thirty axe heads of
guaranteed iron, three candelabra, eighteen pairs of
red trousers, and thirty suits of slop clothing guaranteed as worn by convict subjects of Her Most Excellent Majesty Queen Victoria. That was the wording.
The aborigines admired the yellow of the convict uniforms. They had been unable to explain why they
wanted statuettes of the Virgin Mary, but had insisted
on them. The fact was that one chief had seen such an
effigy, three feet high, in the shanty of an English missionary with High Church leanings, and had reasonably assumed it to be a totem representing in one

figure both the white man's God and the white man's Queen. Three were demanded because the three chiefs wanted one each.

When his deed was voided, the younger Redmond talked darkly about executive interference with that freedom of contract which was the right of all British subjects. His father, when he saw the deed, called his son a fool and apologized to the governor.

So the governor was an honest man, and one of the reasons for his offer to Robert had been the wish for an upright judge.

"He asked me if I would think about it for a week," said Robert, "and I said yes, because to refuse him that would have been uncivil."

"Will you think about it?"

"No."

His mother smiled. "He knows that too. He only asked you so as not to be—what was your word?— uncivil."

They let the subject drop.

"Susannah?" said Robert.

He rarely called her by that name. She sat up. He told her about Elizabeth, Elizabeth's question, his reply, and then hers.

"You say she is like Leah? Is that all?"

"If that were all it would be a very great deal. But no, it is not all, is it? But she is only seventeen."

"I was only eighteen," said Susannah.

Robert repeated aloud, but really to himself, the words Elizabeth had spoken to him, "And I should love to give them to you."

Susannah said, "This time you will not need to ask Jane what wedding gowns are made of, as you did in Dorchester. But you must go and ask her for her daughter."

Susannah gave the silk for the wedding gown, this

time not from Piedmont but from Canton. It was a
marriage blessed with grace. Within two years there
were two children—a girl, Susannah-Jane, named after her grandmothers, and a boy, George-Nicolas,
after his grandfathers. Robert was at peace. The colony was not.

But before the affairs of the colony erupted and em-
broiled the lives of them all, especially Susannah's,
there were two private deaths, and both of these
struck hard at Susannah.

A new Government House was at last built in Sydney. As she saw the pile of quarry stone and marble
rising in the domain Susannah remembered Bligh's
scathing inventory of the faults of the old Government
House nearly forty years before, ending with the
growled phrase, "Wants being new." Since Macquarie's time there had been plans. She remembered
that Greenway, the architect who showed her how to
brush Sydney sandstone, had built such magnificent
stables that successive governors, when they chose to
live at Sydney rather than retire to Parramatta, were
worse housed than their horses, a state of affairs
which generations of convicts had thought only reasonable. Now at last there was to be a viceregal palace worthy of the colony. It was designed of course by
an Englishman. He was special architect to Queen
Victoria. His list of works was formidable. He had
patched up Windsor Castle and Hampton Court, and
put the final heavy touches to Buckingham Palace.
He had built country seats for the English nobility,
and his masterpiece was an Oriental-Tudor-Jacobean
folly for a Russian count in the Crimea. He was therefore very eminent. New Government House at Sydney
lived up to his reputation. Its first ceremonial use was
for the queen's birthday ball in May 1843. The waltz
—no longer considered indecent, riotous, and Ger-

man—was danced by all the society of Sydney and the colony. There were the naval and military officers and their ladies, the stays-and-blubber men and theirs, and, of course, most prosperous of all, the sheep kings and their queens, princes, and princesses. For the first time Susannah saw her two sons at one gathering, Robert dancing with Elizabeth, and John with Mrs. John Redmond. The older Redmond was there too. Half-way through the evening he beckoned to Robert and asked to be introduced to Elizabeth, and, when they had talked for a while, asked Robert to take him over to Susannah.

She saw them approaching.

"Good evening, William," she said. She held out her hand.

He said, "I am pleased to see you so well, and Robert and his wife so happy." They were the first words they had spoken for twenty years. They said little more, but Susannah hoped it would be the end of what had been first an enmity and then a long estrangement, and that they would be friends. She asked Redmond, "Will you tell John that I should be glad to meet him too, and his wife?" Redmond said he would ask, and he did ask his son, who declined. He then told his son to do it, and he refused. There was nothing more to be done.

The governor came over to Susannah, stood with her watching the couples on the floor, and then said, "Your son dances with his wife as if he loved her."

"He does, doesn't he?" said Susannah. Whenever people said "your son" they meant Robert. It was natural, but at that moment she could not help noticing it.

The governor asked her to dance. She had never danced a waltz before, but liked it. The governor saw she liked it and was pleased with himself. Well, he

said, she must come and see how her pictures had
been hung. He meant the two portraits of George III
and Queen Charlotte which Governor King had
brought out, which Bligh had loyally toasted, which
Susannah had kept in her house for many years, but
which she had just presented to Government House.
She thought them better suited to the vast rooms
created by a man who had built a palace for a Russian
count in the Crimea. They had been hung well, with
the king on the left of the mantelpiece looking across
at his queen on the right. Then the governor took her
into the great hall to show her the coat of arms of her
father, which were displayed there with those of the
other governors. Her father's blazon, and hers for that
matter, was a single golden lion rampant on a grey
ground. He had never used it in office. Susannah had
never used it once either, and could barely remember
it. It was by then getting on for midnight on an evening of late autumn, drawing near winter, and it was
not warm. But there was no wind so they stepped for
a moment on to the terrace, and looked back at the
house.

"What do you think of the palace they've given
me?" said the governor.

Susannah looked at the man, and then at the sil-
houette of his viceregal palace. "Crenellated," she
said, "castellated, Gothicized, and superlatively bedecked."

"Um. That's what I think. Turreted too. Superlatively turreted, for bows and arrows. Against the Rus-
sians, I should think."

She was tired, said good night to a few friends, and
then went to her carriage. When she got home, her
maid said they had not sent for her earlier, not wanting to disturb her at the grand ball, but a man had
come from the cottages to say John Easty was dying.
Susannah turned sharply on the girl, but then said

nothing. The girl could not have known Easty was worth a hundred grand balls in a hundred viceregal palaces. Susannah went straightaway to Easty's cottage, to find one man watching over his body, and one candle lit.

Here was Easty, the man who had taught her to plant fruit trees to comfort her, the man who, when Bligh was governor, had moved the toy ships on the blue cloak as Bligh told Robert the story of Captain Dance's most famous victory.

He had come out as a soldier with the First Fleet in 1788, and now had died at the age of eighty-one, so far as she knew the last survivor of that fleet. Easty was also, though Susannah did not know it, the man who, on that October evening so long before, watched her as she stood waiting on the lawns of the domain for the *Géographe* to come to her moorings and for Baudin to walk up from the cove. She was ashamed that for some time she had hardly seen Easty. He had not been in the gardens for a month. She might have asked after him. He was the governor's gardener, not hers, but she might have asked, and found that he was ill, and gone to him. She was ashamed that she had not.

She stayed with him for a while, and then went back to the house and in the early hours of the morning wrote a letter to the governor saying he might wish to know what might otherwise escape his notice, that John Easty, lately dead, for many years head gardener in the domain, had come out to the colony as a private soldier, had served for many years in the army, and to her knowledge had been a particularly loyal and trusted servant to Governors King and Bligh. The governor saw that a flag was provided for the coffin, and a volley fired over the grave.

Very soon afterwards Jane Bryant began to die. Susannah did see this. Jane was not eighty-one. She

had not reached a great age like Easty. It was a
rapid deterioration. Susannah asked the governor for
his physician, who came. Redmond, hearing of
Jane's illness, himself recommended the best man he
knew, who gave a second opinion. Susannah was grateful for this. But neither doctor could get near a diag-
nosis, let alone a remedy. Jane did not die alone.
Elizabeth, Robert, and Susannah were constantly with
her. But she said no last words which were remembered, because she lost the power of speech two weeks
before her death. Another grave. Susannah stood with
Elizabeth on her left and Robert on her right as Jane
was buried. It was a fine day. The sky was unclouded.
She told the other two to take the carriage, and walked
the mile back to her house alone. She was in full
mourning. Jane had been sixty-two. Susannah was
only three years younger. It was absurd, she told herself. Her friend was dead and she could walk under a
blue sky back from the grave.

With Easty and Jane gone so close together, there
was now no one in the colony who had ever seen her
and Nicolas together.

But she was alive. She was vigorous.

30

~~~

The Clamour of a Summer Evening

IT WAS IN THE NAME OF LIBERTY that the sheep kings
called the great public meeting whose real purpose
was to further their own financial interests.

"I suppose," said the younger Redmond, "that it
will have to be an outdoor clamour?"

His father replied that this was obvious. No hall in
Sydney would hold the three thousand men confidently expected to turn up. "Though as to clamour,"
he said, "the less clamorous the better."

So the graziers held their assembly in Hyde Park.
Since it was summer, and no crowd would stand long
in the Sydney sun, the meeting was announced for an
hour before sunset. More than three thousand came.
There were benches for a few hundred, others
perched in the lower branches of trees or sat on the
roofs of carriages, and the rest stood. On a raised
wooden platform sat the graziers who for this evening
had turned into statesmen, for this was, as the posters
plastered all over Sydney had proclaimed, *A Grand
Meeting of Citizens to Determine the Future Conduct
and Government of the Colony*. The governor had
been invited, but regretted his inability to attend. On

the platform, William Redmond was chairman. His son, John, was to make the opening speech. By him sat his undoubtedly pretty wife.

John rose.

"Gentlemen," he said, "you will have thought it a large thing that we are all assembled here tonight to determine, a large thing that you have all come to determine. The future of this colony is a large thing, and we *can* hope to determine it, because we are young. This is a young country. We are not hampered by traditions. We are gathered here to make traditions."

At this there was a first small cheer. The graziers had been thoughtful enough to provide kegs of best beer for the refreshment of their guests, and most had drunk a pint or two already.

"Our country is young," continued Mr. John Redmond, "but do we love her the less for that? We all married this country as each man here married his wife, in the pride and beauty of her youth. . . ."

A cheer. Mrs. John Redmond was undoubtedly pretty. Applause, at which John modestly spread his arms in acknowledgement, and then continued.

"And as each man shapes the character of his youthful spouse, so each man here tonight may shape the character of the country which is also his bride."

More applause. The crowd consisted almost entirely of men.

"Now," said Redmond, "as to the future government of this bride, their beloved country . . ." But at that moment someone, remembering the older Redmond's apostrophes to that Great Oak, an hereditary aristocracy, began to sing "The Four-Legged Oak." John took a chance. He listened, paused, but not long enough to allow others to take up the song, and then said, "I hear an old song, almost a traditional song? I was talking of tradition just now. I am proud that my father has made that contribution to the tradition of our country. I am sure he too is proud."

Applause.

But now, said John, they were almost at their coming of age. The time was coming, as it came to every man, when he should determine his own affairs, when the colony should determine its own affairs. But what did they see? They in the colony were taxed, but had no voice—in the colony itself, let alone in the Westminster Parliament of which he spoke—in the spending of the revenue raised. It was another people, in another time, which had raised the cry of no taxation without representation. That was, he emphasized, another people, a rebel people. The citizens of Sydney were Her Majesty's loyal subjects. (Hurrah.) But the time had come when it might not be inapt to remark, no more than remark, that New South Wales was now being taxed by the mother country at ten times the rate which led the American colonies to seize their independence in 1776. But that was another time. He would say no more as to that. He would talk instead of something with which they were all familiar. Wool. They would all know he was a sheepman. He would assert that he was a sheepman. But he would also assert that it was wool which enabled them all, all of them gathered there tonight, to live prosperously. It was wool on which the colony had prospered, and the prosperity of the colony was their prosperity, theirs to protect. Now was the time to call upon the Westminster Parliament, even if it dragged its feet on the great issue of independence, to act quickly to protect if not their prosperity, at least their means of livelihood. He would go so far as to say livelihood. Wool was the staple of the colony, and yet the price of labour had risen by one-half in the last year. Such was the plight of all connected with sheep—and he was a grazier but spoke not only for graziers but for all who earned their daily bread. (Cries of "Mutton and damper.") Very well then, their daily mutton and damper (laughter) from wool—such was the plight of them all that they might soon have to face the prospect of flocks and herds melted down for mere tallow. And that, he said, would be the melting down to mere tallow of the prosperity of them all. (Prolonged silence.)

It was in these circumstances, and in these circumstances alone, that he proposed that this meeting should petition Her Majesty's government to renew the transportation of convicts to New South Wales; those convicts who, as they all knew, had for the past few years been diverted to Tasmania. They would all know that the draft regulation to permit this continued emigration of exiles had been laid before the secretary of state in London. That gentleman was known to be favourable to the interests of them all. He needed only to sign. But he must sign now.

Mr. John Redmond considered, however, that he must allude to the moral arguments from which it would be un-Christian to turn away one's face, arguments which he knew would be advanced against their proposal. He would only say in reply that the life of a shepherd or hut-keeper could often humanize and restore a fallen human being. He had often seen this effect. He would only say, and would leave this thought in their minds, that this was the system which had given birth to a new and splendid civilization, of which they were all members. It had succeeded in this to a degree unparalleled in history. Here John paused to pick up a tankard set before him, and then, with the tankard raised high, he cried, "Yours is the making of tradition. Yours is the making of history. These things are in your keeping." Then, still standing, he drank.

It took much less of an invitation than that to induce a citizen of Sydney to raise a tankard of beer. Thousands drank with Mr. John Redmond. He sat down, and the cheers were great. Not all present cheered, but most did, and yet most were themselves emancipated convicts. They cheered because the beer had put them in good humour, because Mr. John Redmond spoke well, and, most of all, because they did not in their minds associate themselves, or their former wretchedness and present injustice, with the "exiles" Mr. Redmond wished to be shipped out to herd his flocks. They had put their past behind them. They were also all city men. Few had ever known the delights of the pastoral life. So they cheered.

Robert rose. It was just past sunset. Flares and torches were beginning to be lit here and there at the edges of the crowd and by the platform. Robert stood on the driving seat of a cart, waited until the older Redmond acknowledged him, and then began to speak as quietly as he could and still be heard.

He lifted up a copy of the poster which the graziers had printed to advertise the meeting, and read from it. *"A Grand Meeting of Citizens to Determine the Future Conduct and Government of the Colony.*

"Gentlemen," he said, "since that is what we are here for, I will make two points about the form of government. While the previous speaker was on his way to reminding us—but no more than reminding us, as he made plain—of the fact that the American colonies once seized their independence, he forgot I think to mention that his father, who is in the chair of this meeting, has already submitted to the governor the draft of a new constitution, which I have seen. It does not read at all like the American Declaration of Independence. I do not think the word independence anywhere appears in it. It provides for an elective lower chamber, but proposes a property qualification which would give the vote to perhaps one in five of those present at this meeting. It also provides for an upper chamber, to be composed of an hereditary peerage very much on the English model. 'The Four-Legged Oak' may, as a song, have passed into tradition, but the idea of the great oak of aristocracy is still very much alive, certainly as a proposal."

The crowd was silent now.

"But the speech we heard was really about transportation. That is what this meeting is about. Men may speak out for their own interest, and that is what has happened this evening. Mr. John Redmond has spoken for the graziers' own interest. That is a perfectly proper thing for him to do. But it is also right for us to be very clear that this is what he was doing. Very well then, transportation. Mr. John Redmond told us that in his opinion the life of a shepherd could humanize and restore a fallen human being. He did not say that these words are a quotation from a memorandum addressed by him and his fellow graziers to the secretary of state in London at least a year ago, or that this memorandum was debated in Parliament and reported in the newspapers. He also did not say that this same memorandum contained these words, which I now quote. They are as follows: 'No other country in the world could furnish such an effectual penitentiary as the sheep-walks of Australia.' Mr. John Redmond is offering to provide a penitentiary. Those of you who were transported here will remember the years before you became free again. And when you remember them, will you wish to inflict a punishment of the same severity on others, so that they can live the lives you led?"

Most of the men in the crowd had stopped drinking, and were listening intently. There was hardly a sound.

"Mr. John Redmond fairly stated his own interest. He stated openly that he was a grazier. I must state my interest. I have for many years worked as counsel

for many men who had served their sentences but
then found they were not really free. It is a man's right
to do what he considers in his own best interests, so
long as that does not hurt the legitimate interests of
other men. I feel bound to say that Mr. John Redmond has consistently opposed grants of land to
emancipists, their right to sit on juries, and their right
to hold all but the pettiest public office. His interests
are those of perhaps one hundred other graziers. They
are called the sheep kings. What he proposes would be
in the interest of those one hundred men, but I believe
against the interest of almost all the other one hundred
thousand inhabitants of this colony. And I cannot believe that what he proposes would be in the interest
of the thousands of convicts who would once again be
transported here. Wool is the staple of this colony,
and the prosperity of everyone does depend on it in
some way. But flocks are not yet, I think, being
melted down into tallow. Wool is, perhaps, the Golden
Fleece of this colony. It has been called that. But we
must not sell our souls for the Golden Fleece, particularly when the profits from that sale would go largely
to others, and to so few others."

He sat down. The points he made had gone home.
The graziers' cause was as good as lost. The crowd
gave almost a sigh. The men on the platform asked
each other what to do. Then Susannah stood up.

It would have been better if she had not, so much
better, but at that moment she stood. The light was
now quite gone, and her figure was picked out by the
flickering flares. Everyone there knew her as the governor's daughter, though most likely they did not
know of which governor. They all knew she was the
older Redmond's estranged wife. She was cheered before she said a word, and then she asked, "Would the
chairman say whether he believes, as his son does,

that men should once again be transported to this colony?"

The crowd made Redmond answer. Yes, he said, he favoured the return of transportation.

Susannah said, "We were speaking just now of 'exiles.' That is the new word. I have been here more than forty years, and I have heard many words used. There have been fashions in words. First men were felons, then convicts, then government men, and now there may be others called exiles. Most have been slaves. Some have been lucky. They were pardoned early because they were useful, because they could be useful as teachers, or architects. It has been a lottery. Some have been lucky, but most have been slaves. I have had many friends who were transported here. My dearest friend came here as a convict. She married here as a convict, from the female factory. And her husband, although he was an emancipist by then, was later sent to Newcastle, where he died."

Everyone in the crowd still remembered what Newcastle used to mean. Susannah would have told them how Bryant died in chains, except that his daughter Elizabeth was sitting by her at the meeting. "And now," said Susannah, "are we really standing here, so many of us, to ask for other wretches to be sent out to us?"

She addressed her husband again, this time directly. "William, do you want it?"

He could not answer. Susannah would not have said what she then did say if the death of Jane Bryant had not been still so much in her mind. And if Redmond had managed to say almost anything to her, any words, he could have stopped her. But he said nothing.

She said, "Very well," and went on. "If I talk of my father you will smile, and say it is many years ago. It is many years ago. But he always said that a man

while he was a convict was no slave, and that after he
served his sentence, and was freed, he was less than
ever a slave. But my son John—whom you all know
to be my son—wishes to retain a virtual slavery of his
own emancipists, and now wishes to import more convicts, more exiles. As for the convicts themselves, some
were no angels, but I think no less of a man who has
been a convict. How could I, seeing that I married
such a man?"

She paused. At first the crowd did not take it in.

Susannah said, "William Redmond came to New
South Wales as a convict. He was soon emancipated,
because he was a surgeon. I married him when he was
a surgeon."

This was unknown. Few there knew Redmond had
ever been a surgeon. None knew he had been a convict. At first there was silence, and then the murmur
of three thousand voices grew, and became a shout.

"And now," Susannah continued, "he wishes to
bring others? My son John, my son and William Redmond's, is himself the son of an emancipist, but will
not associate in the least with the other sons of emancipists. And now he too wishes to bring out men to a
kind of slavery."

John was on his feet shouting, but could not be
heard over the crowd which was yelling, "Answer, answer." William Redmond closed his eyes and sat looking straight ahead. He had given up trying to control
the meeting. But when the roaring of three thousand
voices died away, he looked to his side and saw John
about to launch into a furious refutation of Susannah,
who still stood facing him. He reached over and took
his son by the arm. Redmond was a big man and he
half-pulled John off his feet and said to him, in a silence which made his words audible to those near the
platform, "Say nothing against your mother. *Nothing.*"

John shook him off, and turned again to Susannah,

who was being urged by Robert to come away. She
would not. But John was not finding it easy to speak.
He was so angry, so evidently shaking with anger,
that the gathering, which he had so easily swayed
an hour before, now laughed aloud at him. The laughter of three thousand men is terrible to face. The scene
was almost too much for Susannah. She could not
stand and watch him derided in this way, and she
would have left there and then, but she found she
could not move out of the press of bodies round her.
She looked round, and saw there was nowhere to go.
Robert stood by her to prevent her from being carried away by the crowd, which was now swaying
rhythmically from side to side and picking up once
again the tune of "The Four-Legged Oak."

Then a huge man, who had once been dismissed by
John, stood and shouted and waved the crowd into
silence.

"Great Oak?" yelled the man, gesturing towards
John. "Him a Great Oak? Sheep king? Sheep king he
may be. But as to a Great Oak, the cove's no oak. He's
a scrubby cottonwood."

This got a laugh, but it also made a pause in the
bedlam, and John was at last able to speak.

"You have heard my father's wife speak. She lied
to you. My father was always free. Everyone knows
that. And now my father's wife, to make a political
point, to make a fraudulent political point, declares he
was a convict. I call her my father's wife, and not my
mother, because she long ago abandoned the rights of
a mother. She has been no mother to me."

There was an angry howl at this. It was splendid
entertainment to hear the greatest of the sheep kings
called a former convict. It was splendid entertainment to watch Mr. John Redmond making a fool of
himself. But when he attacked his mother he lost
any tatter of sympathy which still remained for him in

all that crowd. And it was sad. Because John believed what he said. He had never known that his father was once a convict. This had been kept from him as carefully as it was kept from the colony.

He believed that Susannah had lied. And he had also, for many years, believed bitterly that it was she who had abandoned him. When his father first took him away, he expected to return to his mother, and asked to see her. But then, two years later, he was told that his mother and a man called Wyndham were lovers. The groom who saw Susannah come down so eagerly to meet Wyndham in the night described the scene in the lighted doorway not only to Redmond but later to John. He was hurt, and horrified. His mother had a lover. He did not even know what the words meant. But he carried that picture of the lighted doorway with him in his mind—his mother in her nightdress embracing the man who came to her in the night. The idea haunted him. His child's mind believed, and his man's mind persisted in the belief, that it was because of his mother's treachery that his father left her. After that John refused to see his mother, even when Redmond relented and offered it.

So when John called his mother a liar, he believed it. When he said she had abandoned the rights of a mother, he believed it.

Then he saw Robert standing by Susannah in the crowd, the pair of them now lit by the flares. As a boy, thinking himself abandoned, he had hated Robert, who was cherished. He knew the history of Robert's birth. It was no secret. It was accepted. Now John prepared himself for another onslaught. Once again Redmond caught him, and said to him, quietly and steadily, "Say *no more* against your mother." John, in spite of all his hardness, feared his father, but he was carried away with bitterness.

He spoke again to the crowd. "My father's wife is

no mother to me, and for years has been no mother to me."

The older Redmond brought his fist down with a crash on the table, but there was no stopping John.

"If my mother has a son, it is a certain gentleman, standing by her now, whom you can all see. He is a gentleman half-French, the son of a Frenchman. He is her only true son. And this true son, who stands so nobly by his mother now, is a man who has disgraced her. . . ."

Here the crowd growled, but John rushed on, now almost having to scream to be heard.

"A man who has disgraced her, and himself, and his new wife. For what did this true son do, a few years past? He is now a husband and father. His young wife sits near him at this moment. Yet it was he who took as mistress . . ."

More howls from the crowd. Many men there knew and liked Robert. But it was a crowd in which John had hardly a friend left. Still he persisted.

"It was he who took as mistress the wife of the very man who saved his life."

At this several men tried to drag John from the platform, but still he shouted on.

"That true son took as mistress the wife of the Yankee captain who rescued him. And that man, Robert King, is the only true son. For she is no mother of mine."

John stopped. The cries of three thousand men died away. In a silence which was the silence of John's disgrace, they turned their backs on him to a man.

Robert put his arm round Susannah's shoulders. The roar gradually fell away. Robert looked down at Elizabeth, who rose and took his hand. Anna was no news to her. With one woman on each side, Robert began to make a way slowly through the throng. Men stood aside and made a wider passage for them. Robert then let his mother go first. She walked across the park, through the crowd that opened to let her pass, and as she walked she looked straight ahead.

And it was all for nothing. It had been an entertainment for a summer evening. Few men, even the other sheep kings, thought the less of William Redmond for learning he was an emancipist. The younger Redmond had discredited himself. The meeting was disastrous to the political ends the sheepmen meant it to advance, but that did not matter either. The secretary of state in London, the other side of the world, had already signed the piece of paper placed before him, and exiles were on the high seas on their way to New South Wales.

But John Redmond had publicly repudiated his mother, and because of that he and his half brother Robert King were ever after enemies.

Part Four

31

The Wildest Flower Is Gold

EDWARD HARGRAVES SAT WHITTLING a stick with his knife, sharpening it with quick strokes to a point, then slicing away at the stem, not rapidly but pensively, thinking between slices. When only the stub was left, he tossed it on the floor. Then he drank a little whisky, the last in his glass. He never drank much, but he called, "Boy," and the Negro waiter glanced easily at him and came over, bringing another glass and, without being asked, another handful of whittling sticks which he placed on the table. There were ten other men in the room. Six of them were whittling as they talked languidly to their companions. Most were American, but there were a German, a Frenchman, and a Chilean as well. The San Francisco Hotel supplied whittling sticks by custom. One day a few weeks before, the hotel had run out of sticks, and the customers had whittled the table legs instead. The marks showed. Hargraves took up a new stick, shaved it smooth with sweeps of his sharp blade, and then cut accurate notches one by one along its length. Twenty-eight. He had been there twenty-eight days and it was time to move on to Sacramento and the Sierra Nevada.

Hargraves' Hotel in Sydney had done well at first, but soon other hotels had opened and taken away his monopoly, and then his restless nature became bored. He bought houses too, but in the slump of the 1840s rents fell until they were not worth keeping. Late in 1848, a president of the United States whose name Hargraves could never remember announced to Congress that gold was discovered in Upper California. He read the report in the Sydney newspapers and turned over in his mind the golden phrases of the leader writers. El Dorado existed—not in the minds of dead Spanish adventurers, not in Utopia, but in a place ships could sail to. He took aside the captain of a British brig that he knew had lain in Sydney three months looking for a cargo.

Hargraves said, "What is this place called San Francisco?"

They went to the brig, and spread out the charts of the western coast of North America. The captain had never sailed those waters. He traced the coast northwards with his finger.

"Ciudad de los Angelos," he said, "San Luis Obispo. Monterey. Yerba Buena." There was no San Francisco.

But they found a range of mountains called the Sierra Nevada, and a River Sacramento, and these names also appeared in the newspapers Hargraves had brought with him.

The captain said, "And the name California is on the Admiralty charts, but I dare say that's its closest relation to the civilized world, being on the map I mean. As for your Saint Francis . . ."

The captain owed Hargraves for two months' board and lodging. Hargraves made him a proposition.

"But there may be no gold," said the captain. "There is *probably* no gold."

"And if there is not?" said Hargraves.

The captain looked at him as if he were mad.

"If there isn't gold," said Hargraves, "there will still be ten thousand men who think there is. Men wanting shovels, trousers, tents, coffee, guns, hats, rum. How plentiful do you think those things will be in a town not on the map?"

The captain said, "It is the other side of the world."

"No, the other side of the Pacific."

The captain shook his head.

"Man," said Hargraves, "how far is it to sail from New York to California round the Horn?"

"Sixteen thousand miles. Six months."

"They'll be American ships. Let's say five months. Right. Five months. And how far from Sydney to California?"

The captain agreed it was half the distance, and in calmer seas. He had also begun to despair of a cargo of any sort, and he certainly could not pay his bill at Hargraves' Hotel. He accepted the proposition.

It remained for Hargraves to get a cargo. He sold his houses, but that did not raise nearly enough. He visited Robert King to ask how to mortgage the hotel.

"I could do that for you," said Robert. "The banks will lend on the security of the hotel. But times are very bad. What will you do if they call in the mortgage and your venture has failed?"

"It will not fail."

"Why not?"

Hargraves had the gift of bold sight. It was then that he saved his venture, and raised the money he needed, by putting more simply to Robert what he had explained step by step to the captain of the brig. He pointed out the undoubted fact that it was easier to get to San Francisco from Sydney than from New York.

"You are telling me," said Robert, "that Sydney

and San Francisco are two Pacific ports, and not to be afraid of distances on maps?"

"I am."

Robert could hear Anna saying that. She would have thought in the same way. He told Hargraves to keep the hotel free of mortgage, and himself lent him the £3000 still needed.

In three weeks Hargraves assembled a cargo and one hundred and fifty passengers, gold-diggers to a man. By agreement with the captain, Hargraves took a commission of twenty per cent of their fares. The brig was the first vessel to sail from Sydney to San Francisco, and the men were the first of six thousand who left the colony for America that year.

They were three months on passage. It was no wonder they could not find San Francisco on the Admiralty chart. Francis Drake never saw that bay, though it is a fine legend that he did. He sailed past. It was first seen by white men, a small party of Spaniards, only a year before Captain Cook saw New Holland. At the time gold was discovered, a few hundred people lived there. It was only the year before the gold strike that the United States sent a sloop to take possession of the place, and only then was the city given its name. But it was not a city. It was a collection of shacks when Sydney was a metropolis.

As they entered, Hargraves did not give a glance to the splendid bay. What he saw was a forest of masts, and he knew that his speculation had succeeded.

"Three hundred sail?" he asked the captain.

"Three hundred vessels," said the captain. "Perhaps four. But as for sail, not a sail among them."

There was not. The masts and spars were bare, and the canvas was shrouded and reefed. The crews had deserted to the gold fields. As soon as the brig anchored, where she could, her crew also deserted. Hargraves and the captain bribed three passengers to remain and unload the merchandise at a dollar an hour. When he was later received in audience by Queen Victoria, Hargraves mentioned modestly that he had voluntarily stayed to help the captain unload when all his crew had fled, and the queen commended him.

"Mr. Hargraves," she pronounced, "that was a British act. We are always pleased to hear of such. For it is the sum of such small deeds, unsung though they be, that creates and maintains the good name of a great nation. And unsung such deeds, by their nature, must be. Or, we should rather say, by nature of their authors. For it is not in the nature of the authors of such deeds—as, Mr. Hargraves, it was not in your nature—to advertise such selfless acts." Hargraves inclined his head in grave assent. He did not tell the queen the goods were his, and were sold at a whacking, tenfold profit, and that he smothered the town in handbills for his shovels, trousers, tents, coffee, guns, hats, and, above all, rum.

By the time he was whittling sticks in the San Francisco Hotel, so-called because it was the only one there, Hargraves had sold the last of his ten thousand shovels at ten dollars apiece, keeping only a hundred or so which he would take inland to sell at thirty, and his thoughts were turning to gold. He tipped the black waiter with a tiny nugget of gold, at which the man scarcely nodded, but ran a finger-nail through it to see that it was soft, and was gold. Hargraves was waiting for his companion to return in a few minutes' time from the cathouse, and then they would be off.

His companion would be more than a few minutes, and he was not in the cathouse, but he was with Yvette Rivière. She was a singer, and was therefore naturally thought a whore. She was not. She was an opera singer, and had got to San Francisco by a chain of events possible only in an operatic libretto or in life. She was young. She had her chance early. She was in the chorus of the Paris opera when the director attempted a revival of Bellini's *Norma*. The prima donna of that season, wishing to assert that she was indeed prima donna, agreed to sing the performances but not to rehearse them. "Dear lady," said the director, "I am desolated." Then he threw her down the stairs and offered the title part of Norma to Yvette, whom he had noticed. This earned him the enmity of the entire company, but he was old and honoured and did not care. The girl Rivière did not have a large voice, but it was true, excellent for the *bel canto* arias of Bellini, and she sang as if her heart was in what she sang. She even sang as if she understood what she sang. In a week she was beloved of all Paris, and in two weeks the mistress of Ingres, who painted her. At Florence a year later she sang Lady Macbeth in Verdi's new opera, but Verdi, as usual, quarrelled with both his leading lady and the impresario. The impresario, in a pique, cancelled engagements in Milan and London, and took Yvette as his prima donna and mistress to Mexico City, where *Macbeth* was ill-received by the critics. After shooting the most outspoken critic, but missing, the impresario fled north to a town where money was to be made from entertainment of any sort. He took Yvette to San Francisco, rapidly made a lot of money, but then was lured by gold into the interior. He deserted Yvette, taking the money with him. There was nothing for it. She continued to sing programmes made up of arias from this and that. Hargraves and his companion heard her one night. Next morning the companion went back to the makeshift, shake-up theatre, sat unseen at the back, and heard her rehearse again and again and again a couple of phrases she was unhappy with. A San Francisco audience could not have told if she were singing "Three Blind Mice," but she wanted to get that line right.

Qual cor tradisti, qual cor perdesti

She was recalling the role which made her famous in
Paris, the unfashionable Norma, and was going through
her part in the last duet. "What a heart you have betrayed and lost."

San Francisco was a cosmopolitan place, and after
she sang the line the fourth time she was not taken too
much by surprise to hear a voice answer her in Italian
from the unseen back of the theatre.

Ah, troppo tardi t'ho conosciuta,
sublime donna.

"And I have come to know you too late, lovely
woman."

Yvette was a self-possessed woman. She could look
after herself in San Francisco. She had been painted
by Ingres. She was statuesque.

She stood onstage with her hands on her hips and
answered the voice. Her Italian was operatic. She could
demand a chalice of poison in that language, but not
ask for a cup of coffee. Her English was no better. She
replied in her native French, telling the stranger to get
the hell out and come back, if he must, that evening.
"And pay at the door," she said. Her dealings with
impresarios had a little coarsened her natural sweet-
ness.

The man begged her pardon, thanked her for her
invitation to return that evening, and said it had been a
great pleasure to hear a voice that would grace the
Paris opera.

"Monsieur," she said, "it has. But my God, you
speak French like Louis Seize."

"I suppose it must be archaic," he said. "I will return this evening."

As he stood up to go she saw him.

"Perhaps," she said, "a glass of wine first?"

That is how they came to know each other, and to spend many hours together, and that is why he was with her the afternoon Hargraves was whittling sticks.

She was singing for him and herself in the same shake-up theatre where they had met almost a month before. She ended with the same lines from *Norma*. Then she walked to a sofa, the only prop onstage, and arranged herself on it.

"Come, come," she called out.

He came up from the auditorium.

She took her long chestnut hair in her hands, and swept it forward across her face.

"Tell me I am a filly, with the handsomest mane in the golden west."

With both hands he parted the shining hair, just enough to see her eyes.

"I have said that, Yvette."

He sat on the other end of the sofa, by her feet, stroked her ankles, and then smoothed her skirt and petticoats up to the waist. She *had* been painted by Ingres.

"*Et ainsi,*" he said, "*je retrouve le marbre*. And so I discover the marble again."

He was leaving next day, and she knew it, and did not too much mind. She would probably never see him again. She would have other men. She did not think coldly, but what use to kick against such things? They had the moment. They had the hour.

Hargraves had to wait rather more than an hour for his companion to return.

It would be impossible to give a coherent account of why Robert left Sydney, because his reasons were not themselves coherent. It was those words of Hargraves' that did it, Hargraves' bold look at the world, and his bold way with distances. Robert had no need for gold. He did not want gold. He had no interest in trading shovels either, and was taking no profit from the transactions. He had lent Hargraves the money to buy the supplies, but had not bought a partnership. Robert loved his wife and his children. He would return to them. "If I were a sea captain," he had said, "it would be as if I were making one voyage." He never intended to stay, but he wanted to see. It was his father's restlessness coming out in him. He wanted to see, and so he went.

Next day Hargraves, with Robert and four other men, moved inland, two days up the San Joaquin River, and then seventy miles farther on to the goldfields in a wagon drawn by eight bullocks. The driver eyed the baggage. "Mighty lot o' plunder." Hargraves was suspicious. His profits, in gold nuggets and gold dust, were disposed about his person and in his various bags and trunks. He and Robert were dressed in blue shirts, mud-caked trousers, filthy boots, and wide-awake hats, like any diggers. To be thought prosperous in San Francisco was dangerous. Hargraves did not like to hear the word plunder, and was only reassured when it appeared that the man used it, as all the drivers did, to mean baggage of any kind. Hargraves then recalled his own days as a baggage-snatcher in Liverpool, took the word plunder as a good omen, and felt relieved and at home. He still kept his eyes open, but there were six of them in the party. All were armed. All but Robert were getting a small share of Hargraves' profit, the size of which he had concealed. A party of six strong men was safe.

In the high country, winter came on. They camped, having to wake several times each night to shake the heavy snow off the tents, to prevent the weight caving the canvas in on top of them. They did not know the country. No one they met knew the country. All were strangers. None knew when spring would come. Robert cut with his knife into the trunk of an oak tree to see how far the sap had risen. Then the buds sprouted, the birds sang, and the snow was gone at last.

They moved on to Sacramento City, a city of tents without a single bed or bedstead in it. Hargraves wrote home, entrusting his letters to bullock drivers or prospectors returning to San Francisco. Some of the letters arrived in Sydney. He wrote, "Treasure smiles at the feet of the seekers, and woos them to clutch it. They pick it out of the ground just as a thousand hogs, let loose in a forest, would root out ground nuts."

The six of them, in the first week, made two dollars.

Hargraves wrote, in another letter, "Men open a vein of gold as casually as you would a potato hill."

The six of them, in the second week, made twenty-two dollars.

Robert wrote back more circumspectly to Susannah, Elizabeth, and the children.

They worked throughout the year 1850. They did not make much. But Hargraves watched. He observed the landscape—quartz, slate, flat-topped iron mountains, gravel. He learned how gold was panned, and though he panned very little himself he put this knowledge to two good uses. First, he took a dozen frying pans which were unsaleable at his asking price of twenty dollars each, removed the handles, and sold them to pan gold, at thirty. Second, he noted and remembered how gold was panned: he stored it in his mind. Then he saw how gold was separated by sluicing, and by rocking pay dirt in wooden cradles. Robert watched too. He saw all Hargraves saw, and he also watched the dealings of the diggers with the gold merchants and banks. The diggers were always cheated.

But Hargraves kept something to himself, telling not even Robert. His eye kept going back to the land. It was summer now. He walked through tall pines in the lower foothills of the Sierra and idly picked wild flowers. He said to himself, "Slate, quartz, granite, red soil, gravel, blue clay, brooks and creeks, and everything else that appears to constitute a goldfield." He remembered New South Wales.

One day he and Robert agreed that the time had come to leave. Hargraves sold the dozen shovels he still had left, which by then fetched forty dollars apiece, shared the rest of his effects among the four men who were remaining, and then he and Robert, carrying only Hargraves' profits, wandered as if they were defeated miners back to San Francisco. Robert asked after Yvette, but she had moved on. No one knew where. Hargraves and Robert took the first ship that offered. On shipboard, Hargraves read his Bible a great deal. By January of 1851 they were back in Sydney.

Robert was reunited with his family. He embraced his mother. He lay with his wife, at peace. His son and daughter were disappointed that he had brought back only a few specks of gold, as souvenirs. He told them Hargraves had more, and would show them. Hargraves promised. On the third day back he went to Susannah's carrying in his arms a brilliant bouquet, and also a smaller posy of the same flowers. Susannah's grandchildren were her delight, and were with her that afternoon. Susannah-Jane was twelve. In every way she had Susannah's features. George-Nicolas, a year younger, was Baudin strengthened by the Dorset blood of the Bryants. Hargraves gave the bouquet to Susannah, and the posy to her granddaughter.

"Now *you* tell us about gold," said George-Nicolas.

Hargraves described San Francisco, Sacramento, the sap rising in the oaks, and the gold falling in the streams of foothills.

"The gold of Ophir," he said, "in the stones of the brooks."

"What is Ophir?" George-Nicolas asked.

"The city," said Hargraves, "where King Solomon sent to find the gold to build his temple."

"What is gold?" asked the little girl.

She was sure there must be more to it than her father made out.

"You have seen gold rings," said Hargraves.

"Real gold," said the girl, "not made gold."

Hargraves regarded the children and their grandmother, paused, and then broke into what was a soft incantation. Susannah, remembering how the blacks "sang" an object to make it theirs, would have said Hargraves was singing gold.

"Precious," he said, "opaque, lustrous, dense, the densest of metals, ductile, the most workable of metals. Sometimes found as flakes, less often as nuggets, rarely as crystals. It does not tarnish. Some say that in the beginning it was carried up from great depths, when the world began; others, that it descended with a hot lava and was precipitated in crevices. I have seen it glisten in streams."

He stood up, looked at them all again, and then opened one hand in front of him, to display a gold nugget of two ounces weight. He held it between his thumb and first finger.

Susannah saw that the eyes of the children were full of awe. She thought Hargraves had a great deal of the conjurer in him, a good juggler, a good entrepreneur, with a touch of the alchemist.

"I could beat this to a sheet so thin that it would cover the room, the floors, and the ceiling, and the walls, and then it would reflect greens among the gold."

Silence from the children. Hargraves took a small pen-knife from his pocket and opened it.

"Or I could cut it with this knife."

Susannah-Jane called out, "No." It was too lustrous to cut.

So he did not cut it, but offered it to her. She held out her hands cupped and he placed it in them. She took it between her fingers.

"Feel it," said Hargraves. "Press it with your fingernail. Your nail will go into it."

She tried, and it happened. She offered it back.

"Keep it," he said. He took two more nuggets from his pocket, gave one to George-Nicolas, and offered the other to Susannah, who shook her head.

"I will keep my flowers," she said.

She picked up the bouquet from the table. "I recognize the Banksias. What are the others?"

"All wild flowers," he said. "You know the Banksias. And there are the geebung, with pine leaves, and the wattle." The flowers of all three were yellow, orange, or gold.

"And what will you do now you are back?" asked Susannah.

"Trade," said Hargraves. "I went to California as a trader. I'm not a miner. Those nuggets were paid to me, a nugget for a shovel. I am not a gold-man. I walk a lot. California taught me how to walk. I have become a botanist, in a modest way. My first day back I took a long walk, and again this morning. I shall go farther. I picked the flowers I brought you. I shall look for wild flowers."

Susannah smiled. "And, Mr. Hargraves, the wildest flower is gold?"

He was right to say that he was not a digger. Susannah was right to think that he was nevertheless a gold-man, with something of the juggler in him. Practical men who dig for gold sell it for what it buys. The getting is a fever, but the possession, for its own sake, no joy. But for Hargraves, gold was an idea. He revealed himself by the incantation.

The next day Robert went back to his law practice.

Hargraves went to the governor. If he could find gold in the New South Wales, what reward would the government offer? The governor sighed to himself, but told Hargraves that the government would not be ungenerous. He could of course not be more precise than that. Mr. Hargraves would appreciate that he could not commit the colony further than that? Of course. Good morning. And Edward Hargraves, a good man of business when it came to shovels, changed, when he was overcome by an idea, the idea of gold, into a man who gave his entire energy and resource in return for a promise that promised nothing.

The governor mentioned the meeting to his secretary as they lunched together. "Well," said the governor, "if this is gold country, it will stop the emigration that is costing us so many men. Nobody will go to California from here anymore."

"And the government back home will send us no more convicts."

"Presumably not," said the governor. "But if it is gold, it will come on us like a clap of thunder."

That was all they said. Then they forgot the matter.

Hargraves began to ride out every day. Then he rode farther, over the Blue Mountains, always going where he had been before, in previous years. In his time he had travelled over large parts of New South Wales. Before he left for America he had earned a living not only as a lodging-house keeper and landlord but also as a small dealer in sheepskins. He had acted as agent for American shipping lines and had often ridden far into the interior to procure cargoes of wool. Now, as he rode, he was searching for the formation of landscape that had come so clearly to his memory once he saw its like in California. He could see it before his eyes, but he could not remember where. Wherever he went he wore in his buttonhole one of the species of yellow wild flower. Australian wild flowers are abundant. It is part of the circle of life in a continent where nectar-eating birds abound, and where small animals, like possums, feed on nectar too. The wild flowers of Australia are by and large yellow or red, or of the tinges between yellow and red. Golden. Hargraves' wild flowers became a joke.

"Wilts soon in the sun, Hargraves," said John Redmond, meeting him one day. Wild flowers wilted in a few minutes when they were picked for buttonholes. Hargraves waved back at Redmond. After that he dismounted regularly to renew the flower, sometimes ten times a day. He never spoke of gold in public, but it was assumed that was what he was after. Any man back from California must be after gold. There could be no other explanation. It was obvious. Just as obviously, he was assumed by everyone to be mad. No one bothered to ask him, or follow him. He hired a black guide. He was several times seen on horseback, standing in a circle of twenty blacks describing to them in pidgin English the landscape he was searching for. They had nothing to tell him. Then he dismounted and drew landscapes on red sandstone for them to see. They brought him yellow and black dyes, and he carried white chalk with him. He drew many landscapes.

As he rode he began to talk to his own black fellow, although the man could not understand him. It was a monologue.

"I tell you," he said, "this is gold country. But mind, unless you knew how to find it you could live a century here and never know it." A shepherd overheard him, and the monologue spread by word of mouth to the taverns of The Rocks in Sydney, where it became a familiar amusement to draw landscapes on pub walls, complete with the figures of Hargraves, his horse, his black fellow, and his golden flower.

On February 12, 1851, Hargraves found his landscape. He dismounted. He said to his black, "The same class of rocks. Slates, quartz, granite, red soil. A creek."

"Where him?" asked the black.

In a gesture, Hargraves took from his pocket a nugget of gold, the largest he had, four ounces. It came from Monterey. That is a large nugget. It was the only sizeable one he ever found himself. He held it above his head so that it took the sun's rays, and said, "I feel myself surrounded by gold."

"Where him?"

"We are now in the goldfields. Here. Under our feet."

The black uncomprehendingly agreed.

Hargraves took a small pick, and in the bed of the creek scratched the gravel and dug a panful of earth. Then he took the pan hanging from the saddle of the black's horse, and washed the dirt with the elliptical motion he had learned in the Sacramento Valley. The creek water slid round the pan, the sludge moved to one side, and the heavier particles were precipitated to the other rim. The particles were gold. At his first panning he had found gold.

"I am a great man," he said.

The black stood grinning at him, understanding nothing. Then Hargraves said his ever-memorable words. He took the black by the shoulders, and said, "This is a famous day in history."

The black smiled widely. Then Hargraves spoke exultantly, still to the black, as if to convince him, "Man, I shall be a baronet, you will be knighted, and my old horse will be stuffed, put into a glass case, and sent to the British Museum."

32

~~~ ⌒⊙⌒ ~~~

Never So Many Craft in the Cove

THERE WAS A GENTLEMAN with a letter for Mr. King. He was shown in. He was very young, only twenty-two, and very American, just off the ship that morning from New York. He introduced himself, "Cobb's the name, sir."

"Cobb?" said Robert.

"Freeman Cobb, sir." It was the American "sir," spoken without a shade of deference, between equals, simply a polite form of address. "And I have this for you."

Robert took the letter, asked his visitor to sit, and opened the envelope. He looked at the signature first. The writer signed herself in full, Anna Cobb. Robert had not heard of her or from her since the day they parted fifteen years before. It was a letter of introduction. The young man was a cousin from Massachusetts who intended to set up business in New South Wales. "You will think him young," she wrote, "but he already has several years' experience in the express business, and manages his men, his horses, and himself soberly and well. He has prospered in California. He has what I think we once agreed to call get-up-and-

441

go." She asked Robert, for the sake of their old friendship, to do what he could for her cousin. She said very
little about herself. Her husband was dead. She had
heard from American captains who called at Sydney
that Robert had married and had two children. She
sent him her love.

Robert folded the letter, and offered Cobb some
wine. He declined.

"I knew your aunt well, Mr. Cobb. I am sorry to
hear of her husband's death."

"Six years ago, sir."

"What can I do for you? Your aunt says you are
in the express business. I do not know what that is."

Freeman Cobb explained. He ran a stage line. He
figured the miners would need to get to the diggings,
and he could take them. He figured they would need
to ship their gold back from the diggings to the city, and
he could do that. He had come out with four of his
boys, all young men his age. He had brought two
coaches to start with, and was aiming to ship out two
others later.

"One of them's just being hoisted onto dry land, sir,
if you'd care to look."

Robert's house was three hundred yards from the
quay, and several of the wharves and docks could be
seen from the windows. Cobb was sitting by a window
and jerked his head. Robert crossed and saw a coach
being lifted by two cranes onto a dock. It was swung
up from the ship's deck, to which it had been lashed
all through the passage, and was now poised in mid-
air. He had never seen such a contraption. It was as
large as the biggest coaches he remembered from London and Paris, but much heavier. It was still covered
with tarpaulin canvas, but the parts he could see were
painted a brick-red.

"Care to walk down and see?" asked Cobb, very
much at his ease, sitting with his long, booted legs

stuck out straight in front of him, and his hands in his trouser pockets.

They went down to the dock together. Cobb's boys were superintending the lowering, watched by a hundred sightseers.

"Bigger'n you have them in this country, Mr. King?"

Robert said it was.

The coach was lowered gently, the canvas covering removed, and Cobb pointed out its features, not only to Robert but to the crowd in general. The wheels were heavier than a farm cart's, with iron tyres shrunk on. Inside, the seats were plush, but the floor was bare. Six passengers rode inside, three on each of the facing benches; or eight at a pinch, four on each bench. Two more could ride up front beside the driver.

As the crowd pushed round it and against it, the coach swayed. There were no steel springs, just heavy leather straps, running longitudinally.

"See," said Cobb, "some of our roads back home are a mite rough. Steel springs won't take it."

"Some of our roads," said Robert, "are not roads at all yet."

Cobb nodded unconcernedly, as if he had expected this. Robert thought he was a cool young man. While the second coach was being lifted from the deck, they strolled back to the house. Freeman Cobb was already at home in Sydney. He was also very evidently the boss, although casual about it. While his boys got on with the unloading, he explained what he wanted. Who should he see to get the mail franchise? Robert supposed the postmaster-general, and he imagined the young man presenting himself to that high official, leaning back in a chair with his boots stuck in front of him and his hands in his pockets, and stating the terms on which Cobb and Co. would carry Her Majesty's mail. He smiled to himself. He liked the young man, and he knew the postmaster-general was a pompous ass. And where, asked Freeman Cobb, could he find a good man who knew the goldfields? Robert said that was easily answered. If Mr. Cobb would wait, Edward Hargraves would be coming to dinner in half an hour's time. No one knew better than he did. Robert said he had been to California, but never to an Australian goldfield.

"That so?" said Cobb. He was very pleased to wait. He had heard a lot about Hargraves. He declined another offer of wine, saying he never drank alcohol. Robert remembered Anna never had.

"How is your aunt?" asked Robert.

"Anna?" said Cobb. "Well, sir, maybe this will tell you more than I rightly could," and he fished from his pocket a crumpled pamphlet and handed it to Robert. It was a paperbound copy of a publication entitled *The Wealth and Biography of the Wealthy Citizens of New York*. It was much thumbed.

"Always carry it with me," said Cobb, "seeing as I mean to be in it one day soon."

The booklet contained an alphabetical list of the citizens of New York whose personal fortune was one hundred thousand dollars or more. Robert flicked through the entries at random. *"Pease, John* $100,-000)"* was the famous horehound-candy man. He laughed at *"Slocum, Daniel* ($100,000),"* who made pins at Poughkeepsie. "Yankee industry," he read, "has so far superseded the old 'plod on your old way' of the English manufacturers that the market is now almost wholly supplied by the Slocum solid-headed pin which, besides giving an excellent profit, encourages home industry."

He read a few more entries. *"Astor, John Jacob* ($25,000,000)"* had come from Heidelberg and made his money in the fur trade. *"Cavanna, Augusta* ($150,000)"* was the distinguished hairdresser. Then he came to *"Harper and Brothers,* James, John, Joseph, and Fletcher ($500,000)." They were jobbing printers, went broke, and turned to publishing. And then it said this, which Robert read aloud: "They retain many literary men in their employment to pronounce their opinion on manuscripts submitted for publication, to revise those that are imperfect, and to write notices and puffs for the more important newspapers and magazines which they have either directly or indirectly subsidized to their interest."

Cobb smiled. "I'm not a man for books myself, Mr. King, except for that one you have in your hand. Anyways, the paragraph I always like in there is the one on John B. James, Junior. Take a look at that. It's kind of short."

Robert turned to *"James, John B., Jnr., ($200,000)"* and read these words, the only ones that described how he had come by his fortune: "Married Miss Johnson."

Robert looked up Anna last.

"Cobb, Anna, formerly Mrs. James Cobb III," had by her flair and diligence increased the Cobb line of packets from two vessels to sixteen, the finest fleet of its kind in the American mercantile marine. "Would not appoint Noah himself to be master of a Cobb vessel until he had served five years as a mate, most of that under her personal superintendence."

Robert looked at the figure against her name. The young man spoke it out for him. "One million five hundred thousand dollars; for real. Some of it is in those coaches. She owns half the equity in those."

Hargraves arrived with Elizabeth, whom he had brought back from a drive round the bay to Vaucluse, which commands a view of the harbour from the headlands to the cove.

"We took your mother," said Elizabeth to her husband. "She said she had never seen so many craft in the cove."

Hargraves remembered his Bible once again. "And

they came to Ophir and fetched gold from thence in a navy of ships."

A few months before he had named the first of the Australian gold towns Ophir. He and the young American talked gold, and the roads to goldfields.

That night, after Hargraves and Cobb had gone, Robert and Elizabeth sat in their drawing-room together. She read. He pretended to read, leafing through the tattered *Wealth and Biography* which Cobb had lent him, pressing it on him, saying it was always good to read about the people who had made it, and how. Robert was not reading the booklet, but thinking of the letter in his pocket. Anna had asked him to help her cousin for the sake of old friendship. They had not been friends, but lovers. It was a formal letter. She said so little about herself. And yet, under the signature Anna Cobb, she had written in Pahlavi script, as she had once before, the name Anahita.

Elizabeth looked at him. Earlier that evening she had entered just in time to hear Freeman Cobb pronounce the figure of his aunt's wealth, and she knew there had been a letter.

"Anna?" she said.

He nodded.

"Long years," she said.

He opened the booklet and read aloud the sentence, "Would not appoint Noah himself to be master of a Cobb vessel until he had served five years as a mate."

"A good journalist's fanciful phrase," she said.

"No, I can hear her voice saying it. She once told me, I remember it, that the first Armenian king was descended from Noah. She was Armenian."

"She is American now. And in New York. And it is how many years?"

"She was from Boston when I knew her. I asked Cobb why she went to New York. He said she insisted they should move there soon after they returned from

Sydney. She said the city was growing faster, and would be the capital of the world." Robert did not say it, but he supposed that New York must have seemed to her a city where one could demand even more of the Cosmos than one could in Boston.

He had a feeling that New South Wales was about to demand more of the Cosmos. It was true there never had been so many craft in the cove. Hargraves believed that what they were seeing was only a beginning, and Robert thought he was probably right.

Elizabeth came over, and stood by her husband. She was peace, peace, peace. She took him to bed.

John Redmond was also confident that it was only a beginning, and he wanted to be in at the beginning. So he left the management of the sheep kingdom to the old emperor his father, and went to Ophir. He did not propose to prospect for gold. The colony had started charging all diggers a licence fee, and he secured the post of licence-commissioner. The salary meant nothing to him, but he reasoned that the power to licence or withhold licences would give him some control over a rabble of emancipists, new English immigrants, disappointed European revolutionaries, and Yankees. The Americans were the worst of the lot. The revolutions of 1848 in France, Sicily, Prussia, Hungary, and Poland had sometimes succeeded, sometimes failed, but whether the insurgents succeeded or failed, the most extreme of the extreme had been rejected and had emigrated to America or Australia. John Redmond would have thrown them back into Sydney harbour, along with the Chinese who were coming in, but he comforted himself that they would in any case murder each other on political principle. He was not too worried about them. Americans were different. They worked. And the damned insolence of them! The few he had already met talked to him as if they were his equals. Ten thousand Americans had come. He thought they were the first of many more. It would be convenient to know who they were and where, and that could be achieved if he had the discretion to grant licences.

That was not his only interest. Men of whatever nationality drank rum and whisky. Redmond was a justice of the peace, and could grant and revoke licences. He naturally favoured the grog shops which sold rum from the distilleries in which he held large shareholdings. And then he noticed that diggers, when they once found gold, had one thing uppermost in their minds, to sell it. They did not want to carry it round long enough to be robbed. They had no way of getting it back to Sydney. Under the cover of various nominees, Redmond set up companies to pay cash or notes of hand for gold, on the goldfields. He contented himself with a discount of twenty per cent, offering three pounds sterling for an ounce, if it was pure. His powers as commissioner also enabled him to assay gold. So he was buying, at his own price, gold which had been assayed by his own agents. There was not a shred of speculation in all this. He stood to lose nothing because he risked nothing. Whoever profited from the goldfields, Redmond would take one-fifth of that profit.

His first instinct was to run this racket honestly, but he was frustrated in this desire by second thoughts which arose from experience. It was impossible to find anyone to work honestly on any terms. It was no good offering double or even treble wages. A digger stood one chance in a hundred of becoming rich, but that was a chance a man would take more eagerly than treble pay.

Redmond cursed at this and called it greed. So it was. He was incapable of seeing that it was also hope. To thrive on sheep, a man needed capital to buy them. On the goldfields, five minutes' luck could make a man a fortune for the price of a shovel. Gold could make the poor rich, as well as the rich richer.

Convicts would have been ideal men for Redmond to hire, but there were now so few. Only a couple of boatloads of "exiles" had come to the colony in recent years, in spite of the sheep kings' frequent requests for more. But there were still a few convicts serving out long sentences as ticket-of-leave men. It was these men who seduced Redmond into his second thoughts.

He took six from his Tongala Section and put two at each of the first three gold-purchasing branches. Each branch was guarded by an armed policeman. The men first shook the gold dust round in a burnished copper pan, to spread it and see no dirt remained in it, and then tipped it onto scales to be weighed in front of the diggers. The policemen, who were well bribed by Redmond's nominees, kept a close watch but saw nothing. His picked villains were apparently honest.

Then a large Dane named Olofsen was brought before Redmond in his capacity as magistrate. He was accused by his mates—a German, a Swede, and a Frenchman—of stealing gold dust they had jointly worked to get. After they had worked for three weeks, and the time came to sell their gold, he was trusted to divide the amount. He had golden-blond hair. It was only by chance that it was noticed afterwards that his hair glinted in the light of an oil lamp. It had not shown by day, but his hair was dusted with gold. As he divided the dust, he had passed his hands through his hair. Redmond jailed the man, and afterwards put on a shabby wide-awake hat and corduroy trousers and watched his own men weighing gold dust. The transaction was carried out in the shade of a tent, so the diggers, coming in out of bright sun, were at a small disadvantage. Redmond watched the men weighing the dust, and saw nothing. He watched twenty times and noticed nothing. None of the weighers had blond

hair, or passed his hands through his hair. Redmond was about to walk away satisfied, when an original thought came to him. Instead of watching the men
weighing the gold, he watched the eyes of the diggers.
They watched their dust tipped into the pan. They
watched closely as it was swished round the pan.
They watched as it was tipped onto the scales, and
watched closely as it was weighed. Then Redmond saw
it in a flash. Where were the eyes of the diggers? Always on the gold, first in the pan, then on the scales.
When it was on the scales, they were so intent on the
weighing that they did not give a second look at the
pan, which was left on the table in plain view. But
Redmond looked at the pan and there, barely visible,
in one patch only, high up against the rim, was a fine
coating of dust.

Redmond reached across and picked up the pan.
He passed his finger under the brim, and it came
away gilded.

The man at the table sat stock-still.

Redmond felt the pan again. The dust had adhered
to the spot just beneath the brim, because that spot was
lightly greased. In the shade of the tent, and against
the burnished copper of the pan, the dust could not be
seen unless you knew it was there.

"Stand up," said Redmond.

He felt in the man's hair. Nothing but lice. He ran
his hands over the wrinkles in the man's neck. Nothing
but dirt.

"Hands," he said.

The man held out his hands. There was nothing in
the creases of the palms, but something was wrong.
Then Redmond knew what it was. They were not the
hands of a working man. The nails were not long, but
neither were they as short and cracked as those of his
shepherds. Under the finger-nails was gold. This was
discovered near the end of the day. In his nails the

man had half an ounce of gold, worth two pounds sterling. Redmond did not charge the man or have him flogged. He sent him and his mate back to Tongala that night, to get them well out of the way. Within a week all Redmond's buyers were growing their nails; only the proceeds came, through his nominees, to Redmond. To add to his discount of twenty per cent, he made another two or three from long finger-nails and greasy pans.

John Redmond never spoke up publicly for the gold interest as he had for sheep. He kept in the background. Gold needed no champion. Hundreds of diggers came by every ship. They were frequently met by Hargraves who urged them to go inland to his Ophir where, he said, there was more gold to be picked up than Mr. Cobb's coaches could carry away, with the coaches running day and night and loaded so heavily they had to be drawn by teams of six and eight horses. Hargraves was the great golden man of New South Wales, but took no interest in the realities of mining. He still mined nothing for himself. He accepted a reward of £10,000 from the colony for making his discovery known, and was spending the money fast. He planned to go to England to see the queen. He assumed that the queen would see him. He was famous, and fame is what he wanted.

At Ophir he addressed gatherings of diggers at night, after the day's work was over. In the midst of enormous real wealth he told them tales of the fabulous. He told the story of Croesus, king of Lydia, and the noble Athenian who helped him build a temple to the oracle at Delphi. To reward the nobleman, Croesus told him to enter the royal stores and take as much gold as he could carry on his person. The nobleman put on a cloak with large pockets, boots several times too large, and stuffed the cloak and the boots with gold

dust so that he could hardly walk—and then, into his
mouth, he crammed as much gold dust as he could
carry there. And when Croesus saw this he laughed,
and gave the man as much again, for his ingenuity.
"The gold mines of Ophir," declared Hargraves, "are
your Croesus, and every digger among you is an
Athenian nobleman. To every man that digs, twice as
much shall be given."

In Sydney, he also addressed other assemblies, not of
diggers but of bankers, gold changers, and bullion
shippers. He was in an especially elated mood one
evening. That day he had received an indirect assurance that Her Majesty would receive him if he went to
England. He intended to go there as soon as he had
done what he could to help the citizens of Melbourne.
This city, only six years old, was being swamped by
the increasing prosperity of Sydney, and seeing all its
men lured away to the gold mines. Melbourne offered a
reward if he could find gold within two hundred miles
of the city. Melbourne wanted a gold rush of its own,
and sent as an inducement a golden goblet filled with
sovereigns. So Hargraves' confidence was at its height,
and to the bullion men he proposed this toast, "Gold—
the mainspring of commerce; gold—the forerunner of
civilization; gold—the handmaiden of Christianity."

The toast was drunk in silver goblets. The next time,
he assured them—raising the golden goblet sent to
him that day—they would all of them drink from
gold. Wild cheers.

John Redmond was not at the banquet. Fearing
tumult and uproar if miners of so many different na-
tionalities continued to pour into the goldfields, he got
himself a major's commission in the cavalry militia. He
was a believer in peace and order.

33

The Absurdity of Conveying Offenders

IN ONE MORNING two messengers came to Susannah.
One was from Government House, and she sent back
a reply that she would come that evening. The second
was from her husband. He had written only twice, in
regard to the comtesse d'Estaing's bequest, in all the
years of their separation. Now he asked her to come
and see him, and to bring her grandchildren if she was
able. He very much hoped she would be able. The note
ended, "I would come to you, but do not get about so
easily."

"Is Mr. Redmond ill?" she asked the messenger.

"No, ma'am."

She glanced at the letter again.

"Are you sure he is not unwell?"

"Not that I have seen, ma'am, though I do not see
much of him. He does not leave the house. But ill, no."

The note said that any day would be convenient,
and any time. Would she please come? She gave the
messenger a note in reply: "Yes. Soon."

That evening she went to the governor in his turreted,
crenellated, gothicized Tudor palace.

"My dear Susannah," he said, welcoming her.

"Charles, what is it?"

There was something odd in his demeanour. She could not tell what.

"Good news," he said. "Do I look solemn because I have good news? Perhaps I do."

Of all the governors since Brisbane, Sir Charles Fitzroy was the man Susannah had known most intimately. When he reminisced with her, as he often did, he was fond of describing his earlier career as that of "obscure governor of obscure places." He had spent four years at Prince Edward Island, quite the smallest province of Canada, and then another five in the Leeward Islands. "In the Antilles," he would explain. "The Lesser Antilles." In New South Wales he was hit hard by the death of his wife in a carriage accident for which he could not stop blaming himself. Afterwards, in his loneliness, he got to know Susannah well. And at the end of his career, a sad man, he had suddenly become no longer obscure. To become governor of New South Wales was a great promotion after the Leeward Islands, but now, since Melbourne had grown and Victoria had become a separate colony, he was governor-general of both New South Wales and Victoria, the first governor-general of Australia.

"It is good news," he said again. "I have a dispatch from London, and before I publish it I should like you to see it. It is a long document. I have folded back the page which says what matters." He gave it to her.

She sat down to read it. The document said: "It would appear an absurdity to convey offenders, at the public expense, with the intention of at no distant time setting them free, to the immediate vicinity of those very goldfields which thousands of honest labourers are striving in vain to reach."

She looked up at him.

He nodded. "Just like that," he said. "But read the next couple of sentences too."

She did. They said: "It is quite true that the offenders have to undergo a preliminary period of imprisonment and labour; but these are not likely to daunt reckless minds. It must be admitted by every impartial observer that transportation would be disarmed of its terrors, and that a very undesirable impression would be produced in the minds of the criminal class, if offenders should long continue to be sent to the immediate vicinity of the goldfields of Australia."

Susannah put the papers down. She was almost angry. "Rotten reasons," she said.

"Rotten reasons," said the governor. "But it is done at last. That's an end to it all, an end to convicts, and I knew you would be happy to know."

"I am happy. But I see all those men and women in my mind; the men and women of my whole lifetime. I see Tyrone at Newcastle." She had told Fitzroy that story long ago. She also saw herself cheered by a convict road gang as she walked up from the jetty the day she took the children to Manly, just before Redmond left her.

Fitzroy said, "Well, it is done. I shall publish this tomorrow. Now . . ."

He stopped.

"Now," she said, and took his arm, and they walked through the open French windows onto the terrace. They would not walk far. He was younger than her, but tired more easily. A man never easily recovered from years in a Caribbean climate.

"Do you know," he said, "I was looking through my father's journals the other day. Oh, papers of sixty years ago. And, it was the strangest thing, I came across the time when he was aide-de-camp to the old king. And he mentioned the visit of a black called

Bennelong and a Lieutenant King, about seventeen
ninety-five I suppose. That must have been your
father."

"It was. He took me to the concert at which Bennelong would only make legs, and couldn't be induced to
say a word."

"The journal said the king took to your father."

"They talked about Virginia. The king had not liked
to lose America."

"Sixty years ago," said Fitzroy. "Nearly sixty years.
Your father and mine, and now the two of us here. It
is strange."

"No. Things go in circles. Events go in circles."

They went in again. Her mind went back again to
the convict gang cheering her, and Redmond leaving
her, and then jumped years to the message she had
received that morning. She said, "My husband wants
to see me, Charles. Does *that* strike you as strange? He
wants to see me and the children."

"No," said Fitzroy. "It doesn't." He had seen the
older Redmond more recently than she had. "You
will go?"

"Of course."

"Susannah, when you do, ask him—I don't know
how I can put this—but somehow suggest that he might
keep an eye on his son."

"Yes?"

"I can't put it more clearly," he said. "But, goldfields. I don't know very much. But there's something."

Susannah went to Redmond's mansion the next morning, taking the two children. It was a drive of two
hours. At the outer gate they were met by two armed
men, who passed them on to a butler at the door, who
passed them on to the man who was now Redmond's
sole companion. It was Halloran, the man who for
years had looked after the Abandon Hope shanty at

Tongala, and had now come to look after Redmond. Halloran said, "You will not mind if I say a word, ma'am? Mr. Redmond will be very happy to see you. He has talked of nothing else for days. But, you see, he may not show it. He does not show much at all. He is an absent man."

He took them along darkly panelled corridors lined with dark paintings and the spoils of great wealth— Meissen vases, Sèvres porcelain, Gobelin tapestries, brocaded sofas with cabriole legs, all acquired by agents, paid for, and then forgotten. The only life in the house was in the huge kitchen, which Susannah glimpsed across a wide courtyard. The food cooked there was no longer for banquets but for the battalion of servants.

"Mr. Redmond is not ill?" she asked.

"Not ill, ma'am," said Halloran, and then they were ushered into the great drawing-room, which contained the most magnificent of the great house's spoils, and Redmond. Although it was summer, he was sitting in a screened armchair by a crackling fire. He tried to rise. Susannah saw it was difficult for him, and walked rapidly to him. He settled back in the chair.

"And you have brought the children," he said. "It is good of you to come to me."

Susannah-Jane was presented. She dropped the lightest curtsy. George-Nicolas was presented to the old man, and they shook hands. Redmond looked at the boy's features and saw Baudin again, almost as much as in Robert. He looked at Susannah-Jane until she lowered her eyes.

The two children looked openly around.

"Yes," said Redmond. "I am a sheep king—you will have heard me called that—I am a sheep king who has not seen a sheep for many months, and this is my palace."

Susannah had not seen him since the night of the

open-air meeting in Sydney seven years before. Then his red hair was turning grey. Now it was white. His face still looked as full as ever, his hands as strong, and his frame as large, but he had lost all energy.

"I never see my other grandchildren," he said.

"Where is John?" asked Susannah. She knew he was often at the goldfields, but did not know he was constantly there.

"They prefer to live away, his wife and the children," said Redmond. His mind was still on the children he never saw.

"And John?"

"Oh, the sheep station is mine again now, you know. I had made the running of it over to him, but now he has given it back to me. Not that I do much. My overseers manage it. And I think Halloran manages my overseers. Halloran is the man who brought you in." And it was true. The keeper of the Abandon Hope shanty was now running the entire sheep kingdom of the Redmonds.

Redmond recollected Susannah's question. "Ah, *where* is John? Gold. He is at the gold. Where are the goldfields?"

It was then that Susannah saw that there was no point in mentioning the governor's fears about John. It was then she saw the extent to which her husband's mind had gone.

Halloran entered with champagne in a bucket.

Redmond said, "You will take champagne with me? It is my own. It is my own make. Morning is the time for champagne. It gives a fizz to the day. The children?"

Halloran had opened the bottle and Redmond was offering the children champagne, as he had once given it to John.

"No," said Susannah. Then she said, "Mr. Halloran, would you show the children the gardens?" He met her eye, and took the children away. Susannah had never entered this house before. She crossed to the long windows and opened the curtains wide so that the sun streamed in.

Redmond did not notice. He poured two glasses, and held out one to her by its long stem. His hand was steady enough.

She saw he had something to say, and knew he would have difficulty saying it. She remembered her own great pride as a young woman, and could understand how heavily the burden of pride rested on an old man.

He did manage to speak, starting with the smallest matter. "When I took that legacy, from France. . . ."

"William, you did make two offers to me. I have not thought of legacies. Do not let that be on your mind."

He said, "I have provided equally for all four of my grandchildren. But it was not that, or any thought of that, which made me want to see them now."

"I know."

"Yes, I think you do."

He refilled his own glass. She had not finished her first. He continued, "That meeting in Sydney, what was said that night. I did not wish it, what John said."

"I know that. I too said what I wish had not been said."

"And when I took John . . ." He could find no more words, but she knew he was trying to make some amends, by saying whatever he could say, for having taken John when he was a boy, and left her.

Susannah watched the man who had once been her husband, and who still was. She knew that when he left her it had been for the best. She knew the marriage had been hopeless. She could not have continued to live with him. But she knew also that this did not matter anymore. All that mattered now was that he should be able to say some words which would unburden his mind of the guilt of that long-ago desertion. She willed him to be able to say what would ease him. She waited. He could not say it. But she saw he wanted terribly to be able to say it. She had to say it for him.

"William, I know what you are thinking. And it's all right."

"I think you do know," he said. The relief showed in his face, but now his hand shook as he raised his glass. This moment was the nearest they approached, in the whole of their marriage, to a community of feeling and understanding.

She let the moment stay, and then pass. Then she said, "I shall call the children back."

They came back, and Redmond said good-bye to them.

Susannah said, "Good-bye, William," and he held her hand. The children went first, and Susannah was almost at the door when Redmond said, "You. . . ."

She turned.

"You will not see it so clearly, but the girl will be you. She will be you as I first saw you."

She nodded. "I see it."

Redmond said, "Good-bye, Susannah."

The last word he ever spoke to her was the first time he ever called her by her name.

By that evening the governor had published the dispatch, and there were fireworks in Sydney. It was a night for memories, but above all for rejoicing. It was a night that was itself remembered. The Chinese, who had been arriving in great numbers, somehow had fireworks. These were almost all bought up or stolen, and the end of transportation from England was celebrated with Canton crackers that blazed in the streets of Sydney in the form of snakes and dragons. The vessels in the cove lit flares. The American and French ships sent white and red rockets high into the Sydney sky. The English ships followed their example.

To some it was a display. To others each rocket represented someone remembered. Susannah took her two grandchildren to watch from the flat outcrop of sandstone at Bennelong Point. They were joined by Elizabeth and Robert. A red flare, climbing and then extinguished, was for Jane. Another, for George Bryant. Another, for Tyrone's man, with his back flogged to the polished bone—for him, whoever he was, because Susannah never knew his name. The crackers and whirling fire-wheels were for a multitude of others. It was not just that transportation was gone, and that there would be no more felons, convicts, government men, exiles, or offenders, and no more chain gangs of men in yellow slop-clothes with the broad arrow. The fireworks also celebrated the confirmed freedom of those who watched. There would be no more shuffling convicts to remind the citizens of Sydney what they or their parents had once been. All that was past.

Susannah-Jane, standing with her brother and grandmother, wore the blue broadcloth cloak with fur collar and silk lining stolen by her grandfather from the town house of James, Lord Bishop of Peterborough. She had become attached to it. It had become hers. She knew its history well. She was fourteen. George Bryant had been only two years older when he stole it. The night of the fireworks she wore it for him.

On the semicircular quay, in front of old Government House, an English actor-manager, directly arrived by public demand, as he expressed it, from the California diggings, drummed up an audience and declaimed, in very actorly fashion, the well-remembered old lines in praise of the felonry of New South Wales.

> *From distant climes, o'er wide-spread seas they*
> *   came,*
> *Though not with much éclat or beat of drum:*
> *True patriots all, for, be it understood,*
> *They left their country for their country's good,*
> *And none will doubt but that their emigration*
> *Has proved most useful to the British nation.*

So ten years—a speck in time—before the United States abolished the slavery of black men, England abandoned the slavery of white men, because of the absurdity of conveying them to gold.

34

Ballarat

EVEN a god could have been seduced. Even a god surveying the terrain of eastern Australia at the turn of the year 1853 into 1854, looking down from an infinite height on a sheep-run called Balla'arat, letting his gaze wander sixty miles to the south-east over a rainforest until it reached the city of Melbourne, and then letting it wander a few hundred miles north-east to Sydney—observing the events of those places, knowing the minds of the men beneath him, and then giving a quick dismissing glance across the Pacific to San Francisco, just to check—even a god could have been seduced into the opinion that the New World was no longer America.

In Melbourne business was at a standstill, the schools closed, and not a man left in the police force. The population was transient. No one stayed more than a week before going on through the rain-forest to the goldfields. But that transient population was on any day five times the size of the resident population of a year before. The banks and hotels were still open. In the marble hall of the principal bank, a miner took off his encrusted boots, pared off the two-inch soles with the sharp end of a spade, and extracted from the space between the lowers and the uppers £1700 in bank-notes, on which he had walked all the way from the goldfields. A man who until two weeks before had been an ostler waited behind him to bank £900 earned since then in tips from diggers for holding their horses outside an hotel. In the banking hall a man lit a cigar with a £5 note. No one took any notice. It was no longer an original gesture.

From the port of Melbourne, Edward Hargraves had departed for England to see the queen, still exhorting the crowd on the quay to go north to the goldfields. "My friends, lumps of gold are to be picked up, any one big enough to make a diadem." For the first time in his life he was understating the truth. The American clipper *Marco Polo* came in from England in seventy-four days. No one believed the captain until he showed them the dates on the Liverpool newspapers he brought with him. No vessel had ever made the passage that fast. Ships from San Francisco anchored every day. All this was because of gold found at Bendigo and, above all, at Balla'arat. Balla'arat is an aboriginal name meaning Place of Rest. In this Place of Rest there was alluvial gold to be picked up or panned from the beds of creeks. But there was more than that. There was also gold to be mined. These were the layers of soil the diggers had to penetrate one by one. First there was turf, then rich, black alluvium, then grey clay, then red gravel, then red or yellow clay. In all these gravels and clays gold was found. Then there was a solid barrier of hard, white pipe clay. Most diggers blunted their picks, turned their backs, and went off to another claim. But one man who broke through this barrier had found a chocolate-coloured clay, rich and soapy. In this layer, nuggets first of 1117 ounces and then of 2640 ounces

were found. Within months, the Place of Rest was occupied by the tents and claims of 132,000 men.

The god looking down, not wishing his opinion to
be decided by the observation of the moment, and not
wishing his judgement to be swayed by the ephemeral,
could have allowed himself to glance ten years into
the future. He would have seen Hargraves, returned
from England, having seen the queen but received no
baronetcy, only words of praise, and so broke that he
was unable to pay his hotel bill in Melbourne. But
that was the fortune of one man. The god would also
have seen that Balla'arat and its nearby fields had in
those ten years produced, in that tiny part of one continent, four-tenths of all the gold mined in the whole
world. Balla'arat was far and away the richest goldfield on earth.

Balla'arat was soon abbreviated to Ballarat. A road
was constructed from Melbourne, through the rain-
forest of ferns and cabbage trees, Livingstone palms
with sheer trunks and dense foliage high up, giving
everlasting shade and dampness beneath. When it
rained, Cobb's coaches struggled through axle-deep
mud. Then Cobb constructed corduroy roads made
from the branches of trees laid like railway sleepers,
only close together, touching each other, forming a con-
tinuous wooden path.

On such a road, in a wildly bucking coach sawing
back and forth on its leather springs like a whaleboat
in a gale, three men and a woman made the voyage
to Ballarat in early 1854. They were Mr. Dryden Hall-
Kean, an impresario, the actor-manager last seen at
Sydney reciting the prologue from the old convict
play; an American who preferred not to give his name;
a travelling lady writer of Polish-Russian provenance
whose name no one could visualize or pronounce; and
a handsome young man in black suit and white top

hat who, when asked for his name, said the one word Cecil, which he pronounced Sissle.

"Mr. Sizzle?" said the American, thoughtfully, steadying himself in the lurching coach by placing his booted feet on the plush bench between the young Englishman and the foreign lady. "Good name, sir. Tells nobody nothing, sir. Good name to give yourself, that one. Now me, sir, I always says—" and at this he said nothing but performed a cabalistic ritual with the right hand. First with his index finger he touched an eye. Then he touched his nose. Then with the index finger and thumb he made a circle, through which he peered in turn at each of his fellow passengers, and then settled back mighty satisfied.

"See?" he asked.

"I do not see." The reply came only from Mr. Dryden Hall-Kean.

The American sighed. "I," he said, pointing to his eye. "Knows," he said, pointing to his nose. Then, forming the circle once again, he said, "Nothing."

Still no reply, at which the American sighed again and repeated, as if he were attempting to make children understand, "I Knows Nothing."

"Very likely," said the travelling lady.

The American spat out of the place where the windows would have been if there had been any windows, settled his two pistols into the holsters at his waist, tipped his hat over his eyes, and went instantly to sleep. The gold rings in his ears swayed with the movement of the coach. The impresario, sitting beside him, mimed the seizing of one ring and the leading of the American by it, as a man would lead a bull by the ring in his nose. The lady allowed herself a smile. The young man lifted the canvas flap and looked at the everlasting rainforest.

The impresario inspected the young man's clothes— the elegant shoes, the waistcoat with the last button correctly unbuttoned, the sit of the coat shoulders, the poise of the white hat. He addressed the young man.

"Are you of the profession, sir?"

The young man turned away from the open flap. "The profession?"

"The profession, sir."

"I do not know to what you allude."

The impresario had concluded from the cut of the young man's clothes, and from his accent, that he had procured his clothes at a good theatrical tailor's, and his accent on the boards of the most fashionable London and provincial stages. The poise of the man also suggested that it assisted him to earn his living, that it was part of his stock in trade. "Sizzle," of course, was a strange name, but it must be, as the vile American surmised, a travelling name, no more.

"Are you of the theatrical profession, sir? Are we fellow actors?"

"We are not."

The young man's tone was final and peremptory. Mr. Dryden Hall-Kean was offended by this, but at the same time relieved that he would not have to face competition at Ballarat. More than a hundred thousand men was a large enough audience, but he would rather not share it. But the impresario still had his doubts, and, in order to learn more, kept the conversation going by offering information about himself.

"You will have wondered at my own name, sir?"

"No."

"Kean, sir, speaks for itself. My father, sir." So far as this suggested that his father was the great Edmund Kean; it was a lie. But it was true that his father had been a Kean, though a butcher by trade.

"And Dryden, sir, my given name, also speaks for itself."

Still no reply.

"But *Hall*-Kean; now that Hall is the proudest part of all, sir."

No reply.

"The great bard of Avon gave his eldest daughter in marriage to one John Hall, a gentleman of Stratford. The Shakespeares in the male line are extinct. The Halls remain."

The young man said, "I know that to be true."

"Yes indeed, sir."

"I have a butler of the name."

The conversation died.

Once the coach slipped off the corduroy road, hurling the passengers in a heap. The American untangled himself, drew both pistols, swore vilely, and repeatedly said, "Put a bullet through his brain, put a bullet through his brain." The travelling lady smoothed her skirt. The actor-manager carefully picked from his elegant grey trousers the bits of straw from the floor which had been thrown round the coach. The American spat in the straw. The young Englishman looked away in disgust. In fifteen minutes they were back on the road again.

Near the end of the second day they came close to the diggings. The bright red of the coach was coated with grey dust. The bright-yellow paint was abraded from the wheels. The travelling lady felt sick from the motion of the coach, and several times they had to stop to let her get down. The American repeatedly spat in the straw until the young Englishman said, "Sir, that is not the conduct of a gentleman," at which the American laughed and laughed, and spat on the floor with new gusto. Then the coach stopped.

On the road in front of them they saw two miners on foot and five uniformed men on horseback. The two men were carrying a sack. An order was given. The men with the sack made a protest, and looked round at the mounted and armed men, and then back at the halted coach. One of the mounted men nudged the man with his horse, knocking him over. He scrambled to his feet. Another of the mounted men drew a carbine and waved it at the sack. The two miners tipped its contents onto the corduroy road. It looked like a heap of gravel. One man dismounted, turned the sack inside out, put it in his saddlebag, and then kicked the heaped dirt in all directions. The two miners watched it as it scattered into the ferns. Neither said a word.

The travelling lady got down from the coach and walked up. She saw that four of the armed men were police constables, and the fifth a major of militia.

"What is this?" she asked.

"Pay dirt," said a policeman. "Pay dirt is what that *was*."

The major said, "Will you return to the coach, ma'am?"

"Why has this been done?" she asked.

"Christ, ma'am, because it's Sunday," said one of the miners. "Three weeks' bloody work gone because it's Sunday."

The lady traveller was protesting, and the major was showing signs of impatience, when one of the Cobb drivers strolled lazily up to the group. Not exactly addressing the major, but rather speaking into the air beside the major's head, he said, "Better take stock before you get your boys to throw her into the trees 'long of the pay dirt, mister. Better take stock who we got inside."

The Cobb and Co. drivers were a free-lance élite on the goldfields, not loved by the police or the militia, but given a lot of freedom. Freeman Cobb, expecting graft and extortion, made tactful and continuing monthly bribes in the right places and bought immunity for his coaches and men. He had come up the hard way. He had seen it all before.

The major rode his horse at a walk back to the coach. "So who?" he asked the driver, who told him.

The major leaned down, glanced at the passengers through the open door of the coach, found his man, and saluted.

"Lord Robert?" he said.

"Good evening, Major? . . ."

"John Redmond, sir."

"Good evening, Major Redmond." The American in the coach went very quiet. The actor-manager congratulated himself on having spotted a gentleman. He had always known there was something distinguished about the fellow. A few words were exchanged. Lord Robert Cecil accepted the major's offer of hospitality at Ballarat. They would reach the camp in another two hours.

The two men on the corduroy road watched the Cobb coach and its escort of four mounted policemen and Redmond disappear towards Ballarat. Their sack had been taken. They searched in the forest for their pay dirt, and recovered about a quarter of it, which they stuffed into their pockets and hats. It was not a fortune. It was not gold dust. It was quartz and gravel containing very little gold which they had not the means of extracting on the goldfields. They would have got ten pounds for the lot. Now they might get two or three. Because they had been detected working on a Sunday, their pay dirt had been scattered. Their only protest had been that they were not working on a Sunday, but just carrying the results of their week-day labour. It had not helped them, and they had afterwards remained silent. Cecil mistook their silence for resignation to a just authority, which properly insisted on the keeping of the Christian Sabbath.

He also found, as soon as he arrived at Ballarat, that he had been wrong to expect only shacks. First he took a bath at the United States Hotel, and, as he

stood allowing one of the hotel servants to towel him
dry, he saw from the back window the panorama of a
slope and then a plain with a thousand tents lit from
inside by candles and oil lamps. He had expected the
tents but not the bath. Redmond gave him a glass of
tolerable port, and suggested that this was a good time
of day, with the sun gone, to take five minutes' walk
along the main street. He showed his guest the Post
Office, the gold office, the auctioneer's, the Chinese
laundry, the apothecaries' hall, the free library and
mechanics' institute, the blacksmith's. The dust of the
day had settled, but the natural town smells were still
there—the pervading smells of horse piss and horse
dung. He was given a guided tour, and shown what he
should see, but what most convinced him that this was
at least an infant civilization was not anything Redmond showed him but a grocer's shop he spotted for
himself.

"The Sabbath," John Redmond was telling him, "is
invariably honoured on the diggings, even by the
French," when Cecil stopped and gazed at a shop window.

"Dog soap," he exclaimed. Cecil had many dogs and
two packs of hounds, which were all washed by his
kennelmen and hunt servants. Well-groomed dogs were
strong evidence of probity.

Then his eye went to an advertisement in the window.

ICE!
ICE!
ICE!

Pure Canadian ice was to be bought, having been
shipped in sawdust, as ballast, in the holds of clippers
all the way from the Saint Lawrence.

Displays of Westphalian and Cumberland hams,

bottles of Scottish marmalade, and tins of tea bearing the label "Jackson's of Piccadilly" convinced him of the civilization of Ballarat. He ate a passable dinner, and retired to a passable bed. He was given a choice between a camp-bed of stretched cowhide and a featherbed. The mattress was a wool bag stuffed with bushfeathers—dry and crumbled eucalypt leaves. It was fragrant, but he reasoned that the cowhide would be freer from lice and took that. He was right. He slept well, being disturbed only once, by the sound of sporadic gunfire. It died away, no one came to rouse him, and he drifted back to sleep.

"Dingoes?" he inquired at breakfast.

"Americans," said Redmond.

"Ah," said Cecil, between sips of Jackson's tea, "they like to discharge their firearms to convince themselves they have them?"

Redmond assured him that this was so. There was no disorder. The Queen's Peace was maintained.

Cecil was shown Poverty Point, a mine which the first prospectors abandoned as worthless, only to see their successors strike it very rich. Then he saw shafts known as the Jewellers' Shops, where lucky diggers made more in a week than they had dreamed of earning in their whole lives.

"How are things going?" he asked, and not one man replied. He came away convinced that this was a satisfactory response. He had been told before that it would be most satisfactory. A miner making money never talked. A man working a rich vein wished to reveal nothing, and was too busy anyway. The only talkative miner was an unsuccessful one.

He left the next day on the same stage as the travelling lady, whom he had not seen during their stay. She was a sharp observer. She had seen what he had not. She had talked to many miners.

"There is no lynching," he said. "No vigilante committees."

"No."

"It is a government not of the mob but of the queen."

"By the police, if you wish; yes. But the miners are harried for their licences, which some lack the means to buy."

"I did not see that. The licence is only three pounds for two months."

"Did you look at their hands?"

"What?"

She said, "There is a sort of terracing, on the slope, extending for two or three miles. You did not walk over it?"

"I did not walk two miles."

"It is like a colander. The earth is dug over and over. Some men have dug two and three shafts. There are more than a hundred thousand men now. I do not know how many have been there before and given up."

"Yes?"

"Their hands suffer horribly. They dig with a pick, or with a spade, or with their fingers when they come to the blue clay. There is a pain in the fingers which starts under the nails. Then it goes up the arms to the shoulders, and from the shoulders to the backbone."

"Did they tell you this?"

"Yes. And I tried for myself. I do not have the hands of a miner, or of a man, so I did not try to do much. But I dug for a quarter of an hour, in soft clay. That was yesterday. This morning I know what they mean."

She took off her right glove. Her fingers were cracked and swollen.

No woman of Lord Robert's acquaintance had ever

worked with her hands. He gazed in horror at those fingers and at the blistered palm.

"I wanted to find out," she said. "Also, they *are* harried over their licences. Sometimes they are required to produce them four times a day. I saw a man chained to a tree because he had not a licence."

Lord Robert Cecil, direct descendant of the first minister of Elizabeth I, a man who would go into Parliament for one of his family's boroughs as soon as he returned to England, a man who would become three times prime minister of England, looked at the hand of the lady travelling writer and admitted to himself that she had seen much that he had not.

"I believe you about the licences," he said.

She thanked him.

"And the shooting late at nights?" he said.

"Oh," she said, "Americans."

At least he had not been misinformed about that.

Two hours after Lord Robert Cecil and the lady traveller left, John Redmond began his burnings of sly grog shops, those not licensed by him. Prodded by policemen, the man and woman who owned one grog tent were forced to bring firewood, bits of timber which had shored up an abandoned shaft, and pile them on their forfeited tent, which first sagged and then collapsed under the weight. The woman pleaded for a small sewing box which had come with her all the way from Ireland. The policemen took no notice. The man stood silently by, watching as the police lit and burned everything he had. The two kegs of contraband rum did not burn with the rest. They were taken into police custody. The policemen rode off with them. The man and woman watched as the last flames flickered and the smoke curled upwards.

From the window of Bentley's Hotel, Frederick Vern watched the bonfire. He was from Hanover, a failed revolutionary, and now a failed miner. He had drunk a lot.

"Europe," he said, "is striking off its fetters."

His two drinking companions, both Irishmen, said nothing.

"The divine right of princes is being scattered to the winds. But here we have a government more despotic than anywhere in the world."

"Better overthrow it then, Fred," said one of the Irishmen. "And by the by, who's king these days in Hanover?"

Vern threw the contents of his glass at the man. There was indeed still a king in Hanover. The Irishman dodged and laughed.

Bentley, the innkeeper, stood polishing glasses behind the bar, listening.

35

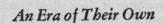

An Era of Their Own

"MR. COBB," said Susannah, "you did promise to take me to Melbourne whenever I wished. You offered it. And now I ask, you will not."

Freeman Cobb caught the eye of Lord Robert Cecil across the room, and then glanced at Robert King, and then at Elizabeth. The eyes of them all said to him, "Nothing will stop her." Cobb looked over at Susannah-Jane, who was sitting with her feet drawn up under her in a chair. He saw that she was already smiling directly at him. Her eyes said the same as the men's, and more. If Susannah went, Susannah-Jane would want to come too. He could see no way of stopping either of them. Cobb carefully put down his tea cup. He had come to tea and found himself surrounded.

"Now, ma'am," he said, "won't you see reason? Sure I promised to take you to Melbourne. Sure it was my idea. But that was when Melbourne was something to see, when the gold country was in New South Wales and people were only just beginning to leave Melbourne. Now the gold's in Victoria. Melbourne's nothing but ships moored as close as they can get, with all their crews deserted, and buildings left half-finished because all the men have gone, and there's nothing there to see but what I would take no mother of mine to see. Drunken diggers and roving women. Apart from them, everyone is gone to Ballarat. I will take you anywhere else; but for the moment, not Melbourne."

"Ballarat then."

"Ballarat? Ma'am, my boys were mostly in California before they came out here, and they say there are more hangable rogues in Ballarat than ever they saw in San Francisco or Sacramento City."

Susannah said, "I am old enough not to be your mother, as you suggested just now, but your grandmother. I lived in Sydney when nine men out of ten were hangable rogues."

Cobb looked at Cecil, who had come to say goodbye. He was on his way back to England. He had already said the government of Ballarat was that of the queen and not of the mob, and he said no more.

"Mother," said Robert, *"why* do you want to go to the goldfields?"

"Perhaps for the same reason that took you to San Francisco? Wanting to see all that's happened. Once upon a time here, a man pounded up two brass doorknobs and it took weeks to discover they were not gold. It was said they were all the gold that ever would be found in New Holland. And anyway, according to Lord Robert, Ballarat is civilized."

Cecil was bound to reply to this. "Well, you can buy there, apart from revolvers, pistols, and bandoliers, Jackson's tea and ladies' side-saddles. The peace is kept." He thought it safer than Melbourne. At Ballarat men were working, not spending.

"Okay," said Cobb, "my boys will look after you, and I'll come right along myself too."

He saw Susannah-Jane flicking her hair from her

eyes and about to pounce on him with her request. He got there first. "Miss King, are you still young enough for me to ask how old you are?"

She considered. "No, Mr. Cobb, I am not." She was fifteen.

"Then," said Cobb, "I guess you are old enough to come, and I guess I have two of you to take now." She sprang up and kissed him on the cheek. Young American women did not do that in Massachusetts. He was very pleased.

George-Nicolas would have wanted to go too, but he was at sea. He showed some of his grandfather's vocation for the navy, and was acting as temporary midshipman on a Royal Naval sloop out of Sydney making a visit of inspection to Fiji, which would keep him another two months. Before he embarked, Robert had given him the sword presented to him by Bligh. It was scarcely longer than a midshipman's dirk, having been made for a boy of six, and the commander smiled at it and let the boy wear it. Its having come from Bligh gave it cachet.

Cobb left with Susannah and Susannah-Jane.

Two days later Robert was offered a brief which would take him to Ballarat as well. The messenger came late in the evening. Robert knew he would have to sail for Melbourne at dawn the next day. He knew he would have to tell Elizabeth.

He lay in their bed waiting. From the closed door which led off to her dressing-room he could hear her voice and her maid's, but not catch a word of what they were saying. He knew the girl was brushing out Elizabeth's hair. She came in, wearing a cotton dressing-gown, walked over to the bed, and stood by him. He reached out an arm, slipping it under the dressing-gown and round her hips. He nestled his head into her, pulling her towards him with both arms, encircling her hips and then sliding his hands up to her waist.

"I have to go tomorrow early," he said.

"Why?"

"Ballarat."

"Don't go," she said. She leaned over him and rubbed her cheek against his hair. "I will make you not go."

He did not reply. She knew he was serious. She stood, then shrugged the dressing-gown off her shoulders and let it fall to the floor. She came to bed. He encircled her and pulled her to him. She was warm. He cupped her head in his hands. He let his head rest on her breasts. She stroked his hair. He raised his head, held her by the shoulders, and then released her and let his head fall sideways against his pillow. They lay side by side, touching at the feet and at the hips, but his head was drawn away from her enough so that he could see her plainly, and see her eyes. He began to tell her.

"I *must* go," he said.

"Yes, but why? When you went to California you said I should think of it as if you were a sea captain and it was just a voyage. I tried to. But it was a year. I hated being alone. I was afraid."

"You knew I would come back."

"I knew, but I was afraid. The sea, and danger. We had not been apart before."

"This is nothing like that. It is not a year's voyage. It is a couple of weeks. I have often been away that long."

"Why go? Robert, I do not want you to go. Susannah has gone there. Susannah-Jane is there. Our son is at sea. I do not want you to go too."

Elizabeth and Robert shared everything. They never quarrelled. She was steadier than he was. He loved her. But he was sometimes unreasonable, sometimes

fierce or sudden. He could not altogether lack these
qualities of his father and mother. When he was im-
patient or angry, and it was not often, Elizabeth left
him alone until he came back to her. She had the
sense to leave him to come to his own senses. He always did. He would come back in a couple of hours,
sometimes saying nothing, sometimes making a gesture of apology with his open hands. They had been
happy. She had never before asked him not to go
away. He told her why he had no choice.

"It sounds like a riot," he said.

She sat up. "What?"

"Look," he said, "Cobb is going to hear this news
too. It will be known tomorrow. He did not intend to
stop in Melbourne, but they will tell him when he
lands. He will not go on to Ballarat. He will bring
them back."

"But he may not hear."

"No, he may not. I cannot think how he may not,
but he may not. And that makes it all the more necessary for me to go. I do not want Susannah-Jane and
my mother there, even with Cobb and his men to look
after them. So I have to go for them. That settles it.
But I think I should have to go anyway."

He told her what he knew. A miner had been murdered by a police spy. The miners were outraged that
the spy had been only cursorily arraigned and had
every prospect of being released by the police magistrate. The military had placarded the streets of Ballarat with posters enjoining all true subjects of the queen,
and all strangers receiving hospitality and protection
under her flag, to help preserve social order and the
supremacy of the law, and to desist from riotous and
violent action. In view of all this, the Australasian
League had asked him to go and represent the interest
of ten thousand miners.

"Elizabeth," he said. "It may be nothing, or it may

be everything. It may have blown over by the time I get there. It may not. But it does look as though Cecil's wrong in his certainty that the Queen's Peace reigns at Ballarat. You see why I have to go, and I must go at dawn."

"Yes, I see that."

There were the beginnings of tears in her voice. He held her and rocked her.

Then they talked about their children. They were very much married in every way, but both knew their children were the strongest bond between them. He had never forgotten and neither had she—as how could they?—her bold first words to him, "And I should love to give them to you."

"George-Nicolas will be all right," she said. "But I wish he had not chosen the sea."

"He will be more than all right. I am not sorry he has gone to sea. I think it will be his career. My father, after all. The pattern of our ancestors is very strong in all of us, you know. I do not know whether it is stronger than in other families, but I do see it clearly in all of us. I never saw my father. But my mother thinks George-Nicolas very like him. I am glad he has gone to sea. I was meant to, you know. The sword I gave him was mine. I do not know whether I still retain the rank Bligh gave me."

"The oldest midshipman in the Royal Navy," she said.

They lay still. Then she said, "But it is Susannah-Jane."

"She is a splendid girl."

"She is a splendid girl, Robert; but she gets what she wants. Did you notice, with Cobb?"

"Oh, yes. There was no chance he would not take her." Robert was amused. He had watched his daughter get what she wanted.

"But all the time?"

"Elizabeth, my dear wife, do not worry about your daughter. She will get what she wants. I think all her life she will get what she wants. It is a natural force of spirit. But hers is a generous spirit, too."

"But it gives her such power."

"*Oh yes*. That is true. But I think she will be one of those few people who enhance everything they touch."

"That will be fortunate for those she loves, but they will still be in her power. Most of all they will be in her power."

"Yes."

Elizabeth and Robert dozed. They did not sleep.

They lay all the short night in the dark, talking sometimes, and then dawn began to break. She slid over her hand and entwined his fingers in hers. He kissed her. The kiss, of all embraces, is the first that goes, even when husband and wife are as close as Elizabeth and Robert. Both knew they had not kissed that way for . . . how long? They could not remember. With the happy ease in which they had always been so fortunate, she enclosed him in her slim arms, and he entered her sweetly. It was an embrace familiar over so many years, in a bed known to them all those years. She clasped him closer. "I do not want you to go, I do not want you to go, I do not want you to go, I do not want you to go."

Cobb, had he heard the news, would certainly have turned back. But he wished to avoid Melbourne entirely, so he landed to the west of the city, at Geelong, and took the slower but safer road from that port to Ballarat. He heard nothing.

Robert, having landed at Melbourne, learned more details from his companions on the Ballarat stage.

"Poor Scobie was just drunk."

Scobie was the murdered man. He was a Scot. He

met another Scot. They drank until the Lord Byron closed at midnight, and then went to Bentley's Hotel, which usually stayed open all hours. But it was closed that night. Scobie smashed a window with an empty bottle, and Bentley chased him and killed him with a spade. The body was dumped in a shallow abandoned digging. Ballarat had enough abandoned shafts to provide a hundred thousand undetectable graves. Scobie was found only by chance.

"Murder," said Robert's companion, "is common enough, but this one smells."

Robert was beginning to think less and less of Lord Robert Cecil's judgement, and to fear for his mother and daughter.

The man in the coach said Bentley was known to be a police informer. The magistrate at Ballarat had been unwilling to issue a warrant for his arrest. When a private warrant was taken out, the magistrate first allowed Bentley bail, which in a case of murder was extraordinary, and then, when he examined him, provided a chair and asked him to be so good as to sit while he answered a few questions. The diggers feared he would be discharged without even coming to trial. This, added to the continuing grievances of the licence fee, and increasing bitterness at the constant burnings-down of tents by Major Redmond, had brought the diggings near riot.

"Major Redmond?" said Robert. "John Redmond?"

"The sheep king. Now the gold and liquor king. The goldfield king."

Robert willed the horses to go faster. He arrived the same evening as his mother and daughter arrived, from another direction. He was looking for them when the diggers burned down Bentley's Hotel.

It was what they had expected. The magistrate who offered Bentley bail, a chair, and all consideration, finally discharged him, finding he had no case to an-

swer. He further announced that Bentley was honour-
ably discharged. This was too much. The news spread
at dusk, the end of the working day when there were a
thousand diggers drinking or lounging in the main
street. There were no apparent leaders. A column
marched to Bentley's. They hardly talked. They did
not shout. There was no shooting of pistols in the air.
The sound was that of shuffling feet on the dirt road.
Those not at the front of the column were choked and
smothered in the rising dust. Their hair was grey. Their
faces were grey. Grey dust lay in the wrinkles of their
faces and in the folds of their clothes. Above the shuffling there rose a sound like a tapping on planks,
magnified an infinity of times. It was the blue trousers
of the men, caked hard with dried mud, knocking
against the leather tops of their boots as they walked.
It was not at first a mob. Outside Bentley's the men
halted, waiting for others to come up, and then a Scottish voice said:

"Shall we drink to Mr. Bentley first?"

A roar of "No."

"In his own liquor?"

They changed their minds and entered Bentley's in
orderly rows. Two bartenders waited petrified behind
the bar. Bentley himself was gone.

"Whisky," said the Scottish voice. "Scotch whisky."

The bartenders poured ten glasses from a bottle,
and waited. The ten glasses stood on the counter.

No one touched the whisky until the counter was
covered with two hundred glasses, all there were in
the house, and then these were handed backwards,
through the windows and doors, to the men waiting
outside.

Then the men inside allowed themselves swigs from
the remaining bottles, until all Bentley's whisky was
gone. They did not touch the rum, gin, beer, or wine.

The Scotsman stepped forward, picked up a full

barrel of Madeira, held it above his head, and threw
it through the back window. It took window-frame,
glass, and all with it and rolled down the slope behind.
Then the men seized more barrels, hogsheads, kegs,
bottles, lamps, tables, chairs, and anything that could
be removed, and threw them through the same back
windows. They broke down all doors, broke all windows, smashed all plate-glass mirrors, and brought the
chandelier crashing down. They stripped the panelling
from the walls of the bar parlour. They smashed
everything that could be smashed. Two barrels remained, too heavy to be lifted. They were staved, and
the rum spurted out all over the floor. Then the men
left. All this was done with hardly a raised voice. The
burning was by accident. A boy at the back tossed a
blazing rag not into the pub but into a canvas bowling
alley at the side.

The Scotsman, who remained inside until the last,
saw the danger and beckoned to the bartenders. "Better come out."

They hesitated.

"It is not you we are after. Better go."

The flames burst in through a side wall. The timber
of the wall caught with a dry crackle, and the two
barmen had barely scrambled through the door when
the spilled rum on the floor caught with a whoosh. The
crowd watched silently, falling gradually back before
the flames. One vat exploded, bringing the roof in. It
had taken twenty minutes from start to finish.

The militia were two miles away in the diggings
carrying out their own, legal burnings of sly-grog tents.
By the time they arrived in force, Bentley's Hotel was
a smoking ruin, the street before it was empty, and
Australian, English, Irish, Scottish, American, German, and French miners were drinking soberly at the
bars of the eighteen other pubs in the main street. It

was Cobb who found Robert, and placed a hand on his shoulder.

"Where?" said Robert.

"Safe. At the hotel where my boys told me Cecil stayed. Good beds. Fair food."

"Look, how could you bring them here into this?"

"Came from Geelong. Heard nothing. Saw the fire first, and then you. Come to that, how are you here?"

"Get them out tomorrow," said Robert. He was angry.

Cobb looked at him. "How close were you to that little bonfire? You're more shaken up than they are, I tell you."

Robert's face was blackened. He had been close to the fire. He put his hand on Cobb's shoulder in apology. "Please get them out tomorrow."

Cobb nodded. "Sun-up," he said. "I already told them. They don't want to go, but I told them, no way do they stay here."

But when next morning came there was, on the contrary, no way at all they could leave. Reports said that one hundred, or two hundred and fifty, or four hundred and fifty Irishmen, having found little gold and not having the money to pay for their next month's licences, had marched off in the night to plunder the bank vaults of Melbourne. No one knew the truth of this. Certainly many of the Irish tents were gone, and others left abandoned. And it was the sly-grog tents belonging to the Irish that the police had been burning the evening before, while Bentley's was destroyed. If they had been four hundred and fifty, and if they were armed, and if they could have reached Melbourne, they could have taken the city. There were no police left there. But it was doubtful if they were more than a hundred, they had only their picks and shovels and a few old pistols, between them and Melbourne lay sixty miles, and twenty miles of that distance was rain-forest. But Major Redmond heard the news and he went in the middle of the night to the police magistrate and recited the rumours. Besides, he said, two of the Cobb coaches had gone from the livery stables, where they had been left the night before, and the Irish had taken them. They must be cut off. On his authority and the magistrate's, horse-police were sent riding cross-country to wreck the corduroy road to Melbourne, and, in case that should be used as a means of escape, the road to Geelong as well. The police found a few Irishmen straggling through the bush, but no coaches. They made a thorough job of wrecking the timbers of the corduroy roads. Then it rained. For two hours it rained, a drenching downpour that completed the ruin of the roads. The Irish had not taken the coaches. Cobb had moved them himself, late the night before, to open ground where he reckoned they were less likely to be burned than at the livery stables. He had coaches but no road. His own boys could repair the roads, but not until the track was dry. Then it would take days. So Susannah and Susannah-Jane had to stay.

Robert watched his mother and daughter as they sat surrounded by amiable diggers in the long room of the United States Hotel. Some of the diggings were flooded and there was no work to be done until the water seeped away. The diggers saw few women. Most of the men were Americans, gentle and full of courteous high-talk.

"And the next nugget I find, ma'am—the next sizable nugget, say more'n a thousand ounces—shall be named for you, ma'am. And the one after that—say five hundred ounces?—shall be named for you, Miss. That do you?"

Robert caught his daughter's eye. She smiled with pleasure and then, remembering that they should al-

ready have gone but for the Irishmen and the roads,
looked suitably grave. He shook his head slowly at
her, but he was reassured in his mind. She would come
to no harm with those men.

He went across to his mother's side. "We will stay
inside," she said. "Today at any rate."

He went to see the representatives of the Australasian League who were his clients. They told him the
name was now the Reform League.

"I am sorry for the change, gentlemen. The old
league did a great deal."

"For convicts," said Frederick Vern, the Hanoverian. "We are not convicts, and what ended all that
was not the league, but what we are getting from the
ground here."

The other three men were John Humfray, an Englishman; John Maguire, an American; and Peter
Lalor, an Irishman. They wanted King to represent to
the lieutenant-governor in Melbourne the iniquity of
the licence fee and the brutality of the police and
militia on the diggings. Could he do that? There was
to be a meeting of ten thousand miners that evening,
and a report of that would convey to the governor the
strength of their feelings.

Robert listened, and surveyed the men. He thought
Vern a liability to any cause. Humfray was moderate.
Lalor, when he spoke, was quiet and convincing, but
he did not say much. The American said nothing at
all, but sat knowing he was being sized up, and sizing
up Robert in return.

"Well, Mr. King?" said Humfray.

"Gentlemen, I am no use to you at all unless we
are honest with each other. I shall play devil's advocate for a few minutes, and tell you how this looks
from Melbourne; how it probably looks to the governor; and how it looks to the military and the police

here. Because if we don't take what they think into account, we shall get nowhere."

"Why bother about the governor?" said Vern. "To hell with him."

"Because he is the only man who can give you any part of what you want. He is a new man. I have never met him, but I know a little about him. He knows nothing whatever about gold, except that it has emptied Melbourne, and ruined the trade of the colony in anything but gold."

The American asked slowly, "And what do you know about gold, mister?"

"I was in California."

"Right," said the American. "We're listening."

"I can complain about the way the licence fees are collected. I think that would be put right. I know the militia officer in charge here, and I think the governor would be heartily glad to get him off the fields. For that matter, if you do nothing, and wait a week, I think he will very likely be removed anyway."

"So?"

"So, that can be done. But I am now going to put myself in the place of the governor and tell you how I think he will see the rest of your grievances. You want the licence fees revoked. He would like to see them done away with himself."

"Like Christ he would," said Vern.

"He would like them done away with because they are too much bother to collect. The inability to collect them makes his police look fools. He would much prefer to drop the licences and levy a simple tax on gold exported from the colony. That is something he could easily collect from the bullion shippers. Naturally they do not like the idea, but he will do it, very likely he will do it; but he cannot do it overnight. So again, wait. Evade paying, but don't attack the principle, forcing him into defending something he wants to get rid of himself."

"Subtle, Mr. King," said Lalor. "But what do you say to the rest of our demands."

"If I were the governor, they would frighten me. First, make a simple concession in your use of words. Don't talk about 'demands' to the governor. Ask him. Make requests. Soften it. He has face to lose. He cannot be seen to lose face. But as to the rest of your points—well, look, manhood suffrage, state parliaments, miners represented in those parliaments, miners' members, and so on. Not new ideas, but add them to your refusal to pay your licences, and then add great open-air meetings, and a hotel burned down, and what does the governor see?"

Humfray said, "What does he see, Mr. King?"

"In a word, then. He sees more than one hundred thousand miners here. He sees he has two hundred policemen here. He sees the miners are not only British but German, French, Irish, and American, and I tell you what he thinks. He thinks of revolts all over Europe: that is very recent. He thinks of English landlords burned out in Ireland: that is the usual state of affairs. He thinks of California and lynch-law: he has never been there but that is what he reads in the newspapers. So, gentlemen, I will do what I can to carry out your instructions. But the burning of the hotel last night will sound dreadful in Melbourne. And I beg you not to hold the meeting this evening of which you spoke earlier. That would only make things worse."

Vern lit a cigar. "You put yourself very easily in the place of the governor, Mr. King."

"I told you why."

Lalor said, "One thing you did not tell us, Mr. King. You said you would tell us in one word what the governor saw here. You did not put it in one word."

"In one word then, what he will see is a revolution."

Robert walked with Lalor and Humfray over to the United States Hotel. The mud in the street was drying out in the steaming heat. Flies were everywhere. "Gentlemen," said Robert, "I am unhappy with Vern."

"Yes," said Humfray.

"And the American said very little."

Lalor said, "Maguire is a man with a head on his shoulders."

They had lunch with Cobb, Susannah, and Susannah-Jane, the six of them together. Robert left them early to visit the three men arrested after the fire. Cobb had found a bakery just down the main street run by a man from New York, and was promising Susannah she should taste American bread. The real thing. Susannah-Jane was leaning back with her hands between her skirts while Lalor told her about the beauty of Dublin. Even as an Irishman he had to admit it, he said; in Ireland it might be, but really it was the most handsome of all English cities.

When Robert had left the hotel, he walked past the Theatre Royal next door where Mr. Dryden Hall-Kean, ringing a handbell, was proclaiming the magnificence of the entertainment to be offered that very afternoon and evening, an unprecedented and never-before-contemplated mélange—he relished the word mélange—of the spoken, terpsichorean, and lyrical drama, of Shakespeare's *King Lear* presented by himself, one of the lineal descendants of the great bard, and of dances and songs by Madame Ophir, as performed before King Solomon and the great Inca monarchs. But Robert had work to do. The police commissioner let him see the three men arrested the night before, who said they were miles away from the burning. The commissioner was reasonable. Robert

was relieved he did not have to deal with Redmond.
He asked after him.

"Bringing up reinforcements from Melbourne, Mr.
King, as far as his ruined road will allow him."

"Yes."

"Mr. King, I hope this evening's meeting will be
quiet. I should welcome a little peace for my men,
and would rather not disturb them or the diggers.
Short of absolute riot, I shall do nothing. I should like
those responsible for the meeting to know that. But it
would be better still if there was no meeting."

But it was hopeless. Five thousand men assembled
that evening, only half the number expected, but a
vast crowd. The voice of moderation was Humfray's.
They were all the loyal subjects of their Sovereign
Lady the Queen, but she was misled by corrupt ministers. They would respect her authority and her person, but they would not respect her menservants, her
oxen, or her asses. This was spoken with Redmond in
mind, and received with irreverent laughter, into
which Vern stepped to seize his opportunity.

"Are we not free men?" A crowd of five thousand
has only one answer to this question. Five thousand
men roared that they were free.

"Why not have a chronology, a date, of our own?"
Vern sometimes played with this idea of starting time
again, at least starting the calendar again with the
Year One, as the French Revolutionaries had done in
1792. This too was cheered. Anything he said would
have been cheered.

"There has been talk of the queen. God may save
the queen, but no one will save the governor in Melbourne." More cheers.

"But I will not talk of the queen. The people are
the only legitimate source of power. As to the associa-
tions of the Old World, let us leave them behind. Let
us leave the Old World, because it is old. We are new.

Why not, say again, have a chronology, a date—an era—of our own?" Five thousand men were so inflamed that they burned their licences on a ceremonial pyre.

Major Redmond returned late and tired.

"What," he asked, "were they saying they wanted, besides not to pay their licences?"

The trooper helping him off with his mud-caked riding boots suppressed the reference to oxen and asses. He said, "They have burned their licences. It's more than licences now, sir."

"What?"

"At the end, sir, they said it was an era of their own they wanted. Which they voted for, raising their hands."

36

~~~~~~~~~~~~~~~~~~~

The Making of the Maiden Flag

WHEN HE GOT BACK to the hotel, after the meeting, Robert could not find Susannah-Jane. His mother was asleep. His daughter's room was empty. The bed was made and not disturbed. It was like looking into the room of a woman he knew intimately, but in some ways he did not know at all. The United States Hotel was marvellously more comfortable than a tent, but its rooms were sparsely furnished. Any furniture had to be made in Ballarat, or brought up from Melbourne or Geelong at great cost. There were no wardrobes. He could see his daughter's dresses, skirts, and petticoats arranged over chairs or hanging from hooks. If she had been a woman he had not known he would have thought, entering her bedroom for the first time, that there was a lovely disorder about her. Then he *did* think that, because of course she was a woman whose bedroom he was entering for the first time. When he last went into a bedroom of hers, at home, she was a little girl of eleven. Now she was fifteen, sixteen in a few months.

And where was she?

It was past midnight, but still hot. He went into the

494

empty lobby. Two last drinkers were sleeping over an empty bottle of whisky. The porter was dozing. Robert woke him. He had not seen Miss King. Robert walked into the empty street. Not a soul. There was still some sound from the nearest tents, a fiddle playing a tune he could not catch, laughter, two voices raised and then dying away. He walked closer to the music. Tents have no windows, but it was the custom to sew panels of calico into the sides of tents, and then saturate the calico in linseed oil until it became translucent. This gave some light. In one tent, through such a panel, lit from behind by an oil lamp, he saw the embracing figures of a man and a woman.

He walked rapidly back to the hotel, and took the stairs two at a time to Susannah-Jane's room. Still she was not there. He walked down the corridor and woke Cobb.

"Take another look," said Cobb. "If you can't find her then, I'll get all my people and we'll go through this town. But take another look."

Robert stood in the middle of the street. The last sounds from the tents had gone, and the last lights. He listened. A dingo howled. A night breeze rustled the leaves of a eucalypt. And, somewhere, horses were restless. He walked towards the livery stables and then stopped and listened again. Why were the horses restless? He half ran the two hundred yards, turned in through the arch of the stable yard, and stopped. One of the stables was lit. Through the open double doors he saw Lalor and his daughter. Lalor was standing looking at Susannah-Jane. She was stooping, examining something at her feet with absolute attention. Then she knelt, and smoothed something in her hands. Lalor must have made some remark, because she turned her face to him and spoke. Robert walked across the yard and showed himself.

"Mr. Lalor," he said.

Lalor turned and met Robert's eyes but said nothing. Susannah-Jane rose from her knees, brushing off her skirt. She said, "You have discovered us."

Robert was possessed with anger against Lalor, fear for his daughter, and anger and bewilderment that she should take part in this mystery. He had recognized, so shortly before in her room, that his daughter was a woman he did not quite know, and now she was exactly that. Most of all he was afraid for her. He turned with anger on Lalor—and then the long, black moment ended because he saw two things. Behind Lalor, in shadow, were two other figures: one was the American Maguire and the other a woman. He hardly gave her a glance. And stretched clean across the stone floor of the stable was a flag. It was on a corner of this that his daughter was kneeling.

His relief was so great that he was not discovering Lalor and Susannah-Jane alone, his sense of gratitude so great that she was safe, that he said no word at all.

His daughter said, "We have made a flag."

It was twelve feet wide, and had been made on the scrubbed stable floor. The fabric of the background was a brilliant blue, except for one quarter where the texture was silkier and the tint darker. It was a flag with a blue ground, on which was superimposed a white cross and five eight-pointed stars, one at the end of each arm of the cross, and the fifth at the centre.

"No flag like that in Europe," said the American. "Well, we'll be going." He and his woman left. Robert nodded to them. He had been standing outside the doors. Now he entered and went over to his daughter.

"No flag so chaste and natural," said Lalor. "A maiden flag, never yet flown."

Robert looked hard at him.

"It is late," said Lalor. "I am sorry for that. But the flag *is* chaste and natural. It is your daughter's.

She told us where to put the cross and the stars, and made most of it herself. She even found——"

Susannah-Jane said, "We just made it."

"She called it the Southern Cross," said Lalor. "The five stars. We shall fly it tomorrow."

He saw the two strands of Robert's disquiet. The first was his daughter. "Mr. King," said Lalor, "I did want to bring your daughter back earlier, but she would not go."

Robert nodded. He could believe that.

The second strand of disquiet was the flag.

"Mr. King, you are putting yourself once again in the position of governor in Melbourne? You are thinking how he will see this?"

"He will see it as your tricolour."

"It is," said Lalor.

They left the stable, Lalor locking the doors, and parted.

Robert and Susannah-Jane walked slowly back together, both with their hands clasped behind their back. He put his arm briefly round the shoulders of his beloved daughter. She met his eyes, then looked down and then quickly up.

"All right," he said.

Then he realized what she was wearing. Round her shoulders was the old cloak of George Bryant, the one she had insisted on wearing the night they watched the fireworks, the bishop's cloak.

"I used the lining for the flag," she said. "For part of it. There was not enough blue. I used the cloak." She opened it to show him. The silk lining was gone.

They were facing each other. He took both her hands.

They were at the hotel, and she ran inside. He watched her fly up the stairs, and then saw a figure by the door. It was Cobb, who raised a hand in greeting. Robert returned the salutation. They went in together.

All his life, certainly since that afternoon in the Bois de Boulogne when he was seventeen, Robert had been aware of the power of women. But he had never felt it so strongly as he did then, when he saw it possessed by his daughter. It was not just the evident sexual force of the girl. She had made the flag, and called it the Southern Cross.

37

The Arraying of Armed Men

THE NEXT DAY was oppressively hot. Flies, the curse of the diggings, were everywhere—in men's hair, in their nostrils, in their ears, crawling at the corners of their mouths. Major Redmond drank scalding coffee from a tin mug which almost burned the lips, and addressed his servant.

"Good hunting weather."

"Sir?" said the trooper.

"You said they burned their licences?"

"I saw it, sir."

"Then this morning we shall require them to show the licences they have already destroyed. But first take a note for me to Mr. King. You will find him at the United States Hotel." The note ordered Robert to desist from further assisting the miners in their rebellion, on pain of instant arrest, and to leave Ballarat, taking his mother and daughter with him.

Then Redmond briefed the senior police officer. The man was in a difficult situation. John outranked him, but his major's commission was only in the militia, and the policeman thought his authority doubtful. If Redmond had not been heir to the largest of the sheep

kingdoms, the man would have questioned his authority. As it was, he did as he was told, assembled a
force of fifty mounted men, and reported back to Redmond, who had just received Robert's reply. It was
brief: "I have always advised the miners to act within
the law. My advice to you is the same. You have no
conceivable authority over my mother and daughter.
They would, however, have left long ago if you had
not torn up the roads." Major Redmond screwed up
the paper in his hands. He swore at the heat, the flies,
and his servant, and mounted his bay. Then he led the
policemen at a canter across the diggings. He was
proud of his horsemanship, but a canter was a reckless
pace. The ground was honeycombed with old diggings.
Old tunnels ran only a few feet below the surface. The
miners watched the approaching cloud of dust hoping
Redmond's distinctive bay would founder beneath him,
and break its rider's neck. "Jo, Jo," went up the warning cry from the miners to their companions—always
the cry when a digger-hunt was spotted—but there was
no need this time for a warning. The horse-police were
so many. Their dust was visible two miles away. They
arrested twenty miners who could not produce licences.
The mass of the miners were so incensed that they
retaliated by throwing stones, timber, and anything
that they could lay their hands on at the police, whose
horses shied and reared. The police fired a volley over
the miners' heads, and then a magistrate read the pre-
amble to the Riot Act, requiring all persons assembled
together to the disturbance of the peace to disperse
within one hour or be adjudged felons and imprisoned
for life.

Vern, Maguire, Humfray, and Lalor took their flag
to a hill and hoisted it on a pole eighty-one feet high
and straight as an arrow. Work stopped on all the diggings. From all over the goldfields groups of twelve or
twenty men conferred together and then walked to-

wards the hill. By early afternoon the workings and the town were deserted. Twelve to fifteen thousand men swarmed over the hill. Troops from the Twelfth and Fortieth regiments were withdrawn into their own camp. There were at most two hundred of them, and they knew they could be overrun.

Robert and Susannah-Jane watched from the foot of the hill.

"It is my flag," she said.

"Then listen to what is said under your flag."

Cobb joined them and stood with his hands on his belt. He had been inspecting the state of the roads, and had found them still impassable. He shook his head.

It was Lalor who spoke. Robert thought this a mercy. It could have been Vern. He could not see Humfray at all. Maguire was by Lalor's side. Robert reflected that Humfray could very likely not have commanded a hearing. Humfray himself had thought the same, and stayed away. Of them all, Lalor was likely to be the least violent, but this time it was Lalor carrying a pistol.

"I look around me," he said; and as he began to speak the meeting quietened. "I look round me and see brave and honest men, who have come thousands of miles to labour for their independence. The grievances under which we have all suffered, and the attack of this morning, are in my mind and in yours. And it is not only ourselves. I know there are hundreds, hundreds upon hundreds, now in great poverty, who could possess great wealth and happiness if they were allowed to cultivate this wilderness which surrounds us, and which without us would remain a wilderness. We will not be stuck up and robbed for what is called a licence. Twenty of us were arrested this morning. We shall demand the release of those twenty."

The cheers were rousing. Lalor waited.

"Gentlemen. Gentlemen." He could now be heard again. "I feel bound to ask you to speak your mind. Should any one of us be dragged to the lock-up—for not having a licence, or for being unable to hear a proclamation telling us we are felons unless we disperse, or for being here on this hill now—will a thousand of you volunteer to liberate the man?"

"Yes. Yes."

"Will two thousand of you come forward?"

"Yes. Yes. Yes."

"Will four thousand of you volunteer to march to the camp and open the lock-up to liberate the man?"

"Yes. Yes."

"Are you ready to die?"

"Yes. Yes."

Lalor then asked men to come forward to enroll themselves in companies, and to take the oath by the flag. Any man who did not intend to take the oath should leave straightaway. Any man who stayed to take it, and then failed to stand by it, was a coward at heart. He waited. No one left.

"Listen to me with attention then. Let all divisions under arms fall in around the flagstaff."

Five hundred diggers carrying pistols gathered round the flag. Lalor knelt, pointed his right arm to the flag, and began:

"We swear . . ."

"We swear," the men echoed.

"By the Southern Cross . . ."

"By the Southern Cross . . ."

"To stand truly by each other . . ."

"To stand truly by each other . . ."

"And fight to defend our rights and liberties."

"And fight to defend our rights and liberties."

A universal Amen rose from the thousands on the hill.

Robert took his daughter's hand. "That is enough," he said. Together with Cobb, they walked back to town. Cobb's boys told him that his two coaches and both teams of horses had been commandeered by the military.

"Thought it best not to shoot it out with half a regiment," said one of the drivers. "They went off Melbourne way. They don't know the horses. The horses don't know them. Way they drive, reckon it would take them a month anyways. Way the roads are, reckon they won't get two miles."

Susannah already knew about the oath from Cobb's boys.

"I have seen two rebellions," she told Robert. "One over rum; this one over gold. The first lot of rebels hardly had a good intention between them. These seem full of high principles. But it doesn't make much difference to the reality of things, does it?"

"Not a bit," said Robert. "Not a damn bit. Not in the least."

The diggers marched from the hill, following the flag as it was carried to the Eureka diggings. There they put up the flag again, and erected a stockade round it. The enclosed area was about an acre. By evening it was an armed camp of fifteen hundred men, though the arms were only pistols, pikes, and a few muskets.

Robert came down from his mother's room and found Cobb and Susannah-Jane returning from the New York Bakery with bread and English muffins. She offered him one. "Now," he said, "this evening you must give me your word to stay in. Above all you must not go near the stockade. But you must not go out at all. I do not know what will happen tonight. Stay with Mr. Cobb if he will have you, or with your grandmother. I shall not go far. You must stay here."

She nodded.

"No, *tell* me you agree."

"I agree."

He did not go far, only to the Theatre Royal. There
was nothing he could do. He was helpless. He wanted
diversion, and so he went to be entertained by Mr.
Dryden Hall-Kean's mélange, along with two hundred
diggers who, after the day's excitement, did not return
to work. It was even more of a mélange than was
promised. First there was a curtain-raiser called *The
Stage-struck Digger,* composed by Mr. Hall-Kean himself. After its performance, only a mad digger would
have remained stage-struck. Then there were great
rodomontades delivered by Mr. Hall-Kean from the
works of his illustrious precursors Dryden and Shakespeare. Shakespeare, as he once again explained, was
his ancestor through the Hall side of the family, the
female line. Then came Madame Ophir, lavishly introduced by the impresario himself. In Ballarat, Ophir
was a name of the past, though of the recent past.
Gold rushes are rapid. But Ophir, thanks to Hargraves,
still had both Biblical and golden connotations.

"We present," declaimed Hall-Kean, "the Queen of
Dance bedecked in the gold of Ophir. She shall be led
unto you, gentlemen, as she was led—I refer to the
Book of Proverbs—unto King Solomon, in embroidered work, her clothing inlaid with gold, and her
garments strewn with myrrh and cassia. And in ivory
palaces, stringed instruments shall make her glad."

At which the impresario bowed off the forestage and
the curtain rose to reveal a girl dressed head to foot in
gilded tinsel, with tinsel veil and tinsel ear-rings, and
banging a tinsel tambourine. The single stringed instrument to gladden her was a fiddle played backstage by
Mr. Dryden Hall-Kean. The girl was handsome but
could barely dance, and the diggers pelted her with
tiny nuggets. It was half derisive, half good-natured,
and she pleased them by dexterously catching a few
nuggets, and at the end of her act making a sweeping
curtsy which enabled her to pick a few more off the

stage. The curtain fell and the rest of the nuggets were rapidly gathered up by Mr. Hall-Kean for his own benefit.

It was tatty revue. The great man roared and yowled his way through the last scenes of *King Lear*—a revised version with a happy ending—and then ended the mélange in a way which showed that, roaring hack though he was, he knew the best act in his show, and how to display it to advantage by putting it last.

"To complete your pleasure, gentlemen, we once more present Madame Ophir [groans], this time not to delight you with her dancing but to seduce the soft air with her voice—the High Priestess of the Inca Gods invoking the golden plenty of the Sun."

Madame Ophir it was again, similarly arrayed except for the veil. This time she held no tambourine. She sang unaccompanied. She did sing in the person of a high priestess, though not of Mexico but of Gaul. And it was not a golden Sun-god she invoked but a goddess of silver, the Moon. Considering the place was Ballarat, Mr. Hall-Kean's slight transpositions were fair enough, but what she sang was "Chaste Goddess," from *Norma,* in Italian. Few of the audience could understand a word. While she sang not a man stirred, or coughed, or made any sound, and at the end there were many seconds' silence before the audience broke into a stampede of applause. That is as great a triumph as any singer can achieve, at Ballarat or La Scala. They showered her with nuggets, made her sing again, and showered her again.

Later, Robert went backstage to her.

She said, "Farther and farther from Paris? That's what you're thinking?"

"Yes," said Robert.

"You know how long it is since I was in Paris? Paris, Florence, then it was going to be Milan, Berlin.

But I ended up in Mexico City—I told you that—
and then San Francisco. Where can you go from San
Francisco?"

"The way the ships are sailing."

"Right. I came here. I last sang in Paris eight years
ago."

"Go back."

She shook her head.

Robert thought she lacked the fare, and said, "You
know me well enough to let me give you a passage
home."

She smiled and half-opened a drawer. It was full of
small nuggets. There was at least five hundred dollars
in gold. "Look," she said. "The dance—I keep the
nuggets I catch. The aria—I take half of everything
that's thrown. I make ends meet. Robert, I make four
times as much here as I ever did anywhere before."

"But you should have heard yourself tonight."

"I did. Paris? I'd do, I know; but for how much
longer? Oh, if you have a big name you can keep going until you sound like a moorhen, and longer. But I
was never much of a name. I would have been. Perhaps. What I was, was a new young voice. There'll
be other new young voices now. How many since me?
I'll stay."

He nodded.

"Build me an opera house in Sydney," she said.

"One day."

Outside the open door the impresario passed for the
third time, obviously wondering who the visitor was.

"Him?" asked Robert.

"My God, no. There's an American. Dryden and I
just happened to come from California. But not together. I never even saw him there. We met here."

"Ah."

"Robert, you have a memorable daughter."

"What?"

"You know, you really were surprised to see me this evening."

"Astonished. But what do you mean about my daughter?"

"You saw me last night, in the stable. Or rather, you were so engrossed you never even looked at me."

"You were with Maguire?"

"My American," she said.

"You helped make that flag?"

"I watched. Your daughter did it. When you came in, you were afraid for her, weren't you? You needn't have been. Lalor has great charm, but she has much more than that. She is utterly memorable. I'm glad she's your daughter. I remember you."

"Yvette, you know where Maguire is tonight?"

"Yes, I pray for him."

At the Eureka Stockade, Lalor drilled his men by the light of flares. Sixty Americans calling themselves the Independent California Rangers rode by and asked, "What's up?" They had Colt revolvers and knives. They listened to Maguire, and then bivouacked in the stockade. A hundred British infantrymen marched into Ballarat late, to reinforce the garrison. The California Rangers laughed at their uniforms. "Greenhorns in red padding," they said. Lalor let it be known that he had appointed a Minister for War. The major in charge of the new detachment roused the printer at the *Ballarat Times* near midnight and ordered him to print, immediately, five hundred posters proscribing all those who had rebelliously and traitorously levied and arrayed armed men in the Eureka Stockade, with a view of making armed war against their Sovereign Lady the Queen.

38

The Eureka Stockade

THE STOCKADE at the Eureka was not a fort. It was
made of timber slabs whose normal use was to shore
up the diggings, boulders, upturned carts, and sharpened staves driven into the ground. "Great works!" exclaimed an Italian, Carboni Raffaello, surveying the
corral as if it were a feat of fortification and engineer-
ing. He was constantly taunting Vern. "Where are
your five hundred Hanoverian marksmen?" There
were none. Vern ignored him and went round encour-
aging the others by promising to lead them to victory
or death. He particularly addressed the Americans,
who in turn ignored him. They sat silently oiling their
Colts, spinning the chambers, cleaning the barrels. A
blacksmith from Mexico worked all through the day
forging pikes that he sold at ten dollars apiece. Raffaello denounced the pikes as poor, rough things, but
they were bought by the Irish, who resolutely drilled
with them.

"Shoulder pikes. Order pikes. Ground pikes."

A broad Irishman, once a sergeant-major in a British regiment, instructed his men in a combination of

remembered ceremonial-drill sequences, and in a technique of defence hardly used since Agincourt.

"Pre-*pare* to receive cavalry." The men formed up two-deep, the first row kneeling, the second standing.

"Ad-*vance* pikes." The men smartly raised their pikes, making a wall of pointed metal rods on which jumping horses would impale themselves.

"Poke your pike into the guts of the horse," said the sergeant-major. "Poke it in, and draw it out by the tail. Now, pre-*pare* to receive cavalry." He drilled them for two hours in the sweating sun.

"Good boys," he said. They were all Irish. Only thirty had iron pikes. Twenty others went through the motions with wooden staves. There were no Hanoverian marksmen, but there was a Hanoverian band. Five men played the "Marseillaise" on trumpet and drums. The Americans observed everything. They watched the pike drill with a feeling that was half-admiration and half-amazement. Some of the Americans did not even recognize the "Marseillaise." Raffaello told them. He was everywhere, addressing revolutionary lectures to anyone, in Italian, English, French, and very bad German. Vern at length seized a half-wrought pike from the Mexican's forge, with the end still glowing red, and hurled it at the Italian. He missed. Lalor quelled Vern, and took Raffaello by the shoulder and walked with him, talking quietly. The Italian revered Lalor, and calmed down. A messenger rode in, reporting large bodies of redcoats coming up from Melbourne. The Americans talked about ambushing them. At six o'clock, a patrol of cavalry militia, a dozen strong, reined in two hundred yards from the camp, on a slight hill where they could overlook the drilling. An officer dismounted, took a pair of field-glasses, and swept them over the stockade and up at the flag.

"None other than Major Redmond," said the Italian, "with his gold-lace cap, and red frock coat, and jingling sword, such a precise Puss-in-Boots."

The long hours of Saturday afternoon and evening dragged themselves out. It was still very hot, a stinker of a day.

At the army camp the men of the Twelfth and Forti-eth regiments were confident for the first time in days that they were not about to be attacked and over-whelmed by armed diggers. They were much encour-aged by the arrival the previous midnight of the reinforcements from Melbourne, and by the young Major Hannay, who commanded them. He had imme-diately posted double pickets but ordered the rest of the men to stand down and rest. He assembled his of-ficers and asked who was the senior. They told him Major Redmond was asleep in his quarters.

"Ask him to be so good as to attend on me now."

He was told that Redmond, though only a major of militia, was heir to an empire of sheep.

"Good," said the young man. "I have some live-stock of my own back in Shropshire. We shall have an interest in common."

He was just the kind of commandant the colonial officers would ordinarily have suspected and disliked. He was English, he had been seconded to Victoria from a fashionable English light-cavalry regiment in which he still held his commission and to which he would return, and he did not give a damn for Red-mond. But as things stood, the officers were pleased to have him.

Redmond, summoned in the middle of the night by a much younger officer who did not even rise to greet him, was not pleased. He was told that the military command was no longer his. He would continue to com-mand his own troops, but was relieved of the garrison.

"Now," said Hannay, "I do not know the terrain. I

have been told that you are intimately connected with the goldfields, Major Redmond. Instruct me."

He listened to what Redmond grudgingly told him, sent out his own patrols in the morning, and then in the afternoon told his officers, "It looks like the Irish and the Americans."

Redmond wanted to attack. He proposed a cavalry charge straightaway.

Hannay said, "I should not care to order a charge by tired horses, ridden by tired men, in the heat of the day. If it can be avoided, I shall not care to charge at all. I shall prefer to pray for rain. If it rains they will go away. That would be best for us all. I have no wish to risk my men, or to make martyrs out of diggers. If it does come to a fight I have no wish to command a massacre. I shall use the infantry, with cavalry in reserve. We will disperse the diggers if we can, or take them prisoner if we can. If they fire on us, we shall return fire. If they drop their arms and run, we shall let them run. There are no field-marshals' batons to be gained from such a little rout as this. We shall do it as quietly as we can. So, wait. And, gentlemen, pray for rain."

It was Susannah in the end who convinced Robert that he ought to go back to the stockade to make a last approach to Lalor. Since the oath-taking there had been nothing he could do. He had come away from a meeting of fifteen thousand men. If fifteen thousand diggers were intent on armed rebellion there was nothing to be done. On the Saturday evening he sat talking late with his mother and Cobb. The United States Hotel was bustling. So were the Eagle, the Excelsior, the Byron, and the Liverpool. The main street was packed with happily drunk diggers. The next day was Sunday. Sunday was kept, according to the way it was looked at, either as the Sabbath or as a holiday. There was at any rate no work. But that Saturday men had been working their claims as usual. And in the evening the street was full. It was still full at midnight. The waiter said it was as full as any Saturday night. Outside, beyond the town, there were still lights in a thousand tents.

Susannah said, "So how many men are still in the stockade?"

"This afternoon," said Cobb, "maybe fifteen hundred. Maybe not."

One of his boys said, "Maybe not. A half hour ago, I was down by the Free Trade Bar, and Maguire and, oh, maybe fifty riders passed by. I saw Maguire and I called out to him, and he said they were out to ambush some more redcoats coming up from Melbourne. 'At night?' I says. 'They did last night,' he says back, and then he says he surely hopes the stockade can hold out till they get back. Now, you can say it was a joke the way he said it; but maybe, maybe not. I wouldn't bet on any fifteen hundred sitting there."

Susannah said, "There were fifteen thousand on the hill, listening to speeches in the sun. Tonight, there may be only a thousand in that stockade, and how many of those would come away if they were given the occasion?"

"I shall go and see," said Robert.

"Good," she said.

"You'll need the password," said Cobb's man. "Vinegar Hill."

"Vinegar Hill," said Robert. "How did you come by that?"

"Just heard talk of it."

It was a bright starlit night. A hundred yards from the stockade Robert was challenged.

"Vinegar Hill."

At the compound he was challenged again. He went

in. He did not look for Lalor straightaway. Another man had slipped in with him at the same time. Robert said, "Good night."

"Good night, friend," said the man exultantly. "The excitement is of Satan."

He disappeared towards one of the three fires still blazing. Robert made for another fire, round which a dozen Irishmen, three Scots, and an American were standing.

"Nobblers all round?" said a Scot. A tot of brandy was pushed into Robert's hand. He knocked it back with the rest, and looked around. The pikemen lay near the perimeter of the stockade, each one nursing his pike. Four hobbled horses scuffed round a fragment of hay. The stockade itself was more insubstantial than he had thought. A horse could easily jump it, or a man vault it. Behind the stockade, against the sky, rose the mass of Mount Warrenheip. The army camp, which lay in the other direction, was not visible, but the stockade and the men in it could be seen by any spy who stood on the rising ground a few hundred yards off. Robert was lost in a survey of the terrain when he was startled by a clashing and hammering close by. What he had taken to be a third bonfire was the Mexican's forge, and he was still shaping pikes. Robert saw the metal glow white and then red, saw the red sparks fly as the hammer beat the iron against the anvil, and saw the steam rise in the light of the flames as the man doused the sharpened point in a trough. The sparks and clatter scared one of the hobbled horses, which neighed. Its call was answered from somewhere in the dark, outside the stockade.

Robert asked for Lalor. The man indicated the group round the other fire. Lalor was not there, but a group of Irishmen were lying back listening to a story intensely told by the man who had come in with Robert. It was a tale the Irish liked, as fantastic as a story of Brian Boru, ancient king of Ireland, as exotic but more recent. The little man was talking in English and half-translated bits of Italian about his defence of Rome a few years before, with Garibaldi, against the might of the French. And when the battle was won in Ballarat, he said, and in all Australia, and the tyrants had all fallen, then he would be back to his native country to overthrow the oppressors in all the states of Italy.

"You have a fine command of the English," said one of his listeners, "being an Italian as you are."

The man said he had lived in London after being driven by the French from Rome. But he and Garibaldi would enter Rome again. They would conquer all Italy, starting from the very toe, from Sicily, from Palermo. They would stop in Palermo only long enough to construct in honour of freedom an opera house grander than Milan, and then they would fight their way up through all Italy. "And I shall write a grand opera of the Revolution for Palermo; and a pantomime; and historical dramas; and comedies and ballets." He saw in his mind the opera house they would build at Palermo when he and Garibaldi entered. "Great works!" he exclaimed. "The greatest opera house in Europe or the world."

"That is a fine thing," said an Irishman. "And I wish you well. We have a fine theatre at Waterford too; and your grand comedies, if they were translated, could be performed there to the applause of thousands, when the English are gone."

Then the Italian overstepped himself. He began composing, to the accompaniment of much hilarity, a satirical letter to Her Most Excellent Majesty Queen Victoria, London, inviting her to the diggers' celebration dinner six months hence in Melbourne, when the Diggers' Parliament was inaugurated. He went too far when he proposed to extend the invitation also to His

Holiness Pius the Ninth, Pontifex Maximus, Rome.
The Catholic Irish diggers would not mock the pope.
The Italian had already launched into a mock blessing
of them all in Latin—for had he not once spent a
year in a seminary intending to be a priest before he
saw the light?—when he saw that his audience was
now silent and offended.

Robert found Lalor alone at the edge of the stockade, gazing at the sky above Mount Warrenheip. He
came up on him unawares.

"They will not attack from that direction," said
Robert.

"Mr. King," said Lalor, "I did not expect you. But
shall we be attacked?"

"How many men have you here?"

"How did you get in, Mr. King?"

"Your password is known in town."

"And I dare say in the barracks as well?" asked
Lalor.

"I dare say."

Lalor said, "As for men, see for yourself."

There could not have been more than four hundred.

"The Americans were seen to go," said Robert.

"Off starlighting," said Lalor, "intercepting reinforcements from Melbourne. They call it starlighting.
Now tell me why you have come. With an offer from
the commanding officer?"

Robert did not answer him.

"I beg your pardon, Mr. King, that was foolish of
me."

"Where is Humfray?"

"He never came in here with us, and has been persuading others not to join us."

"You and he, and Maguire, all seemed to have
heads on your shoulders; when we first met."

"Maguire would be here too. He is out with the
Americans."

"Mr. Lalor, why did you speak as you did on the hill? Why the oath?"

Lalor stared at the sky, but did not answer.

"Mr. Lalor. If Vern had said what you said, I could understand. I was glad when you spoke and not Vern. But you asked four thousand men if they were willing to die. I do not know why you selected that figure, but you said four thousand. And they took the oath. Well, Mr. Lalor, there are not four hundred left here to die with."

Lalor said, "I would not say now what I said on the hill. That does not mean we shall not fight. We shall fight. I would not say it now, but I have an hereditary disability which is apt to show itself sometimes. My name in Irish is O'Labhaimir, which I am afraid means 'descended from a man who is a great speaker.'

"Mr. King," Lalor continued after a pause, "do you have a brother?"

"A half brother."

"I had a brother. Mr. King, I am from Queen's County, Ireland. My father was what the English call a gentleman farmer. He was in the Westminster Parliament as member for the county. That was only ten years ago. He is dead. As an undergraduate I went to Dublin—Trinity College. I was telling your daughter about Dublin. A city not in England, but the loveliest English city of them all. My elder brother would have been angry to hear me say that. He was oppressed in spirit by the English, and brooded over the English, and did not wish our father to sit in the English Parliament. My brother brooded over plans for Irish freedom. I could meet the English and drink with them. He could not in any way. He said the land was for the Irish. He wrote that Irish tenants should not pay rent to English owners of Irish land. I could follow his grievance, but did not feel it. He wrote again and again, for the newspapers. Then a friend of his, who had done no more than write just such articles, was transported. I think he will still be serving out his days in Tasmania. The newspapers my brother wrote for were suppressed. When the last was suppressed, he founded another. It was called *The Irish Felon.* After five numbers, that too was suppressed and he was arrested. He was imprisoned. He was a persuasive man. A man of original and vigorous mind. After nine months he was so broken by the jail that the English released him, not wanting him to die in jail. He died afterwards, out of jail. Now, I was the one who could always talk with the English, and drink with the English, but when it came to it, I said what I said two days ago on the hill. And now I suppose I too am an Irish felon."

While he listened, Robert had been looking up at the flag, looking anywhere so as not to see Lalor's features as he spoke about his brother. Against all usage, the flag had been left to fly all night. A flag by day can be an inspiriting sight; at night, when its colour and features cannot be seen, it can hang like a damp sheet.

It was half past two in the early hours in the morning.

Robert kept silence for a long time. "Well then," he said. "I see. You have told me about your brother, and about Queen's County, about Dublin, about Ireland. Now, forgive me, I have also heard Vern speak about Hanover—and what he hopes will be one Germany. He speaks differently, violently, and senselessly, but the point is that he is thinking of Hanover, and of what he did not achieve in Hanover. An hour ago, here, before I found you, I heard a man speaking in English and Italian, with Latin thrown in as well, about a triumphal march through an Italy of the future. Starting at Palermo."

"He is Italian," said Lalor. "In Italy his name was

Raffaello Carboni. When he came here he said he would change it round to Carboni Raffaello, to fit the southern hemisphere."

"Lalor," said Robert, "this is not Ireland, or Hanover, or a notional Italy that may exist one day. Men are here in this stockade for far-flung, different reasons which have nothing to do with Ballarat. And look around. Count. Tell me how many are left now."

The fires had died down. The groups of men were sparser. While Robert and Lalor had been speaking, men had melted into the night. Raffaello had gone, though only to his tent a few hundred yards outside. The rest had considered, had second thoughts, and left.

"How many?" said Robert.

"Two hundred?"

"Lalor, listen. You may be an Irish felon, but you are not an Australian felon yet."

"My dear King, what does that mean?"

"I want to speak to these men."

"Do."

"You must tell them who I am and why you asked me to come here in the first place."

It was done.

The men gathered round the last of the fires. Most of those who remained were Irish.

"Gentlemen, there's precious little legal advice left for me to give. I can give you a couple of pieces of information, and then an opinion or two. The rest is up to you. Now, the new commander of the troops has stuck up posters proscribing those who have traitorously and rebelliously levied and arrayed armed men with a view to make armed war against the queen. That is you. That on the face of it is what you have done. He will have got that proclamation out of his manual of military law. It's a matter of form. But the form is more ancient than the reality. Those words date back to the year dot. He can no longer declare the lot of you outlaws and say there's an end to it. I have been talking to Mr. Lalor. He said a few minutes ago that he supposed he was an Irish felon. I don't know whether he is or not. But he certainly isn't an Australian felon until he's been tried and found guilty of felony in Australia. It can't be done by a magistrate. And the commander here has not declared martial law. Either he's forgotten or he's had the good sense not to, or he hasn't got enough officers to make up a court-martial. So if there are trials, they will have to be trials by jury. That's all the *legal* advice I have. Now, opinions. If the new major were to send a patrol tomorrow and find nobody here, he'd write a report to Melbourne saying how successful he had been in preserving the peace. I doubt if he would pursue anyone. But suppose some men *were* later found and charged, how easily do you think a jury could be empanelled in Ballarat, or Melbourne, to find anyone guilty of treason—which, since he's put up that poster, is about the only charge left open to him? My opinion, gentlemen, is that if you left, no jury would convict any digger of treason."

And that was all he would have said, praying that it was enough, except that Vern said, "So you are telling us to run? That is your coward's advice?"

"I am telling you what I think will happen if you leave. And I am advising you to leave. Yes, I am."

"You talk of traitors," said Vern, "but you are the only traitor here. We"—here he indicated those around him with a sweep of his arm—"we shall not be traitors to our own destiny. Our destiny is in our hands."

Robert said, "Lalor, tell them to go, for God's sake."

Lalor hesitated. And then something of the same quality of change that came over Lalor on the hill came over Robert. His coolness left him.

"Destiny? Look at yourselves. How many are you?

There were fifteen thousand on the hill taking the
oath, but how many was that compared to the one
hundred thousand on the diggings? There were once
fifteen hundred in the stockade, but how many was
that compared with the fifteen thousand on the hill?
And how many are left now? Two hundred? I doubt
two hundred. For God's sake, go! If you stay here you
will sooner or later be attacked. Vern says you can
decide your own destiny, and so you can. So you can.
Stay here and you will decide your own destiny: you
will decide your own deaths."

And with that he would have left—and how many
would have gone with him?—but it was ten minutes
past three in the morning and at that moment the first
digger sentinel fired the first shot as he saw in the
light of the coming dawn the storming parties of the
Twelfth and Fortieth of Foot with their bayonets, and
the dim forms of the mounted Fortieth standing back
in parade order on the right, the foot-police and horse-
police with their carbines in the centre, and the cavalry militia with sabres drawn on the left. Hannay
knew the Americans had gone to intercept reinforcements. He knew he could take the stockade easily in
their absence. He decided to do so in the minutes before dawn. He did not expect to use cavalry. He had
ordered the captain of the Fortieth to invite surrender,
but the digger sentinel fired first.

In the stockade the Irish pikemen formed their two
rows. They prepared to receive cavalry, the front row
kneeling, the second row standing. They advanced
pikes. There were fifty pikemen in all. They had
stayed in the stockade to a man. The infantry came on
at a march in drill formation. Two diggers had borrowed rifles from the Americans. They picked off the
officers who marched in front of their men, presenting
ceremonial targets, easily distinguished because their
men had bayonets and the officers alone carried

swords. The captain of the Fortieth fell, and the lieutenant leading the Twelfth. Their sergeants took command. One hundred and sixty infantrymen knelt, fired a volley into the stockade, and then advanced at the charge. At the first volley, Lalor was badly hit in the shoulder. Vern ran. The pikemen stood their ground, prepared to receive cavalry. Only it was not cavalry that overcame them, but the bayonets of the Twelfth. The pikemen suffered most. They stood firm and were cut to pieces—a few cuts, kicks, and pullings-down, and all was over with them.

It was really finished by the time the cavalry came, Redmond's militia from the left of the stockade. Major Hannay, holding his own cavalry back on the right, swore as he saw the militia let loose at full gallop and leap the stockade. Two riders were injured, but that was because they fell. It was not the work of the pikemen, who were all lying dead or injured. The diggers fought while they could fight, and then they ran. They were helpless now. The few with muskets had no powder or shot. The two riflemen were bayoneted. They had fought. Now, anyone able to run, ran. The cavalry militia pursued and ran down an already defeated force of men. The sabre wounds were nearly all across the back of the shoulders, neck, or head. Robert dragged Lalor to a heap of timber slabs, and, with the help of an American, hid him there. Lalor was bleeding badly from the shoulder. The American screamed a warning, and Robert turned to see him fall to a thrust from a militia officer, who wheeled his horse and came back. Robert recognized the bay, and then its rider. It was John. Robert crouched, struggling to rise, but the bay ran him down. John wheeled again and then, as if he were at field exercise, trotted up to Robert, leaned to the left out of his saddle, and cut at him casually with a backhand sweep of the sabre. Robert fell. Major Hannay, who had just come up with his sergeant, saw the slash at the wounded man and shouted with anger at Redmond, whom he saw caracoling his bay, turning her on her hind feet, to attack again.

Hannay drew his pistol. "Damn you, man, for a butcher. Damn you and your elegant horsemanship, and damn your bloody men. Call them off or I will shoot them." It took longer to bring the militia to order than to defeat the defenders of the stockade.

At ten past three there had been not two hundred but rather fewer than one hundred and fifty diggers in the Eureka. Ten minutes later twenty-two were dead and three times that many wounded. The attackers numbered two hundred and seventy-four in all, including the regular cavalry, who never took part in the action. Besides the two infantry officers picked off by the snipers in the first minutes of the attack, three other soldiers died.

A police trooper hauled down the Southern Cross, and Redmond's militiamen, having at length been rounded up and brought back to the stockade, tossed it from sabre to sabre, hacking at it, until Hannay's sergeant took it from them and threw it over Robert and the American, who had fallen close together. It was just full light. Hannay's charger cast a long shadow as he stood still watching his men collect the dead. He found that he was still holding his pistol, and put it away. Redmond walked his bay up to the bodies covered by the tatters of the flag. As he looked down at the dead American, and at Robert, he felt the contemptuous eyes of Hannay on him. John had hated Robert, but had not wished to be seen to kill a brother.

39

～◦৩৩৽◦～

In Which Susannah Awaits Her Lover

SUSANNAH-JANE faced Cobb on the boardwalk outside the hotel. It was twenty minutes after the last shot had died away. Cobb had found a light cart, and one of his men was holding the horse's head.

"I will *not* go back," she said.

"Where is your grandmother?"

At that moment he saw Susannah at the top of the hotel stairs and went in to help her, but she walked steadily down herself. None of them had slept since Robert left. They expected him back at one o'clock, then at two. At three they decided he would stay the night and not return till morning. Ten minutes later they heard the first shots. Cobb ran to find a cart. Susannah walked slowly to her room, stripped the sheets off her bed and Susannah-Jane's, for bandages, and came downstairs.

Cobb again told the girl, "Go back," and again she fiercely refused.

"Miss King," he said, "go back of your own accord, or one of my men will hold you back. I will not take you."

She turned to Susannah. "My father is out there."

523

Susannah answered her gently, "Yes. But go back."

The girl defiantly obeyed her, so defiantly that Cobb asked Susannah, "Do I need to leave a man with her?"

"No," said Susannah.

They overtook hundreds of diggers on the way to the Eureka. It was hard going. The light wheels of the car jarred against boulders. When they came in sight of the Eureka they found it was guarded by a double line of police with carbines. They had to get down and walk the last three hundred yards. They met a file of prisoners being led away by soldiers of the Fortieth. They were the remains of the Irish, and the Italian. Those men who still had hats, took them off to Susannah. She looked at them, and no man met her eyes. She faltered. Cobb put his arm round her shoulders, and they went on. A police sergeant let them pass. Six military carts were heaped with dead. They lay with their faces upwards, looking like lead. Cobb and Susannah went from the first to the second cart. Neither had ever seen a battlefield. Some men lay apparently untouched, but lifeless. The sabre wounds were the most terrible. A sabre can remove half a man's face. On the third cart one man was still breathing. At every breath blood bubbled from a wound in the throat, and trickled onto the floor of the cart. Cobb called out to a sergeant of the Fortieth, who glanced at the man and called two orderlies. He also took the sheets from Susannah. There were three more carts of the dead to see, and then the wounded, propped against the slabs of the stockade, some lying still, some moaning and turning, one screaming without stop. Susannah looked over at the man and then at the sergeant, who understood her and said, "There is only one surgeon we have. But believe me, ma'am, if a man screams he has life in him. I have seen it."

Then he recognized her, and took Cobb aside. Susannah still looked towards the screaming man.

Cobb went back and stood before her.

"You have found him?" she said.

He took her arm and led her over to a heap of rags, which was the Southern Cross. The sergeant came with them. "I am deeply sorry," he said. He rolled back the flag from the two faces—the American, and Robert King.

Susannah gazed at the face of her son, disfigured with the dark slash of a sabre. Then she looked at the other face, lying so close that the hair of the two dead men mingled.

"Who was he?"

"An American," said the sergeant. "We showed him to the prisoners but no one knew his name." He looked over at Cobb, who shook his head. He did not recognize the man either. The flag where the sergeant held it was very bloody. He shifted his grip to a part of the fabric that was not sodden and coagulated.

Susannah suddenly knelt, and the sergeant sprang to her and took her shoulders in both hands. "No . . ." he said. He almost cried the word. But Susannah knelt erect, only putting one hand to her son's forehead. The sergeant held her in a firm hold, as if she were his own mother. He wished to spare her what she could be spared of the ordeal. She rose without tears and looked up at the bare flagpole.

Cobb jerked his head to summon his men, who had stayed with the cart. "We will take both," he told the sergeant.

"Take the lady first," said the sergeant. His eyes said, "Do not ask me why."

Coob took Susannah back to the cart himself, leaving his two boys with the bodies and saying he would send the cart back. The sergeant had seen so much blood—not at Ballarat but in miserable African campaigns—that it had made him tender. Only a man already a brute is made more brutal by familiarity with the scenes of violent death. It gentles others. The sergeant had pulled the flag back carefully, and cried out "No . . ." when Susannah knelt, and then held her, because he would not let her see too much. She had to see her son's face. The sergeant could not disguise a sabre wound, which was terrible enough, but he did not uncover the face far enough to show that the chin was mostly gone, or that the chest was caved in by the trampling of the bay.

Susannah-Jane, watching them return, did not need to be told that her father was dead. Her grandmother sat in the lobby of the hotel, not caring who saw her. Her dress was bloody at the shoulders where the sergeant's hands had held her. She would not change the dress for two hours. Susannah-Jane half-sat and half-knelt by her, holding her hands and speaking quietly to her, asking her to go and rest, asking her to . . .

"To do what?" said Susannah. "What should I do?"

"Your shoulders."

Susannah looked at her dress and saw the blood for the first time. "It does not matter," she said.

"It's all right, then. It's all right."

But then Susannah did allow her granddaughter to take her to her room.

Cobb had stood by them the whole time. When Susannah-Jane came down again, he said, "You were brave."

The girl would let no one see her tears. She asked to see her father. By then Cobb's men had brought the two bodies into town, laid them out as best they could in a stable, and covered them with a blanket. At the Eureka, the troopers had taken the remains of the flag. Cobb took her to the stable and did for Susannah-Jane what the sergeant had done for Susannah in the morning, carefully uncovering her father's face, concealing from her what he would by no means allow her to see. She too asked who the other man was. Cobb had discovered a letter in the man's pocket. It was a letter home, saying he had panned forty-four ounces of gold in three days, that he was in good health, and that he hoped the crops in Fayetteville were good and fair. He had not finished the letter, so he had not signed it. There was no address, so not even his family name was known. Cobb said there was a Fayetteville in Virginia, and that it was likely to be very poor.

Susannah-Jane looked at the face of the young man from Fayetteville, and then she went back to her father, standing for a long minute at the foot of the trestle on which he lay. Cobb waited at the door. She bowed her head so that her hair hid her face, and Cobb could not see her features. Then she looked up and round. It was the stable where her father had come to fetch her at midnight only three days before, and had found her kneeling on the floor by the flag she had made.

It was December, nearly midsummer. The burials had to be rapidly done. The coffins were made of wooden slabs salvaged from the stockade. The coffin lids were of rough-hewn eucalypt. The dead Irishmen were supposed to be Catholic. Not all of them were, so the Roman Church took back a few souls that day from the Established Church of Ireland, which was Anglican and Protestant. Robert King, together with the American, a Canadian, and two Germans, was buried according to the English rites. Susannah heard the terrible and beautiful words, which had no comfort for her. She felt the sting of death, and plainly saw the victory of the clay grave. Her hope of the Resurrection was neither sure nor certain. And when it came to that part of the service which recites that the past is no more than faded grass, she denied this with all her instinct and soul and heart. In that triumphant denial she came away, supporting Susannah-Jane, whose courage had at last given way when she heard for the first time the words spoken at the burial of the dead, and the clods of earth striking the coffin.

No one told Susannah—they all thought to be kind so no one told her—that her first son had been killed by her second, or in what way, but she came to know, because it was common talk and not to be kept from her.

Then she cursed John. If she could have spoken a formal commination it would have lessened her anguish, but she had no easy anathema to pronounce. When she knew, she said, with soft intensity, "Oh may he live in Hell. Oh may he live in Hell." And that was all. But then she wept bitterly, and her spirit broke.

Cobb would have killed the man. Many men in Ballarat would have killed him, but he was gone. Susannah-Jane would have killed him. Cobb held her hard by the wrists until her fury exhausted itself and she sat with her head between her knees. When she lifted her head again, he said, "Go to your grandmother." She did, mourning her father, but most of all comforting Susannah in both their griefs.

They took Susannah home to Sydney. Susannah remembered nothing of the journey from Ballarat to Melbourne or the passage from there to Sydney. Only as the ship entered the harbour, and rolled in the swell between the north and south heads, did she look up at the rocky outcrops on the right, then at the wooded slopes of Vaucluse on the left, and then, as they entered the cove, up at the domain. The news had preceded them. Governor Fitzroy had taken Elizabeth to the residence, not caring for her to stay in

Robert's house the first weeks, and it was to Government House that he ordered Susannah to be brought too. She was put in the old sandalwood bed in which she had not slept since it was hers as a girl. She had slept there alone, and with Baudin. When she married she left it with the governor's furniture: she had never shared it with her husband.

Already the legend of Ballarat had begun to grow. It was as she had once told Wyndham when she was speaking about the myths of her own life—legends are the spiritual side of events. The spirit of Ballarat grew, as it had been destined to grow. The charge of the militia cavalry into the Eureka Stockade was five weeks almost to the day after the charge of the Light Brigade at Balaclava, and the first event became as memorable a legend as the second. The diggers had demanded a great deal of the Cosmos, and got it. *The New York Times,* reporting the skirmish, called it the Battle of the Southern Cross. The legend became no skirmish, but a revolution. Lalor, hidden by Robert King and the unknown American from Fayetteville, Virginia, escaped detection that night and recovered. When he was found, and became one of thirteen diggers to be tried for high treason, no jury would convict them. Licences were done away with and the diggers enfranchised. Cobb and his boys became the Wells Fargo of Australia. Carboni Raffaello, becoming again Raffaello Carboni, did march with Garibaldi, five years later, through the length of Italy, and they did land at Palermo, where they built a stupendous opera house. Carboni wrote his grand operas, ballets, dramas, and pantomimes, but they were never performed. In Australia, Lalor became speaker of the state parliament. Yvette Rivière, once of the Paris opera, lived to coach the young Nellie Melba.

But Susannah knew nothing of even the first beginnings of the legend. The two months after she learned that her second son had killed her first, Baudin's child, were a chaos of near madness. When she saw Elizabeth, she recognized her and comforted her as she would have comforted anyone in distress for the loss of a husband. By instinct she comforted a bereaved woman, but her reason did not see that they shared the same loss. She did not identify Elizabeth's lost husband with her lost son. They were not in her mind the same man. A letter came from William Redmond. When she was told of this, she did not recognize her husband's name. Elizabeth opened and read the letter herself. It was written in the sharp, illegible scrawl of old age, and expressed sympathy, deep regret, and deeper shame. Elizabeth knew there was no point in reading it to Susannah. She replied to Redmond herself, explaining. Redmond had disowned and disinherited his son. John Redmond appeared once in Sydney and was met everywhere with contempt. No house or hotel was open to him. No one would give or sell him food or drink. No one would stable his horse. He left —it was said for California. No one knew. Old Redmond lived on in his palace. The Redmonds were long-lived.

Susannah was never left on her own. Elizabeth and Susannah-Jane took turns to be with her. She and Elizabeth had been close, but it was to Susannah-Jane that she talked now.

"Bring me my pictures," she said.

The girl went to Susannah's house and fetched the sketch of Susannah by Wyndham and the framed engraving of Baudin. Susannah smiled at the sketch, looking into the eyes of the woman she had been, and gave the drawing to Susannah-Jane.

"This is for you."

Susannah-Jane took it. It was familiar to her. She

had known it since she was a child. For the first time she saw that it could be a sketch of herself.

A letter came one day from Bengal. Elizabeth recognized the handwriting of the address. As long as she could remember, Susannah had received letters addressed in that hand, once or twice a year, most from England but others from all parts of the world. Elizabeth did not remember Wyndham and so did not know the handwriting was his. She saw by now that Susannah spoke to her young granddaughter more freely than to her. She did not know why, or whether there was any knowing why. Perhaps it was because the girl had been with her at Ballarat. She asked her daughter to give the letter to Susannah.

Susannah did not open it. She said to Susannah-Jane, "Bring me the two boxes."

The girl brought her two rosewood boxes, inlaid with ivory, and the two tiny brass keys.

"You knew where to find the keys?" said Susannah.

The girl admitted it. She remembered from the time she was a very young child the drawer of the writing desk where the keys were kept.

Susannah opened one box and took from it more than thirty years of letters in Wyndham's hand. They were first the letters of a lover, and then the serene letters of an old friend. She replaced them, together with the new letter, which she did not open. She locked the box, put it to one side, and never once looked at it again. She put the second box by her bed.

Susannah-Jane knew what she was witnessing. She had known for a week now what no one else knew—and she had told no one else, not even her mother. She had realized that Susannah no longer remembered Robert's death. His death had broken her, but she had forgotten it. Ballarat and all recent events were forgotten. Susannah was living in herself. It was not that she had forgotten Robert. But she remembered him only as a boy, as a child. She had forgotten his death, but still remembered his birth. She talked about his birth. She told Susannah-Jane about the naming of Australia.

"He said, 'I will call you Australia.' And the next day, at dinner, I asked if it would not do very well for a name for the whole continent. And Sir Harry said he would willingly abduct a continent of that name."

She often talked like this. Susannah-Jane sat and listened, and came to understand very well. The recent past no longer existed in her grandmother's mind. And now, by laying aside the letters, and by giving her the sketch by Wyndham, she was also putting away any flickers of memory from her middle years and earlier. Now, only the events of Susannah's earliest womanhood were alive to her.

One day a high wind rose from the south. In the gardens, not fifty yards from Susannah's window, a clump of giant bamboo strained, creaked, clattered, and sang as bamboo does in a high wind, like the spars and rigging of a hard-driven ship. The wind fell as suddenly as it came. But it had stirred Susannah. From the second box her granddaughter had fetched for her, she took Baudin's last, sea-stained journal in which, a week out from Batavia, he had written his last words to her.

She gave Susannah-Jane the box, the key, and the journal. "That is for you to read and keep," she said.

Susannah-Jane took the box to the edge of the domain lawns and sat down, folding her skirts around her. She took out the journal and read. "Heavy seas all night, pitching, labouring, spraying all over. . . . Morning and the sea is fair. Susannah, you were the greatest gift that was ever made to me. . . . May you be cherished in your heart, and in your mind, and in your bed. . . . I believe we are at latitude 7 degrees

30 minutes S. and longitude 95 degrees 41 minutes E., but I do not know where I am."

Then she sat for a long time, surrounded by the scent of the frangipanni, with her head on her knees. Her grandmother had given her the Indian Ocean in the year 1803. Susannah had put from her mind the dying Baudin, and kept for herself only the living Nicolas, whose portrait still stood by her bed.

That night, when Susannah-Jane went to see her grandmother, she found that she had left the sandalwood bed and was at the window.

"What is it? What is it?" the girl asked.

Susannah was searching for the Southern Cross. "My father had a gardener," she said, "who used to say it was the evening star and the seven stars all intermixed, as he never saw in his life in any part of the world before."

"It is too early in the year," said Susannah-Jane. "It is February. It is in the south-east, too far round to see from the window."

"I cannot see it."

"Not in that part of the sky, not now."

"No," said Susannah. "It was an October evening that he came."

On the last night, Susannah-Jane found her again at the window, looking not at the sky but over the lawns and the acacias and the tall, grown cedars of the domain, down into the cove at the lights of the ships riding easily. She said she was waiting for a ship.

"What ship?" asked Susannah-Jane, but as she asked she knew what ship.

"She will come in under topsails," said Susannah. "She will anchor first, and then she will come to her mooring. She will come to her mooring in an hour, and I will wait for him. When I am on board, there is something, there is a feeling, I could be in the gardens of the domain. I asked. I told him. He says she is

made of cedar, which is a fast wood for a ship; and
that is what I sense. He says her timbers might be
from the young cedars of the domain—when they are
a little grown. I will wait for him."

Peralta, Sydney, Ballarat, Papeete, Deptford
1977-78

A Note, and Acknowledgments

THIS IS a novel, not a history, though I hope the characters who live through it are true to the spirit of Australia and of Sydney, that magical city. The principal historical events of the story, particularly the more terrible, are based on fact. They happened. Sydney was settled by the convicts of the First Fleet. A group of such convicts, a woman and two children among them, did escape in an open boat to Timor and around the world. The flag of the Southern Cross flew over the Eureka stockade, and the battle between diggers and the military was fought around it. Some of the people of the novel are real. They lived, and I have used some of the words they spoke. Captain Bligh of the *Bounty* did become governor of New South Wales, where he suffered a second mutiny. Philip Gidley King was third governor of the colony, and I have portrayed that courageous man much as he was, though his acquisition in this novel of such a daughter as Susannah has necessarily changed the course of his life a little. The French explorer Nicolas Baudin, Susannah's lover, was sent by Napoléon to New South Wales, and sailed into Sydney Cove one day in 1802. Susannah herself is a creature of the imagination; and the hearts and souls of those around her are, also, created.

I owe a debt of gratitude to many people: to Peter Kay, Ian Dawes, and Peter Davison of the Australian Information Service in London and Sydney; to the staff of the Observatory, the Royal Botanic Gardens, and the Mitchell Library in Sydney; to Nina Valentine of Sovereign Hill, a marvellous reconstruction of the Ballarat gold diggings; and to the staff of Old Sydney Town. I particularly wish to thank Alan D. Williams and Georgette Felix of The Viking Press, New York; Harold Harris and Chris Chippindale of Hutchinson, London; and Elizabeth Douglas of Hutchinson, Melbourne.

Now, a great debt. I first saw the Eureka flag on December 2, 1973, when its tattered and restored remains were unveiled at the Ballarat Fine Arts Gallery by the Prime Minister of Australia. That was on the anniversary of the battle of the stockade. I never forgot Ballarat or Sydney. In 1977, when I returned to London after a second visit, a history of early Australia was proposed to me, but I doubted whether I should dare undertake any history of a continent that has been and is blessed with fine historians. It was then that Rosalie Swedlin, herself a publisher of distinction, told me to write it as a novel.

And, last, I thank her whose generous heart gave me the means to write *Southern Cross*.

Bestsellers from BALLANTINE

No one who buys it,
survives it.

THE HOUSE NEXT DOOR

A terrifying novel
by
Anne Rivers Siddons

28172 $2.75

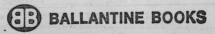 BALLANTINE BOOKS

G-1c